THE BLONDE IN LOWER SIX

Also by Erle Stanley Gardner available from Carroll & Graf:

Dead Men's Letters and Other Short Novels.

THE BLONDE IN LOWER SIX

ERLE STANLEY GARDNER

Carroll & Graf Publishers, Inc.
New York

"The Blonde in Lower Six," *Argosy*, September 1961
"The Wax Dragon," *Black Mask*, November 1927
"Grinning Gods," *Black Mask*, December 1927
"Yellow Shadows," *Black Mask*, February 1928

This Carroll & Graf edition is published by arrangement with Argosy Communications, Inc. in cooperation with Thayer Hobson and Company, representing The Erle Stanley Gardner Trust, Jean Bethell Gardner and Grace Naso, Trustees.

Library of Congress Cataloging-in-Publication Data

Gardner, Erle Stanley, 1889–1970.
The blonde in lower six / Erle Stanley Gardner.
p. cm.
ISBN 0-88184-633-3 : $18.95
I. Title.
PS3513.A6322B56 1990
813'.52—dc20 90-43553
CIP

First Carroll & Graf edition 1990

Carroll & Graf Publishers, Inc.
260 Fifth Avenue
New York, NY 10001

Manufactured in the United States of America

Argosy Communications wishes to extend its grateful appreciation to the following people who helped to make this volume possible:

Jean Gardner and Grace Naso, who approved it;

Lawrence Hughes, who sanctioned it;

Betty Burke and Katharine Odgers, who coordinated its manuscript;

Mary Bowling and Mark Dunn
of the New York Public Library, who came to its rescue;

Herman Graf, who demanded it;

James Mason, who cultivated it;

Robert Weinberg, who guided it;

and

Eva Zablodowsky, who inspired it.

The Blonde in Lower Six

CHAPTER ONE

It was a night when swirling fog scurried over the high peaks of San Francisco, to settle down in the comparatively windless tranquillity over Chinatown. Having hurried in from the ocean, the fog now became leisurely, settling down slowly upon the carved dragons, the distinctive roofs with their peculiar upturned corners—down to the level of the second- and third-story windows—and stopping.

As I emerged from the Stockton Street Tunnel, I couldn't help noticing this vagary of the fog and wondering about the reason for it. So many nights I had seen the fog rush breathlessly in over the peaks, pause to hover over Chinatown, then settle to a point where the red neon signs gave it the appearance of fine blood particles suspended in the air in little ominous eddies—and down on the sidewalks there would be no fog at all, only a peculiar hush, a dampness—and a menace.

Behind me, lay the city of San Francisco, modern, up-to-date, plagued with those problems which are brought about by the complexities of civilization. Ahead of me was a section which, so far as the eye could tell, might well have been eight thousand miles away—a section of old Cathay. San Francisco's Chinatown is like that, and the line of demarcation is as sharp as though it had been etched with the blade of a keen dagger.

When one is being used by the police as a convenient scapegoat upon whom to blame unsolved crimes, it behooves one to be careful. And when one has, moreover, incurred the enmity of the organized underworld, it behooves one to be doubly careful. But tonight I had an even greater incentive to seek the dark byways. I was calling on Soo Hoo Duck, the king of Chinatown.

There was a time when one who had the proper credentials needed only to pass the point where San Francisco's ornamental street lights became crested with dragons, the sign of the beginning of Chinatown, to go about carrying on the business of Soo Hoo Duck with absolute impunity.

Now, with the war, there were spying eyes and listening ears. There were those who would give much to learn, even to within a block, the nerve center from which the activities of organized Chinatown are conducted. One bomb dropped from a submarine-borne airplane, or perhaps skillfully planted in an adjoining building would have done much to wreck the Chinese espionage system.

I entered a narrow alley. Only too well I realized the dangers which might lurk here, but I realized also that no one could follow me into this alley without my knowing it.

I walked half the length of the alley and waited.

The fog-filled silence was broken by the occasional moaning of fog signals from the bay. The muted noises of the city, merged by distance into a continuous murmur of sound, were not loud enough to be audible unless one deliberately listened.

As the sound of my breathing became more quiet, I could hear the steady, monotonous drip . . . drip . . . drip of moisture from the eaves of the houses.

There was no sound that would indicate the presence of any other human being.

Years of practice in threading my way through the darkness stood me in good stead. Long before any of us knew what vitamins were, the eating of carrots to enable one to see at night was one of the most carefully guarded secrets of the underworld. I counted doorways, paused before an innocent-appearing door, opened it and entered a smelly little passageway. The door swung shut behind me and I was in darkness so intense that it was difficult to keep even a sense of direction. I waited a full five minutes. Then I walked slowly through the smelly darkness, perhaps a hundred feet. Again I waited cautiously.

When I opened the door that was now barring my way, I was in a crowded anteroom, merely one human atom in a composite whole, a stream of packed humanity that was flowing ever forward toward the lighted stage of a Chinese theater.

Cymbals clashed.

A thin, reedy note of a Chinese flute snarled at the auditory nerve, screaming, at times, into a pitch of sound so high that it was all but inaudible.

The stage at the front of the theater held no curtain, no scenery. It was merely a raised platform containing three or four chairs, a large table, a small table and a couple of stools. The Chinese feel that imagination is a rare attribute, something to be cultivated, and so they refrain from giving an audience all the facilities the occidental theatergoer has learned to require before his imagination can visualize that which is happening on the stage in terms of actuality.

The Chinese flute skirled into a new ecstasy of sound. The cymbals clashed again.

A player walked out on the stage, strutting with that exaggerated swing which characterizes the Chinese actor. He was portraying a military hero.

A hand touched me on the shoulder.

An old Chinese, stooped and palsied, let his yellowed talon slip carelessly down my arm, then turned and wormed his way through the crowded darkness. I followed, taking advantage of that moment when the attention of all spectators was on the stage.

A few seconds later, I was groping through dark underground passageways. Doors opened and closed. Sliding panels moved back so that shrewd eyes could size me up as I passed, until I came at length to that familiar flight of stairs with the door at the top—a steel-cored door that seemed to be a particularly flimsy portal of checked wood, the varnish dark with age and grimed with dirt.

The door swung open on massive ball-bearing hinges and Ngat T'oy was waiting on the threshold to greet me.

"Ed Jenkins!" she said. Just two words, but the tone of her voice spoke volumes.

I entered. The door whooshed shut behind me.

She gave me her hand, a hand so long and slim and fragile that instinctively one touched it as one would hold the petal of a flower.

"It's been a long time," I said.

"Too long," she told me.

For a moment, her face held that inscrutable expression of oriental impassivity which is the property of a race that can mask its feelings; then she was laughing up at me. Full red lips parted to show teeth that were as pearls in a setting of rare old ivory, eyes that might have been covered with black lacquer—eyes that glistened with vitality. "It was nice of you to come. Must you wait for a summons?"

"My presence brings danger, Little Sun," I said, using the American translation of her name.

"Danger!" she said scornfully. "Since when," she asked, "has Ed Jenkins become afraid of danger?"

"My fear," I said, "is for you."

Of a sudden, the smile faded from her face. "My race does not fear danger, because it has never had security. For centuries your people have basked in security and therefore fear danger. But as for us—we have never known anything but danger—floods, famine, pestilence, marauders, conquerors. Death is always jeering at our elbow. Therefore, we do not fear danger—nor do we fear death."

And she was right. One never knows a Chinese to worry. That is because, as a race, they are threatened with so many potential misfortunes it would be impossible to catalogue them all, let alone fear them, and worry is but an attenuated fear, long drawn-out, clutching constantly at the mind.

"What," I asked, "is new?"

"Father wants you to do something as a favor to him. It is something very, very important."

"So far as I am concerned, it is done," I said.

"Wait until you hear what it is."

"Do you know?"

Her eyes were mischievous. "I do but I'm not supposed to tell."

"Give me a hint, Ngat T'oy."

"To do that would rob my father of the pleasure of asking for himself," she said, and her face was suddenly the inscrutable, demure countenance of a dutiful Chinese daughter.

Ngat T'oy was like that. Educated in California, she was pure Chinese beneath the flippant veneer of Western civilization and casual slang. Her mind was just like that, a mysterious well of oriental mysticism beneath a layer of the Occident. There could be no mixture of the two. At times, she was merely a casual American girl with breezy informality and a mischievous give-and-take of repartee. Then, when the going got tough, she became as Chinese as Cathay itself.

"Come," she said, "and bring your ears and your wisdom to the house of my father."

CHAPTER TWO

Soo Hoo Duck had the air of benevolent wisdom which comes with age. The eyes that peered out at the world from behind horn-rimmed spectacles were kindly, shrewd and penetrating.

Dressed in a loose Chinese costume with baggy sleeves and wearing those awkward Chinese shoes which shuffled along the floor as he walked, the man, nevertheless, had that about him which made his carriage solemnly dignified.

The older Chinese prefer to shake hands with themselves rather than with you. And it is etiquette to clasp your own hands over the heart, agitate them gently, and bow.

I returned Soo Hoo Duck's courteous salutations.

"It is as though warm sun gladdened my heart on a winter morning," Soo Hoo Duck said in Cantonese. "I was stumbling in the dark, but now with your presence, warmth and light illuminate my path. My feet are to follow."

"I am but a mirror," I said. "The light which you see comes not from me, but is the reflection of your own wisdom illuminating the pathway the Gods have selected for your feet."

"You have the modesty of wisdom," Soo Hoo Duck said. "It has been written that only the very wise are very humble. It is the stupid man who has the loud voice. Will you join me in a cup of tea?"

Soo Hoo Duck, bowing again, escorted me across deep Oriental rugs that seemed to the feet like a springy mat of pine needles in a virgin forest. Overhead, chandeliers of cut and polished crystal glittered in myriad coruscations. The furniture was of teakwood and Chinese mahogany inlaid with mother-of-pearl. Suspended from the walls were wide banners of silk on which had been embroidered the words of various prominent scholars, black ideographs against a red silk background.

We seated ourselves on those straightbacked chairs which only the disciplined spines of the Chinese can find truly comfortable. A servant brought tea, melon seeds, thick, sweet almond cakes, placed them on the carved, inlaid table and departed noiselessly. Ngat T'oy placed cigarettes and matches at my elbow.

Soo Hoo Duck glanced at his daughter. "You will interpret for our distinguished visitor," he said.

My knowledge of Cantonese is such that I can follow ordinary conversation and reply in kind, and I happen to know that Soo Hoo Duck has an excellent knowledge of English. Yet when he wishes to be doubly certain that he says what he intends to say and to scan closely the replies of his visitor, he presses Ngat T'oy into the job of interpreter, which gives him the advantage of listening to his own statements after he has uttered them, as well as hearing the replies of his visitor twice.

Recently, however, Ngat T'oy was becoming inclined to take liberties with the utterances of her father, masking her short cuts by the use of slang which, being completely foreign to Soo Hoo Duck's vocabulary, left him very much out on a limb.

"Tell him," Soo Hoo Duck said, "the preliminaries."

Ngat T'oy said, "You know, Ed, these days, you never can tell what you're up against. You'll get what looks like a live lead and it will turn out to be a dud. Then something will come along that looks like an absolute washout and it will be the real goods. That's what's bothering the paterfamilias. He's in touch with a jane by the name of Betty Crofath who has something he can't afford to overlook, *if* she has it."

I glanced at Soo Hoo Duck.

The old man's eyes were puckered in puzzled bewilderment as he listened to what his daughter was saying. She paused and he said to her sharply in Cantonese, "What is this language you are using?"

She met his gaze guilelessly. "The language of the white barbarians."

"Truly it is barbarous," the old man sighed. "Go ahead."

"Okay," Ngat T'oy said to me. "This jane tries to make a build-up without first putting an ante in the jack pot or letting us know how many cards she wants to draw. She writes Dad a letter that she'll be in San Francisco day after tomorrow at the Pelton Hotel. She has certain information which is definitely authentic and which she wants to turn over gratis.

"That's the payoff, Ed. That Annie Oakley business. You know, we get all sorts of propositions from people who want to turn over information for a payoff. We have certain definite ways of playing them, but this jane is different. It's a purely voluntary contribution to the cause as far as she is concerned. There's only one condition. She has to deliver the information to my father personally."

"What," I asked, "is the general nature of the information?"

Ngat T'oy said to her father in rapid Chinese, "How much am I at liberty to tell him about this information?"

Soo Hoo Duck's face was utterly without expression. "To this man," he said, "I bare my soul."

Ngat T'oy said, "Secret data on the entire construction program of the Japanese Navy, and the exact location of the different yards where carriers, cruisers, destroyers and other ships are being constructed."

I gave a low whistle.

"And," she went on, "that isn't all. It seems that just as everyone misjudged the Japanese before Pearl Harbor, they are now making the mistake of misjudging them afterward. There has been a lot of talk that, according to the true oriental concept of things, the Japanese will never make a peace at which they will lose face; that they will go on butting their heads against a stone wall—that if they can't win, they will commit military hara-kari by fighting to the last soldier."

I nodded.

"It is," she said, "sound psychology except for one thing."

"What," I asked, "is that?"

"There is a very strong amount of evidence dead against it."

"Evidence that can be believed?"

She nodded. "The Japanese have absorbed much from their contact with occidental civilization. The Japanese would be extremely reluctant to admit defeat and taste the bitter dregs of the cup of humiliation."

"I can well understand."

"But," she said, "Japan is cunning. Japan remembers what happened to Germany in nineteen-eighteen. In place of carrying on until the Allies trampled her so completely in the dust she could never rise again, Germany accepted the best terms she could get, pretended an external docility, and within twenty years, was in a position to try again. And that time, she came within an ace of doing it.

"There is some talk in Japan that it would be better to accept even humiliation and an apparent loss of face for another quarter of a century and then conquer the world, using the hard-earned knowledge gained in the present war, than to carry on until the last gun is fired. Because the smart ones in Japan realize now that when the last gun is fired, it will be pointed at Japan's heart and secret bombs will be used that will leave nothing in Japan for the Allies to shoot at."

"And so?" I asked.

"And so," she said, "we do much speculating about Betty Crofath. The information which she has is vital if it is true. It is deadly dangerous if it is untrue. If it is true, it could only have been obtained in one way. But there is one other piece of information she has that bothers us," Ngat T'oy said, an anxious expression on her face.

"The fact that she got in touch with your father?"

Ngat T'oy nodded. "To a few of the influential Chinese, my father is well known. To the mass of Chinatown, he is but a name—yet even the name is well guarded. Go into any place in Chinatown and ask for Soo Hoo Duck, and the person whom you ask will look at you with the peculiarly courteous disinterest at which my race is so adept. But thereafter, just try and leave Chinatown without being shadowed; try and conceal yourself so well that within twenty-four hours we would not know all about you—all about your background and how you had learned of the name, Soo Hoo Duck."

I nodded.

"And now," she said, "out of a clear sky, a woman writes from Buenos Aires a letter addressed to my father at the post-office box where he receives his mail under the name of Tai Yat. If our enemies have that information, it is important to know where they got it."

"And what," I asked, "do you wish me to do?"

"Are you free to do it for us, Ed?"

I merely nodded.

"No, please, tell us. We know it will be doubly dangerous for you, but there is no one else."

"What I can do," I told her, "I am glad to do."

She said, "Betty Crofath is on a train that will arrive in

Tucson at midnight tonight. She is in lower six of car four. She will be suspicious of anyone with an oriental background. But an attractive white man who is traveling with her could get a lot of information about her, which we need."

Soo Hoo Duck interposed once more in Chinese. "A man," he said, "who has that bearing that is attractive to women, who can charm the heart so that the ears hear his voice as the tinkle of running water; a man who has the power to draw women to him as a magnet draws iron. Tell him all of this, Ngat T'oy."

Ngat T'oy turned to me. "A guy who is lousy with S.A.," she said.

Soo Hoo Duck looked with surprise at his daughter as she ceased talking. "You have told him this?" he asked.

"I have told him that."

Soo Hoo Duck sighed resignedly.

"Are you trying to flatter or to kid me?" I asked Ngat T'oy.

"Neither, Ed. You can do it."

"Where do you get this Clark Gable stuff?" I asked her.

"How do *you* know what you do to a woman's heart? Peace now, and let us plan what we are to do. Can we count on you?"

I nodded.

Ngat T'oy clapped her hands. A servant appeared in the doorway. Ngat T'oy asked him in Chinese, "You have a report?"

He came forward, bowing, and laid a plain Manila paper envelope on the table. Then he bowed and withdrew.

I opened the envelope.

It contained a plane ticket from San Francisco to Tucson—a railroad ticket from Tucson to San Francisco via Los Angeles—and a Pullman ticket for lower seven, car four, Tucson to Los Angeles.

Soo Hoo Duck's sharp eyes slithered over the contents of the envelope as I pulled out the colored strips of paper.

"It is well," he murmured approvingly. "Time has been short."

There flashed through my mind some idea of what those tickets on such short notice must have meant, the pre-emption of outstanding reservations, the frenzied telephone calls, embarrassed official explanations. And it had all been done with the swift efficiency of an organization that ran as smoothly as a piece of high-speed machinery.

I put the tickets back in the envelope, and the envelope in my pocket.

A look of serenity established itself on the face of Soo Hoo Duck. "The problem is now gone from my mind," he said, "as the morning mists leave the lake."

I wished I had shared his assurance. Problems were being turned over in my own mind, problems that presented many angles. "You and I will have to arrange a few details," I said to Ngat T'oy.

Her eyes laughed into mine. "Your words," she said in Chinese, "have ever been the masters of my ears."

Soo Hoo Duck beamed at us. So far as he was concerned, the matter was all disposed of and his mind could devote itself exclusively to the things of beauty in the world.

So for some ten minutes we split dried melon seeds, sipped tea and discussed the thought processes by which the sweeping curves of conifer bows had been translated into the Chinese architecture, which gives to its eaves that peculiar concave sweep.

At the end of that time, I made my farewells, giving a glance at Ngat T'oy as I bowed myself out of the room.

She joined me in the corridor beyond the heavy door.

"It's going to be up to you to make the contact at the hotel, on behalf of your father," I told her. "I'll find out what I can. She must have a reservation at the Pelton Hotel. See if you can get a room across the corridor, or perhaps an adjoining room. Her train should arrive about nine. At eleven o'clock on the dot, you are to knock on the door of her room. But if, for any reason, anything should have gone wrong—if she doesn't check in, for instance—you are to meet me at the Golden Lotus Petal at exactly ten-thirty. Do you understand?"

"At eleven," she said, repeating after me, Chinese fashion, "I am to knock on the door of her room, if everything has gone without a hitch, if she registers at the hotel and there are no suspicious circumstances. Otherwise, I am to meet you at the Golden Lotus Petal at ten-thirty. Right?"

"Right."

"And why it is so important that I get a room near hers?" she asked me.

"Because I don't want anyone to know that you have gone

to her room—anyone who might be waiting in the lobby. And when and if we decide she is to meet your father face to face, you will only need to spirit him into your room, then take a few quick steps across the hall. Under no circumstances is this girl to know that you are registered in the hotel. Understand?"

"Yes. Where will you be, Ed?"

"Around."

"Okay."

I patted her shoulder. My arm dropped to her waist. She abruptly came close to me with a lithe, cuddling motion, then swiftly twisted free.

"Good-by, Ed, and good luck! And don't worry about not having the S.A."

I left immediately to make my plane connection for Tucson.

CHAPTER THREE

Dry desert heat held the nightdarkened city of Tucson in an inexorable grip. This heat was different from the high-humidity, smothering heat of the tropics. It was a heat in which perspiration evaporated so fast that the skin felt dry while the body suffered from dehydration.

Fine particles of abrasive desert dust seemed to be suspended in the air—particles so small as to be invisible, yet making the clothes seem harshly abrasive to the skin. A few months later this air would be as invigorating and almost as intoxicating as wine. Tourists would flock from the snow-bound East to soak up the dry sunlight, the tang of the pure air. But now, for a period of six weeks, heat held sway in the desert.

The train was late, and no one seemed to have any very definite information as to when it could be expected.

The railroad depot was crowded with tired, dejected bits of human flotsam, some of them people who had been trying in vain to get on trains for nearly twenty-four hours, sprawled wearily in postures of dejection, getting up when they heard the sound of an approaching train, picking up their baggage, plodding wearily out to the platform, standing in long lines, being pushed and jostled, hearing the discouraging voice of a tired conductor, the slam of a vestibule door, and then trudging wearily back to the depot to resume another period of waiting.

I preferred to wait in the fresh air out on the platform—air which had no sign of a breeze, yet into which almost imperceptibly was beginning to creep that before-dawn freshness that gives tired mortals the courage to face another scorching summer day.

The block signal changed. I heard the distant "*who-o-o-o*" of the train. Then, a few minutes later, the long, weary line of cars rumbled tiredly into the station.

The conductor looked at my reservation, turned me over to a porter, and a few minutes later, I was walking down the green-curtained Pullman aisle.

I sat down on the edge of lower seven and looked across at the buttoned green curtains of berth six. In all probability, the girl would sleep late in the morning, but I couldn't take any chances. I needed to be on deck as soon as she was stirring.

I slipped out of my clothes, relaxing already in the cool, air-conditioned train. By the time the long line of coaches creaked into protesting motion once more, I was sliding down between the sheets. I raised the curtain on the windows so that I would be sure to waken at daylight.

It seemed that I had no more than closed my eyes when light stung them awake. It was just about sunrise and the desert clicking past the window was a disorderly procession of saguaro, ocotillo, cholla cactus and the lacy branches of smoke trees.

There was only one other man in the washroom. He looked me over speculatively, laughed, and said, "I don't know what *your* hurry is. We're not going anywhere—at least we're not *getting* anywhere."

I sized him up—a man in his forties, jelly-jiggling fat, good-natured, moonfaced and bald. In the nineties, he would have been a drummer with a fund of naughty stories and an air of worldly wisdom. As it was, I couldn't place him. A fat man who liked the creature comforts of food, drink and sleep. Yet he was up in the early morning, shaved, dressed, and waiting. For what?

"Lost more time?" I asked.

"Another forty-five minutes during the night."

I said, "I hate crowded washrooms."

"Same here. I can't shave with other people jabbing me with elbows, jostling me with bags and suitcases. Going to Los Angeles?"

I nodded.

I let him see that I was too occupied with my shaving to care about engaging in further conversation.

He was still sitting there as I left.

There was no sign of motion in lower six when I checked.

The dining car wouldn't be open for more than an hour, so I walked out to the vestibule for a couple of cigarettes. The porter found me, expressed surprise that I was up so early, tactfully mentioned that he couldn't make up the berth until the person in the upper berth got up, and then went straggling off in the direction of the dining car.

I stood in the vestibule until my legs got tired. I went back to the smoking room. A couple of other early risers were there, also the man with whom I had spoken earlier. He was engaged in some sort of an argument with one of the men. He looked up, saw me and, for a moment, his voice seemed to undergo a change of pace. Then he was back in his verbal stride, hardly giving me a second glance.

I went back to stand in the swaying vestibule.

The man who had slept in the upper over my berth rang for the porter. As the porter brought the ladder for him to use in getting down. I saw the curtains billow into motion on lower five. An attractive young woman with unruly golden blonde hair pulled a robe around her and scurried for the washroom. Still no sign of motion from lower six.

I waited fifteen minutes, then strolled through to the men's room. It was now a crowded mass of humanity. I went back to my station in the vestibule.

Some ten minutes later, the car door opened. I glanced around casually. The unruly blonde hair had now been carefully combed and brushed. Wide, frank blue eyes regarded me with just the right twinkle of good nature. The girl who had slept in lower five said, "I came out here for a before-breakfast cigarette. The dressing room is a mess. I hope you're not going to object to smoke."

"I'll join you," I said. "Or perhaps you'll have one of mine."

She took one of mine.

"Beastly, isn't it," she said as I held a match for her.

"It could be worse."

"Not without concentrating on it."

The sun was now beginning to pack a wallop. We moved over to the shady side, stood there smoking.

"Do you know if the dining car is open?" she asked.

"The waiter just started through for the first call."

"Ouch! I suppose that means I'll have to stand in line for coffee."

I took a glance back into the aisle of the car. The porter was making up berths. There was still no sign of life from lower six.

I decided I'd have time for a quick cup of coffee before she could possibly get up. I felt that coffee would just about save my life.

"I'm going up," I told the girl from lower five. "Want to trail along as I open doors?"

She nodded.

It was a long, interminable journey but there was a pleasant surprise at the end of it. The dining car wasn't as yet completely filled. The steward saw me coming, held up two fingers and motioned us to a single table.

"This," I said, "is luck."

"A gift from the gods," she announced. "You've really no idea what coffee does to my disposition."

She was watching her figure. Grapefruit, black coffee, dry toast, fresh strawberries with a bare sprinkle of sugar and just a touch of cream.

With the train so crowded, I knew I could count on quick service. I had a rush order of ham and eggs, toast and coffee, and was ready to go back by the time she had finished her light breakfast. The strain of the heat and the grime of dust and travel seemed to have eased. I felt much better. The blonde's name was Hazel Deering. She was from the South and going to San Francisco. She led me to believe, in a vague way, that she was going to San Francisco to be near a boy friend who had been stationed at the Presidio. It was nothing definite that she said, merely a casual impression I derived from a lot of little things.

Lower six was still sleeping.

My section had been made up, so Miss Deering settled down with me when we returned. The man who had the upper was in at breakfast.

We talked about the desert, about the South, about the war, about politics. She had a quick mind, a way of making herself thoroughly at ease, and, as became a traveling acquaintance, was completely casual in her manner.

It was eight-thirty when the porter came and tugged at the green curtains of lower six.

"Eight-thirty, ma'am," he said.

He stood by the curtained berth, waiting for a few seconds.

Then he reached his hand down between the curtains, caught the blankets and started jerking them. "Eight-thirty, ma'am."

Hazel Deering and I were both watching him. He flashed white teeth at us, shook the mattress violently. "You wanted to be called at eight-thirty, ma'am," he said, raising his voice.

There was no answer.

The porter hesitated, glanced at us, apparently to see if we were the type that would disapprove, then having reassured himself, parted the curtains and peered very discreetly through the opening. A moment later, he was clawing the curtains apart, then, with a face the color of raw liver, trying to get them back together again.

"Fo' Gawd's sake! Call de conductor. She's *daid!*" he screamed.

CHAPTER FOUR

The conductor was sympathetic, overworked, and immersed in so many troubles that the death was merely one more straw on an overloaded camel's back. They found a vacant drawing room into which they could move the body temporarily and then, some time later, unloaded it at Indio.

The passengers gathered in morbid little groups, huddled against the terror of a death which had appeared in their midst, very much as young chickens scuttle for safety at the threatening shadow of an approaching hawk.

Hazel Deering seemed particularly influenced by what had happened. She kept very much to herself, staring moodily out of the window at the gray monotony of the desert as it clicked by.

My genial, paunchy friend, on the other hand, became even more talkative, made it a point to accost me when I entered the men's room.

"Tragic, wasn't it?" he asked.

"Very."

"Beautiful, young girl. Noticed her particularly at dinner last night."

"Did you?"

"You weren't aboard the train last night, were you?"

"No."

"Got on sometime during the night?"

"Yes."

"Where?"

"Tucson."

He chuckled. "Lucky thing for us it wasn't a violent death."

"Why?"

"Because you and I were the first up this morning. Everyone else was sleeping. You know, ample opportunity and all that. Damned nuisance to be questioned by the police."

"It was a natural death?" I asked.

"Apparently. Heart failure or something." He pushed his hand out at me. "Name's Rendon," he said, "Herb Rendon. Real estate."

I shook hands gravely. "Glad to meet you, Herb."

"What did you say your name was?"

"Sabin."

"Los Angeles?"

"San Francisco mostly."

"Terribly tragic. Can't get over it. Keep thinking about it. Lucky for us it was a natural death. Hate to be questioned by the police, myself," he said, shaking his head solemnly.

"I can imagine it might well raise the devil with a man's plans," I said, and escaped back to the silent companionship of Hazel Deering.

The last part of the trip seemed interminable as the long line of tired Pullmans snaked its way through the pass between San Gorgonio and San Jacinto.

Then, almost immediately, the character of the country changed. The train picked up speed as it started on the long down slope toward Los Angeles. The desert gave way to well-kept orange groves where golden fruit and snowy blossoms splotched against the dark green of glossy leaves, with snow-capped mountains seeming to hang suspended in the blue distance like well-rounded dishes of celestial ice cream.

When we were pulling into Los Angeles, I managed to avoid both Hazel Deering and Herb Rendon by moving up three cars. I caught the Lark for San Francisco that night. And, after a leisurely breakfast, strolled into the Golden Lotus Petal for my appointment with Ngat T'oy.

I wasn't certain whether Ngat T'oy would read of Betty Crofath's death in the paper, but when Betty Crofath failed to register at the Pelton Hotel, that would be Ngat T'oy's signal to meet me at the Chinese restaurant. So I ordered a bowl of tea and some of the bent rice fortune cakes and settled back to a period of waiting, knowing that Ngat T'oy would be right on the minute.

But Ngat T'oy wasn't right on the minute. I frowned at my

watch as she became five minutes, then ten minutes late. Surely something was wrong.

I waited anxiously for another five minutes. Then I thought for the first time to send a boy out to a stand where I knew he could get a Los Angeles paper.

It took me a few minutes search to find what I wanted. I located it on a third page under the heading "TRAIN DEATH MAY BE SUICIDE."

From this account, I learned that the death of a young woman found in a Pullman train between Tucson and Indio had apparently been caused by an overdose of sleeping tablets. The body had been tentatively identified as that of a Miss Daphne Strate of New Orleans.

Miss Strate had, it seemed, left New Orleans rather hurriedly and under somewhat suspicious circumstances. She had been employed as secretary for a wholesale chemical company. The manager of her department had admitted to police that Miss Strate had left there without any notice whatever. More than that, he declined to say. He did state, however, that it came as a distinct surprise to him to learn that she had taken a west-bound train. Other employes in the office had remembered that, for a few days, Miss Strate had seemed rather moody and preoccupied.

I rushed through the few paragraphs in the newspaper, then made a dash for the Pelton Hotel.

"You have a Miss Crofath registered here?" I asked.

"Yes, in 309. Shall I ring?"

"She's expecting me," I said. "Tell her Mr. Smith is on his way up."

I left the elevator, walked down the third floor, tapped on the door of 309.

"Who is it, please?" a woman's voice asked.

"Smith," I said, keeping my voice low and guttural.

Hazel Deering opened the door and then recoiled with a gasp of startled surprise as she saw me standing there.

"Good morning," I said, and moved on past her into the room.

She moved back to let me by, leaving the door swinging wide open, her eyes, wide with consternation, following my every move. There was no sign of Ngat T'oy in the place. A small trunk was in the middle of the room, a suitcase on a baggage stand.

"Close the door," I said.

She hesitated a moment then closed the door.

"All right, Hazel, why did you do it?"

"Do what?"

"Kill Betty Crofath."

"Kill her!" she exclaimed. *"I* kill her? You're crazy. *I'm* Betty Crofath!"

"Then why the Hazel Deering?"

"It's a name I took so I wouldn't be annoyed while I was traveling."

"Let's see your driver's license."

"I don't have to."

I simply stood, waiting, exerting silent pressure on her.

She hesitated a moment, then went to her purse, opened it with hands that were trembling, took out a driving license and handed it to me with an air of proud defiance.

The description fit. Betty Crofath, age twenty-seven, height five feet four and a-half, weight a hundred and thirteen pounds, eyes blue, hair light.

I said, "All right, so you're Betty Crofath. You pulled a slick dodge. Now, what do you want?"

"What do *you* want? Why did you come here?"

"On business."

"What sort of business?"

I kept my back to the door, trying to hurry through this before Ngat T'oy's knock would complicate the situation. "You came here to meet someone, didn't you?" I asked.

"What if I did?"

"I'm the person you were to meet."

"You can't be."

"I am to take you to that person."

"You'll have to show me."

"Okay, but first I'll need something more than this," and I indicated the driving license I was still holding.

"You will! I'm the one to be shown."

I merely smiled.

She said, "You've had some preliminary contact with me. Tell me just what it was. Describe all the details."

I kept smiling and let it go at that.

"What's wrong with that?" she asked.

"Everything."

"Tell me one thing that's wrong with it," she insisted.

"It won't work."

"That's what I was afraid of. You aren't the proper person for me to talk to. You're simply—simply chiseling, simply horning in on this thing. You—you followed me here to this hotel. You met me on the train and followed me."

I heard a couple of faint sounds, the sort someone might make by pounding on a wall.

The girl got up, dashed over to her trunk, jerked out a tray and banged the lid shut.

"What's that for?" I asked.

She stood there for a moment, then threw the lid back, started rummaging around among the contents, dumping quantities of books, shoes and clothing out on the floor.

"What's the idea?" I asked.

"I'm looking for something."

"What?"

"Something to show you, to prove I'm the person you think —and something that will enable me to identify you."

I heard another thud. She impatiently slammed a book to the floor.

I said, "I think it came from the closet."

"What did?"

"The noise you're trying to keep me from hearing. You slam things around in the trunk every time it happens. Shall we look?"

Her hand had been down in the trunk. It came up carrying a businesslike revolver. "Suppose you take a look at this instead."

I sat very still. "I'm looking at it, Hazel," I said.

"Betty."

"All right, Betty. I'm looking at it."

She said, "Raise your hands above your head, walk over against that wall and turn your back."

I sat perfectly still.

"Go on."

I shook my head.

"I'll shoot!"

"That would be very, very messy—not a nice, clean job like you made on the train."

Watching her eyes, I put my hand on the arm of the chair, made as if to rise. It was well past the time for Ngat T'oy to show up. I didn't want her to run into this.

The gun snapped to a rigid steadiness.

I settled back in the chair.

"Called your bluff, didn't I?"

I kept looking at her.

"Get your hands up."

I shook my head.

"I *will* shoot. I really will!"

She started circling the room away from the window. Abruptly she jerked open the door of the room and left.

I got up out of the chair, walked across the room, locked the door and opened the closet door.

There was nothing in there except a few clothes.

I heard the peculiar thudding noise again. As I stopped to listen, the knob of the corridor door turned slowly. I stood perfectly still, making no sound no slightest motion.

The thudding sounds were more rapid now.

Knuckles were tapping gently on the outer door.

"Hoh shai kai mäh?" I said in a low voice—the greeting of certain types of Chinese, meaning literally, "Is the whole world good?"

Instantly, Ngat T'oy's voice answered. *"Hoh shai kai"*—"the whole world is good."

I unlocked the door and let her in.

"What is it Ed?" she whispered.

"I don't know. You're late."

"I was just opening my door to come over here when I saw you entering this room. I thought something was the matter, so I waited. Then I saw her go out, pushing a gun down in her purse as she walked toward the elevator, so I came. Is anything wrong?"

"Plenty. I . . ."

More poundings interrupted me.

"Let's take a look in the bathroom Ngat T'oy," I said.

She moved to my side. "You want me with you?"

"I—yes. Come along."

She was a step or two behind me as I opened the bathroom door.

A man, a Negro, was lying in the bathtub. His shoes had been removed. A gag had been tied in his mouth, and his hands and feet were tied. He was making noise by pounding his bare heels down on the porcelain of the tub. He rolled his eyes up at us as I opened the door.

For a moment the gag which virtually covered the lower

part of his face made it impossible for me to recognize him, but there was something familiar in the livid fear, as well as in the rolling whites of the panic-stricken eyes that tugged at my memory. Then I knew who he was—the porter of the Pullman car—the one who had found the body in lower six.

I bent over him and untied the gag—a woman's nylon stocking holding in his mouth a wad of lingerie.

He was too frightened to talk.

I sat down on the edge of the bathtub, said reassuringly, "How about a cigarette?" and took out my cigarette case. I didn't make any move to untie his hands or feet.

He rolled his head from side to side in a gesture of refusal, moved his tongue around in his mouth, glanced apprehensively over my shoulder at Ngat T'oy, took a deep breath, and said, "Hones' to Gawd, boss, if'n yo' let me loose and doan' kill me, ah won't ever tell nobody you killed dat girl in the Pullman."

"Don't be silly," I said abruptly. "I didn't kill her."

I saw that my words simply didn't register with him. He was looking at me with pleading and panic in his eyes.

I said, "Who tied you up, George?"

"You know."

"No, I don't know. Who did it?"

"Ah'm promis'n, you square, boss. If'n yo' let me out of here, ah won't tell nobody."

I said, with a trace of irritation, "I'm trying to help you, you fool."

"Untie me then and lemme out o' here," he answered.

I said, "Don't be silly. If I untie you now, you'd dash out of that door screaming bloody murder, and I can't afford to have that. I only have a few minutes leeway and can't wait. Now, *when* did you get here?"

He took one look at me, opened his mouth and sucked in a prodigious breath. I knew he was going to yell. As he threw his head back, I clapped the gag back into his mouth, whipped the stocking into place and tied it in a swift knot.

The porter in the bathtub was so frightened he all but passed out. Once he realized I had slapped the gag back into his mouth, he twisted and squirmed around in the tub like a trout that has wiggled free of the hook to fall on the stream's edge.

I stepped back out of the bathroom, said to Ngat T'oy, "Come on. Let's take a look. We can't tell when she'll be back."

"Can't we turn him loose?"

"Definitely not. He'd tear the door off its hinges getting out of here and have the place around our ears before we could get out. Tell you what you *can* do. Turn on the water in the bathtub. He can keep his head above the water, and by the time it overflows and starts trickling through the ceiling of the room below, the hotel will send someone up to find him. By that time, we'll be out."

Ngat T'oy went into the bathroom. As I heard the water start running in the tub, I dropped down on my knees in front of the open trunk in the middle of the floor.

It was Betty Crofath's trunk. There were books dealing with the Orient—books that an ordinary person wouldn't have; books on Chinese temperament, customs and language published by Kelly & Walsh of Hong Kong and Shanghai; maps and guides of Japan, "The Symbology of the Shinto Religion," "The Essence of Buddhist Philosophy," a little pamphlet dealing with a dramatized story of the forty-seven Ronin.

I turned to the front of these books. Those dealing with Japan were all inscribed: *"To Betty, so that she may learn more of the dignity of my country and the significance of its customs. With love, from Numatsu."*

Ngat T'oy came to stand behind me, peering down over my shoulder.

"He can keep his head up all right?" I asked without looking up from the books.

"Yes. If he doesn't faint from fright. I was most considerate. I regulated the temperature of the water so it's just right to be comfortable. He can push his foot against the overflow outlet. As long as he holds it there the water will run over the tub—as soon as it reaches the top. If anything happens, and he faints or anything, he'll automatically remove his foot and water won't overflow. Are you finding anything interesting, Ed?"

"Interesting but not vital—so far. You've got to get out of here, Ngat T'oy. Meet me at nine o'clock at the Dragon Tooth night club. I simply can't afford to have you taking these chances."

"Nonsense. I can take them if you can," she said.

"In just about ten seconds, as soon as I reach the bottom of this trunk," I told her, "I'm going to take a look out at the hallway. If it's clear, out you go."

I found several yards of Oriental silk, a Japanese pigeon-blood cloisonné vase, the usual assortment of feminine wearing apparel, and down near the bottom of the trunk, a nineteen-forty-three diary.

The diary had been kept in a neat feminine handwriting in an expensive leather-backed book just the size to fit the side pocket of a man's coat.

I put the diary in my pocket.

I said to Ngat T'oy, "You've got to get out of here—in fact, we both have."

"You go first," she told me, "for your way is the more dangerous. I have but to cross the hall and be in my room."

I shook my head. "You first. I'll have to make certain the corridor is clear. I'll do that, then come back."

From the way she twisted her eyebrows, I saw she didn't understand what I meant.

I pointed toward the door. "The way the hinges are hung, the door opens outward. Once you open that door, you've got to step all the way out into the corridor. You don't dare to just poke your head around the door and then step back in, in case there's someone in the corridor. We don't know what the girl in here has done. If she wants to clear herself of responsibility, she'll go out and telephone the desk, telling them she's forgotten to turn off the water or something and ask to have a bellboy sent to the room. Get me?"

Ngat T'oy nodded.

As we stood there, I heard the first faint splashings of overflowing water from the bathtub.

"All right," I told her. "I'm going out now and explore the hallway. If there's anyone in the hall, I'll say something to him —even if it's nothing but a good morning. When I get to the elevator, if the corridor is clear, I'll cough twice. You keep the door partially open, wait and listen. When you hear my cough, slip out and go to your room—fast. All ready now?"

She nodded.

I approached the door.

"Open it gently, Ed," she whispered.

I laughed at her. "That's the worst way on earth to leave a hotel room. It looks furtive. Jerk the door open, march boldly out in the corridor as though you owned the joint. And if you meet someone, give him a casual glance. Listen for my signal at the elevator," I told her.

I unlocked the door, jerked it open, stepped out into the corridor, turned boldly toward the elevator—and found myself face to face with the house detective.

He was walking toward the room I had just left, carrying a slip of paper in his hand. And I didn't need to be a mind reader to tell either that he was the house detective, or that the number on the slip of paper he was carrying was the number of the room I had just vacated so boldly.

I had approximately half a second to size him up and decide what could be done about it while he was getting ready to approach me in just the right manner.

I beat him to the punch. "You're the house detective here, aren't you?"

I saw that he was a bit taken back. These chaps like to kid themselves into believing no-one can ever spot them. They are usually just a bit past middle age, inclined to an oily firmness, a certain fastidiousness of dress, usually with a bald spot over which hair has been carefully trained to cover just as much of the dome as is physically possible. Most of them are inclined to be paunchy, but all of them have a certain self-effacing manner that is a synthetic mask they throw up to hide an underlying firmness. Don't ask me why they should run to type this way. I only know they do.

He cleared his throat. "May I have your name, please?"

I grabbed him by the arm. "I'm with the Motor Vehicle Department. I've just taken up a driver's license."

I slipped my fingers down into my inside pocket and jerked out the driver's license that I had neglected to give back to the girl.

"Betty Crofath," I said. "Three-oh-nine. I was going to look you up when I got downstairs. Let's go talk with the manager."

He har-r-r-umphed and said, "I was on my way to see Miss Crofath. And I sized you up as a State man as soon as I saw you."

"The devil!"

He nodded.

I let admiration come in my eyes. "Say, there's not much gets past you birds, is there?"

He smiled. "You might like to go in the room with me."

"Not me," I told him. "I just came out, and once is enough." I lowered my voice, "You'd better talk with me, however, before *you* go in." I glanced back over my shoulder at the door, took his arm and led him gently toward the elevator.

"We can talk right here," he said.

"No," I said firmly, "what I have to say is not alone for your ears, but for those of the manager as well."

He didn't argue any more after that. We went down in the elevator and he piloted me into the office.

The manager was a disillusioned individual with tired gray eyes, pouches under them, and a general air of misanthropic skepticism.

The house detective did the talking. "I met this man up on the third floor just coming to the elevators," he said sapiently. "I spotted him just as soon as I saw him—figured he was from one of the State departments. I asked him, and he said it was Motor Vehicle."

"How'd you spot him?" the manager asked warily.

"Just the manner—the way he was walking. I don't know exactly how," the house detective said with a certain synthetic modesty as though trying to belittle something which was a very smart piece of detective work indeed.

The manager looked at him, started to say something, then turned to me.

I said, "I've been up taking Betty Crofath's license. She'd been in trouble before and made a lot of false statements. I thought you ought to know."

"I didn't know you had the right to go up to any person and take his license," the manager said.

I showed surprise. "You didn't know that?" I asked.

"No."

"You'd better keep up with changes in the motor-vehicle law. We're adding to it all the time, trying to make conditions better for drivers."

"They're passing laws so fast these days," he said, "you can hear them whiz by, but you don't have time to read them. That's a hell of a law."

"On the contrary," I told him, "it's the only sensible law. That places the authority in the hands of the people who have the responsibility—the Motor Vehicle Department."

"I'd hate to have some guy just come walking up to me, flash a badge, say he was from the Motor Vehicle Department and demand a surrender of my license without a hearing."

I looked authoritative. "Don't violate the vehicle law and

you won't have any trouble. Now, in case this young woman gets into a car, I want to know it. If you see her getting into a car, get the license number, pass the word to your bellboys and whatever clerk comes on duty. Just telephone the Motor Vehicle Department and leave a message for the field representative, Mr. E. L. Dickers. By the way, she tells me she had a reservation here. How did she make it, by letter or wire?"

"Wire—relayed on through a New Orleans hotel."

I started for the door. "Well, if you fellows have any trouble with your motor-vehicle stuff, let me know. Glad to do anything I can, and lots of times I can do a great deal—renewal of licenses and stuff of that sort. And be sure and let me know if Miss Crofath so much as sets her foot in an automobile unless there's a chauffeur at the wheel."

I bowed and swung around to the door which led from the office to the lobby, gave them an affable grin and headed for the street.

As I passed through the lobby, a chunky figure suddenly held up an open newspaper in such a way that it concealed his face.

The man might have found something in the paper that greatly interested him, or he might have been trying to keep me from seeing him, or from letting me know that he had seen me.

My only way of identifying him was from his clothes. It was the same suit of quiet brown with a white pin stripe that my jovial friend, Herb Rendon, had been wearing.

I pushed through the exit door and turned right, noticing from the corner of my eye as I hit the sidewalk that the newspaper had been abruptly jerked down from Herb Rendon's face.

No-one followed me from the hotel.

Back in the modest little apartment which served as my headquarters, I settled down to read the diary of Betty Crofath.

I would have given much if the diary had gone back for a full year, but it didn't. Starting on January first, nineteen hundred and forty-three, I picked up Betty Crofath in Buenos Aires. I didn't know what she was doing there, how long she had known the people whose names appeared so casually in her diary, or, except by inference, how she felt toward them, or what her past had been with relation to these men.

There was a German, Karl Wilkers, a man by the name of Ramon, whose last name never appeared in the diary. Also one named José, who was also only a first name. Then there was an N. K. who appeared only as initials. However, the name Numatsu appeared once or twice and once the name N. Kamchura, which gave me the name, Numatsu Kamchura to stand for the N. K. There was a girl named Felice, and another named Mae. And there were scores of references to people and initials who came and went casually across the pages, but Karl, Ramon, José, Felice, Mae and the mysterious N. K. seemed to dominate the book.

I started to get acquainted with the girl of the diary, beginning with the first entry on January first, nineteen hundred and forty-three. There were two separate entries for that day. The first one, in a somewhat scrawling writing was:

"Hello Diary! Happy New Year!

"Mama's been out all night, staggering in well after daylight. Ramon bought me a breakfast and we had an argument. Going shut-eye now, diary."

The second entry seemed a little shaky. *"Oooo, Diary! Mama shouldn't have done it!"*

That was all for the first day of 1943.

I couldn't be certain whether the argument with Ramon was over the obvious, or was related to some other matter which was locked away in the nineteen hundred and forty-two diary.

Nor could I get any clue as to the real feelings of the writer of the diary. She referred at times to the Japanese, the British, the Germans and the Italians with no prejudice whatever. If one could judge from the pages of her diary, she didn't think of herself as a citizen of the United States, but regarded the moves of the various warring nations as a spectator would review a gridiron struggle—not without emotion, not without appreciation of the terrific fight that was being waged, but definitely without becoming identified with either of the teams. Was this because she was afraid her diary might be read by someone who would try to accuse her of espionage? Was it because she had been on relations of close friendship with a Japanese, or was it because her nationality really wasn't an *"Americano del norte?"*

Apparently she considered herself as holding the status of citizenship in a neutral country.

One thing I did definitely conclude. The girl I had met in that room, the one who had told me on the train that her name was Hazel Deering, had never written the pages of that diary. The entire style of writing, the very detachment in mental outlook simply didn't fit in with Hazel Deering. Was it possible then that the dead girl on the train was in reality Betty Crofath and that Hazel Deering was in reality the Daphne Strate who had left New Orleans so abruptly and under such strange and suspicious circumstances?

On January twenty-first, Karl had made her an offer to "go to work," saying that she possessed the qualities of resourcefulness and daring which were required by his "superiors" whom he wanted her to meet. She had chronicled his proposition, but not her answer. After making brief mention of the compliments Karl had paid her resourcefulness, daring and mentality, she had added as a humorous afterthought, *"and during all of the time he was bestowing such lavish praise upon my intellectual attainments, he said nothing whatever about my figure—the beast!"*

The mysterious N. K. seemed to have been well established as a friend at the time the diary opened. He was, I gathered, rather an interesting personality, filled with racial ideas of the destiny of his people, their invincibility in combat, and a sublime faith in the outcome of the struggle. On February twentieth, she had written: *"N. K. has such a peculiar mentality. Even now, when the most ardent and patriotic enthusiast at home must be assailed with doubts, N. K. still retains his sublime faith. But the man is unbelievably cunning and resourceful. He doesn't minimize the bad news, simply adopts the position that his work will be that much more difficult. It is fascinating to watch him, and yet—I am terribly afraid of him."*

In April, she had been to the races and *"had the uneasy feeling which comes from being followed. It was impossible in that crowd to tell whether any one person had singled me out for attention, but I certainly had the feeling all afternoon and evening that such was the case. Ran into Karl in a nightclub lounge. We had a dance together and he asked me how I was feeling. I told him of my uneasiness. I will never forget how he looked. His face was a mask of cold fury. He tried to keep up the small talk, but I could feel him stiffen to a rigid military efficiency. Trying to make his voice sound casual, he asked me if I had seen Numatsu. It was a ghastly job of acting. The man looked as though he had been ordering an execution. I noticed that he left the club a few minutes after we danced. And, strange to say, from that moment on, I lost all feeling of being under surveillance. Is there some connection—I wonder?"*

One thing about the woman, one peculiarity, furnished a key to her character. She seemed to have a certain flair for interior decorating. Whenever she saw a room which impressed her as being beautiful, she would go into enthusiastic details in her diary. I began to wonder if she might not at one time have been connected with interior decoration, or if perhaps this might not account for her presence in South America.

However, aside from that one clue, although there was a period of some six months covered in the diary, there was no word which would tell me anything of the woman's nationality, her occupation, if any, the manner in which she received her funds, or the reason for her trip to the United States. On the first of May, there was an entry saying, *"I am to go on one of the coffee boats. It has been all arranged. I will arrive in New Orleans, and it will be such a pleasure to see that city again. Yet, definitely, this is not to be a pleasure trip. What will be its outcome? I wonder."*

She did well to wonder. Lying cold in death, one couldn't help but speculate whether she had ever had any premonition that, before the year was finished, the hand that had penned the entries in the diary would lie cold and still while another girl would have usurped her belongings and tried to take over her identity.

Or was this woman dead? The body on the train had been that of a blonde girl. Betty Crofath's license showed that she had light hair. But Betty Crofath seemed to be a citizen of the United States. Surely no girl who had been born in the United States would have been on terms of friendship with the Japanese and the Germans. Was the identity of Betty Crofath a mask?

I spent the entire afternoon studying the diary, then shortly before nine o'clock, taking due precautions to see that I was not followed, went to keep my appointment at the Dragon Tooth night club with Ngat T'oy.

CHAPTER FIVE

The jazz orchestra squeezed out a syncopated rhythm of popular music. Very few people tried to listen. All about was the sound of conversation. Some woman, her voice keyed up with alcohol until it had all the strident insistence of a locomotive's whistle, kept shrilling above the other voices. Over at the table next to mine, a man was telling a low-voiced story. The women of the party were waiting for the proper moment when they could be moved to shrieks of laughter by a story they had probably heard somewhere or other at least six months ago.

Over on the right, a middle-aged man was talking insistently, persuasively to a woman half his age, who was beginning to become bored. The man kept pouring out words.

At the table behind me, two rather quiet, reserved men sipped sparingly at liquor and exchanged occasional words. Their manner indicated that they had some joint purpose, some sort of perfect understanding.

I shifted my position slightly so that I could give them the benefit of an oblique scrutiny. Situated as I was, I could never afford to overlook those about me, even for a moment. These men seemed not in search of entertainment. Definitely they were not on the prowl. They. . . .

And then I was pushing back my chair, for Ngat T'oy was coming toward me. These public meetings in Chinatown were risky for us both. She knew it as well as I. Yet the danger was only to ourselves, whereas if I went to see Soo Hoo Duck too frequently, the danger would involve not only a great man, but a cause as well. Therefore, for necessary conferences, Ngat T'oy and I met as we could. One thing I had long ago learned, an Occidental and a young, attractive Chinese girl may mingle without attracting too much attention in a Chinese night club or a Chinese restaurant—and nowhere else.

I held Ngat T'oy's chair for her.

A woman who tries to be seductive usually merely flaunts herself, just as a woman who dismisses sex from her mind tends to become a biological nonentity. Occasionally, some woman manages to strike just the right note. Such a woman will never be whistled at but every masculine eye will follow her across a room, and when she is seated, an almost audible collective sigh will go up from the onlookers.

I could all but hear the sigh as I seated Ngat T'oy and went back around the table to seat myself opposite her.

"We would give much to have known more of this woman," she said. "Did you find out anything at all?"

"A very little. I have clues."

A waitress appeared to take our orders, and we ordered *'ng ga pay,* that spiced oriental cordial which has the tang of herbs, a flavor as distinctly pungent as that of a dried litchi nut, and the kick of a mule.

At that moment, a gong filled the room with strident sound. The lights dimmed to a purple and all conversation ceased as though the flow of words had been cut sharply off with a knife.

Oy Ching Wong bounded to the little stage.

Various races have different standards of beauty. And there is a world of difference between the Orient and the Occident, but I have yet to meet any competent judge who has had the advantage of walking the streets of Shanghai in the evening after the theater hour who has not been willing to admit that China produces some of the most beautiful women in the world.

Oy Ching Wong was from Shanghai. She had that peculiar lithe grace and the smooth, flat stomach which is the heritage of rice-eating peoples the world over. Her dance was a combination of tawny-skinned nudity, oriental mysticism, and that rhythm of motion which makes it seem as though the body is writing poetry.

One could hardly hear a sound in the entire audience while the low strains of music pulsed through the half-darkened room and the lithe young body on the stage, with its smooth, old-ivory skin, held the audience in a trance.

When it was over, when Oy Ching Wong had gone, and after that first dazed moment during which the audience was coming back to earth, and before the roar of applause beat against the confines of the small room, I saw one of the two men at the table behind me move unostentatiously over to the telephone booth.

Then, for as much as a half a minute, everything at the night club was at a standstill. The audience went wild with enthusiasm, beat the applause up to a crescendo, begging for an encore.

But Oy Ching Wong—like one of those priceless adventures of life itself which are so frequently encountered unexpectedly—gave no encores.

When things had quieted down, I said to Ngat T'oy, "There are two men at the table behind me. It is difficult for me to watch them. One of them is telephoning. Do you know the other?"

I waited for her inscrutable black eyes to shift over to the other table—and I waited in vain. She said, without taking her eyes from mine, "I have never seen either of them before, Ed."

I smiled as I realized that Ngat T'oy would no more have seated herself at my table without having first appraised the persons around me than she would have thought of crossing a busy street intersection without looking at the traffic.

The Chinese waitress hovered around our table ostensibly putting down our glasses. "The man in the telephone booth," she said in Chinese, "is talking to someone, and his eyes keep shifting to this table. He has taken a newspaper clipping from his pocket."

The dance orchestra struck up music. I raised my eyebrows in a question to Ngat T'oy.

She smiled her assent, said casually to the waitress, "In the office. Have an evening paper for us."

We moved out onto the dance floor.

Ngat T'oy had that peculiar something which makes dancing seem a music-filled dream, and we floated along just over the floor, not quite touching it with our weight, but having just support enough to use our feet for guidance. For the moment, wars and murders were distant, remote things that peopled an outside world of grim nightmares while we were drifting smoothly along a stream of music headed toward the stars.

All too soon, the dance was over. We were back in the realm of reality, my arms still tingling with the feel of Ngat T'oy's warmth, but the ice-cold realization of danger stinging my brain into action.

The manager's office had been fixed up as a background for interviews with influential customers, publicity agents and sight-seers. It contained carved wood, deep rugs, crystal chandeliers, an elaborately carved, massive incense burner and several of the wooden figures of Longevity which the Chinese like to keep for good luck. The place was heavy with cloying incense. A green-shaded desk light threw white illumination on the pages of an evening newspaper lying on the desk.

Nor did it take us long to find that which we felt was significant. In the lower right-hand corner of the front page appeared in a small headline: "PULLMAN DEATH MAY HAVE BEEN MURDER."

Below that was a very brief dispatch under an Indio date line:

"Daphne Strate, who it was first believed met her death in a Pullman car from an overdose of sleeping medicine, may have been deliberately poisoned. Autopsy surgeons have found traces of a very unusual poison similar in its effects to one of the barbiturate group so extensively used for the purpose of inducing sleep. In fact, the similarity was so pronounced that had it not been for the curiosity of one of the assistant autopsy surgeons who carried his investigations a step beyond the routine requirements, the poisoning might never have been discovered at all.

"Miss Strate was a passenger on a west-bound train, who, seemingly in good spirits, left word with the car porter she was to be called at eight-thirty a.m. When the porter tried to arouse her, he found she was dead.

"Making the suicide theory seem possible was the fact that New Orleans police have announced they were seeking Daphne Strate in order to question her in connection with the embezzlement of a large sum of money from the Crescent City Chemical Manufacturing & Supply Company. Police are still inclined to the theory that the poison may have been self-administered, but there is always the possibility, in such cases, of a crime having more serious repercussions, and an investigation is going forward."

Ngat T'oy looked at me, a puzzled frown creasing her forehead. "Was the dead woman Betty Crofath or Daphne Strate?" she asked.

I studied the paper. "Betty Crofath, I think. But I don't see just how this fits in. Those two men behind us were waiting and watching. They took no great interest in me when I entered, nor in you when you entered, but when you came to my table, when you joined me, that's it! They were planted there, looking for a Chinese girl in the company of an American man. Quick! Let's see that paper!"

I spread the paper out on the desk, turned back to page one, and then over to page two.

Headlines struck me with the force of a blow.

"What is it, Ed?"

I pointed.

Together we read the story which had all but escaped our attention in turning hurriedly to continue the story of the death on the Pullman car.

Headlines stretching across four columns read: "NEGRO MURDERED IN GIRL'S BEDROOM."

Down below that appeared headlines in smaller type: "WEIRD CRIME UNCOVERED IN HOTEL ROOM OCCUPIED BY BEAUTIFUL BLONDE."

Below these headlines was the story:

> *"When Arthur Harryman, house detective at a downtown hotel, entered a room which had been rented to a beautiful blonde who had registered as Betty Crofath from Buenos Aires, he was confronted by a peculiar gurgling noise which aroused his curiosity.*
>
> *"Tracing the mysterious sound to the bathroom, Harryman found the body of a giant Negro, bound, gagged and slumped in death in the water-filled bathtub. Water running from the taps had evidently, for a few brief moments, overflowed to the floor of the bathroom, presumably when some obstruction had prevented the overflow drain from functioning. As Harryman entered the bathroom, water was still running briskly from the tap, filling the tub to within an inch or two of the top and then swirling down the emergency overflow drain. The water was a sinister crimson.*
>
> *"In the tub, wrists and ankles carefully tied together with strong cord, gagged with a woman's silken under-*

things and an expensive nylon stocking, lolled the inert body of the Negro.

"His throat had been cut from ear to ear.

"Police, summoned to the scene, at first pronounced the murder a sex crime, but with the development of additional evidence, are inclined to the belief that some weird, exotic gathering took place in the hotel bedroom. And the Negro may have been offered as a human sacrifice in connection with some bizarre religious rites.

"Significant is the fact that the water turned into the bathtub had been carefully regulated so as to be warm without being hot, as though the murderer had wished the body to be comfortable in death.

"Police are inclined to the theory that the crime was committed after the helpless Negro had been placed in the bathtub and water deliberately turned on to assist in removing evidence of the crime. Several good fingerprints have been developed from the faucets on the bathtub. And Arthur Harryman, the house detective, reports having seen a suspicious-looking individual on the third floor of the hotel not more than fifteen minutes before the body was found.

"Having been spotted by the alert eye of the house detective, this individual was accosted and taken to the office of the manager where he gave what appeared to be a satisfactory account of himself, explaining he was an officer from the Motor Vehicle Department. Subsequent investigation proved this to be false.

"Police have an excellent description of this individual, who is described as being about five feet ten and a-half or eleven inches in height, somewhere in the late twenties or early thirties, with an abundance of dark wavy hair, a thin straight nose, high cheekbones, penetrating gray eyes, broad-shouldered, slim-waisted, well-dressed in a dark gray, double-breasted suit. His weight is given as about a hundred and sixty-five pounds.

"Because certain literature discovered in the room indicates that the murder might have an oriental background, police became interested in the fact that a day or two ago, a beautiful young Chinese girl had registered in the hotel, asked particularly for a room on the third floor, and had been assigned a room almost directly across the hall from the one in which the body was later

discovered. There is, in fact, evidence leading the police to believe that this Chinese girl may actually have been in the room where the body was discovered shortly prior to the time the murder was committed. The clerk remembered that she had paid in advance for her room and that she was seen leaving the hotel shortly before the crime was uncovered.

"Police have as yet been unable to identify the victim. Apparently every bit of evidence which might give any clue as to the man's identity had been carefully removed prior to the murder. This, coupled with the water in the bathtub and the fact that the man had been bound and gagged before being killed, convinces the police they are dealing with a premeditated murder—one which may have weird ramifications founded in oriental mysticism or voodoo eroticism.

"The authorities are not as yet divulging the name of the Chinese girl, pending some clue which will connect her more definitely with the crime. But a preliminary test by fingerprint experts indicates that it may have been the slender, tapering fingers of a woman's beautiful hands which turned on the water in the bathtub.

"The Chinese girl is generally described as having smooth skin with a very faint trace of tawny color. She is perhaps twenty-seven or twenty-eight, slender of figure, and with features that the hotel clerk could only describe as very high-class Chinese.

"The woman who had rented the murder room under the name of Betty Crofath, is reported to be a quiet, rather beautiful blonde young woman with a distinctly Southern accent. Police feel confident that if she is innocent, she will communicate with them; or, if she is trying to avoid questioning, that they will have her in custody within another twenty-four hours.

"In the meantime, police are taking steps to identify the body, and they feel that when this is done, they will have additional light to throw upon the murder itself."

I looked up from the paper to meet Ngat T'oy's eyes.

"How long were you in the room after I left?"

"I left the moment the elevator door clanged shut. I went down to my room, waited for perhaps five minutes, then went down in the elevator and out to the street."

"When you left, did you notice a man in a brown, double-breasted suit with a white pin stripe sitting in a chair near the plate-glass window in the front of the lobby reading a newspaper?"

"No."

"You didn't notice him?"

"He was not there."

I drummed nervously on the corner of the desk. "The water," I said, "had begun to run over the bathtub before I left the room. That was because the Negro was holding his foot against the overflow escape. But not much water ran on the floor. That means he was murdered almost immediately after you left, Ngat T'oy."

"Those two men in the night club?" she asked. "They suspect?"

I said, "We walked into a trap. Those two men are simply typical of two headquarters men who are waiting tonight in every Chinese café, every night club, every cocktail lounge. They have been instructed to watch for a couple—an American man and a Chinese girl. The man at the telephone was reporting to headquarters. He was checking our descriptions against the newspaper clipping he had taken from his pocket. You know what that means? The place is probably being surrounded right now."

She nodded.

"Is there," I asked, "some way out of here other than by the entrance?"

Her hand came over to rest on mine. "Ed," she said softly, "when you are in Chinatown, there is always a way out—for you."

CHAPTER SIX

The greatest danger to Ngat T'oy was my presence. The greatest danger to me was hers. We came to a parting of the ways at a drab little door in an alley where we had been taken by secret passageways from the office of the night club.

Her hand touched mine lightly. " 'Bye, Ed," she said.

"Keep your chin up, Little Sun," I told her.

Impulsively, she raised my hand, brushed the back of it against the smooth skin of her cheek. Then she was out in the alley, moving with swift steps on feet so light that they hardly tapped an echo from the fog-shrouded buildings on the side of the alley.

I gave her thirty seconds. Then I slipped out the door and walked down the alley in the other direction.

Somewhere in the distance, I heard the sound of a siren. A police car roared past as I turned the corner. Aside from that, there was no trouble gaining my dingy little room, and making myself comfortable, awaiting the first move which would be made by Soo Hoo Duck when Ngat T'oy had told him the news.

While I was waiting, I turned on the radio, both the short wave set which was tuned to police calls and the conventional long-wave outfit that brought in the news every hour.

I learned that police had by now identified the dead colored man as George Bronset, the Pullman porter. That, in turn, reopened the case of the dead woman in lower six whose body had in the meantime been positively identified as that of Betty Crofath of New Orleans and Buenos Aires.

And since New Orleans police were making frantic inquiries concerning the whereabouts of Daphne Strate, broadcasting descriptions and photographs of her, it looked as though Miss Strate was mixed in something a little more sinister than a pleasure trip to the West Coast.

From the police description of Daphne Strate, I recognized her as the girl I had met on the train—the one who had first given me the name of Hazel Deering, then, later on, had posed in the hotel as Betty Crofath.

An employe of the Crescent City Chemical Manufacturing & Supply Company, Daphne Strate had, it seemed, simply disappeared into thin air. At the same time, a shortage of some six thousand dollars had been discovered on the books of the corporation. From the manner in which the coincidence was announced, it was plain that the police were not as yet definitely ready to pin that six-thousand-dollar shortage on Daphne Strate, but they were very anxious indeed to locate Miss Strate and ask her some questions.

The ticket seller remembered a young woman of Daphne Strate's description who had purchased a ticket to Los Angeles. A check-up on the Pullman space had disclosed that Miss Strate occupied lower five, while Betty Crofath had occupied lower six. The police let it go at that, merely commenting on the numbers of the Pullman berths, and mentioning also that George Bronset, the Negro whose body had been discovered in the room apparently rented by Daphne Strate under the name of Betty Crofath, had been the porter on that car—the very one who had discovered the body.

No-one needed to say any more. The whole thing made a series of damning coincidences that built up into a wall of circumstantial evidence. The only trouble was that I had been trained to distrust circumstantial evidence. I had seen too much of what it could do.

Minutes ticked away while I waited for the hand of Soo Hoo Duck to show itself.

A knock sounded on my door.

"Who is it?" I called in Chinese, and I flatter myself that no detective on the force would ever have suspected it was a white man calling the question.

I thought I recognized the voice, but I could not be certain. "You order food from restaurant," came from the door in the singsong of the *say yup* variation of the Cantonese dialect. "I bring food. Open the door so food does not get cold, please."

I stepped over to the wall and placed my eye to the little

periscope device I had installed. What I saw reassured me. The lone Chinese who was standing in front of the door clad in a loose-fitting blouse, light blue trousers, and embroidered Chinese shoes was Yat Sing.

Yat Sing was virtually the head of the Chinese Secret Service in San Francisco. He was a man of uncertain age, his moon face perfectly round and cherubic in its expressionless innocence, his eyes glittering with the concentration of attention, and his mouth schooled in silence.

On a first meeting, one never knew whether Yat Sing understood everything that was said to him, because he merely listened. He seldom spoke, asked very few questions, did not nod. He merely listened to what was said and then went out and did what was required. Anyone familiar with the results Yat Sing obtained never had any doubts whether he had understood what was said. Only at the first meeting could there be any question.

Yat Sing not only invariably carried out the missions he was called upon to undertake, but he usually added little artistic finishing touches, so dear to the heart of the true oriental diplomat.

I opened the door.

Until the door was safely closed once more, Yat Sing never once departed from the part he was playing of a gruff, good-natured but somewhat crude and inexperienced waiter.

"Get out table," he said. "The belly makes complaint at cold food. Cash in advance, please."

And Yat Sing had brought me a real meal—fresh fried shrimp with that peculiar Chinese sauce, made of catsup, with a little island of red hot mustard on top, hot fried rice, tea, chicken-almond chop suey and those delightful little pickled leeks the Chinese call *son kieu tau.* He brought all these on a series of trays, one atop the other, the whole expertly balanced. Had any detective stopped him, Yat Sing would have been able to show a complete Chinese meal. And, if he was not molested, he would be bringing me sufficient food so I need not run the danger of leaving my room for a full twenty-four hours.

I was hungry and the food looked good to me.

I pulled out a table, as he suggested, and closed the door.

Yat Sing sat and watched me while I ate, and talked in between mouthfuls.

"The secret of that girl in the hotel," I told him, "is the key to the whole business. If Daphne Strate were merely an innocent bystander sucked into the vortex of events, she ceases to have any real significance, *unless* Betty Crofath gave her something to keep for her—something that, to a girl such as Daphne Strate, would seem to be a trivial article of no particular importance. If she is not an innocent bystander, then her connection with the case is of the greatest importance."

I stopped to dip a fried shrimp into the tomato-mustard sauce and see how Yat Sing was taking it.

His eyes were bright with attention, his face merely a round frame for eyes, nose and mouth.

I said, "The police will cover the hotels, the rooming houses, keep an eye on the outgoing buses and trains. All that is routine, as you probably know." My chopsticks scooped up the chicken-almond chop suey.

Yat Sing said nothing.

"Daphne Strate," I said, "worked for the Crescent City Chemical Manufacturing & Supply Company. She is supposed to have been short six thousand dollars in her accounts. Let us suppose she was. What did she do with the money?"

Yat Sing might not have heard the question.

"There is," I said, "one answer, and only one answer. When a girl of that type is short six thousand dollars in her accounts, the money has gone to some man—either a ne'er-do-well brother or a glib-tongued lover who is short of cash and gets her to sacrifice everything in order to get him money.

"If, on the other hand, the girl is not guilty, then why did she run away? Why would the New Orleans chemical company feel that it had enough evidence to go to the police?

"Now then, in either event, she came to San Francisco. She had some reason for coming to San Francisco. I want to find out what that reason is. I want very much to find Daphne Strate before the police do."

I poured a little of the dark Chinese soy-bean sauce—which the Chinese call *shee yeu* but which is known virtually in every Chinese restaurant as "bettle juice"—over my fried rice.

The police are not dumb. Yat Sing, no matter what people may say about them. They will search for the *reason* Daphne Strate came to San Francisco. The obvious assumption is, of course, that Daphne was running away from the New Orleans police, that she learned in some way of Betty Crofath's death and, by taking possession of her purse, thought she could assume the dead girl's identity. As far as the baggage is concerned, having acquired a purse containing a trunk check, Daphne Strate had the trunk delivered.

"But suppose there is another explanation. Suppose, before Betty Crofath went to bed that night, she arranged to change identities with Daphne Strate. Suppose Daphne Strate was asked to come to San Francisco in connection with Betty Crofath's mission. Suppose her pretense on the train was not merely a coincidence but the result of carefully laid plans."

I stopped talking and looked intently at Yat Sing.

He slowly blinked his eyes.

I said, "I want to know all about the background of Betty Crofath in Buenos Aires. I want to know about a Karl Wilkers. I want to know who is the Ramon and who is the José in her life. I want to know all about Numatsu Kamchura. And," I went on, "the hell of it is, I want to know all of this before the police can possibly find Daphne Strate. I want to know it by tomorrow evening."

Yat Sing merely picked up the empty dishes. "All right," he said. "Can do. Maybe-so, can do."

I put in the biggest part of the night and most of the next day getting acquainted with Betty Crofath through her diary. Not only did I have the things she had written as a measure by which to gauge her character, but I had the things she had *not* written. For instance, I noticed there was never a word of complaint in the diary. On New Year's day, she had apparently been suffering from pretty much of a hangover, but she had made no complaint. She had made whoopee the night before and was paying the price. She paid it without comment other than one humorous line.

And there was a certain whimsical philosophy which ran like a thread of gold through the entire diary, connecting all of the incidents—a thin thread on which the events were strung into a necklace draped around the personality of a dead girl.

Then, abruptly, realization dawned on me that *I* might have in my hand a possible key to some of the problem I propounded to Yat Sing.

I ran through the diary, locating the date the coffee ship had docked in New Orleans. The entry was innocent enough on its face, yet, in the light of after events, it became significant:

"Docked at New Orleans at one p.m. Some trouble getting through customs. Hot and sticky, but New Orleans ever remains the incomparable city, the queen of them all. Bathed and changed at hotel then went out to wander through streets of the French Quarter. Had warned D. Not to meet me at boat. Once more am having peculiar sensation of being followed. Ate bouillabaisse, shrimp, good old Southern cornbread, chicken and Spanish rice. Bill for the two of us only $2.20, including wine with meal and cocktail before. Truly, there is no other city in the States quite like New Orleans. Leaving on train tomorrow night. In meantime, plan to keep very much to myself. As ticket is already purchased, will not do anything about that. Walked around until after midnight soaking up the atmosphere, dropping in at little bars. Had a wonderful time all by myself. Let a few of the boys buy me a drink but got rid of them afterwards by saying I was going to meet my husband. Afraid I was a bit crude about it, but they seemed to take it in good part. I have often noticed that about New Orleans. A girl can let herself get picked up for the evening and then go home alone if she wants to without making a scene. There is a certain give-and-take tolerance in the French Quarter that makes for good fellowship in the best sense of the word. Yet what is this feeling of nervous apprehension which is settling over me? D. laughs at me. It will be a relief when I am safely aboard the train and can enjoy a long sleep."

I debated over that entry. She had settled into a long sleep all right, poor girl. She had been apprehensive. Yet she had anticipated safety when she was once on the train. Why? Why would the train with its swaying, crowded Pullmans have offered more safety than her locked room in the New Orleans hotel?

She had gone to dinner with a certain D. That could have well been Daphne Strate. Some agreement had been reached —perhaps an agreement to switch identities. When I had first glanced through the diary, I had thought her statement that, since the ticket had already been purchased, she would do nothing about it, meant she had decided it was not necessary to secure any validation. It was, however, quite possible that if she made some agreement to switch identities with Daphne Strate, she had decided not to do it until after they were on the train.

Yat Sing showed up at eight o'clock with roast-pork chow mein, spareribs with bittersweet sauce, tea, almond cakes and rice. He had information to impart so he talked—a peculiar combination of Chinese words, pidgin English and motions.

"Numatsu Kamchura velly impo'tant. Die already." And Yat Sing clinched his hand as though holding a knife, and drew it rapidly across his abdomen from left to right.

"Same thing, *Jee saht.* Karl Wilkers alla same German man. Him boss send for him come back home, chop-chop."

"How go home?" I asked.

"Chiemm soey taung."

"You're certain he go by submarine?"

Yat Sing repeated with dogged persistence, "Am certain for sure. He go *chiemm soey taung."*

I waited for more.

"Betty Crofath alla same catchum one cousin, liv'em apartment house *tai fow.* I write 'em down paper."

Yat Sing handed me a piece of paper. On it written in a pencil scrawl: *Genevieve Hotling, 632 Medville Arms.*

I waited to see if there was any more.

"Betty Crofath write letters New Orleans. People no savvy much her pidgin. Keep alla same shut up. Ramon—José—too damn many. No can do."

Yat Sing ceased talking.

"Anything else?"

"No more."

I ate my dinner in silence and Yat Sing watched me in silence.

"Maybe-so by-and-by you find out more?" I said when I had finished.

He put the dishes back in the suitcase. "Maybe-so," he said as he started out of the door, which was loquacious indeed for Yat Sing.

CHAPTER SEVEN

When a man is on the lam, there are certain elemental things he must remember if he has to go out in public. He must never seem to avoid other people. He should mingle in crowds as though unconscious of them, should neither try to hold the eyes of persons who look at him nor to avoid their glances. He should not hurry. He should not loaf. He should be just an average citizen going somewhere. And, most important of all, he should never, under any circumstances, glance back over his shoulder.

The amateur tries to avoid crowds, tries to keep off the beaten path, acting on the theory that the more people with whom he comes in contact, the more eyes there are watching him. As a matter of fact, the exact opposite is the truth. The more people who are about, the more faces there are for eyes to see, the more weary the eye gets of seeing them.

Which was why I went by streetcar to the Medville Arms rather than by taxicab.

There was a list of names and a row of buttons to the left of the door. I didn't bother with any of them. I had the number I wanted, and the electrically-controlled lock on the street door was definitely not an obstacle to a person who knew anything about locks. It was not even an inconvenience.

I opened the door and entered the automatic elevator, whizzed up to the sixth floor and found 632 without any difficulty.

Noiselessly, I tried the knob of the door. It was locked.

I knocked.

I thought I heard surreptitious motion from inside the room, but I couldn't be certain.

I knocked again.

A feminine voice on the other side of the door sounded distinctly frightened. "Who—who is it?"

"Telegram, Miss Genevieve Hotling," I said, making my voice sound weary and without expression. "Charges, twenty-five cents."

"Oh," the voice said with relief.

The sound of a lock snapping back preceded the opening of the door.

I pushed forward.

Daphne Strate—alias Hazel Deering—fell back with panic-stricken eyes.

I kicked the door shut behind me.

"It's time for you and me to have a little talk," I told her.

She couldn't get her lips together. She backed three steps to the edge of a studio couch and dropped down on the cushions. "What . . . Who . . ."

I said, "Let's come clean for once. You doubled back to your room after I left. You found George Bronset, the Pullman porter, still in the bathtub with the water running. You cut his throat."

"I did nothing of the sort. You're crazy! Why should I have killed him?"

"We'll talk about that, too. You killed him, all right."

"I certainly did not! *You're* the one who killed him!"

I kept my eyes on hers. "It *had* to be you. He had something on you. He came to blackmail you. You pulled the gun on him and scared him to death. You didn't know what to do next. You tied and gagged him and put him in the bathtub. Then you realized that didn't help any. The gun had frightened him stiff, but he was still a blackmailer and sooner or later you'd either have to turn him loose or else leave the place and let someone else turn him loose. In either event, you were no better off than when you started—worse off, in fact. You can't stop a blackmailer by tying him up. You either have to pay up, tell him to go to hell, or kill him. You realized that, after a while. That's why you came back and killed him.

"You were just debating what to do with him when you heard my knock on the door. You were in a blue funk. You finally decided that the porter was all right in the bathroom for a while, so you opened the door. . . . Then the prisoner started making a noise, and you had to go out—until after you saw me leave; then you went back, with a knife."

I waited for her to speak, and it was a long wait.

"No," she said at length, "I didn't. It wasn't like that at all. You make it sound true, but it isn't."

"What did he have to blackmail you about?" I asked.

"Don't be silly! He didn't have a thing on me."

I laughed.

"Well, what's wrong with that?"

"In the first place," I said, "you had the berth next to Betty Crofath. Betty Crofath was poisoned. You go to the hotel where she had made a reservation, register under her name. You show up with her baggage checks, claim her baggage, have it sent up to your room, open it and go through it. Come on, sister. Let's at least be reasonable."

She looked as though I had hit her in the stomach.

"And don't take it out in bawling," I said. "We haven't any time for that."

"I don't cry. I'm not that kind. What do you want?"

"Suppose we try the truth for a change," I suggested.

She was silent for a few seconds, thinking. I didn't crowd her any, I simply sat there, waiting.

In that silence, the sound of a key in the lock sounded inordinately loud. I jumped to my feet and whirled.

The latch on the door clicked back. The girl who stood on the threshold was neat, trim, twenty-two or twenty-three, and cool as a test pilot. She looked at me with hazel eyes that held frank curiosity and not a trace of panic. Her hair, neatly combed along the sides of her head, was dark and glossy. The skin was of tawny smoothness.

"Hello," she said, and smiled. "Who are *you?*"

"You're Genevieve Hotling?" I asked.

"Yes."

"Related to Betty Crofath?"

"Yes. Are you a newspaper reporter?" she asked.

Daphne Strate said, "He's . . . he's. . . . You know who."

Genevieve's eyes didn't waver. "Oh," she said, "like that, eh?"

I saw her gloved hand grope back toward the doorknob.

I said, "It's too late for that. You can't get out now. Come in and join the party, Miss Hotling."

She sized up the situation, said suddenly, "Very well, I will."

She slipped out of her light overcoat, started taking off her gloves with a certain calm precision.

I said, "I'm trying to talk some sense into this girl. Perhaps you can help."

I liked the way she moved, liked the way she wore her clothes—a smooth, unwrinkled trimness about the way her garments fitted over the curves of her very good figure.

"Let's hear what *you* have to say first," she said, and seated herself over by the reading light. "Why did you kill the man?"

"Cigarettes?" I asked. "I didn't kill him," Miss Hotling."

"Yes, thanks. One would hardly expect you'd admit it."

I handed her a cigarette, offered one to Daphne Strate. Daphne drew back as though my hand had held a knife.

I reached for a match, but Genevieve had one going before I scraped mine into flame. She lit her cigarette with a steady hand, settled back in the chair, crossed her knees, said, "As I gather the situation, you've located Daphne. You're holding her a prisoner. I blundered in, so you're holding me."

"It's not quite that bad."

"Well, am I free to leave here?"

"No."

"Is she?"

"No."

"That makes us prisoners, doesn't it?"

"Let's call it material witnesses."

"Why did you make me come back?"

"I thought you might be going to call the police."

She glanced at Daphne.

Daphne said, "He killed the man, Jen, he *must* have killed him. He was starting for the bathroom when I left. If he'd going to . . . well, just find out who was making the noise in the bathroom, he'd have turned the man loose. He didn't. He turned on the water and cut his throat. . . . Ugh!"

Genevieve Hotling looked at me with a certain impersonal appraisal. "Yes," she said, "you'd have turned the man loose if you hadn't—done that other."

"Want to try listening to me for a while?" I asked her.

"Yes."

I said, "I met Daphne on the train. She gave me an assumed name. I located her in San Francisco after Betty Crofath was found dead. Daphne drew a gun on me and got out of the room. I found this porter bound and gagged in the bathtub. I took the gag out of his mouth and asked him questions. He was too frightened to talk. When he started to yell, I shoved the gag back in his mouth. I turned on the water so the room below would telephone in to the office and they'd investigate. That would give him a chance to get out, *after* I'd got in the clear."

She glanced at Daphne but didn't try to interrupt.

I said, "It didn't work that way. I walked out of the room and smack into the arms of the house detective. I had to think up a good stall, and had to think it up quick. I had Betty Crofath's driving license. I beat the house detective to the punch by pretending to be from the Motor Vehicle Department."

Her eyes met mine steadily. "And just how do you happen to be so interested in the girl who was my cousin? Why were you on the train? Why did you follow Daphne to the hotel?"

"I didn't follow Daphne to the hotel. I went there to see Betty Crofath. I didn't know the woman who was found dead on the train was Betty Crofath. I only knew Betty Crofath had reserved a room in the hotel, and had registered and gone to that room."

"Then you must have—wanted to see Betty," Genevieve said.

"I did."

"On the business that brought her up here?" she asked.

"You might put it that way."

Daphne said, in sudden panic, "Then why was he on the train, Jen? He must have gone there to . . . kill her."

"Or to protect her," I said.

"You didn't do a very good job," Genevieve flashed back at me.

"The train was late. I didn't have a chance. Daphne had already slipped her the poison. She was dead when I boarded the train at Tucson."

Genevieve looked speculatively at Daphne.

"Damn you!" Daphne said to me.

I took a drag at my cigarette.

"You don't know Daphne—or her relations with my cousin," Genevieve said. "If you did, you wouldn't make accusations like that."

"Perhaps not."

"Tell him," Genevieve said to Daphne.

"Damn him! I'll tell him!"

"Tell him," Genevieve interrupted her insistently.

Daphne hesitated, met Genevieve's eyes and started talking.

"I first got acquainted with Betty two years ago. We were working in the same office. Betty wanted to go places and do things. She went. I stayed on and worked. Betty wrote to me from time to time. She wrote she was coming back from South America and wanted to see me.

I met her a short time after she docked in New Orleans. She told me she had something very important that I could do, something that would fix it so I didn't have to keep on working in the routine of an office job. She made it sound very fascinating. She looked exceedingly prosperous and well-dressed, and had acquired a certain poise and polish. It made me feel I'd been missing a lot. So I told her I'd go along with her.

"On the train, she told me for the first time what she wanted. When we got to San Francisco, I was to take her identity, go to the Pelton Hotel, get her baggage, wear her clothes."

"Suppose you met someone you knew?" I asked.

"She didn't know a soul in San Francisco—except Jen."

"And what were you to do?"

"She was to give me instructions from time to time."

"How did you get her purse?"

"She gave it to me."

"When?"

"That night on the train. We exchanged purses. I took hers and she took mine. We kept out, of course, the personal things we wanted—lipstick and things of that sort—but we exchanged everything that would identify us."

"When did you see her last?"

"That night about eleven o'clock."

"What time did she go to bed?"

"That was when she went to bed—when we had that conversation."

"Did you know she was going to take a sleeping tablet?"

She hesitated. "Yes," she said.

"Did you see her take it?"

"Yes."

"Were you near her when she took it?" I wanted to know.

"Yes. We stood at the water cooler. We both had a drink. She . . ."

"Go on," I said, as she hesitated.

The sleeping tablets had been left by mistake in her purse—the one she'd given me. She said she needed them, that she forgot to take them out. So I took them out. She drew a glass of water and held out her left hand. I unscrewed the top of the bottle and tapped one of the tablets out of the bottle into the palm of her hand. She took it and washed it down with the water that was in the glass."

"Then what happened to the bottle?"

"I gave it to her. She dropped it in her bag—really my bag, you understand."

"And where was the porter when this was taking place?"

Her eyes faltered.

"Where was he?"

"He was . . . there."

"Near the water cooler?"

"Yes."

"He saw you give the tablets to Betty Crofath?"

"I guess so, yes."

"Did he tell you he had—later?"

"No. I never talked with him."

"Not in your room at the hotel?"

"No. I went out to get some things. I had arranged to have the baggage sent up. When I came back, the baggage was there. Then, as I was opening the trunk, I heard those funny noises in the bathroom. I looked in. He was there, in the bathtub, tied and gagged. I screamed. He rolled his eyes. I took a step toward him . . . and then you knocked on the door. . . . I felt I had to answer. . . . I went to the door. It was you."

I said, "You must realize how that would sound to a jury."

She didn't say anything.

"That porter saw you giving poison to Betty Crofath. He came to your room. He's found with his throat . . ."

"Stop!" she screamed.

I ground out my cigarette in the ash tray. She wasn't crying, but she was trembling.

"Why did you tell me your name was Hazel Deering?" I asked.

"Because it was the first name that popped into my mind. I

didn't know just what name to give you. I didn't know whether I was supposed to be Betty Crofath before we got to San Francisco or not. I hadn't asked Betty about that. I thought if I gave you my name as Daphne Strate and then you met the other girl and *she* gave you the same name it would be ridiculous. And, of course, the same thing would have been true if I had given you the name of Betty Crofath. So I compromised. I thought I could square it afterward if Betty wanted me to start in right away using her name."

"You had no idea she was dead until the body was discovered?" I asked her.

"None."

"Why did you come on to San Francisco after her death?"

"Because, for one thing, Betty had all my baggage and I had hers. The trunks had been checked through to San Francisco. I had to come here to get hers. And then—well, I heard from New Orleans."

"About the shortage in the company where you'd been working?"

"Yes."

"You hadn't embezzled anything?"

"Of course not."

"You weren't short in your accounts?"

"No. Absolutely not."

"You didn't see Betty in New Orleans, tell her you were in a jam—that you were short in your accounts and didn't know what to do and she advised you to come with her and take her name?"

"No. Certainly not."

"Any other reason for coming to San Francisco?"

"The president lives here."

"Who's the president?"

"Mr. Ruttling."

"You mean the president of the chemical company?"

"Yes. He's quite a big shot, Benjamin Colter Ruttling."

"Seems to me I've seen the name in print. Did you think you could get in touch with him; get a personal interview or the like?"

"I feel certain of it."

"What makes you think so?"

"Well . . ." she hesitated and shifted her position.

"Go ahead."

"Well, I don't know just how the company is organized. It's

a national organization, but the different state units are incorporated separately, and then, there's some holding company or something that co-ordinates all the activities of the state companies, and Mr. Ruttling is the president of this company. They put on a contest between the different companies and the different states for a certain type of efficiency. And, while the Illinois company won first place, the New Orleans company was second; and there was a banquet in New Orleans and some speech-making and dancing—and the president was there."

"And you met him?"

"Yes."

"You mean there was a little dancing and some joke-cracking,—and the president thought you were attractive and danced with you and handed you a line?" I asked.

"Well, in a way, yes."

"And you thought he'd remember you?" I asked.

"I'm quite certain he would."

"Why?"

Well . . . after the formal part of it was over—the dinner and the speeches and that stuff—the president told me he was bored stiff with so much formality and said he'd heard a lot about New Orleans and some of the more unconventional night clubs, and wanted to know if I knew any of the spots and I told him I knew where they were. So he suggested that he'd like to go and look around. He didn't want to go alone and wouldn't I break away and go with him."

"So you did."

"I certainly did. I'd been curious about some of those places myself. One or two of them I'd been in, and there were others I wanted to go to. And then, of course—well, the president."

"I see. So you and the president went out and looked the town over?"

"That's right."

And he told you that you were a very smart girl, and a very clever little girl, and a mighty good-looking little girl; and didn't you think, perhaps, you were wasting your talents working for one of the state companies in New Orleans, and that if you came to San Francisco didn't you think you might be able to better yourself. . . . ?"

"Why, yes. That was almost *exactly* what he said. He said

that he thought he could get me a position in the parent company where there was a chance for advancement."

"How long ago was this?"

"Oh, perhaps four or five months."

I said, "It's a fifty-fifty bet whether he'll remember you. What is he, a pompous old stuffed shirt?"

"No. He's . . . he's nice."

"And you came up here to see him?"

"Well, in a way, yes."

"Why?"

"Because I thought he might do something about that New Orleans situation and keep the company manager down there from telling a lot of lies about how I was short in my accounts."

"Are you bonded?"

"What do you mean?"

"I mean, did any bonding company guarantee that you wouldn't be short in your accounts?"

"Why, I don't think so."

"No application for a bond was made when you went to work for the company?" I asked.

"Noo that I know of."

"You haven't seen the president since you came here?"

"No."

I said, "All right, now, let's get down to brass tacks, Daphne. There was money in the purse Betty Crofath gave you, wasn't there?"

She nodded.

"How much?"

"Quite a little."

"How much?"

"A hundred or two hundred dollars."

"How much?"

"Over four hundred dollars."

"How much?"

She got mad again. "Four hundred and fifty-eight dollars and thirteen cents—if it's any of your damn business."

"And there was no money in the purse you gave her?"

"She told me to take my money out and put it away, and that I was to use her money for expenses."

"Then she must have had some more money?"

"I guess so."

I said, "Let's look at it the other way. You were short in your accounts in New Orleans. You were trying to get away. You knew that the officers were hot on your trail. You took the name of Hazel Deering. You got on the train and noticed the girl in the next section looked a lot like you. You noticed she seemed prosperous. You wished you were in *her* shoes. Then the idea occurred to you that you might get in her shoes. In your purse, you had some poison that you'd picked up through the chemical company where you'd been working. You decided that you'd never go to jail. If the police caught you, you'd take poison. Then the girl you'd been looking at came to you and asked you if you had any sleeping medicine. You said you had. You started to give her some. Perhaps by accident, perhaps deliberately you gave her the poison. If by accident, you happened to wake up along toward morning and realize you might have given her the wrong tablet. You went to her berth to see if she was all right. She was dead. The car was quiet; everyone was asleep. You switched identities with the dead woman. Later in the morning, the porter discovered the body. At the time, everyone thought it was a natural death. Later on, when the question of poison entered into it, the porter remembered what he'd seen. He didn't go to the police. He went to you. He wanted more than you were willing to give. You pulled a gun on him, tied him up, gagged him, and were wondering what to do with him when I knocked. Later on, you went back and killed him. It was your only way out."

"I did nothing of the sort," she said. "I was so frightened, I never went back to that room."

"What did you do?"

"Betty had told me about her cousin here. I walked the streets for a while—after I got out of the room in the hotel by pointing the gun at you. Then I remembered about Jen. I came up here and told her—everything."

I looked across at Genevieve.

"Check," she said.

"If I'd done the things you said," Daphne went on, "I wouldn't have known anything about Jen."

"Unless you got her address from a book in Betty's purse."

Genevieve said, "I don't think she did. I think Betty told her about me."

I asked Daphne, "Did you ever meet a man named Herb Rendon?"

"No—not that I know of."

"He was on the train, a heavy-set chap in a double-breasted brown suit."

Oh, I remember. No, I didn't talk with him, but I remember seeing him in the hotel lobby as I went out."

I asked Genevieve, "Did your cousin tell you anything about what she was doing in South America?"

"No. I'm a poor correspondent, and so is she. We only exchanged short letters. She sent me some postal cards."

"What's her nationality?"

"American."

"Her mother living?"

"No."

"Did Betty speak German?"

"No. She spoke Swedish. Our ancestors were Swedes."

I turned back to Daphne. "You haven't been in touch with Ruttling, haven't let him know you're here or made any attempt to get into communication with him?"

"No."

I got to my feet. "Well," I said, "I'm going to take a chance. The only thing in your story that supports your statement is that you may have actually been too frightened to have doubled back to your room."

"I've been telling you the truth," she said, "the absolute truth."

Genevieve Hotling studied me for a few seconds, then asked, "Could I help any if—if I went along?"

I moved out into the corridor, said, "No," almost closed the door, then turned, pushed it open and added, "thanks."

I heard her say, "You're welcome," as the door closed.

CHAPTER EIGHT

The home of Benjamin Colter Ruttling sat high on a ridge where, on a clear day, the eye could range out across the ribbon of blue water, looking over Alcatraz Island on the right, out through the Golden Gate on the left. On days when it wasn't clear, the house was a cold, bleak monument wrapped in chill uncomfortable fog.

At the rate at which real estate sold in the neighborhood, one could almost do mathematics with the weather statistics and tell exactly how many thousand dollars an hour the view was worth on those days of the year when it was available.

Tonight it was wrapped in somber mist—a thick, wet blanket that muffled sounds, distorted the perspective, and suited my purpose admirably.

I rang the bell and waited.

A Filipino who was no longer a boy, but a man nearing middle age, answered the bell.

I didn't waste any time with him. "I'm a private detective," I said. "My name is Sabin. I want to see Mr. Ruttling personally on a business matter which is important and which can't be put off. Tell him it has to do with his last trip to New Orleans and that it won't take over fifteen or twenty minutes to discuss."

The servant ushered me into a reception hallway, asked me to please be seated, and left.

The house was evidently air-conditioned. The reception hallway, illuminated with an indirect lighting that gave a uniformly gentle glow, was regulated as to temperature and humidity so that there was nothing to indicate that just just outside the door, a chill, wet fog blanket was blowing along the street or dripping monotonously from the eaves.

Somewhere in a distant part of the house, I could hear the occasional mumble of voices, and once or twice, the distant sound of laughter. Then the servant was back. Behind him came a tall, thin gentleman in evening clothes who looked as though he'd been laughing at a funny story before he entered the room, but was striving now to compose his features into a mask of cold, efficient business.

"I am Mr. Whitney, Mr. Ruttling's confidential secretary," he said, and waited.

"Good evening, Mr. Whitney," I said.

"I take it you can tell me something of the nature of your business?"

"Oh, certainly. First, I would like to ask a question about Mr. Ruttling."

His educated eyebrows indicated that this was not quite the conventional manner of doing business.

"Mr. Ruttling, I take it, has a sense of humor?"

"Oh, yes."

"If it should appear that the shortage in Mr. Ruttling's New Orleans office is laid at the door of the attractive female employe with whom Mr. Ruttling went out to see the town, that wouldn't bother him in the least?"

"I can see no reason why it should."

"Or if the most sensational tabloid newspaper in the country is offering the young lady in question a large amount of money for diary concerning the night Mr. Ruttling made his visit to New Orleans . . ."

"Just whom do you represent?"

"No one at present. I'd *like* to represent the Crescent City Chemical Manufacturing and Supply Company."

Whitney said, "If you'll get in touch with me at ten o'clock tomorrow morning, I think I can give you an answer."

"Doubtless you could," I told him. "Between now and tomorrow morning, I could get in touch with half a dozen other people who could also give me definite answers."

"What do you mean?"

I said, "You damn fool, I mean that *I* have the diary."

"Oh," he said. "Wait here just a minute, please," and walked out.

He was back within five minutes, evidently acting under

definite instructions. "This," he said, "sounds omniously like blackmail."

"Perhaps it does to you. To me, it sounds like business."

"Do you have any proposition you would care to make—to me?"

"No."

He said, "Step this way, please."

I followed him through a door, up a flight of stairs and into a room that was evidently fitted up as a species of supplemental office with some filing cases, a couple of secretarial desks, typewriters and built-in cases.

"Just a moment, please," Whitney said, and crossed the office to knock at a massive walnut door.

After a moment, he opened the door an inch or two, peeked inside, then he eased his lath-like figure through the opening. He called back over his shoulder to me, "Just a moment, please," and closed the door gently behind him.

I stood there waiting, very careful not to touch anything, feeling certain that appraising eyes were watching me from concealed peepholes.

At the end of some three or four minutes, the door opened again and Whitney jackknifed himself into the room. His face was twisted into a smile that was evidently meant to be cordial.

"Step right this way, Mr. Sabin," he told me.

He opened the door wider this time and stood to one side, ushering me into the presence of greatness.

Benjamin Colter Ruttling sat in a room that was a cross between a den and a private office. He was at his ease in a deep-cushioned, russet leather chair that matched the bindings of rare books that filled the bookcases. He was an expansive, genial gentleman with merry, twinkling eyes, a neck that was slightly inclined to washboard, a forehead that was high and round, with the hair thinning just a bit. The eyebrows were well shaped, and if the man had taken that jovial grin off his face he could have looked deadly and dangerous.

He was wearing a dinner jacket with a black tie, a pleated white shirt, and he exuded an air of well-fed prosperity.

"Ah, yes," he said, "Sabin, a private detective. Sit down, Mr. Sabin, and tell me what I can do for you."

I said, "Apparently there's been a shortage of six thousand or so in your New Orleans office."

"I'm afraid I don't keep up with the details of things, Mr. Sabin. I leave the minor matters to my local managers, who are capable of handling them."

"And," I said, "the girl the newspapers are going to play up in connection with the shortage is a Miss Daphne Strate—and when you were in New Orleans, you and Miss Strate went out to see the town."

"There is the matter of a diary?" he asked—not of me, but of Whitney.

"So this man says."

"Naturally," I said, "Miss Strate considered that evening as the highlight of her life. She was flattered, excited and intoxicated. She came back home and confided to her diary."

"Dear, dear," Ruttling said deprecatingly, "such a naïve habit!"

"Isn't it? You can, of course, get the picture of a young woman completely losing all perspective, thinking that Mr. Big was paying quite a bit of attention to her, and she *might* well have an opportunity some day to preside over the destinies of Mr. Big's household if she just played her cards right. She wanted money for culture, for clothes—and for traveling expenses to San Francisco."

"And so she dipped into company funds?" Ruttling asked.

"Exactly."

"Hardly an auspicious way to advance her career," Ruttling said. "I'm afraid that wouldn't make a very convincing story, Sabin."

"Expecting,"—I went on as though he hadn't said anything — "to be able to pay it all back. Then, when sudden financial misfortune overtook her, and she realized she was trapped, her last forlorn expedient was to come to San Francisco and throw herself on the mercy of the man she had learned to really love."

Ruttling frowned.

Whitney said virtuously, "One, of course, can't be held responsible for the adolescent emotions of those with whom one comes in casual contact."

"Which," I said, "is precisely why much hinges on what is in the young woman's diary. It depends *so* much on what you mean by a *casual* contact."

That brought them up with a jerk.

"Precisely what *is* in the diary?" Whitney asked.

I smiled at him.

"What," Ruttling asked, "is your proposition?"

"I want some information."

They exchanged glances. "What information?"

I said, "Let's suppose, for the moment, that Daphne Strate didn't take the six thousand from the New Orleans company. Who did?"

"I'm afraid I don't understand."

I said, "Let's concede, for the moment, that six thousand dollars has been taken from your New Orleans company. It just didn't get up and walk out by itself, did it?"

"Naturally."

"How do you know Daphne Strate took it?" I wanted to know.

"My New Orleans manager has charge of all such details. I wouldn't know. I'd have to ask him."

"Get him on the phone and ask him."

He frowned, then said, "No, I don't think I'd care to do that —not as yet, at any rate. You haven't shown your hand, as yet."

"You've seen all you're entitled to see—the backs of the cards, my ante and the chips I'm putting in."

"The backs of cards all look alike."

"I'll put them on the table when someone calls for a showdown."

"I'm calling for a showdown now."

"Oh, no, you aren't. You haven't called my bet yet."

"What's your bet?"

"I want this information."

He thought for a moment, then said, "The manager of the New Orleans office is a very responsible individual. We have quite a large business out of Louisiana. He wouldn't make such an accusation if it weren't fully substantiated."

"What's his name?"

"Randolph Holaberry."

"You do quite a business out of New Orleans?"

"Yes."

"Foreign trade?"

"To South America, yes."

"Fool around any in international politics?" I asked.

"Absolutely not."

"Don't care a hang about who runs those South American countries, about what party is in power?"

"Certainly not."

I got to my feet. "When will you be able to get in touch with Holaberry?"

"I don't know. I'll—I'll put through a call for him."

"By the way," I said, "would it make any difference to you who happened to be in power in Argentina, for instance?"

"Absolutely not," he shot back, the words snappy as musket fire.

"Or," I asked, "do you have any foreign competitors—perhaps the Japanese, for instance?"

He smiled. "No Japanese competition. The only Oriental competition we have is Chinese."

I raised my eyebrows.

"The Bak Shui Wong Company," he explained. "They undersell us on certain competitive lines in some foreign countries, but our products are worth the extra price."

"And you don't know anything about a Miss Betty Crofath?"

"I never heard of her."

"You have agents in Argentina?"

"We do business through local distributors in the South American countries. Of course, we keep in close touch with those distributors, but . . . I think you have everything you are entitled to, Mr. . . . er . . . er . . ."

"Sabin," his secretary supplemented.

"Oh, yes, Mr. Sabin," Ruttling said, smiling an affable smile of dismissal. "I'll get in touch with my New Orleans manager, just to see what he can tell me about this girl, this Miss . . ." He looked at his secretary.

"Strate," Whitney said.

"Oh, yes, Miss Strate. I want to find out about her. I don't think I remember her, Mr. Sabin. And, as far as the diary is concerned, I don't think I'm interested. You said some newspaper was interested? Well, I think I'll let you deal with this newspaper."

I frowned at him. "Yet when Whitney told you about me, you left a dinner party to see what I had to offer."

"Perhaps that was merely curiosity."

"And now you're no longer curious."

"Perhaps my curiosity has now been satisfied."

I walked out of the room, down the stairs, the footsteps of the secretary pattering along behind me. The Filipino opened the door and I went out. For the life of me, I couldn't tell where I had said the wrong thing, but I'd stubbed my toe somewhere.

Where had I missed my cue? Ruttling had been jarred enough and frightened enough to leave his dinner party and see me. Then he'd recovered his assurance. He didn't give a damn what I did now. Where had I said the wrong thing—or failed to say the right thing?

I kept going over and over the conversation in my mind. Suddenly I got an idea. I walked down to a drugstore and called Genevieve Hotling.

"Don't say anything that would tell anyone who might be listening who this is, but . . ."

"There's no-one here," she said. "I'm all alone."

"How long since Daphne went out?" I asked.

"About twenty minutes. How did you come out in your interview?"

"I came out," I said, "the same way I went in—through the front door." And I hung up the receiver.

CHAPTER NINE

Soo Hoo Duck wore a wide-sleeved Chinese coat embroidered with fanciful dragons, crawling and squirming about the silk background, chasing always the elusive pearl of wisdom which is shown just in front of their gaping jaws. The long nails of his hands were incased in sheaths of wrought gold in which jade had been inset and cunningly carved. The sheaths protected his nails against breakage, but made a peculiar rasping sound as his hands trailed across the map of South America which lay spread on the table before him.

He looked across at Ngat T'oy and his right hand swept over Argentina in an inclusive motion which brought the gold and jade nail sheath on the right index finger against Buenos Aires.

He glanced up at Ngat T'oy.

Ngat T'oy turned to me. "He wants to know what you think, Ed."

"I have told him the facts," I said.

Soo Hoo Duck's eyes stared steadily at Ngat T'oy. He didn't speak.

"My father says," Ngat T'oy went on, "that facts are food for thought which the mind of the truly wise man digests into wisdom."

I said, "I'm afraid my digestion is not too good."

She said nothing, merely waited.

"Oh, well"—I surrendered—"Betty Crofath was on the trail of something big. She was afraid. She got in touch with Daphne Strate because she was afraid. Daphne has lied to me. I don't know where the truth leaves off and the lies begin. Daphne has some hold on Benjamin Ruttling, the president of the chemical company. She knew I was going to see Ruttling. I delivered my message to Whitney, Ruttling's secretary. It brought Ruttling to me on the run. But, before I reached him, something happened. That something must have been a telephone call from Daphne herself. Ruttling played with me as a cat plays with a mouse. And Daphne gave me the double-cross.

"Betty Crofath had something. She was playing a shrewd game, evidently posing as a neutral, possibly Swedish. She was on the trail of something that was carefully developed for months. There must have been something—some map, some clue, some documentary evidence. Daphne Strate must have that. She must know its value, and she is going to use it to feather her nest. She may offer it to us, but not until she sees how much the other side will pay to get it back. . . . Unless Genevieve Hotling is the one who has it, and the one who telephoned Ruttling."

Ngat T'oy translated.

Soo Hoo Duck mumbled in Chinese, "The cat which has eaten the canary always starts purring."

Ngat T'oy said, "Which one of the women will be the first to buy new clothes, Ed?"

I said, "It isn't that. It's bigger and deeper than that. I don't think the canary has been eaten—not yet. The person who got the information Betty Crofath had hasn't been able to use it. That may be just a hunch, but it's my best guess."

"What makes you say that, Ed?"

I said in Chinese, "When the canary cage is open and none of the cats are purring, it is a good sign the bird has flown out the window."

I felt Soo Hoo Duck's shrewd eyes fastened on mine, probing my thoughts.

I said, "I have looked up The Bak Shui Wong Chemical Company. It had headquarters in Shanghai. Ostensibly, it is still Chinese, but you know what must have happened to the control of that company. It has extensive trade in Argentina. Large stocks were piled up there for distribution before transportation difficulties developed."

Ngat T'oy flashed a glance at her father. "You have a plan, Ed?"

I nodded. "I will be the canary," I said, "and see which cat tries to pounce upon me when I am not looking."

There was a moment of silence, then Soo Hoo Duck's hands

moved once more over the map. The nail sheaths made his motions slightly awkward as he fumbled over a carved ivory rosebud in the decorations of the inlaid table.

His thumb joint pressed down. I heard a metallic click, and the drawer slid open. It was filled to the brim with currency. Soo Hoo Duck said nothing.

Ngat T'oy's delicate fingers scooped out the large denomination bills. "You will," she said, "need the sinews of war. As a canary, you must have golden feathers, Ed."

CHAPTER TEN

A full moon riding high in the heavens turned Lake Pontchartrain into a pathway of gold. The New Orleans airport loomed ahead and the plane dipped its nose.

The stewardess came by, adjusting the dark curtains over the windows. "Sorry," she apologized, "but we have to come down with the passengers blind."

I said, "You got my wire off to Mr. Holaberry?"

"Oh, yes. That went hours ago," she assured me.

The motors gave forth that peculiar swishing sound which is so characteristic of a big plane coming down. A few moments later, a series of faint, muffled jolts running up through the plane indicated that we had landed.

It was still a long, tedious ride to the city, but when I arrived, my reservations were waiting for me. I had just finished with the luxury of a good tub bath when the telephone rang and Randolph Holaberry was on the line.

"Is it too late to run up for a chat, Mr. Sabin?" he inquired.

"No. I was rather hoping you'd call. You got my wire?"

"Yes. I'll be right up."

He was a brisk, alert chap in the late forties, with the restrained, jovial manner of a man who wants to be the perfect host and furnish just the right entertainment, but is carefully feeling his way.

"You're familiar with New Orleans?" he asked.

"I've been here several times."

"We have some unique night spots in the Vieux Carré."

"I know you have."

"Some of the atmosphere has been ruined by the influx of such a large number of people—conditions due to the war and all that—but you can still find—well, just about anything you may be looking for."

His eyes, slate-gray, prominent and alert, twinkled at me from behind rimless spectacles.

"So I understand. I'm afraid I won't have time to do much prowling. I'm leaving almost immediately."

"Your wire said you were interested in detergents?"

"That's right. In quantity, delivered at Buenos Aires."

"I think we could make you a very attractive offer."

"You have an agency there?"

"A distributor. We, of course, would work very closely with our distributor on matters of this kind."

"My purchases," I said, "would run somewhere around twenty-five hundred dollars a month—in gold."

"Could you tell me something of the nature of your business?"

"Not now. I want to know just what you manufacture, and get your prices first. I presume you'd want to get in touch with your South American distributor," I said.

"Well . . . well, yes and no. However, I can give you approximate data."

He was fumbling with the snaps of a brief case as he talked. Once the fastenings came off the case, he was the suave, persuasive manager of an important business. He took out illustrated folders, showed me his line, showed me testimonials, gave me interesting information on competitive prices, on local conditions, on shipments and deliveries.

"I see," I said at length, "that your line is most complete. Have you made any attempt to segregate those chemicals that are dangerous?"

"What do you mean by being dangerous?" he wanted to know.

"Poisonous."

"No. Many of them are very deadly to man. We, of course, see that purchasers of those chemicals are duly warned."

"There isn't anything then in the shape of tablets that might be confused with. . . ."

"Oh, no. Our stuff is in bulk. Wait a minute—we have one chemical that is put up in small, white tablets that is—well, it could be . . ."

"Poisonous?"

"Well, yes."

"In small doses?"

"Yes."

"What would the symptoms be?"

"Something similar to an overdose of sleeping medicine, I believe. And, of course, there are some of the cyanides . . . But surely, Mr. Sabin, you aren't apprehensive that . . ."

"I am," I interrupted. "I insist that any company with which I do business shall take all responsibilities in connection with labeling. The laws of various countries differ, and I am not familiar in detail with the laws of Argentina in this respect."

His face showed relief. "Have no fear, Mr. Sabin. We will assume all responsibility."

An hour later, he extended his hand and clasped mine in a cordial handshake. "That will give you a general idea," he said. "I'll see you tomorrow around ten o'clock. By that time, you'll have had a chance to think things over."

"By tomorrow morning," I said definitely, "I'm going to reach a decision. Good night."

I followed him out into the corridor, went down as far as the elevator with him, then went back to my room and sat down and waited.

If that particular cat had been eating any canaries, he had given no indication of the fact. But, perhaps he was too shrewd to be caught licking his chops.

I waited ten or fifteen minutes, then went out to stroll along the narrow, uneven paving blocks of Royal Street.

Everywhere, the night life of the French Quarter was going full-blast. The narrow streets were crowded with people who were there for pleasure—the warm, tropical air, heavy with the scent of lush greenery; the round moon riding toward the meridian; the carefree tinkle of feminine laughter; the low pitched insistence of masculine voices; couples strolling casually from place to place or standing in the narrow doorways talking in low tones; curious sightseers from out of town; the little friendly bars crowded with people chatting back and forth as though they'd known one another for years. It was all a part of the gay Bohemian night life distinctive to the New Orleans French Quarter and for the moment, I all but forgot the grim nature of my errand.

I dropped in at a corner bar for a drink. A young chap who was there with two attractive young women started talking to me. In no time at all, we were a foursome. And, despite my intentions, it was after three o'clock in the morning before I finally re-entered the hotel and asked for my key.

A swarthy gentleman seated over near the cigar stand casually arose and approached me. "Mr. Sabin?" he said.

I didn't need to simulate surprise. My emotion was genuine.

"I know that it's very late, and yet here in New Orleans we so frequently take advantage of the cool of the night. If I could talk with you for five minutes—perhaps ten?"

I glanced at the clock. "About what?"

"About chemicals."

"What about them?"

"Permit me to introduce myself. I am Señor Ramon Vasquo Gomez. I am what you would call a citizen of the world, but I am exceptionally familiar with the South American countries and the problems confronting one who would engage in business there."

I gave him my hand, bowed low, with a politeness that matched his own. At the moment, my first thought was to determine whether he was the Ramon referred to in Betty Crofath's diary.

"As you say," I observed, "where the days are hot, the cool nights seem to hold back the hands of the clock."

"Exactly."

He was olive-skinned, unusually dark of eye, and it was hard to place his exact age. I put him somewhere in the late thirties, a well-knit, wiry little chap who had just that selfish veneer of suave polish which would enable him to send a girl orchids one night and stab her in the heart the next.

"You intend to establish a business in South America?" he asked.

I was cautious. "At present," I told him, "I am merely traveling."

"In certain South American countries," he said, "business is done upon a more intimate—more personal basis than here in North America. A person's contacts can do him much good, or . . ."

"So I understand. I have certain South American contacts."

"Are they tentative, or shall we consider that they are absolutely permanent and irreplaceable?" he wanted to know.

"It might be better to call them tentative," I told him.

"Ah!" he said, and his exclamation was velvet-smooth in satisfaction. "It is quite possible that I can be of assistance. I have heard very indirectly, Señor Sabin, that you are looking for certain commercial chemicals. Here in this country, where you have tariffs and trade restrictions, it is unusual to consider Oriental products. But in South America, I can assure you it is not. The Bak Shui Wong Company, as I happen to know, is in a position to furnish any quantities of commercial chemicals at the right prices."

"Indeed," I said. "That is most interesting." I started to say something else, then suddenly caught myself and snapped my fingers. "Now I've got it."

"What?" he asked.

"I have seen you before," I said. "Let me think. Buenos Aires . . . January first, nineteen hundred and forty-three. There was someone with you—an attractive young woman. It was shortly after daylight. You were talking in front of a hotel . . . an argument."

"It is," he announced, "quite possible. I was in Buenos Aires on January first, nineteen forty-three—and surely, Señor Sabin will realize that any South American gentleman would be accompanied on New Year's morning by an attractive companion." And Señor Gomez preened a little smile in my direction.

I nodded. "Quite so. But it has been worrying me ever since I met you, where I had seen you before. I'm quite certain now that I place you."

"That," he said, "is fortunate, because it is not well that those little haunting thoughts should mar a potential friendship. It is much better when one is able to dismiss those haunting memories so as to relax and drift along on the stream of mutual liking."

His dark eyes twinkled a friendly message into mine.

I glanced at the clock. It was three forty-five. I had a reservation back to San Francisco on the six-o'clock plane.

"Perhaps," I said, "you would care to have breakfast with me. We might talk about chemicals. Unfortunately, I have a very early appointment with another gentleman—an appointment for ten o'clock."

"But any time suits me!" Señor Gomez exclaimed.

"Would eight-thirty be too early?"

"Not at all. I might even suggest eight o'clock because there might be certain details to be discussed before your ten-o'clock appointment."

"Eight o'clock," I said, "will be quite all right. Here at the hotel?"

He bowed and extended his hand.

I felt the long, sinewy fingers grip mine, and there was something in the grip that made me want to jerk my hand away. It was as though the tentacles of an octopus had twined themselves about my wrists. But his eyes were smiling and very friendly.

Quite ostentatiously, I wished the clerk good-morning, left a call for six o'clock, and took the elevator up to the floor where my room was located. But I didn't go to the room. Instead, I walked down the corridor to the stairs, walked down the stairs, waited until the clerk's back was turned, then moved casually across the lobby and out the side door to the street.

The office and factory of the Crescent City Chemical Manufacturing & Supply Company was down near the waterfront in an old part of the French Quarter where dilapidated commercial buildings filled with musty atmosphere and haunted with hoary antiquity offered plenty of space and cheap rents.

Under the circumstances, effecting an entrance to the building was mere child's play for a man who had at one time in his checkered career specialized in locks and combinations; nor did the door of the big vault offer any difficulties other than the necessity for locating and disconnecting the burglar-alarm system and brushing up a bit on some of the technique that was a carry-over from the old days.

Once inside the vault, I had no difficulty in locating what I wanted.

Quite apparently, auditors were going through the books to determine the exact extent of the shortage, and their progress through the various ledgers was denoted by a series of orderly check marks against the numerous items which had been gone over.

I moved on ahead of the audit, locating figures which denoted liquid assets, wherever possible moving a decimal point or skillfully changing a figure. Then, with a pencil, I made little checks just as the auditors had done, so that it appeared the work had progressed farther than was actually the case, and that the figures I had changed and manipulated had been approved by the auditors.

There was not one chance in ten thousand that such manipulation would go unnoticed. It was the last-minute, clumsy attempt of a desperate criminal who was being cornered.

When I had completed my work, I replaced the books, closed the vault, slipped out of the door, and noticed that the first gray light of dawn was beginning to illuminate the French Quarter.

I walked through the deserted streets to the Roosevelt Hotel, found a taxi and was taken to the airport. I sat in the waiting room, dozing until my plane was ready to take off.

At about the time I entered the plane and fastened the safety belt, I had the satisfaction of knowing that I had left behind me a trail which would lead to a bewildered confusion which, in turn, would set in operation certain activities that promised to have some very startling repercussions.

When I failed to respond to the call I had left at my hotel, a bellboy would be sent up with a passkey. He would find the bed had not been slept in, that my personal belongings were spread about the room. The night clerk would remember that I had wished him a good-morning at around four o'clock, that I had gone directly up to the room, that shortly before that I had been in earnest conversation with a dark-complexioned man who might have been a South American. And at about the time the police were being notified, Señor Ramon Vasquo Gomez would enter the lobby to keep his early-morning appointment with me, and find a police officer ready with a warm welcome.

Shortly thereafter, auditors checking the books of the chemical company would begin to puzzle over certain discrepancies which had, apparently, been duly checked in the progress of their audit. Sometime within the next forty-eight hours, the discovery would be made that the books had been tampered with in a desperate attempt to distort the facts with reference to liquid assets.

On the whole, it looked rather promising. New Orleans police would definitely be puzzled to account for the manipulation of the books. Such falsification of records was hardly compatible with the theory that Daphne Strate was the guilty party. Perhaps now Benjamin Colter Ruttling would begin to concern himself with the details of his New Orleans branch, while Daphne Strate could begin to wonder at what was happening.

So I settled back in the cushions and let the rhythm of the

pulsing motors lull me into restful slumber. I doubted if the New Orleans police would connect the west-bound passenger who had secured reservations under the name of John Harper with the east-bound passenger named Sabin who had been bound for South America.

At any time now, the cat which had eaten the canary might well begin to suffer the first premonitory pangs of acute indigestion.

CHAPTER ELEVEN

Yat Sing was waiting for me in front of the dingy little Chinese-owned apartment house where I had my hideout. His eyes slithered up to mine in quick appraisal, then glided away without his having made the slightest sign; but I knew he had news to impart, and would join me in a few minutes.

I got under a shower, changed my clothes, and was half dressed when I heard Yat Sing's knock at the door, and the rattle of dishes.

I opened the door. Once more, Yat Sing was the perfect characterization of a Chinese waiter. He raised his voice in the sing-song pidgin English of Chinatown, and said, "My bossey man say long time now you no pay. You going catchum food my restlaunt, you must catchum pay me money tomollow suah."

I said, "Things have been pretty tough. I can let you have two dollars today, perhaps two dollars more tomorrow. How's that?"

"All-right. Maybeso I tell bossey man," Yat Sing replied.

The dishes rattled as Yat Sing set the tray on the table. Then he went back and closed the door, came over to sit beside me, and took a long breath, priming himself for the unwelcome chore of carrying on a long conversation.

"You go airplane," Yat Sing said. "Maybeso two hour later, white man comes, ask questions, look over list of people who go on plane. Then he go sendum telegram. No can find out what's in telegram. I find out two telegrams to New Orleans."

"What did this man look like?"

"Face have expression alla same happy bull. This man thick."

"Clothes?"

"Clothes alla same yours, but different color—brown."

"You mean double-breasted brown?"

"Alla same."

"A little stripe?"

"White."

I knew now that Herb Rendon had given me a line on himself. I asked confidently where this man lived.

"This man," Yat Sing said, "velly smart. Velly hard follow. He go all around circles. He go in one door; he come out another."

"Where did he go finally?"

"Montelley House Hotel."

"Under what name is he registered?"

"No find out yet."

"Benjamin C. Ruttling, president of Chemical Company—how about him?"

"He go see police."

"What about?"

"Not find out yet."

"Daphne Strate and Genevieve Hotling—what about them?"

"Still same place."

"Has Daphne Strate seen Mr. Ruttling?" I asked.

"No see."

"Have the police found any more clues to the killing of George Bronset, the porter?"

"No clues."

I ate my dinner silently, thinking that over. Yat Sing smoked a cigarette, saying nothing.

"Ramon Vasquo Gomez," I said at length, "in New Orleans. I saw him there and . . ."

Yat Sing was ahead of me. "You leave hotel. Ramon Gomez come see. Police talk long time. Ask many questions. Take him headquarters."

I said, "I also had an appointment with Randolph Holaberry for ten o'clock. What did he do?"

"He not come."

Once more, I was silent, and once more, Yat Sing returned to his cigarette. No use to ask him how he knew these things or to question the accuracy of his information. He was head of a far-flung system of celestial espionage and transmitted accurate, up-to-the-minute information of cold, hard facts. He wasted no time in idle surmise. When Yat Sing had established something as a fact, he would communicate it. Until that time, his thought processes were locked behind a bland, moon-faced tranquillity that was as hard to penetrate as the armor of a battleship.

Abruptly, Yat Sing, noticing that I had finished, got up and arranged the empty dishes on the tray.

"That's all the information you have?" I asked.

"No more." He turned at the door. "Maybe so you go out," he said. "Maybe so you have trouble. No matter. Chinaboy plenty close."

And he was out, closing the door behind him.

Soo Hoo Duck had spoken. The mysterious, ubiquitous hand of the Chinese would be protecting me.

I smoked two cigarettes and did much thinking. Then I put on a light overcoat, drew on thin, very soft and flexible gloves, pulled a hat down low on my forehead, and went out into the night.

CHAPTER TWELVE

I tapped gently on Apartment 632 at the Medville Arms.

Genevieve Hotling opened the door. "Hello," she said.

"May I come in?"

"It's almost midnight. I was just going to bed."

I didn't say anything.

She smiled then and said, "Oh, all right, come on in. I was interested in a story and was sitting up to finish it. Usually I'm in bed by eleven."

"Where's your friend, Daphne?"

"She hasn't come in yet."

"Been out all evening?"

"Since about nine. Did you hear about what happened in New Orleans?"

"What?"

"They've virtually cleared her of the embezzlement."

"How did that happen?"

"I don't know the details, but something happened that convinced the police the embezzler is still in New Orleans. Apparently he tried to take some advantage of the auditors who were working on the books."

"So Daphne's out in the clear?"

"Yes."

"And about the hotel business?"

She said, "I'm satisfied that will straighten out."

"You don't think Daphne Strate had anything at all to do with your cousin's death?"

"Naturally not. Otherwise I wouldn't be protecting her."

"And you don't think she had anything to do with the death of the Pullman porter?"

"Of course not."

"What makes you so positive?"

"She couldn't have done it; she simply couldn't have done it."

I offered her a cigarette. She took one, and I struck a match.

"Mind if I get personal?" I asked.

"Now or later?" she asked in a calm, very noncomittal tone of voice.

"Does it make any difference?"

"Some."

"Why?"

"Nearly all men get personal sooner or later. It's the rapidity with which they rush the point that makes it more or less objectionable."

I deliberately misunderstood her. "Meaning that the delay makes it more objectionable?"

She met my eyes, smiled, and said, "Sometimes."

"But not always?"

"Definitely not always. It depends upon the personal equation and the—well, the approach."

I said, "All right, I'm going to get personal now, and there won't be any subtlety about the approach."

"That wasn't exactly the way I had you sized up, but go ahead—get it off your chest."

"When I went out to see Benjamin Colter Ruttling the other night, did you telephone him that I was coming?"

The surprise on her face could hardly have been simulated unless she was a darned good actress. "What on earth made you think I did anything like that?" she asked.

"Someone did."

"Well, *I* certainly didn't."

"Did Daphne?"

"I don't think so. She knew you were trying to help her."

"She didn't seem too certain of it when I left."

"She did afterwards."

"What changed her mind?"

"I talked with her."

I said, "Daphne went out. She could have telephoned Ruttling."

"Yes, she could," Genevieve admitted.

"And you were left alone. You could have telephoned him."

"Yes, I could have. I didn't. I don't think Daphne did."

"Then who did?"

"I don't know. The whole thing is new to me."

"Do you think Daphne went to see him tonight?"

"I hadn't thought of it, but—well, she may have."

"Who was it telephoned her about the New Orleans matter?"

"I don't know."

I said, "The poison that killed your cousin was a chemical worked out by the Crescent City Chemical Manufacturing & Supply Company. It's something they're using in connection with a treatment of brush bristles. A tablet dissolved in water has the effect of stiffening the bristles on a brush—toothbrush, hairbrush, nailbrush, etc. It's particularly advantageous in the treatment of toothbrushes, and when it's used according to directions, there's no danger. But taken internally it would produce symptoms similar to those of an overdose of sleeping pills."

"Daphne didn't kill my cousin."

"How do you know?"

"Because I think—I think I know . . ."

"Go ahead," I said.

She changed her mind and quit talking altogether.

"You mean that you think you know who did?"

"I didn't say that."

"Your cousin didn't write to you?"

"She was a poor correspondent."

"When was the last time you heard from her?"

She said, "Mr. Sabin, I'm going to be frank with you. My cousin telephoned me from New Orleans. She told me she was coming to San Francisco, that she had reservations at the Pelton Hotel. She told me she was on a very dangerous mission and that she thought it would be better for me if she didn't see me after she arrived in the city. She seemed to think that we might meet on the street or somewhere and that—well, you know, she intimated she was in some danger and she didn't want to drag me into it. And she said she was bringing someone with her, that if I *did* meet her on the street, not to use her name, not even her first name."

"It was from New Orleans that she telephoned?"

"Yes."

I got up and walked over to the bookcase in the corner of the room, resting my elbows on it, studying Genevieve, trying to frame my next question.

I was still debating which particular lead I wanted to follow, when I heard the sound of a key being fitted into the lock. The bolt clicked back.

Daphne Strate burst into the room. "Hello, Jen! It's really true! I'm in the clear on that New Orleans business!"

She hadn't seen me, and she ran over to Genevieve Hotling, throwing her arms out in an embrace.

Genevieve narrowed her eyes and jerked her head in my direction, but Daphne didn't see the signal.

"And there's something else, Jen . . ."

"That's fine, honey," Genevieve interrupted firmly, "and I'm sure Mr. Sabin will be as pleased as I am to hear it."

"Mr. Sabin! He . . ."

Genevieve's fingers clasped Daphne's forearm firmly, exerting a gentle pressure, and turned her in my direction.

Daphne got the idea, swung to face me, said, "Oh, hello, I didn't see *you!* The New Orleans business is being cleaned up. I'm exonerated. Isn't that wonderful?"

"That," I said, "is very wonderful indeed. I appreciate how you must feel."

She hesitated a moment, then came over to me, her hand extended. "I think I owe a good deal to you," she said.

"For what?"

"For going out to see Mr. Ruttling. I think you made quite an impression on him—in my behalf."

"Indeed," I said. "You've seen him?"

"Well, I . . . Yes."

She threw her arms around my neck and pressed warm red, grateful lips to mine. I could feel her body straining against me, could feel the rapid *pound, pound, pound* of her heart.

Then she had taken her arms away, slipped out of my grasp, and was waltzing across the room to Genevieve.

I took out my handkerchief and wiped lipstick off my mouth. It was flavored with raspberry.

"Oh, I'm so happy!" Daphne said. "I feel like two-million-dollar's worth of champagne bubbles."

She swung Genevieve around in a swirling turn, clasped her once more in an embrace, and said, "Jen, you were just wonderful to me!"

Genevieve said, "Why, I didn't do anything, Daphne."

"You took me in when . . . when things looked dark."

"I knew you hadn't done anything wrong, honey."

Daphne said, "How about a drink? Have we got anything to drink in the house, Jen? Let's celebrate."

"I've got about half a bottle of Scotch in the kitchenette."

"Let's bust it, Jen. I'll get you another one tomorrow. Mr. Sabin wants a drink with us, don't you?"

I said, "I'm not certain I do."

They both looked at me in surprise.

I said to Genevieve, "You told me that the New Orleans business had been cleaned up, before Daphne came in."

"Why, yes," Genevieve said, meeting my eyes.

I said to Daphne, "Then you knew it had been cleared up earlier?"

"Well—in a way. Nothing I could be sure about. It wasn't until after I talked with Mr. Ruttling that I knew that—well, you know, that Mr. Ruttling understood it."

"And when did you talk with him? What time?"

"This evening."

"Who told you about the New Orleans matter having been cleaned up?"

"Why—why, I don't know what right you have to cross-examine me on that."

"Go on," I said. "Who told you?"

"It's none of your damn business."

I looked across at Genevieve, to make certain she was going to get it. I said, "I tried to put a deal across for Daphne. I thought someone in the company might be making her the goat. I knew she wouldn't get to first base if she went to the president of the company and reminded him that she was the little girl he had taken out in New Orleans on the sneak-away party. He'd brush her off, and tell her to go jump in the lake. Moreover, he'd undoubtedly have turned her over to the police.

"So I went to Ruttling's house and told him my name was Sabin, that I was a private detective, that Daphne had kept a diary, that her account of what had happened that night when she went out with Ruttling would make very interesting reading, that I had the diary, and that a tabloid newspaper wanted it."

Genevieve Hotling's eyes were without expression. "You mean you blackmailed him?"

"You're damned right I blackmailed him," I said. "I put it up to him cold-turkey, the theory being that as long as he thought I had Daphne's diary he would never permit her to be arrested by the New Orleans police on a six-thousand-dollar embezzlement charge."

"I'm afraid I don't get you," Genevieve said.

I said, "It's simple. No one would care a hang about Daphne Strate's impressions of going out with her boss on a whoopee party in the French Quarter unless it was tied up with some news story. But if the company of which Ruttling was president had her arrested for embezzlement, and then, as she sobbed out her story of innocence, she referred to a diary she had, and the diary contained some very interesting statements concerning the evening she had spent with the president of the company—well, *then* it would be news. Do you get me?"

"I get you," Genevieve said.

Daphne didn't say anything.

I said, "Therefore, I thought that once I could impress upon Ruttling the fact that such a diary was in existence, he would see to it that nothing was done about apprehending Daphne. I thought he would telephone his New Orleans office, and the New Orleans police would drop the charge."

Genevieve said, "You mean that you're the one who's responsible for Daphne's exoneration?"

"What I was doing didn't pan out. Do you know why not?"

"No."

"Because," I said, "your dear little friend Daphne sneaked out and telephoned Mr. Ruttling, telling him I was coming out there to see him, but that I didn't have authority to speak for her. That she wanted to see him personally."

"How you talk!" Daphne said.

I said, "I've been wondering about that ever since I went out there. Now I can put two and two together. The missing fact that I didn't have is now in my hands and it all fits together to make a perfect picture."

"I still don't get it," Genevieve said.

I said, "I went up to Ruttling's house. I handed a good jolt to the servant who answered the door. That brought Whitney, Ruttling's secretary. I handed it to Whitney straight from the shoulder. Whitney went back and told Ruttling. Ruttling was in a panic. He went to his office upstairs in the house and told Whitney to bring me up. Whitney came back to get me and bring me up. They kept me waiting for a few minutes in the outer office. Then, when I went inside Ruttling played with me as a cat plays with a mouse. What brought about the change?"

"Are you certain there was a change?" Genevieve asked.

"Of course, there was a change. Ruttling would never have left his dinner party and gone to his upstairs study to receive me unless he'd been badly frightened. Then something happened to make him get over being frightened. It was something Whitney didn't know anything about until after he had taken me to the upstairs office. There's only one thing it could have been. A telephone call."

Daphne Strate said, "Listen, there are about two million telephone subscribers within a ten-mile radius and. . . ."

I smiled at her. "And how many of them would be smart enough to sit up all night and fake a diary?"

"What do you mean?"

"You know what I mean. You put through a telephone call to Ruttling's house. You'd been trying to get him off and on all day. You couldn't get past the barrier of secretaries. But after I had gone and delivered my message to Whitney, and Whitney had in turn taken it to Ruttling, you telephoned, and Ruttling received the call with open arms. He talked with you on the telephone and asked you what you were trying to do, blackmailing him with a diary."

"Phooey," she said.

I said, "You are a quick-thinking little girl, Daphne. You listened to what Ruttling had to say, and he let the cat out of the bag. So you told Ruttling that *you* had the diary, that *I* didn't have it; that he had nothing to worry about as long as he was *your* friend. You asked him if he didn't remember how friendly you had been in New Orleans, and he handed you a nice little package of hooey over the telephone. You hung up, feeling very, very smart and very, very smug, leaving me holding the sack.

After that, they let me in to see Ruttling. He was too shrewd to let me see that his attitude had changed while I'd been on the stairs. He talked with me at first as though he were interested, and then, all of a sudden, he changed his entire attitude, trying to make me think I had said the wrong thing somewhere along the line.

"You went down to a stationery store first thing in the morning, got yourself a neat-looking little diary and started in with January first, nineteen hundred and forty-three, faking entries. It didn't make any difference what you put in the diary, because Ruttling didn't have any way of checking up on you. Then you came to that fateful evening in New Orleans, when Ruttling had taken you out, and you *really* went to town. You had found out by that time that Ruttling was afraid of what you might put in the diary, so you confided everything to the diary, everything you could think of that had happened and perhaps something that only might have happened, didn't you?"

"That's a lie!"

Then," I said, "you began to do some more thinking. You learned that the New Orleans matter had been cleared up, that your name was vindicated. That left Ruttling in rather a peculiar position. As long as he had the threat of prosecution for embezzlement to hold over you, it was sort of a stalemate, but when that blew up, you had the supposedly genuine diary, and Ruttling had a headache. So you telephoned Ruttling again, and Ruttling suggested you come over there tonight. You went out and had a very satisfactory talk. You came back feeling like the two million dollars' worth of champagne bubbles. Now suppose we see why."

I made a quick grab for her purse, which lay on the table.

For a moment, she didn't realize what I was doing, then she screamed and flung herself at me.

It was too late. I had the purse open. It was full of money.

I dumped it out on the table. "You little fool," I said.

"Why am I a fool? How dare you open my purse!"

"How much did you get, Daphne?"

"It's none of your business. My own affairs aren't to be bandied about and . . ."

"How much, Daphne?"

"I hate you! I could kill you!"

"How much?"

"I tell you, it's none of your business. I'll mind my affairs and you can mind yours."

I said, "Are you foolish enough to think for one minute that the money isn't marked?"

"Phooey! You talk like a gangster movie," she said.

"Just a minute, Daphne, and I'll show you just how much you can trust people. You thought *you* were smart. Did you give up the diary?"

"I. . . . That's something else that's none of your business."

I looked up Ruttling's number in the telephone book, went over to Genevieve's phone, called the number and assumed the hard-boiled, expressionless voice of a police-radio broadcaster. "Police Headquarters. Let me have Ruttling's secretary, please."

Whitney's voice said, "Yes, Sergeant, this is Mr. Whitney, Mr. Ruttling's secretary."

"Give me the dope on that dough again," I said. "There seems to have been a mistake on some of the stuff."

"Just a moment," Whitney said, and I heard the rustle of paper.

"There's fifteen hundred dollars in five one-hundred-dollar bills, ten fifty-dollar bills, and twenty-five twenty-dollar bills. Now, what numbers did you want?" he asked.

"The numbers on the hundreds."

"Just a moment," Whitney said. "Here they are."

He read off five numbers. I copied them on a sheet of paper, said, "Okay," and hung up.

I passed the list across to Genevieve. "All right," I said. "There are the numbers of the hundred-dollar bills."

It was Genevieve who reached forward and picked up the list of numbers. She turned to Daphne Strate and said, without any expression whatever in her voice, "Pick up the hundred-dollar bills, honey. Let's see if the numbers check."

Daphne Strate stood perfectly still. She might not have heard either of us.

Genevieve matter-of-factly started pawing around the bills on the table, pulled out five one-hundred dollar bills and spread them out.

"Come on, honey," she said, "check the numbers."

As one in a daze, Daphne Strate leaned over the table. Genevieve read out the five figures.

It didn't need any affirmation from Daphne Strate to show that the numbers checked.

"There you are," I said to Daphne. "You've traded your diary for a one-way ticket to San Quentin."

"What—what do I do now?"

"Now," I said, "you grin and bear it. You started out to be a grownup little girl. You started double-crossing those who were trying to do something for you. You've got yourself in a sweet mess, and now you can try to find a way out."

She looked at me steadily without batting an eyelash, then she walked across the room to the studio couch, flung herself face down on it and remained motionless. If she'd started crying, it would have eased the tension all around, but she didn't cry, just lay there stretched out and rigid.

I walked over and shook her. "Tell me," I said, "does Rutling know where he can get you? Did you give him any address?"

She shook her head.

"Not even any telephone number?"

"I—I—told—him he could reach—me—through a friend."

"Come on," I said, "snap out of it. He told you he wanted to take you out again, didn't he? Suggested that you might have an evening together in San Francisco, now that things were all straightened out; that he held no ill-feeling and wanted to know how he could reach you. Is that right?"

She straightened up on the couch. "Damn him! I could kill him!"

"Never mind that," I said. "Is what I said correct? Did he ask you where he could get in touch with you, and did you give him an address?"

"He told me he didn't mind paying me for the diary; that he didn't mind giving me money at all; that he thought I was entitled to something; that he was acting under the advice of his attorney and his secretary, but that if I'd scribble some way to reach me on a piece of paper and leave it under the blotter on his desk, he'd get in touch with me later on and—well you know, we could talk with each other—informally."

"What address did you give him?"

"I told him to call here and ask for Genevieve."

I nodded to Genevieve Hotling. "Grateful little devil, isn't she? How soon can you pack up?"

"Do I have to?"

"I think you'd better."

Genevieve didn't say a word. She walked over to the closet, pulled out her suitcase and a bag and started packing. "How long do you suppose I've got?" she asked.

"Probably not to exceed ten minutes. Getting all the numbers on those bills copied will hold things up a little while and the police won't have any idea she's going to run out on them. They'll think they have all the time in the world."

Daphne savagely jerked her own suitcase out from under the studio couch, threw a few things in it, walked over to the table where the money was lying, said bitterly, "Two million dollars' worth of champagne bubbles!"

She swung her arm in a sweeping gesture and knocked all the money onto the floor.

CHAPTER THIRTEEN

I said to Daphne, "Pick up the money, Sweetie."

"Why should I? I don't want a one-way ticket to jail."

I said, "You aren't going to leave it on the floor and give all of us a one-way ticket to jail."

"What am I going to do with it, then?" she asked.

"Do you want to burn it?"

"Why not?"

Genevieve said, "We can't burn it. I do all my cooking with gas here in the apartment, and there isn't any fireplace."

"Pick it up," I said to Daphne.

She looked at me for a second or two with a surly negation in her eyes. I didn't wait for that to turn into defiance. I turned away from her and said to Genevieve, "Turn on the radio."

She walked over without a word and turned on the radio.

Daphne was picking up the money, putting it together in a sheaf. "Why do you want the radio on?" she asked.

"It will keep anyone from standing out in the corridor and hearing anything we say. Try and get a news broadcast, Genevieve, and turn it up good and loud."

Daphne had the money all picked up now. She pushed it out at me and said, "Since this seems to be your party, you take charge of the refreshments."

I took the money from her, folded it once, snapped an elastic around it, and pushed it down in my coat pocket. Gravely, I took out my wallet, crammed with greenbacks Soo Hoo Duck had given me for the sinews of war. I took out half a dozen twenties and handed them to her.

"What's this for?" she asked.

I said, "In the underworld there are men who make a specialty of taking hot money and giving clean cash in return for it. If you're going to be a crook, you'd better start learning the ropes."

Her eyes blazed. She said, "I could . . ."

"Don't pull that favorite expression of yours," I said, "that you could kill me. That's something else that could get you into trouble, if it hasn't already."

Genevieve brought in a news broadcast, tuning it up so that it was level with the sound of our voices.

"What are you going to do with that money?" Daphne demanded.

"What do you care? You wanted to burn it up."

"Well, I'm beginning to think you just threw a scare into me so you could climb aboard the gravy train. When you come right down to it, *we* don't know anything about *you.*"

"That's right," I agreed. "You—"

Knuckles tapped on the door.

Genevieve looked at me with eyes that held no fear, only a silent question. Daphne's face twisted into a spasm of expression. She glanced wildly about her as though looking for some means of escape.

"Are there any back stairs?" I asked Genevieve.

She shook her head.

I said, "All right, we're in for it."

"What shall I do?" Daphne asked.

I said, "Sit down on the davenport, act as though you were just about ready for bed, and keep the panic off that face of yours."

"Shall I answer it?" Genevieve asked.

I said, "I think I'd better. One just can't tell."

The knuckles sounded again, a more imperative and authoritative summons than the first knock.

I walked over and opened the door.

Señor Ramon Vasquo Gomez stood on the threshold, his face twisted into that smirk with which he would have greeted an attractive woman who opened the door. It was amusing to see that expression play tag with a whole series of expressions as he recognized me.

"My dear Señor Gomez," I said, "won't you come in?"

"It is a pleasure, Señor Sabin. I had hardly expected to find you here."

"Business," I said, "forced me to change my plans."

He entered the apartment, was careful to close the door behind him, looked at Genevieve Hotling, then turned to Daphne Strate. An expression of triumphant satisfaction flooded his face. "Well, well," he said, "what strange things happen! One follows Daphne Strate to see where she will go, and she leads one to the Señor Sabin, who is so interested in purchasing large quantities of commercial chemicals for his South American business."

"And Miss Hotling," I said.

He turned to Genevieve with a bow.

"Miss Hotling," I said, "may I present Señor Ramon Vasquo Gomez, once resident of Argentina, and murderer of your cousin, Betty Crofath."

Gomez, in the midst of a bow from the hips, jerked upright as quickly as though I had yanked him by the coat collar and snapped him back. "What was that?" he asked.

"I merely wanted Miss Hotling to know that you had murdered her cousin," I told him.

"My dear sir, I was in New Orleans at the time of that unfortunate occurrence! Please, may we not have the radio turned off if we are to engage in conversation?"

I nodded to Genevieve.

She was watching me for signals, as a base runner watches his coach. She reached toward the radio.

At that moment, the announcer said, "Turning now from National affairs to our own city, police have uncovered new evidence in connection with the murder of George Bronset, the porter who . . ."

Genevieve Hotling clicked the radio into silence.

I turned suavely to Gomez, and said very casually, "That may be quite true, *señor*. Perhaps you *were* in New Orleans at the time the young lady met her death, but—"

Gomez jumped from his position at the far end of the room, to grab the dial on the radio. He snapped it back on, turned to me with glittering eyes.

I moved toward him. "You asked to have the radio . . ."

His right hand came up from his hip pocket holding a blued-steel automatic pointed squarely at my stomach.

The voice of the radio announcer came blasting into the room. ". . . dead in a downtown hotel under circumstances which for a time baffled the police, who have thrown out a dragnet for the young woman who registered at the hotel under the name of Betty Crofath, as well as the man who was seen leaving the room shortly before the body was discovered. With the identification of fingerprints found in that room and after a careful check of the description of the man who passed himself off on the house detective as a representative of the Motor Vehicle Department, police are now convinced that the man they want is none other than Ed Jenkins, known throughout the underworld as The Phantom Crook because of his ability to slip through the fingers of the police."

Señor Gomez' black eyes were glittering at me with an intensity of concentration. His lips twisted in a smile.

The announcer went on: "Edward Jenkins has had perhaps as adventurous a career as any man alive. He is reputed to be both hated and feared by the organized underworld, which misses no opportunity to pass on any information it may have concerning him to the police. Yet so clever is this master crook that he has become almost a legendary figure. Earlier in his career, police had him in custody half a dozen times, only to have him slip through their fingers. Later on, they set trap after trap, only to have The Phantom Crook vanish into thin air. Of late, there has been some attempt to enlist public sympathy by presenting the claim that Jenkins is used as a scapegoat by the underworld; that any crime which momentarily baffles the police is blamed upon Jenkins by the stool pigeons who obey the orders of their underworld masters. Police, however, brand this claim as absurd. They say that, despite all reports to the contrary, Jenkins is still carrying on his nefarious activities, albeit so cleverly that it is next to impossible to secure proof which would result in his conviction in front of a jury.

"However, police have definitely identified several of the fingerprints found in the room where George Bronset met his death as being those of Ed Jenkins, The Phantom Crook. Arthur Harryman, the house detective, when shown a police photograph of Jenkins, leveled an emphatic finger at the pictured likeness and said, 'There's the man!'

"Police are also convinced that the beautiful blonde young woman who registered at the hotel under the name of Betty Crofath was, in fact, Daphne Strate of New Orleans, who was for a time sought by the police of the Southern city in connection with a shortage of funds in a chemical company where she had been employed. More recently, however, her name has been cleared in connection with that shortage, and police are convinced that insofar as the murder of George Bronset is concerned, she is an innocent bystander who has been frightened into flight by events for which she is, in all probability, blameless. Police insist that if she will surrender herself and submit to questioning, they will extend her every possible consideration.

"At the request of police, we are broadcasting a description of Ed Jenkins, The Phantom Crook. Anyone having any information concerning the man who answers this description will please communicate with police headquarters immediately. According to police, Jenkins is about five feet ten and a-half or eleven inches in height, somewhere in the late twenties or early thirties, with an abundance of dark, wavy hair, a thin, straight nose, high cheekbones, penetrating gray eyes, broad-shouldered, slim-waisted, well-dressed in a dark gray double-breasted suit. His weight is about a hundred sixty-five pounds.

"Turning now to the local political scene, it has been announced that two of the candidates for mayor. . . ."

Ramon Gomez switched off the radio.

"So," he said with a smooth, purring note of satisfaction in his voice, "the man who left the room in the Pelton Hotel was none other than Ed Jenkins, The Phantom Crook—and how well the description fits you, Señor Sabin. But come, we are all wasting time, standing here tense and dramatic. Suppose we be seated and relax for a friendly discussion. But do not think that I will hesitate to use this weapon. And, my dear Señor Jenkins—or perhaps you prefer to be called Sabin—please note that I don't make the mistake of holding the weapon extended, where you could reach it with a swift blow or a well-placed kick. No, *señor,* I have learned how to use these little toys. You will note that I keep it held back and closely against my body. I can assure you that at the first unexpected move on your part there will be most unpleasant consequences."

I held a chair for Genevieve. "We may as well be seated," I told her.

Daphne Strate sat on the davenport, looking from Gomez to me. Her forehead was creased in a thoughtful frown. Her eyes were intent upon missing nothing that happened.

"May I reach for a cigarette," I asked Gomez, "without causing unpleasant complications?"

"Oh, but certainly. You see, *señor,* it is necessary for one in my profession to acquire and remember many things. And among the odd bits of knowledge that I have picked up is some rather detailed information about the character who is known as The Phantom Crook. I know, for instance, that he never carries a gun. He has rather a unique philosophy upon this point which appeals to me."

Gomez turned to Genevieve Hotling. "Would you ladies perhaps like to hear about it?"

"I would," Daphne Strate said, speaking so quickly that her reply came on the heels of Gomez' question.

Gomez favored her with a little more detailed study. "Ah, yes," he said, "the young woman who had the room in which the Pullman porter was found with his throat cut wishes to know more about The Phantom Crook. Most interesting—perhaps we should say most significant."

"What about his philosophy concerning guns?" Daphne Strate asked.

"It is very, very interesting," Gomez announced in the voice of an enthusiastic collector praising some very rare item. "You will correct me if I am wrong, Señor Sabin, but as I gather the story, The Phantom Crook relies entirely upon his wits. He says that to carry a gun is like carrying a crutch. One grows to depend upon it, and to the extent that one relies upon the symbol of brute force, one loses the ability to think with that quick-witted cunning which takes advantage of every situation. And that is correct, is it not, *señor?"*

"You're doing the talking," I said.

Gomez turned to Daphne Strate. "Moreover," he said, "The Phantom Crook has been known to remark that if one depends upon a gun, someone can take the gun away from him, and he is disarmed. But if he depends upon his wits, he can always keep his wits about him. Rather a neat bit of an idea there, don't you think?"

"You mean he *never* carries a gun?" Daphne Strate asked.

"I personally cannot vouch for it. This is only the second time I have met the gentleman. The first time was in New Orleans, when he was posing as one about to embark upon a business in South America. However, my dear young lady, rest assured that if my information is inaccurate and the hand which is exploring Señor Sabin's pocket, ostensibly for a cigarette case, should come out with anything more sinister, you will promptly proceed to stick fingers in your ears, because four or five explosions will take place with very great rapidity, and the stomach of Señor Sabin will be perforated with holes arranged in a very neat circle. I pride myself not only upon my accuracy with a gun, but the quickness with which I can pull the trigger. I am interested in the philosophy of The Phantom Crook, but I do not subscribe to it. I find a gun a very convenient weapon—but then I do not have a police record. I can appreciate the fact that as Señor Jenkins—or Señor Sabin, as he undoubtedly prefers to be called—would express it, the police can arrest a man with a police record simply for having a gun in his possession. But they can hardly arrest him for merely having his wits about him."

I said to Daphne Strate, "He's rather vain, you know. Don't deprive him of his moment of temporary triumph. He is basking in the warm light of his own self-approval."

For a moment, there was anger in Gomez' eyes. Then he was smiling at me. "Perhaps you are right, Señor Sabin. Who knows. But, in any event, *señor,* this little steel baton that I hold in my hands makes me the master of the orchestra. I can command the tune that is to be played and the tempo with which it will be played, as well."

I didn't say anything.

"Come, come, Señor Sabin. I do not want to steal the entire show. I have shown you the efficacy of my weapon; now perhaps you would like to give these very beautiful young ladies a demonstration of the weapon which is supposed to serve you in such good stead—the use of your wits."

"Why not?" I said.

"Why not, indeed, *señor?* We are waiting impatiently for you to proceed."

I said to the girls, "How about a cigarette?" and extended my case toward Genevieve.

"I'm sorry," Señor Gomez interrupted, "but if the young ladies wish cigarettes, they must get them themselves from their own supply. I do not wish to seem impolite, but when one has heard stories of the remarkable agility of The Phantom Crook, one wishes him to keep his distance. I am only too well aware, *señor,* of the limitations of a gun at very close quarters. To keep your victim at least seven feet eight inches away is my motto."

I lit a cigarette.

"We are waiting for the demonstration of your particular weapon, *señor,*" the South American reminded me.

I said, "Let's do a little reasoning, then. Betty Crofath, it seems, was killed by a rather peculiar poison, which resembled one of the barbitals in its action. It seems that the Crescent City Chemical Manufacturing and Supply Company has recently put out a chemical for the treatment of brush bristles which comes in small white tablets, which is quite poisonous, and which, when taken internally, produces rapidly fatal symptoms that are very similar to those accompanying an overdose of the more powerful hypnotics."

"You interest me very much," Gomez told me.

Now then," I went on, "I went to New Orleans. I sent Randolph Holaberry, the manager of the Crescent City Chemical Manufacturing and Supply Company, a wire stating that I was arriving by plane, that I was leaving almost immediately for South America, and that I wished to get some information from him as to prices and deliveries on commercial chemicals.

"Mr. Holaberry came to my hotel very shortly after I arrived. I talked with him for some time about chemicals and prices. Mr. Holaberry was the only person in New Orleans who had any reason to believe I was interested in commercial chemicals.

"Around three o'clock in the morning, I returned to the hotel. Señor Gomez was waiting for me. He told me that from sources of information which were purely his own, he had learned that I intended to engage in business in Argentina and that I was in the market for commercial chemicals. He wished to tell me about the chemicals of the Bak Shui Wong Chemical Company of Shanghai."

I turned to Genevieve Hotling. "Under the circumstances, would some idea suggest itself to your mind?"

Señor Gomez said delightedly, "This is enjoyable, *señor*. Pray, proceed."

I said, "Since I was not engaged in business in Argentina and had no intention of doing so, since Randolph Holaberry, the head of the chemical company in New Orleans, was the only person on earth who had any information to the effect that I intended to engage in business, it is obvious that Señor Gomez' information must have come through Randolph Holaberry.

"That brings up a very interesting situation. Mr. Holaberry

calls upon me, apparently attempting to sell me chemicals. He leaves, and passes on information to Señor Gomez which enables that individual to call upon me as the representative of an Oriental competitor, and offer to deliver the same merchandise at a much lower price than that quoted me by Mr. Holaberry. A very interesting situation."

"But don't stop there!" Gomez said. "Please, *señor*. Please go on. Surely your next step of reasoning is obvious."

"Exactly," I said. "Señor Gomez was the friend of Betty Crofath. He knew her in Argentina. He comes to New Orleans. Betty Crofath comes to New Orleans. Betty Crofath had information which might have been of some military importance, something that would have hurt the Japanese Empire had it been divulged to certain parties. Betty Crofath is murdered. The instrumentality of that murder is a poison which very much resembles a sleeping tablet in appearance and in effect. It is a chemical worked out by the Crescent City Chemical Manufacturing and Supply Company. A very interesting chain of circumstances, don't you think?"

Señor Gomez made a little bow. "You express it very forcefully, *señor*. Now, perhaps, may I say a word?"

"Go ahead."

"Let us look at it from the other viewpoint. Betty Crofath leaves New Orleans for San Francisco. At approximately that same time, The Phantom Crook takes an airplane to Tucson. He boards the train. He has a berth directly across from the one occupied by Miss Crofath. Shortly after The Phantom Crook boards the train, Miss Crofath dies. Also on that car is a Daphne Strate, who is a friend of Miss Crofath and who had been seen in earnest conversation with her the night before. The next morning, The Phantom Crook is seen engaged in earnest conversation with Miss Strate. Then Miss Strate goes to San Francisco, assumes the name of Betty Crofath, steals Betty Crofath's purse, her driving license, her baggage. The Phantom Crook calls upon her in her hotel bedroom. Daphne Strate leaves. The Phantom Crook leaves. Almost immediately after the last departure, the body of the Pullman car porter is found in the room. His throat has been cut from ear to ear."

And Gomez made a little bow, smiled at us, and said, "I rather like that presentation. I doubt if a prosecuting attorney could have done better."

Daphne Strate was watching me with thoughtful, speculative eyes.

"But come, come," Señor Gomez said. "We are above all of these petty matters, my dear Señor Sabin. The game we are playing is far removed from that elemental cops-and-robbers pastime. You are not going to say anything to the police about me, and, by the same token, I am not going to say anything to the police about you."

"What, then, *are* you going to do?"

"You mentioned when you first met me that you had seen me on New Year's morning."

"Something to that effect."

"In a restaurant."

"I said in front of a restaurant."

"With an attractive young woman."

"That's right."

"And we were engaged in an argument," Señor Gomez went on.

"Correct."

"That was in Buenos Aires?"

"Yes."

"Could you tell me the name of the restaurant?"

"No."

"Could you tell me what street it was on?" he asked.

"No."

"Could you tell me what hotel you stayed at there?"

"I see no reason for doing so."

"Could you tell me exactly, or approximately, even, what time it was?"

"Shortly after daylight."

"Come, come, *señor,* you should do better than that. Was it eight o'clock, nine o'clock, ten o'clock?"

"About eight o'clock, I should judge."

His smile showed even rows of white teeth. "A very conservative guess, *señor,* but as it happens, a wrong guess which betrays you to your undoing. In short, my dear Señor Sabin, much as I dislike to question the word even of one who has a police record, it is now quite evident to me that you have never been in Buenos Aires, that you did not see me on New Year's morning at all, that you were simply bluffing about the whole business. If you will note carefully, Señor Sabin, you will realize that Buenos Aires is far south of the Equator, that, therefore, the seasons are completely reversed; that New Year's day comes in the middle of our summer; that in place of getting daylight around seven or seven-thirty in the morning, the sun is high in the heavens at eight o'clock on New Year's. In short, my dear Señor Sabin, it has now become apparent to me that you received this information from something Betty Crofath had written—perhaps a diary."

"And so?" I asked.

"And so, *señor,* if it is all the same to you, I will take custody of that diary."

"I am afraid it is not all the same to me," I told him.

"I will take custody of it anyway."

Daphne Strate sat suddenly upright. "So *that's* it!" she exclaimed.

Señor Gomez looked at her with thoughtful eyes.

"That is what, my dear?"

"That's where it was."

"The diary?"

"Yes."

"And," Ramon Gomez said, suavely, "that is where what was, my dear?"

I said to Daphne Strate, "You keep your tongue moving, and you'll talk your head off—and I don't mean that merely as a figure of speech."

Ramon said, "Don't let him frighten you, my dear."

Daphne Strate said nothing.

"What was it you had reference to, Miss Strate?"

She shook her head.

Gomez turned to me. "I'm afraid, Señor Sabin, you are causing me much trouble. Come, which one of you has the diary?"

Señor Gomez turned to Daphne Strate. "My dear," he said, "you need not be afraid of me. I am perhaps your best friend. I perhaps could get you out of rather a tight scrape. All that I would ask in return would be your assistance."

She watched him silently.

"I have reason to believe," he said, "that there was something in the personal effects of Betty Crofath that would have been very valuable. I have, I believe, gone through all of those personal effects and I have not found that which I wanted. Therefore, it never existed or it has been removed.

"I have good reason to believe that it existed. So, my dear, let us suppose it was removed. Do you suppose that you have it?"

She slowly shook her head. "I didn't have a chance to go

through her things—I just gave them a hurried glance when I —when I heard this noise."

"The noise?"

"The man who was bound and gagged and placed in the bathtub."

"Oh, yes," Ramon Gomez said, and tilted back his head and raised his eyes to the ceiling, as one who wishes to appraise certain various ideas and does not want his judgment to be influenced by any visual interruption.

"There must have been a diary," he said almost musingly, "and that diary must contain more than . . . No, how absurd, how foolish of me! I know where it is now." He threw back his head and laughed. "Not in the diary. Of course not! It was in the one place where no one ever thought to look—the place that . . ." He broke off abruptly.

I grinned at him.

Daphne Strate looked disappointed.

Abruptly, Gomez got to his feet. "My *dear* Miss Strate, I think that you and I can be of some mutual assistance."

She looked him over with a certain tentative appraisal. "What's your proposition?" she asked.

"Come, come," Ramon said. "One should hardly make his proposition to a beautiful young woman in the presence of hostile witnesses. What I say might be misconstrued. I notice that you have a suitcase there. Yours, perhaps?"

"Yes."

"You were leaving?"

"Yes."

"Splendid! Excellent! After we get into the corridor I shall carry your suitcase. But here, since the Señor Sabin has such a reputation for baffling speed and swift dexterity, I will not be quite so gentlemanly. You had better go first."

She looked at Genevieve, looked at me, looked back at Ramon Gomez, then without a word, picked up the suitcase and started for the door.

"A most interesting young woman," Ramon Gomez said, as he beamed at me. "She has the power of decision—a realist. I fancy we shall get along splendidly."

Gomez stood near the door, the automatic pressed close against his side. His eyes swept the room as Daphne Strate marched through the doorway into the corridor.

"I followed her here from Ruttling's house, and what a fortunate bit of shadowing *that* was."

I met his eyes and said guilelessly, "And when am I free to go?"

"My dear Señor Sabin," he said, "go any time you damn please," and stepped out into the corridor and pulled the door shut behind him.

CHAPTER FOURTEEN

Genevieve Hotling said, "Are you really the one they call The Phantom Crook?"

I ground out the end of my cigarette in an ash tray and merely smiled.

She said almost wistfully, "I remember when you cleaned up your record and started going straight. What happened after that? Did you slip?"

I said, "Something happened that made it so I didn't care one way or another. The police did the rest. You know, it's very difficult for the police to say to the newspaper reporters, 'We just don't know. We haven't any clues'. Much easier to say, 'Yes, we know who did it. We'll have him in custody within another day or two if he stays in the state, but he's probably gone down to Mexico or back East somewhere.' "

"Meaning you?" she asked.

"Meaning me. The public have an idea I'm responsible for about ninety percent of the unsolved crimes."

"How many of them are you responsible for?"

"None."

"It's difficult to believe that."

"I'm not asking you to believe it; I'm simply telling you."

"Don't you care whether I believe you or not?"

I started to say no, then at something peculiar in her eyes, said yes instead.

"What," she asked, "do we do now?"

"What would you like to do?"

She said, "We can go out and—"

"Don't be silly," I told her. "He stayed here long enough to bait his trap. If we went out now, it would be fatal. Got any playing cards?"

"Yes. Why?"

I said, "Get me a deck. Where are the bedclothes?"

She nodded toward a closet.

I went over to the closet, pulled out the bedclothes, cut blankets into strips and started tying the strips together.

"A rope?" she asked.

I nodded.

We tied them together in a long rope, and tossed the loose end out of the window. Then we tied the other end to the radiator.

"We go down that?" Genevieve asked me dubiously.

I smiled and said, "We go up. I noticed a couple of blank spaces on the directory. Probably those apartments are vacant."

I walked across to pick up her suitcase. I didn't trust to the elevator, but took the stairs, located one of the vacant apartments and did things to the lock.

The place was completely furnished.

I switched on the lights and closed the door. I held a chair for her and said casually, "After all, there aren't very many good two-handed card games. How about a cigarette? And then let's try cribbage."

She took one, said, "I simply can't understand Daphne."

I lit her cigarette, shuffled the cards, said, "I understand her, all right. Cut the cards."

We played two or three hands. Then there were sounds coming from the apartment house, below us, the sounds of doors opening and closing, of heavy feet in the corridors. Outside on the street, cars roared into noise and sped away. We could hear the rumble of men's voices.

"I'm frightened," Genevieve said.

I scooped up the cards. "Just to be on the safe side, we'd better turn out the lights and sit in the dark. They won't search the apartment house, but if they should happen to see a light in an apartment that's supposed to be vacant, it might cause trouble."

I turned out the lights. We went over and sat on the davenport. There was enough light coming in from the street to show objects in shadowy outline.

"After all," Genevieve said, "you don't need to be so standoffish. I'm scared."

I slid my arm around her shoulders, drew her over close to me. "There's nothing for you to be frightened about."

"Why?"

"If they catch us, you simply tell the truth. I forced you to come up here."

"You aren't frightened?"

"Not in the way you mean."

"Don't you think they'll catch you?"

"They may."

"How long have you lived like this?"

"Like what?"

"Being on the dodge?"

"Almost ever since I can remember."

"Do you want to tell me about yourself?" she asked me.

"There's nothing to tell."

"How did you get started?"

"The same way most of them get started. My parents were divorced. My mother took my custody. Then she fell in love and married again. The man didn't like me. My mother had another child by this man. When you're young and sensitive and hungry for love, and find you can't get that love, it does things to you. You get bitter. You get harsh. You get a mental maturity which hasn't been properly seasoned. I turned to the companionship of other boys. We weren't particularly vicious; we simply wanted action. Then something happened, and they blamed our gang for it. Circumstantial evidence pointed pretty strongly to one of the boys, but I knew he was absolutely innocent. They brought him into Juvenile Court. The judge was a misfit. He tried to break the boy's spirit. After a while, they sent him to reform school. It made me bitter. I learned to hate the law.

"After that, it was an easy step to find myself outsmarting the police. Then there came a time when I wasn't clever enough. By that time, I was old enough to take the jolt. They threw the book at me.

"In the Big House, I made up my mind that if I was going to be a crook I'd be a top-notcher. There's plenty of chance to pick up miscellaneous information in stir. I kept my eyes and ears open. Then, about a year before I got out, I realized it was a game you couldn't beat. I decided to go straight. That shows all I knew about what we call justice.

"When a man gets out of prison, he either has to have a job and friends who are interested in seeing that he goes straight, or he has to team up with the underworld and make a living out of crime. Otherwise, you can't beat the game. I know, because I tried. I tried to be a lone wolf. The underworld couldn't understand me—thought I'd gone soft. Men whom I'd met in stir and who had educated me in all the tricks of the profession, thinking they'd have a young, skillful apprentice to help them later on, felt that I'd betrayed them. In a way, I had."

"But surely," she said, "that didn't drag you back into the underworld!"

"No, the police did that. They started using me as a scapegoat. I was the fall guy for any crime the police couldn't solve."

"It doesn't seem possible," she said.

"It wouldn't have been," I told her, "if I hadn't been so young and thought I was so smart. I decided that it would be easier to let the police try to catch me, and to outwit them, than to go into court and try and clear my name."

"But I can't understand that."

"To understand it," I said, "you have to know something about our system of law. Well-balanced justice permeates our law in theory but not in practice. Getting justice implanted in laws which, for the most part, go back for decades is quite a job. Because we have been so jealous of our liberties, we have fought to retain many of our ancient laws, and some of those weren't too good. They go back to a day when public executions were as exciting and as well attended as a country fair.

Our laws are very smug and sometimes hypocritical. Theoretically, if a man is on trial for a crime, you can't prejudice the jury against him by showing that he has ever been convicted of another crime. The theory of the law, set forth in self-righteous complacency, is that a man can only be tried for the one crime he is accused of committing."

"That's fair," she said.

"Very fair, if it worked that way. The trouble is, it doesn't."

"Why?"

"If you don't deny the charges against you, the prosecution can't show that you've ever been convicted of another crime. But if you take the witness stand and become a witness, the law says that your testimony may be impeached by showing that you have been convicted of a crime."

"Why is that?"

"That's because from time immemorial it has been permissible to impeach a witness in a *civil* case by showing he's been convicted of a felony. And when they apply the same rules of evidence to criminal cases, the man with a criminal record doesn't dare to take the stand.

"Wait a minute," I said, as she started to say something, "don't get me wrong. The law, in its smug complacency, says, 'Oh, we'll fix that all right', and throws a statute on the books saying that if a man accused of crime doesn't take the stand and testify in his own behalf that isn't to be considered against him; the jury aren't even allowed to think about it, much less comment on it."

"But can jurors do that?" she asked.

"Only the judges think so."

"You mean, if you don't take the stand . . ."

"If you don't take the stand," I said, "you're licked. The jurors listen to the judge tell them that inasmuch as the defendant hasn't taken the stand, they aren't allowed to consider that in any way, and then go back to the jury room, look at each other, elect a foreman, and for a while nobody says anything. Then someone says, 'Well, what do you think?' and someone else says, 'I think the so-and-so is guilty.' Perhaps there's an argument, and somebody blurts, 'Well, he didn't dare to take the witness stand; you can see that,' then someone says, 'But we're not supposed to consider that,' and then someone laughs, and then they have another ballot and the foreman announces they've agreed on a verdict, and that the defendant is guilty as hell."

"But suppose you had taken the stand?" she wanted to know.

I smiled. "Then the district attorney tries to trap you on cross-examination. If he can get you mixed up, he pours a lot of sneering sarcasm at you and then gives you the works. If he can't get you mixed up, he pauses for a long moment, then looks at you and says, 'Let's see, Mr. Doe, you've been convicted of a felony, haven't you? Back in nineteen-twenty-eight, I believe?'

"You look him in the eyes and say, 'Yes, sir,' and you can feel the sympathy of the jury turning to ice. It isn't alone the way the district attorney says it, but it's the tone of voice he uses, as much as to say, 'Look at him, ladies and gentlemen of the jury, a graceful, gifted, talented, accomplished liar. He wants you to believe he's innocent and yet I've just forced him to admit that he's a crook, a professional criminal.' "

I stopped talking, so that there was a sudden dramatic silence.

After a moment, Genevieve asked, "And what does the jury do?"

"The jury," I said, "loses interest in everything connected with the case. The only thing that concerns them is how soon they can get a chance to write a verdict of guilty and go home. What's the use of wasting time on a crook? Throw the book at him. There should be a law against letting a crook have a jury trial, wasting the time of twelve good men and true."

"But can't you appeal?"

I laughed. "You can appeal only on questions of law. The verdict of the jury is final on questions of fact. You've been found guilty by due and proper legal procedure, and that's it."

"So what happens?"

"So," I said, "you go to the Big House for the second time. This time, they give you quite a jolt. When you get out, you're pretty apt to be sour and bitter at the whole thing. Then's when you *really* start going wrong. And if you get caught again there's nothing to it. The D.A. dangles *two* prior convictions in front of a jury. That time they send you up for life. You're an habitual criminal. No, it's a game you can't beat—not unless you have some luck, some friends, a lot of determination, and a job with a boss who knows your past history and is willing to give you a chance to go straight."

"But I should think society would make it easy for a man who has been convicted of crime to go straight. I always thought it was that way."

"Lots of people do."

We were silent for a little while. Then I said, "Pretty soon, when things have cooled off a bit, I'm going to leave here. After I do, give me about ten minutes, then call the police. Tell them that I knotted the blankets together and tossed them out of the window for a blind. Then I made you come up here with me and wait; that you were frightened stiff and didn't dare not to do everything I asked. But give me a break on one thing."

"What?"

"Say that you came with me because I *asked* you to; that

you *thought* I'd kill you if you didn't, but that at no time did I make any threats. All I did was to *ask* you to come. And when I left, I told you that, as a personal favor to me I'd appreciate it if you didn't say anything for ten or fifteen minutes."

She thought that over. "And I'm to tell them you didn't make any threats?"

"Not right off the bat," I said. "Think it over and . . ."

There were footsteps coming down the hall outside. Then the footsteps stopped in front of the door.

I heard Genevieve's breath suck in, in a quick, gasping intake.

We sat perfectly still for a matter of some ten seconds. Then the steps moved slowly away.

I turned to Genevieve, whispered "Take it easy."

She breathed my name.

Then, abruptly, the steps came back, paused once more in front of the door. Then, very gently, fingers tapped against the panels.

Genevieve's hand came over to rest on mine. Her fingers were cold.

We sat perfectly still, waiting.

I heard the scrape of metal against the lock of the door—not a key. Somebody picking the lock.

It seemed that we sat there for more than a minute while we could hear the gentle scratching and scraping of metal against metal. Then the latch clicked back, and the door opened.

Silhouetted against the vague light of the outer corridor were two figures, two men moving with surreptitious stealth.

Every muscle in Genevieve's body tightened. I knew she was going to scream. I slid my left arm up from her shoulders, clapped my hand over her mouth. That brought her back to sanity and got her nerves under control.

The two ominous figures moved on into the shadows of the apartment. I heard fingers groping along the wall for a light switch. Then abruptly the room clicked into brilliance.

Yat Sing and another Chinese stood peering into the room. Abruptly, Yat Sing gave an exclamation of satisfaction and gently closed the door.

I held my hand clamped over Genevieve's mouth.

"Velly hard time to find," Yat Sing said. "Police men big fools. See blanket hang from window. Think you go way. Yat

Sing tries knots on blanket. Find too loose. If you go down blankets, knots be velly tight. Yat Sing think maybeso you somewhere in house. Findum all vacant apartments. Pick lock each apartment. Take long time. Velly solly not come sooner," he said impassively.

Genevieve realized now that these men were my friends. I felt her relax and removed my hand from her lips.

"What is it, Yat Sing?" I asked.

His beady, glittering eyes bored into mine. "Ngat T'oy," he said, "go way. No come back."

CHAPTER FIFTEEN

I was on my feet, facing Yat Sing with no recollection of having moved from the davenport. I could feel a deadly, cold rage taking possession of me, sharpening my faculties until I saw the things in that room with a clarity and attention to details that made it seem my eyes were photographing motion pictures upon my brain.

And beneath all of the rage, there was a chill of apprehension.

The people with whom we were dealing knew too much. They had repeatedly made use of information which was closely guarded as a secret locked in the minds of Chinatown's leaders—and information which is kept secret by an Oriental is very secret indeed.

I met Yat Sing's eyes and saw the consternation on his face. I looked at Genevieve Hotling sitting on the davenport, still open-mouthed with amazement. I looked at the Chinese who had entered the room with Yat Sing, and knew him instantly for what he was. He was a Foo Tow Chi, a Chinese hatchet man. At one time, these men were the executioners for the tongs, the gunmen who roved about, killing members of rival tongs, chosen for their skill with a gun, their cool nerve and daring.

"How," I asked, "did it happen?"

Yat Sing said, "Get automobile. Start for see you. My men watch her go; wait for her come. She no come."

I knew that Ngat T'oy had always prized her freedom of action. She had remonstrated with her father that there was no necessity that he should know where she went or what she did, because of what she was pleased to call her unimportance. But I knew also that her father had instructed Yat Sing to keep an eye on her wherever it was possible to do so, without letting Ngat T'oy know that she was being protected. And a moment's thought convinced me that Yat Sing had had men on my tail; otherwise he would not have known that I was at the Medville Arms.

I said swiftly, in Chinese, "The woman with hair like straw that has been left in the sun—did you see her?"

"I saw her," Yat Sing said in his native language.

"You saw her when she came to this apartment house?"

"When she came, and when she left."

"She came alone?"

"Alone."

"No one drove her to the place?"

"No one."

"Was she followed?"

Yat Sing said, without hesitancy, "Not followed. She came from the car that goes over hills, with a bell that clangs. The car stops. She gets off and walks one block to apartment house."

"The car that is pulled by a rope up the hills?" I asked.

"The same thing," he affirmed.

"Let's go," I said simply to Yat Sing.

"You want me to—stay here?" Genevieve asked.

"Not now," I said.

"Why?"

"Because you are no longer safe in this apartment house—anywhere in it."

I turned to Yat Sing and said in English. "This woman is to be given protection. Take her with you. Keep her safe until such time as I tell you there is no longer danger."

I swung my eyes over to meet Genevieve's. "This man," I said, "is my friend. With him you are safe. Go with him. Do as he tells you. It may be inconvenient, but it will be safe."

She said, somewhat angrily, "Who are you to come to my apartment in the dead of night, involve me in a crime, carry me up to a vacant apartment, hold me there, then turn me over to some Chinaman and tell me to go with him wherever he wants to take me?"

"I am your friend," I said, "and they will like it better if you refer to them as Chinese rather than as Chinamen."

She met my eyes for a long moment. Then the flash of anger

faded from her eyes. She got up from the davenport. "Very well, friend, I will go with these Chinese," she said.

I saw the faintest flicker of expression on the face of Yat Sing, nothing so crude as a motion of the facial muscles, but only a very slight softening of the lines of tension about his eyes. I knew then that Yat Sing approved of her, and that she had made a friend.

I said to Yat Sing, "I wish to make certain there are no police remaining to watch the house. I will stay with you until you have told me the coast is clear, and then I will go."

"Alone?" he asked.

"Alone."

He glanced toward the Foo Tow Chi and said in Chinese, "Dead enemies can do no harm."

"Where I am going there is danger for one; for two—death."

Yat Sing said, "Lead the way."

We left the apartment, didn't trust to the elevator, but walked down the stairs, the Foo Tow Chi in front, Yat Sing in the rear, Genevieve and I in the middle. Had any prowler tried to stop us on those stairs that night he would have received a surprise which might well have been fatal.

On the floor below, Genevieve hesitated a moment. "Could I," she asked, "get a few things from my apartment?"

I shook my head.

"Please. It will only take me a few seconds—less than a minute. I promise."

We stood there in the corridor while I weighed that which was prudent against the pleading of her eyes.

Her eyes won.

"Very well," I said, "but you have only a few seconds."

We moved down the corridor to her apartment. She unlocked the door and went in. It was quite evident that police had been through the place. The blanket rope which I had thrown out of the window had been pulled back and coiled on the floor. Doors had been opened. Clothing had been pulled from the closet and tossed carelessly on the bed, in an effort on the part of police to make certain that I was not hiding behind clothes in the closet.

Abruptly, the telephone started to ring, and the sudden sound of that bell shattered the silence in such strident summons that Genevieve jumped, with that jerky motion which is the fear-inspired reflex of taut nerves.

The sound of that ringing telephone forced me to change my plans instantly.

Either someone had been ringing the telephone at intervals, and it was merely coincidence that the phone happened to ring as we entered the apartment, or someone knew that we had entered the apartment and wished to talk with us.

I whirled to place my hand on Genevieve's arm, gripping her so she would concentrate her attention upon what I had to say.

"In a moment, Genevieve, you will answer that telephone. Your voice will sound sleepy. You will say that you went out shortly after Daphne left your apartment; that I left at the same time you did, telling you I was going out through the basement; that I said I would return and kill you if you said anything to anyone; that you were terribly frightened. You walked the streets for awhile, then decided that you would return to your apartment because there was no place else for you to go. You found that I had apparently returned in your absence; that I had torn up some of the bedclothes into strips; that I had searched the apartment and thrown clothes onto the floor. You will never admit that the possibility entered your mind that the police had been here and searched the apartment in your absence. You will say that you found other blankets to put on the bed, crawled into bed and went to sleep; that you were awakened by the ringing of the telephone. Do you understand?"

She nodded.

"But you are not to say that, unless your presence in the apartment is questioned," I warned.

Once more she nodded, and then said simply, "Ouch, you're hurting my arm."

I realized, then, the tension with which I was gripping her.

"All right," I said. "Answer the telephone now."

She moved over to the telephone, picked up the receiver, yawned and said, "Hello," in a voice that was thick with sleep.

I watched the expression on her face.

The receiver snarled rapid, metallic sounds that were audible to me only as a rapid-fire, rattling sequence of noises—noises that clattered forth some crisp message, then quit abruptly.

But those noises made Genevieve Hotling's eyes pop wide open.

She picked up a pencil and started writing rapid shorthand notes on a pad.

We heard the businesslike click at the other end of the line as the person who had spoken dropped the receiver into place, without giving Genevieve an opportunity to ask a question.

Genevieve replaced the receiver back into place and turned to me.

"Well?" I asked.

She said, "The person at the other end of the line didn't ask who I was, simply started delivering this message."

"And the message?"

She read her shorthand notes:

"We wish the return of the maps you have taken from the trunk. Tomorrow morning, after Fred Collette has made his morning deliveries, you will see our hand. The one whom you thought in danger, whom you will later think is safe, can be rescued from the clutches of your law only when we say the word. Otherwise, the Little Sun will be eclipsed into perpetual darkness."

I looked at Yat Sing. "Herb Rendon?" I asked. "The man in the Monterey House Hotel?"

"Him gone bed."

"You're sure?"

"Go room, turn out light, make snore noise," Yat Sing said.

I said, "The woman with the straw-colored hair left with South American, the one who called on me in the New Orleans hotel."

"Heap savvy."

"Can you find that man?"

"Any time."

My face showed surprise.

"He leave here," Yat Sing explained. "Two China boys go along behind."

I looked at the message Genevieve had written out for me. "Before Frank Collette has made his morning delivery." What did it mean?

An idea occurred to me. I consulted the telephone directory, then sat down at the telephone and dialed the morning newspapers.

The second paper I tried gave me the answer I wanted. The Circulation Department told me that Frank Collette was a lad who made morning bicycle deliveries in a section of the residential district.

After a few minutes' delay, I got the boundaries of the territory assigned to Frank Collette.

I said to Yat Sing, "Ngat T'oy is being held a prisoner somewhere within the boundaries of this district. Something that will be published in tomorrow morning's newspaper will change the entire situation. And . . . wait a minute."

I sketched out a mental map of the city, then got up from my chair and said to Yat Sing, "It is easier than that. The residence of Benjamin Colter Ruttling is within the district covered by Frank Collette's newspaper deliveries."

I saw Yat Sing's dark, slanting eyes glitter with emotion.

I said to him, "Not yet. So far, it is a one-man job. In order to make their message dramatic, they gave us too broad a clue."

Yat Sing said, "Maybe-so on purpose."

"That," I told him, "is why I am going alone."

CHAPTER SIXTEEN

We paused at the doorway of the apartment house. Outside, the streets seemed silent and deserted. Yat Sing stepped out to the cement porch, moved down two steps to the street. We followed, Genevieve Hotling, the Chinese hatchet man, and I. A car swerved around the corner and screamed to a stop. I knew the driver. He was a trusted messenger whom Soo Hoo Duck used in times of emergency. But the lad looked at me with no sign of recognition. It was to Yat Sing that he gave his message.

"I am," he said rapidly in Chinese, "the unworthy bearer of a most important message. He who is the Master desires that you and the Vanishing Ghost should seek his presence immediately."

Without a word, I stepped from the curb, opened the rear door of the car and nodded to Genevieve. "Will you get in?" I asked.

"Is this necessary?" she inquired.

"I think it is."

"Why?"

"I think it will insure your safety."

I didn't tell her that since it had been to her the message concerning Little Sun had been delivered, she stood no chance whatever of being released from what virtually amounted to detention by the Chinese. It would take some event of major importance to make the Chinese resort to extreme measures. But once they decided to take those measures, there would be no turning back.

We climbed in the car and in minutes were in the middle of Chinatown.

The car came to a stop. Yat Sing looked at me.

I said to Genevieve, "You'll have to trust me and trust these men. Will you promise to stay with them for a little while?"

"For how long?"

"Until you hear from me again."

Yat Sing was holding the door open for me impatiently. When Soo Hoo Duck summoned one to an audience, it was useless to waste time in polite nothings. Why worry about asking the girl's permission? She would stay, whether she wanted to or not.

I joined Yat Sing on the sidewalk. We crossed to an unlighted doorway, black with sinister shadows.

It was too dark to see the door open, but we could feel the movement of air, hear the slight creak of hinges.

Yat Sing's hand was at my elbow, and we went inside.

We were taken to the presence of Soo Hoo Duck without the loss of a moment; nor did Soo Hoo Duck waste time in the flowery preliminaries which are incident to Chinese conversation.

"My son," he said to me in Chinese, "the minutes have been as hours crawling across the face of the clock like turtles in the sun. Come at once, please."

Not knowing what to expect, my heart filled with dread, I followed him through a door and into a corridor, conscious of the fact that I was hard put to it to keep pace with this little old man, while behind me, Yat Sing was all but running.

We paused before a door.

Soo Hoo Duck did not knock. As far as I could see, there was no way by which he made our presence known, but there was some secret signal of communication, perhaps some beam of invisible light, perhaps we were standing upon a concealed signal which, beneath the heavy carpet, established a contact and flashed a light or actuated a buzzer.

The door opened.

A Chinese woman whom I had never seen before said, "She waits," and flung the door wide open.

Soo Hoo Duck's hand clutched at my arm and I could feel a faint trembling running along my nerves. It was as though Soo Hoo Duck's fear had subtly communicated itself to me.

I entered that room not knowing what to expect.

Ngat T'oy sat in a chair over in a corner of the room. She was wearing street clothes, and at first glance, she seemed to be quite her usual self.

"Hello," she said to me, after making a little Chinese gesture of respect to her father. "Boy, am I glad to see you! I thought you would *never* get here." And then she began to laugh, and a note of wild, fearful hysteria edged her voice.

The woman said to Soo Hoo Duck, "She won't let me undress her; won't let me touch her."

I saw Soo Hoo Duck's eyes soften with sympathy. "My dear," he said in Chinese, "perhaps a doctor of the white race can quiet you with . . ."

"No! No! No!" she screamed. "They drug you. No doctor. I'll be all right. I'm just nervous, that's all."

Soo Hoo Duck and Yat Sing exchanged glances.

"What happened?" Yat Sing asked in Chinese.

Soo Hoo Duck said, "She was crowded into the curb, held a prisoner for a while."

"Was she harmed?" Yat Sing asked.

"Certainly not," Ngat T'oy said proudly. "There is no reason to make so much commotion over this. I want to speak to Ed. Father. And alone, please."

Soo Hoo Duck said to Yat Sing and to the woman, "Come."

They shuffled out of the room.

As soon as the door had closed, Ngat T'oy spoke to me with such rapidity that my ears could hardly follow her words. "Ed, I've got to undress. You've got to find some way of getting my clothes out of here."

"Your clothes!" I said. "What's the matter?"

"Come here."

I moved over closer to her.

She raised her skirt, showed me pink silk, and on that pink silk were ominous splotches of blood.

"Ngat T'oy, you were hurt?"

"Not me," she said. "I'm afraid—I'm afraid I committed murder."

"If you killed someone who was trying to harm you, it is not. . . ."

"No, no, not that. I'm afraid I committed deliberate, cold-blooded murder. I am afraid I killed a man who never harmed me, a man I don't even know."

"But why?"

"I don't know, I tell you."

"Tell me what happened."

"All right. I was driving along the street, intending to run an errand, pay a social call and then see if I could get in touch with you, just to find out how things were coming. A car pulled alongside. A man said, 'A message for Little Sun'—that is the name you use always, Ed, and I thought it must be from you. But I was cautious. I pulled over to the curb on Grant Avenue, where there were dozens of people within earshot. My own countrymen. I had only to raise my voice, and I could have commanded the obedience of a dozen of my countrymen."

"What did he do?"

"Ed, I—I don't know. He came over to the car. He lowered his voice. He said, 'A man who is very dear to you is in danger. He wants you to go to him.'

"I drew away a little. I knew, Ed, that you would never send for me because you were in danger, and I think the man realized that, because he said, 'And there is danger to your father, as well.' And then his hand rested on my arm and I felt something—a pinprick.

"I tried to jerk my arm away.

"He said, 'Don't, you little fool. Can't you see I'm trying to give you this message without letting everyone on the street hear it?'

"And then he started talking, and peculiar things happened. He said that I must get men whom I could trust and go to a certain place, and he started to tell me where that place was. I was to take a certain street, go so many blocks, then turn to the left, and, as I tried to follow him, a roaring noise came into my ears, and my mind seemed stupefied. I tried to concentrate, and the more I tried, the less could I think. I couldn't focus my eyes. My tongue got thick. I felt that my body had been turned into a big head. And then I was unconscious."

"And then what?"

There was more than fear in her eyes, there was terror. "Ed, I don't know. I felt that men were carrying me upstairs. I was placed in a bedroom. Lately, I have been carrying a dagger, something that I could use in defense if it came to an absolute showdown. I don't know what happened to me. I seemed to be hypnotized. I was walking on tip-toe toward a bed. A man was sleeping there. I knew that I must kill him."

"A drug-induced nightmare," I said.

"Ed, look." She raised her blouse. I could see a strip of smooth, peach-tinted skin, a leather sheath. She raised the blouse farther. The sheath was empty.

"And what happened?" I asked.

Ed, I killed him in his sleep. I felt drawn by some power, greater than I was, something over which I had no control, something that pushed me onward as though it had been a big hand. And the moment I struck down with the knife, I felt that I had fulfilled the thing I had been called upon to do. A vast peace and contentment came over me. I slept. And when I awakened, I was in my car, out in the residential district. I was parked at a curb. There was fog swirling all around. I was filled with panic. I started the car and came home at once. Father ordered me to bed. I went into the closet and started to take off my clothes. I saw the blood—and then I remembered."

"What did your dagger look like, Ngat T'oy?"

"You've seen it, Ed. Jade, encrusted with gold."

"The dragon on the handle?" I asked.

"Yes. . . . And my purse, Ed. It is missing."

I reached a sudden decision. "I will tell your father the truth. I will tell your father and Yat Sing while you take a hot bath and dress. And then you are going out with me."

"And these clothes that I have on?" she asked.

I smiled. "Do you not think you can trust Yat Sing for that?"

"Yes," she said simply, "if I tell him the truth, I need have no worry about someone finding these clothes. But, Ed, do you think that I murdered . . ."

"Ngat T'oy," I said, "who knows? There are drugs which destroy the volition. Perhaps you were hypnotized. Perhaps you were drugged and told to dream. . . . The probabilities are that it was merely a dream. You say this man was in bed?"

"He was lying on a bed, but was fully dressed."

I said, "When you have bathed and changed your clothes, you will come with me and we will investigate."

Ngat T'oy clapped her hands, summoning her woman.

I left the room, walked down the corridor to where Soo Hoo Duck and Yat Sing were seated, waiting for me.

CHAPTER SEVENTEEN

I left Ngat T'oy in the car.

The fog had now settled to a thick blanket, muffling sounds.

The big house of Benjamin Ruttling was a white monstrosity, without visible architectural design, a huge, dark bulk suspended in a sea of weak skimmed milk. From the ground, one could not see the roof. Midway along the side of the house, it was impossible to see the corners.

I felt my way carefully along the side of the fog-enshrouded mansion until I found what I sought—a door at the service entrance with glass panels.

What followed was purely elementary in the art of housebreaking.

Ten seconds later, I was inside.

Despite the shortage of domestic labor, a man with the money, resourcefulness and ruthlessness of Benjamin Colter Ruttling would have servants. These servants were probably sleeping in the back wing of the house. My concern was with the front bedrooms.

The job in hand called for all of my skill, all the underworld education I had learned from my contacts with expert criminals, as well as such experience as I had gained in my war with the underworld.

On silent feet, I moved down the long corridor which led to the sweeping staircase that had been so carefully planned for its architectural balance.

The beam of my flashlight, a flashlight hardly larger than a fountain pen, showed me the curving wrought-iron ornamentation of the staircase, the wrought-iron cage for the big indirect-lighting fixture hanging by a massive chain from a hook suspended in the ceiling; showed me the . . .

I froze in my tracks. A shadow had been cast by some object which lay upon the floor.

The pencil of illumination struck a sprawled body, grotesquely inert in death, a sinister red stain welling out from under it, to send a blood-red reflection from the beam of my flashlight dancing upon the ceiling.

Slowly, carefully, fearing a trap, yet faced with the necessity of doing what had to be done, I circled around the dead man.

The beam of my flashlight illuminated the face, showed the death-distorted features of Whitney, the confidential secretary of Benjamin Colter Ruttling. The dagger of Ngat T'oy was plunged to its hilt in his chest.

I moved back from the body, noticing the direction in which it had fallen. Then I looked back toward the stairs.

I found a drop of blood, more blood, a trail of telltale spots which moved along the curving staircase to the upper corridor, down the corridor to an open door.

I listened for fully two minutes in front of this door before I ventured to enter the room.

My flashlight showed a bedroom. The bed had not been turned down, but there was an indentation on the counterpane where someone had flung himself at full length to rest—or perhaps get a cat nap while waiting for some particular event to happen. And there was blood on this counterpane.

I retraced my steps to the body sprawled in the hallway.

A glimpse of the eastern windows showed that the first faint wisps of light were trickling through the thick fog clouds, giving to the windows a faint hint of cold, gray visibility.

Ngat T'oy, waiting outside in the automobile, would be getting impatient.

I took from my pocket the money I had taken from Daphne Strate, fifteen hundred dollars. And I carefully counted out seven hundred and fifty dollars, folded it and slipped it into Whitney's inside coat pocket.

Then I moved up the stairs once more on swiftly silent feet.

This time, I entered the room where Ruttling had received me on the occasion of my first visit. I remembered that there had been an expensive desk set in that room, a paper knife, scissors, paperweight, desk clock, ornamental blotter. With my gloved hands, I gently extracted the paper knife from the leather receptacle and once more went down the stairs.

I bent over the body. Carefully, I drew out the jade-handled dagger, and, as I drew it out, I inserted into the wound the paper knife I had taken from Ruttling's desk.

I pushed the paper knife deeply and firmly into the wound; then I withdrew it, wiped it off rather hurriedly on the coat of the victim, then took it back upstairs and replaced it.

On my way out, I stopped in at the lavatory on the first floor to wash off Ngat T'oy's dagger. I washed it with soap and water, and when I had finished there was no faintest stain upon either blade or handle.

I found Ngat T'oy's purse where I thought it would be, on the table in the reception hallway. I put knife and purse under my coat and slipped out of the house the same way I had entered.

Cold dawn was now making the fog more milk-white than when I had entered. It was possible to see little swirling tendrils of fog in the strengthening daylight, ghastly streamers that drifted on past, caressing the countryside with damp fingers.

Ngat T'oy was waiting impatiently in the automobile.

"Just a minute," I said, and raised the lid in the storage compartment in the back of the car. "I want to get a rag and wipe off that windshield," I said. "Do you have anything in here that I could use?" I asked.

"Not there, silly," she said. "It's in the glove compartment."

I hid her purse and dagger in the back of the car, pulled down the lid, snapped the handle into place, walked around to the front of the car and took the rag she gave me.

"You were in there a long time," she said. "I thought you just wanted to talk with a man."

"I had a hard time waking him up," I said, polishing off the windshield.

"Did you learn anything?" she asked anxiously.

"I think so," I said. "But I've got to go to the Monterey House Hotel to make sure. Are you feeling better?"

"I'm getting more of a grip on myself," she said. "I think the daylight will make a difference—if only we could get out of this fog."

I slid in behind the steering wheel, took off the emergency brake and let the car coast silently down the long incline.

"I think, Little Sun," I told her, "we'll be out of the fog very soon."

CHAPTER EIGHTEEN

I parked my car directly in front of the Monterey House Hotel.

"Will you be long?" Ngat T'oy wanted to know.

"Not long," I said.

"Ed, tell me, can you find out anything—anything at all?"

"Not yet. I think this man I'm going to see will give me what I'm looking for," I told her.

It was that period just before sunrise which is so beautiful out in the mountains, on rolling farmland or along a trout stream, and is so drab and sickly in a city.

A night clerk looked up from a book he was reading.

"You have a Herbert Rendon in the place?" I asked him.

"Yes, sir, room five hundred and six. Excuse me, sir, I hardly think he's up yet," he said.

"Not up yet!" I exclaimed. "He didn't leave that six-o'clock call?"

"No, sir, his call was for seven."

I grinned and said, "That's one on Herb. I'll bet that's the first time he ever forgot an appointment in his life. Connect me up on a room phone. I'm going to have some fun with him. Why, he promised me he'd be all dressed and ready to come down to the lobby the minute I telephoned. Wait a minute. I'll fix him."

I walked over to the room phones, picked one up. The clerk connected me. I could hear the phone ringing, and then Rendon's voice, not jovial this time, but thick with sleep.

"I beg your pardon, Mr. Rendon," I said, "this is the desk. I hated to disturb you, but the young lady says it's *most* important; that it will be all right to ring you; that if I don't do it, you'll be very, very angry."

"What the hell are you talking about?" Rendon asked.

"A Miss Strate," I said. "A Miss Daphne Strate. She seems to be very much upset over something and says you'll want to see her."

"Is she alone?"

"That's right. And, if you'll pardon me, she seems rather distraught."

"Send her up," Rendon said. "Send her right up."

I took my face an inch or two from the telephone and said, "It's all right, Miss Strate. You may go on up."

I hung up the telephone, walked back to the desk and saw by the way the clerk was looking at me that he had been listening in on the conversation.

I slapped my hand down on the counter and burst into laughter. "This," I said, "is one on Herb! That's the way to get him up and dressed in a hurry. I was a little afraid I couldn't get away with it because as soon as he heard the phone ring, he'd remember his appointment with me. He fell for it hook, line and sinker. This is going to be good," I said, laughing and shaking my head.

I took the elevator up to the fifth floor, walked down to 506 and tapped very timidly on the panels of the door with the tips of my fingers.

I heard Rendon's voice saying, "Just a minute, Miss Strate," and then the bolt shot back and the door opened.

Rendon was just pushing the last of his shirttail down into his trousers. His face, which had been wreathed into a smile of pleasant expectancy, dropped about a foot.

Before he had recovered, I walked on into the room, over to the telephone, took pliers from my pocket and cut the telephone wire.

"Don't," I told him, "make the mistake of making any sudden moves."

His eyes narrowed. "Isn't this rather a new role for you, Jenkins? I thought you never carried a gun."

I said, "Sit down over there on the foot of the bed. Keep your hands in sight. Don't make any moves. Don't try to reach under your pillow or into a suitcase."

"What," he asked, "do you want?"

I stood by the doorway. "I want to give you a break."

"On what?"

I said, "Unless I miss my guess, you're either FBI or Military Intelligence. You're working for the Government. I'm Ed Jenkins, The Phantom Crook. Perhaps I have some patriotism, too." I watched him.

His eyes showed interest now.

I said, "The poison that was given Betty Crofath was something that had been worked out by the Crescent City Chemical Manufacturing and Supply Company. It was something relatively new. Someone had been trying to kill her. They couldn't make connections. Finally the trick was done rather neatly. The person took the same train out of New Orleans with Betty Crofath—not in the same car, but on the same train—managed to sit next to her for a few minutes, open her purse, substitute poison in place of the sleeping tablets she was known to use, and move on.

"For a while, I thought it might have been Daphne Strate. Then I began having some other ideas."

"Go ahead," he said.

"Under the name of Sabin, I went back to New Orleans, got in touch with the head of the chemical company there. Holaberry was the only one who knew I was in New Orleans."

His eyes twinkled. "Not the *only* one, Jenkins."

"The only one," I said, "who knew that I was supposed to be in the market for large quantities of commercial chemicals.

"I talked with Holaberry. A few hours later, Ramon Vasquo Gomez came to my hotel and tried to sell me chemicals to be furnished by the Jap-controlled Bak Shui Wong Chemical Company of Shanghai."

"Very interesting," Rendon said. "Very, very interesting."

"At the time, I made the mistake of jumping at the obvious conclusion."

"That is nearly always a mistake."

I nodded, "I'm afraid I did Holaberry an injustice."

"Then how did Gomez get the tip-off?" he asked.

I said, "Holaberry must have telephoned Benjamin Colter Ruttling that night and told him I was there. Then, tonight, Ramon came to the apartment of Genevieve Hotling. He said he had followed Daphne there. That was a lie. Daphne was not followed—but Daphne *had* left her address with Ruttling."

"Then you mean Ruttling called back Gomez and told him to try and sell you on a competitive line of merchandise put out by a Japanese-controlled company?" Rendon said. "Why, the thing is incredible. The president of the company could hardly be cutting his own throat!"

"No," I said, "but the secretary who was double-crossing him could have been listening in—chap by the name of Whitney."

Rendon's eyes narrowed.

"I thought about the president at first," I said, "but he couldn't have been on the train because Daphne Strate knew him. She'd have seen and recognized him. But she didn't know Whitney. The car porter probably saw Whitney fumbling around in Betty Crofath's purse. That was just too bad for the porter. The reason I got a berth out of Tucson was that some passenger got off at Tucson. It would be very interesting to find out if that passenger might not have been a tall, slender chap with a horse face and pale blue eyes."

"Whitney's description?"

I nodded.

Rendon said, "Apparently there were some things in Miss Crofath's trunk which had considerable significance."

I said, "That, of course, is a little out of my line. But if Whitney or his accomplice, Ramon Gomez, murdered the Pullman porter in the room which had been reserved by Betty Crofath in the Pelton Hotel, it is reasonable to suppose that—well, draw your own conclusions."

Rendon said thoughtfully, "A tall, slender man with a horse face. Yes, I noticed him in the Pelton Hotel."

"You might be able to find that he was registered there. Rather a ticklish position, don't you think?"

"What do you mean?"

"Oh, nothing," I said. "But as a crook of some experience, it wasn't a position I would care to have been in."

"Why not?"

I said, "The Japanese are not a particularly tolerant race."

"What are you getting at?"

"Nothing," I said. "Only if I, as Whitney, had taken a contract to search Betty Crofath's trunk and find certain documents which were, in turn, to be delivered to my accomplice Gomez, who represented the Bak Shui Wong Chemical Company of Shanghai. . . . Well—just suppose, Rendon, that after I had made my search, I hadn't been able to find those documents. Would Gomez believe me? Would the Japanese believe me? Wouldn't it be rather reasonable to expect that the representatives of the Bak Shui Wong Chemical Company would take steps to see that, just in case I had made a double-cross, the enemies of Japan didn't profit by it?"

Rendon's eyes showed glittering interest. He gave a low whistle.

I got up and started for the door.

"Wait a minute," Rendon said. "You haven't told me just what your connection is in this."

I bowed and smiled. "My interest has nothing to do with Betty Crofath. To tell you the truth, I was making a play for Daphne Strate."

"Why?"

I said, "I wanted the diary she had. I wanted to sell it to Ruttling. And I *almost* put it across. If the little tart hadn't double-crossed me, I would have. I'm telling you this frankly, because you'll find out when you talk with Ruttling that I tried to peddle the diary to him. It was one of the few failures I have made in such matters."

And I bowed myself out.

That was once when it was much to my advantage to have a reputation for being a crook. He believed me.

I'd cut his telephone line. It would take him a few minutes to get in touch with the night clerk. He'd have to rouse some sleeper to get a telephone, and I was taking the only elevator down.

At that, Rendon was a fast worker.

The night clerk was just answering the telephone as I went out the door.

Ngat T'oy looked up at me with anxious eyes.

I avoided her eyes. My right hand pushed a tack into the tire.

"Nothing, Ed?"

I shook my head. "I can't get a line on a thing. Look here, Ngat T'oy, don't you think it was a simple case of suggestion? You know how it is. There are certain drugs which more or less destroy the volition, make one susceptible to hypnosis. While you were drugged, someone could have repeatedly told you certain things you were to dream . . ."

"But they might just as well have told me certain things I was to have *done,*" Ngat T'oy said. "And then—and then—oh, Ed, I'm afraid I would have done them. It was the most *awful* feeling."

I drove the car away. "I'm afraid," I said, "I'm at the end of my string."

Ngat T'oy's face was hard with fatigue, worry and inner conflict. The growing daylight was not so kind to it.

I had felt lucky to have thought of the long upholsterer's tack I had picked up at home and stuck in my pocket, but now I was in a dither of annoyance for a moment, wondering if the darn thing had dropped out of the tire. Suddenly however, I heard the sound of the rim striking an obstruction, and a moment after that, the peculiar *thump . . . thump . . . thump* of a flat tire.

I pulled in to the curb and stopped. "Got a spare?" I asked her.

"Why, yes, in the back."

I said, "It's too early to find any place open where we can change the tire. I'll have to do it myself."

I took my coat off, folded it neatly, laid it over the seat back.

Ngat T'oy got out and walked around to the back part of the car.

I raised the turtleback, groped around and found the jack and a canvas roll containing tools. I jacked the front wheel up and came back to get the spare.

All of a sudden, I heard Ngat T'oy's half scream.

"What is it, Little Sun?" I asked.

She was staring at the back of the car, her eyes wide. The jade handle of the dagger was peeping into sight from out behind the spare tire.

"Good Lord!" I said.

Ngat T'oy pushed me to one side, scrambled into the car, pulled out the knife, then stood so the light struck it. She searched it with the greatest care.

"Anything on it?" I asked.

"No," she breathed.

She dove back into the car once more, groped around, and came out with her purse, held that up to the light. Then suddenly her arms were around me. She was laughing, crying, talking all at once. I felt her lips on mine, her arms straining me to her.

"Ed! Oh, Ed!" she cried. "It *was* a dream! They planted those things in the back of my car, thinking I wouldn't find them until . . . Oh, Ed! Oh, my *darling!*"

CHAPTER NINETEEN

Soo Hoo Duck listened to so much of my story as I told him. I saw his kindly eyes soften into gentle sympathy as I talked. When I had finished, he waited for a few moments, putting my story in order in his mind, getting ready to ask questions.

I didn't want to answer any of those probing questions.

I glanced at Yat Sing.

Yat Sing's face was as bland as a full moon, but his eyes, glittering, inscrutable, penetrating, were boring skeptically into mine. It was then I played my trump card.

I said, "I have been doing much thinking—thinking that I could have done to better advantage earlier. Everyone seems to think that I have certain valuable documents which I took from the trunk of Betty Crofath. I thought they were all wrong. But perhaps they were right and I was wrong."

"What do you mean?" Soo Hoo Duck asked me.

"Betty Crofath," I said, "was very clever. She realized that, before she left South America, her baggage might be searched by persons who rather suspected she had information she should not have. Therefore she worked out an elaborate code."

"What?"

"I noticed," I said, "in reading her diary, that she always described the furniture in any room which she thought was artistically arranged. At the time, I thought that she had a taste for interior decorating. But lately, a new explanation has occurred to me."

"And that?" Soo Hoo Duck asked.

I said, "Suppose that when she described the location of the table she was talking about a flat top that was under construction in Japan? Suppose that chairs were destroyers? Suppose that beds, pianos or other massive articles of furniture were battleships?"

"The diary," he said sharply. "Where is it?"

I took it from my pocket.

I noticed Soo Hoo Duck's fingers tremble as he opened the pages.

"I have picked out several instances where rooms are described," I said. "Let us orient them with reference to a map of Japan. Notice that invariably she describes the location of the furniture in these rooms according to directions. There was a piano in the northeast corner, while a table was on the west side of the room. Hardly the sort of furniture arrangement which would impress one as being artistic," I said. "And notice that on the south side of the room were a group of half a dozen chairs."

Yat Sing picked up a pencil and began drawing maps.

As these topographical outlines began to form physical features of familiar regions, there was grateful acknowledgement in every expression that Soo Hoo Duck made in my direction. Finally, he turned to Yat Sing and said, "To this man, I shall always bare my soul."

Later, Soo Hoo Duck ordered tea, egg *foo yung,* fried rice and strips of Chinese pork for his guests. For himself, he had that peculiar, tasteless rice gruel which is a standard breakfast dish in China. It is perhaps the only bit of oriental diet my stomach can't quite stand.

When we had finished, I arose.

Soo Hoo Duck looked at me sharply, arose and said, "Excuse me a moment, please," and stepped quickly into an adjoining room.

I could hear him talking in low tones with the woman who was waiting on Ngat T'oy.

When he came back, his face was softened. He looked at me with affection. "My son," he said, "she sleeps."

"Quietly?" I asked.

"Quietly. She sleeps, and there is even a smile which plays about her lips."

"It is well," I said.

"You are leaving?"

I nodded.

"The other girl," Soo Hoo Duck said gently, "sleeps also, and I am advised that before she went to sleep she asked that under no circumstances should she be permitted to sleep so that slumber would rob her of seeing you upon your return."

I hesitated.

"And," Soo Hoo Duck went on, "the woman who watches over her says that in her sleep she has mentioned your name."

I turned toward the door. "It is not well," I said, "that a woman should mention the name of The Phantom Crook in her sleep. Our ways are different. Hers is the way of light and life and laughter. My feet take me through the dark alleys. I travel in the ways of stealth. Better to let her go her way than to encourage her eyes to see the dark shadows of life."

"You have enemies," Soo Hoo Duck said. "You are at war with the law of your own land, but the hand of every Chinese is the hand of a friend. In my family, you are as an honored son. And should you ever go to China, I can assure you that you will be treated as a king. Only here, in your land, where your lawmakers themselves admit that justice is blind, is it necessary for you to follow the ways of stealth—a land which tonight you have served to such great advantage that you would be honored, were the facts but known."

"The facts will not be known," I told him. "Many facts will not be known. When a newsboy named Frank Collette tosses a newspaper upon a certain porch in the exclusive residential district, and the Filipino houseboy goes to get that newspaper, other facts will come to light. Then Ramon Vasquo Gomez will be charged with murder. There will be much confusion among the members of the Bak Shui Wong Chemical Company. And there will be an even greater incentive to eliminate The Phantom Crook. It is well, therefore, that I go before these things are discovered, and that the girls remain in peaceful slumber."

For a moment, Soo Hoo Duck debated the point. Then his eyes slithered over to the face of Yat Sing, his captain who had charge of the far-flung Chinese Intelligence. What he saw in Yat Sing's face made him sigh wearily with resignation. He turned to me, clasped his hands in front of his heart and shook them gently. "Farewell, my son. Your bravery and wisdom have done much for your country and for mine."

I bowed humbly. "I have profited by the light of your wisdom," I told him. "As the moon can but reflect the light of the sun, so have I but seemed to be wise. Now I go out into the shadows and there will be only darkness for me there."

It was a typical Chinese speech, but there was truth to it.

I would leave this magnificent place with its carved furniture, its deep rugs, its crystal chandeliers and go out into the darkness. Only when some disaster threatened would I dare return.

In the meantime, because I had laughed at the law, I was destined to plunge once more into the shadows of night, into the alleys of Chinatown.

The Wax Dragon

CHAPTER TWENTY

It was a tingling of the hair roots which made me feel that the flesh on the back of my neck was crawling. I knew the sensation from past experiences, knew what it meant.

There, in the narrow, smelly streets of Chinatown, I fought down the impulse to turn and confront the man who was following me. By an effort of will I maintained the shuffling, shambling gait of a Chinaman, a gait which belonged with my present disguise. My mind raced on ahead of my lagging feet. If the man behind me knew he was following Ed Jenkins, disguised as a Chinaman, that would be one thing. If he thought he was following Yee Dooey Wah, a Chinese cook, that would be another. I must find out.

Ahead of me a stooped figure shuffled from the door of a cafe. Soo Hoo Duck, parchment-faced philosopher, reputed to be the uncrowned king of Chinatown, awaited me. Twice before he had sought to interview me, and twice before I had avoided him.

This time I could not avoid him. Nor could the meeting have come at a more inopportune time. Complications were piling up.

I was a fugitive—from the police, but not from justice. And there was a price on my head in the underworld. Ed Jenkins, known in many states as "the Phantom Crook," immune from arrest in California because of a flaw in the extradition laws, could never hope for peace. Police wanted to blame crimes on me, crimes which they could not solve otherwise. Leaders of the underworld feared me.

At one time the police had promised protection, friendship. But there had been complications. I would neither be a stool-pigeon for the police, nor a crook for the leaders of the underworld.

And so I found myself, disguised as a Chinese cook, stained of face, shabby of clothes, hiding from the bright light of the day, and venturing forth upon the narrow streets of Chinatown only at night.

For myself I did not fear. I would have kept in the open, defied police and underworld alike. But there was Helen Chadwick. I had been of service to her, saved her from the clutches of a powerful crook. She had sworn her friendship, but I had evaded the issue and sunk from sight. A man with my record dares not even analyze his feelings for a society girl of the four hundred.

Yet the girl's friendship for me, and my feelings for her, were a constant menace. At any time the underworld might seek to reach me through her. At any moment the police might set a trap and bait it with the one bait I could not overlook—threatened injury to Helen Chadwick.

Hence I had adopted a disguise, had slipped through the fingers of police and crooks alike.

And always I was on the alert, pressed every moment by two dangers. One was that I should be recognized, my disguise penetrated by the crooks on the one hand, or the police on the other. The other was that organized Chinatown should demand an accounting of the mysterious Chinaman who remained secreted during the day and came forth only in the dim light of the night.

And now both dangers had materialized at the same moment.

Behind me came mysterious footsteps; ahead of me waited Soo Hoo Duck.

Could I carry through the deception with the old Chinaman? Was my knowledge of that most subtle of all languages, the Cantonese dialect, sufficient to stand the searching scrutiny of the old patriarch?

Even as I contemplated the problem, it was upon me.

My shuffling feet advanced me to the café door and Soo Hoo Duck stepped before me, screwed his wrinkled face into a monkey smile, and peered shrewdly at me over the tops of his horned-rimmed spectacles.

"Hoh shai kai mah!"

It was the Cantonese salutation, a question. Translated literally it meant, "Is the whole world good?"

"Hoh shai kai," I answered—the conventional reply. "The whole world is good."

And so, disguised as a Chinaman, I was standing in a dark, narrow street of Chinatown, seeking to account for myself before Soo Hoo Duck. And ever in the back of my mind, during the first few words of that interview, was the disquieting feeling that the old man was laughing at me—that and the knowledge that someone had followed me, was approaching even as I bandied words with the king of Chinatown.

"A stream which runs in a winding course must have mountains in its path," mused the old man, his eyes peering cunningly over the dark rims of his spectacles.

I bowed gravely.

"And yet, oh Wise One, the stream eventually reaches the ocean. Mountains may obstruct, the stream may swerve, but, in its very swerving, it is fulfilling the law of life."

The wrinkles about his mouth deepened.

"Perhaps the stream may become surrounded by obstructions. What then?"

He was inquisitive, and yet he seemed friendly.

I matched his smile.

"In that event, Learned One, the stream becomes a lake, and the calm tranquillity of its surface mirrors the obstructions which have given it beauty, serenity; which, by damming it up, have become the very creators of the lake."

I spoke the words slowly, sparring for time.

"Then," said Soo Hoo Duck with a trace of impatience in his tone, "you have ceased to be a brook, and have become a lake."

I met his eyes steadily.

"Your excellency will remember that it is the brook which babbles. When water has ceased to run it becomes silent."

He was a good sport, this puckery-faced Chink. He laughed at that, and, at that instant, the man who had been shadowing me, walked slowly past, forced into the bright light of the Yat King Café.

Never have I seen a human being who so resembled a vulture. He was tall, stooped, red-eyed. As he walked, his long nose twitched, a continual, spasmodic snuffling. His reddish eyes blinked constantly, as though the light irritated them. His thin neck dropped forward so that his chin hung out over his shoes, and the narrow collar which surrounded that thin neck was like a wedding ring about a lead pencil.

As for clothes, he was dressed entirely in black, and he slipped softly by on rubber-soled shoes.

Abruptly I became conscious that the Chinese philosopher had riveted me with his eyes, had followed my gaze. Of a sudden the kindly look dropped from his face, and his eyes bored into mine as though they had been twin gimlets of cold, black steel.

"Where the buzzards fly there will soon be carrion," he intoned.

I returned his scrutiny.

"And yet, my brother, it is well known that the buzzard does not kill. He merely devours that which has ceased to live. The wise man should fear the hawk rather than the buzzard."

With that I turned away, left the aged philosopher digesting a little new philosophy. He had been too quick to compare me with a coursing brook, too ready with his comment about the vulture-like appearance of the man who had followed me. Perhaps that man followed me, thinking I was a Chinaman, believing in my disguise. If so, he followed me at the direction of some powerful Chinese, and Soo Hoo Duck was the uncrowned king of Chinatown.

Yet, and this was the disquieting thought, perhaps my enemies had pierced my disguise, knew that the Chinaman who always circled the block before starting on any errand, was, in fact, Ed Jenkins, the Phantom Crook.

I hurried on, seeking to turn the tables, to become the one who followed, and, behind me, Soo Hoo Duck wrinkled his face in silent mirth.

The buzzard had gained a block. His awkward, ungainly shuffle carried him rapidly over the ground and I lengthened my stride. Then I noticed that there was one ahead of me, a beady-eyed Chinaman who was bearing purposefully down upon the ungainly figure.

I dropped back, waiting, watching. Ahead of me the buzzard quickened his pace until it became almost a trot, the arms flapping loosely from the shoulders as though they had been wings. A taxicab swung around the corner and I heard the voice of the buzzard for the first time as he hailed the cab —a raucous, throaty cry.

I pressed on. There had been pursuit and flight in the actions of those ahead. Perhaps I could get the license number of the cab, find out more concerning the identity of the Chinaman who had engaged in the mysterious pursuit. One thing was certain—that Chinaman had not been following the buzzard when I stopped to chat with Soo Hoo Duck.

The license number of the cab I secured. The Chinaman crowded to the edge of the sidewalk, against the shadows of the dingy buildings, and suddenly vanished. As I passed the spot a second later, I could discern no sign of a doorway; yet I knew that in the side of the dark building on my left there was a secret entrance. A hidden door had swung silently open and the Chinaman had vanished within.

Nor did I pause for a careful inspection of the wall of that building. Shuffling steps scuttled along the pavement behind me. Soo Hoo Duck had taken up my trail. His hands were concealed within the loose sleeves of his padded coat and the smile was gone from his wrinkled countenance.

Abruptly, I crossed the street and entered the Mandarin Café, one of the chop suey joints that cater to the tourist trade. For some reason, which I could not quite fathom, Chinatown was becoming too hot for Ed Jenkins. Calmly, impassively, I slippety-slopped my way through the main dining-room, into the kitchen, past the huge range with its brass kettles, into a narrow oblong of darkness which marked a back passageway that went I knew not where.

There were steps, a door, more steps, black darkness, and the feel of the wind on my right cheek. I turned so that this wind was squarely in my face, took a few steps and found myself in a dark alley. Flattening myself against the side of a building, I waited within the damp darkness.

There was the sound of running feet and a slim, stealthy figure entered the alley, paused for a swift glance in both directions, and then trotted toward the patch of dull light which marked the nearest outlet of the alley.

I sighed, and turned back into the passageway, retraced my steps, went through the kitchen, into the main dining-room of the Mandarin Café, and out upon the street. A vacant taxicab stood before the door. I dove within, gave the driver an address, changed it after two blocks, had him drive twice around the next block, and then went directly to the railroad depot where I handed a red-cap a baggage check and waited while he brought me a big suitcase which had been checked at the baggage room. I had previously made all preparations necessary to the changing of my disguise whenever necessity might arise and I could have made a dozen such changes had I cared.

My next address was the most exclusive tourist hotel in the city. I changed my disguises in the cab. The brown stain of the skin remained the same, aiding me in my new role. I had entered the cab as a Chinaman. I left it as a wealthy Mexican. The driver blinked, pocketed the bill I handed him for a tip and drove rapidly away.

Half an hour later I had established myself as Señor Juan Morales, and as Señor Morales I looked up the cab which had borne the buzzard away from Chinatown. The driver consulted his records, pocketed the banknote I gave him, and pointed to a pencilled address with a grimy forefinger.

"There yuh are, boss," he said.

Schooled as I am to conceal my emotions, I could feel the blood drain from my face. The address was that of Helen Chadwick!

That which I feared had taken place.

For years the police stool-pigeons had sought to find some weak point in my defense. For years organized crooks had tried to work out some method by which they could control me, force me to do their will. Their efforts had been in vain. I had been a lone wolf, a creature of the shadows who kept his own counsel. And then had come Helen Chadwick. Recognizing the utter futility of any romance, knowing the danger to her, I had taken stern steps to see that we were not thrown together, that there should be no opportunity for romance to develop, that her name should never be linked with mine.

But the underworld has a thousand eyes which can see in the dark.

And now I was faced with the horrible certainty—the underworld knew.

"I guess that's not the one I wanted," I said to the cab driver, striving to make my voice sound casual, and turned away.

Within fifteen minutes I was frantically undoing the elaborate scheme I had perfected for concealment. Either the underworld or the police were menacing the girl I loved. Through her they sought to strike at me.

Very well. If they wanted to find me they would have no trouble. The disguises I ripped off. The stain upon my skin was removed with a chemical preparation. I had left Chinatown as Yee Dooey Wah, a Chinese cook. I had entered the hotel as Señor Juan Morales, a Mexican millionaire. I left the hotel as Ed Jenkins, the Phantom Crook.

Calling a cab, I stepped within and gave the driver a laconic direction. "The Mandarin Café, in Chinatown."

He nodded and grinned, thinking that I was a tourist going down into the night life of Chinatown for a thrill. Little could he know just how much of a thrill it would be. Stripped of disguises, flaunting my identity to criminals and police alike, I was headed for the place where I had last encountered danger.

I could defend myself. Crooks and police mean but little to me when I have a free hand. It was not by accident that I had become known from coast to coast as the Phantom Crook. But Helen Chadwick I could not watch. I had not dared to even show my interest in her, lest the very display of such interest should doom her. The underworld works its schemes cleverly, and the police are not asleep. Both capitalize most strongly on that attraction which nature has built up between man and woman. Man desires to be near those whom he loves; he will fight to protect his loved ones.

Many a crook is serving time because the police trapped him by watching the girl who meant more to him than anything in the world. Many a man has been framed because the police could count upon his coming to the rescue of the girl he loved.

And now they were trying it with me.

Very well. It would work. It always works. But there would be no sly, slinking shadow sneaking up to the house of Helen Chadwick, seeking to protect her, no Chinese cook nor Mexican millionaire trying to guard her. It would be Ed Jenkins, the Lone Wolf, the Phantom Crook himself, that would descend upon the underworld, and make that best of all defenses—a counter attack. Trap me through Helen Chadwick, would they? Damn them. I'd walk into their trap and smash it.

The cab lurched to a stop before the Mandarin Café, and I discharged it with a flourish, sneered at the inquisitive faces which peered about me, and went slowly up the flight of narrow steps, my coat over my arm, my jaw set.

Ed Jenkins was back in the underworld.

How the news traveled! A slinking hop-head by the doorway took one look and then dashed madly down the stairs. A whining stool-pigeon who held his head low and glanced at things about him with the flickering eyes of a human jackal, paid his check midway in the course of his meal and scuttled for a telephone. The whole atmosphere of the place became suddenly charged with static electricity.

I selected a table, snapped my fingers to a waiter, gave my order and sat back, watching the curling spirals of eddying smoke from my cigarette, speculating on what the events of the next half hour would be. Those who knew me would know that my very appearance in this place was an invitation to a duel, one of those subtle duels in which the weapons are human pawns and in which no quarter is given or asked.

And yet it was in this way, and in this way alone, that I could save Helen Chadwick. The intrigue of the underworld was clutching at her with its slimy fingers, seeking to control me through her. Now that I had disclosed myself, come out into the spotlight, I could probably count on two things; one was that they would leave her alone, the second was that I would be sucked into the swirling vortex of exciting events.

There was a commotion at the door.

Soo Hoo Duck entered, shuffled across the room and paused before my table.

"You eatum noodle?" he asked in bland pidgin-English.

Perhaps he knew who I was, perhaps not. If he knew me for the man who had talked with him earlier in the evening he knew that I could talk Cantonese. Also I fancied Soo Hoo Duck could speak English as well as the average college graduate. Yet now he stood before my table and talked the broken pidgin-English of the Chinese coolie.

I nodded a curt answer to his question. I was in no mood for the subtleties of Chinese diplomacy.

"You eatum all alone?"

Again I nodded.

"Heap no good eatum allee time alone. You catchum some one piecee fliend, maybeso two piecee fliend heap more better. You savvy me? I heap savvy you. I heap fliend you."

I studied the motionless wrinkles of the impassive face and sought to pierce the wall of black reserve which hung before his beady eyes. Was he fishing for an invitation to join me at my meal? I shrugged my shoulders. It was to be a lone game.

"I no savvy you," I said, and turned my shoulder to him.

Without another word he slippety-slap-slipped away, his shuffling feet moving with a slow rhythm which somehow conveyed the impression of offended dignity.

Two men slipped in the door, men who were panting from

a hasty ascent of the stairs, men who glanced quickly about the room before they settled themselves at a table.

I marked their faces for future reference.

From the back door there came a party of three pasty-faced fellows with ratty eyes and vicious mouths. There was a startling similarity of appearance in the three. Stoop-shouldered they were, white, furtive, yet garbed in the most expensively tailored clothes.

There sounded heavy feet on the stairs and a square-toed, broad-shouldered, bullet headed individual slumped his way into the room and jostled over to a table in the corner—a plainclothes detective.

The stage was set.

Evidently three separate factions had been sufficiently interested in the appearance of Ed Jenkins to rush special representatives to the scene. Nor could I be sure that they were not all three working in a common cause.

The two heavy-set fellows who had first entered were typical strong-arm men. They were probably instructed to kidnap me, throw me in a waiting car, take me to some secret destination. The three stoop-shouldered, putty-faced men were "guns," men who represented the typical gangster killers. Now that prohibition had systematized crime, had placed ready money in the hands of criminal gangs, they were a type that was becoming daily more common. The plainclothes man had apparently been sent to watch and listen, and he was more than likely in cahoots with one or both of the other factions.

I leisurely ate my chicken noodles, sipped my tea and looked about me, waiting for the first move that would enable me to plan my campaign, start my counter offensive.

And I was unarmed. I rarely carry a gun. It is a felony for a crook to possess a weapon and I dare not take the chances of having a gun on me. I depend on my wits. A cop might pinch me for having a gun under my arm, but he can't arrest me for having my wits about me.

And now I was without a plan. Usually I try to keep one jump ahead of events, to have a general plan of campaign. But this time I was not my own master. Events had crowded my hand. Helen Chadwick was in danger and I must force things to an issue. Nor did I misunderstand the situation in the slightest. For some reason I had suddenly become a creature of importance in crookdom. This sudden interest in me was not merely because of my record or on account of past scores. Somewhere, somehow, something was happening concerning which I knew nothing, yet the happening of which was making me of prime importance in the plans of somebody, perhaps of several somebodies.

Lord knows there were enough complicating factors of the situation there in that smelly Chinese café, and yet I kept watching the outer door, feeling that there would be still other developments. Perhaps it was the attitude of the men, a sort of tense waiting. Perhaps it was a hunch, perhaps merely the emotional strain. Whatever it was, it kept me watching the outer door.

Five minutes passed, and the swinging door shot back under the impetus of a stiff-armed jab that would have rocked a prize-fighter. The man who stepped into the room and sneeringly contemplated those within was more or less known to me. Twice before he had been pointed out to me, and each time the pointing had been accompanied with a warning.

Bob Garret, a hound for publicity, one of the outstanding figures on the detective force, bold, ruthless, clever after a cunning fashion—and, as he stood there, contemptuously turning his glittering eyes from face to face, I knew his errand. He, too, was interested in Ed Jenkins. I could read it in his glance, in his every gesture.

At length his eyes locked with mine. For several seconds we stared at each other. He seeking to overawe me by his very gaze; I refusing to lower my eyes. Then he came forward.

"Ah, Jenkins. I've never had the pleasure of meeting you, but I've seen many of your—er—photographs."

I said nothing. As a crook, society had labeled me an outcast. I had no rights save such as I could command. I could no more openly resent the insult in the man's voice than I could the brazen assurance with which he drew up a chair and sat at my table.

He extracted a black cigar from his pocket, clipped the end, scraped a match across the sole of his shoe, and regarded me appraisingly through the film of blue tobacco smoke.

"The Phantom Crook, eh?"

No reply was apparently expected from me. The words had been merely in the nature of a taunting preliminary. It is by such methods that the police break down the spirit of those with whom they deal, sneer them back into the shadows whenever they would rehabilitate themselves. I was used to it. Yet I resented it. If society desired to confine me within barred walls that was the privilege of society—provided it could catch me and prove its case. But when I sought to keep within the law I should have been given the privileges of a citizen, freedom from police persecution. However, society creates conditions, not theories. And, in the meantime, here was this pudgy detective sneering at me across the table.

About forty-one or two, he was, and there was the look in his eyes which creeps into the eyes of those who are accustomed to achieve their ends by bully-ragging and hypocrisy. His face was scraped and massaged to plump pinkness. The great knuckles of his ham-like hands were cushioned beneath a layer of soft fat. Plainly he was one who liked the good things of life. Probably he had started as a youth to fight his way to the top, and then sheer animal cunning had served his purpose better. He was a combination of fighter and coward, of a cunning man and a fool—and the law had clothed him with the majesty of its authority, had given him license to do almost as he wished with those who had once been unfortunate enough to incur the displeasure of organized society and to be thenceforth labeled as ex-convicts, crooks.

"Not very glad to have me as a dinner companion, are you?"

The words were spoken with the easy assurance of one who knows that he has the backing of unlimited power; but they, at least, called for an answer.

I raised my eyes from my food, let them bore into his so that he could get the full meaning of my answer.

"No," I said, and spat the word at him.

His eyes shifted somewhat beneath the hostility of my gaze, and the knowledge that they had shifted angered him.

"All right. Let's get down to business."

He flipped a careless little finger across the end of his cigar, scattering ashes over the table, upon my butter, into my food, and his pink face came forward as he lowered his voice.

"Jenkins, you're a crook. You're wanted in other states. Because you've found a hole in the extradition laws you're all clear in California. You've developed a technique with safes that's never been equalled anywhere, and no one knows just how you do it. You always seem to have plenty of money, and you're a Lone Wolf."

He ceased speaking to take a deep drag at his heavy cigar,

and I said nothing. No answer was necessary. He had spoken only the simple truth, the bare facts.

He withdrew the cigar and let his eyes bore into mine.

"All right. You've made a boob of the department long enough. The jig's up."

Again he paused.

"Yes?" I asked, casually.

My tone angered him. I could see the flush come to his scraped cheeks.

"Yes. It's a cinch you're working. And it's a cinch you're holding out on us. Come across with a fifty-fifty split or you're going bye-bye up San Quentin way."

"I'm keeping within the law in California," I said simply.

The words irritated him more than anything I could have said.

"Well, what if you are, you damned fool? Does that make any gravy for me? What'd yuh think this is, a summer resort? I don't give a whoop in hell about your record or your intentions. I want fifty per cent of the gravy; and if you ain't gettin' it I'm losin' fifty per cent just the same as though you was holdin' out on me."

I shrugged my shoulders. It was the same old line. I'd heard it so much that my ears were as weary of it as of last year's popular song.

"Yes, you have no bananas," I said, knowing that this man and myself were bound to become sworn enemies after this interview.

His face became fairly livid.

"All right, you cheap, second-story crook. Try that line and see what I hang on to you. D'yuh think I give a damn whether you're within the law or not? I'll frame a crime on you that'll get a jury to send you up in ten seconds after the case reaches 'em. You don't dare even take the witness stand with the record that's against you. You've got to do what I say and do it damned quick."

He was right as to part of it, wrong as to the rest. The law is a strange assortment of injustices. When a man has once been convicted of crime he becomes absolutely within the power of the police. Charge him with crime and he is done for. Of course the law says that the District Attorney cannot introduce any evidence of prior convictions. Oh, no. That would not be right. The jury must pass on the man's guilt or innocence of the particular crime for which he is being tried. But the law also says that when a "witness" is on the stand he can be impeached as to his testimony by showing that he has been previously convicted of a felony. That makes it delightfully simple for the police. They frame a charge on an ex-convict. If he sits silent the jury convicts him because he didn't deny the charges that were made against him. If he takes the stand to declare his innocence, he becomes a "witness," and the District Attorney smirkingly "impeaches" his testimony by showing that he's been convicted of a felony. It's a fine game, the law. And it's played according to a complicated set of rules; but, as to me, those rules are all one way. Heads, the police win. Tails, I lose.

Bob Garret's face drew even closer and another shower of cigar ashes sprinkled over my food.

"There are two gangs that need you here in the city. Both of 'em are in right. Both of 'em need a good box man. You're it. You make your choice right here and now. Either you tie up with 'em and I get my split, or you wish you had."

I motioned to the waiter.

"Bring me another order of chicken noodles as soon as this *gentleman* has finished with his cigar."

Bob Garret sat back in his chair with a smile.

"Think you can get my goat, eh? All right. Now let *me* tell *you* something. Helen Chadwick's on her way to jail."

I had been half way expecting something like that, and I had nerved myself for it. I believe my face retained its expression without so much as a change of color.

"Who's she? Someone I know?"

The detective gave a sneering laugh and I noticed that his eyes had dropped to my hands.

"Oh, yes," he mocked. "Is she someone you know? That's good," and he pointed his finger.

I lowered my own eyes, looked at my hands. Unconsciously I had gripped my left hand, had bent one of the composition spoons almost double. Even now the skin showed white as paper across my knuckles.

"Now I'll go on from there," he gloated, fairly radiating confident assurance. "It happens we need you in our business. We never could get a strangle-hold on you until you and the skirt fell for each other. Then it was a cinch. She's way up in society, one of the four hundred, but she hasn't got any political influence. Her dad's dead. Just her and her mother, and the old woman's not lastin' long. She got mixed up with you just enough so we could prove that she knows you, that she posed as being engaged to you once, out at Loring Kemper's. That'll make a fine background for what we're going to frame on her."

I interrupted him. Knowing in advance that it was hopeless, I tried it, nevertheless.

"Leave her out of it. She never really cared for me, nor I for her. She was being blackmailed, and it would have killed her mother. I was able to help her out of it, and she had to pose as being engaged to me to trap the blackmailer. That's all there was to that. She's straight as a string. Leave her out of it."

How he laughed, the sneering laugh of those who have power to control the destinies of others.

"Don't make me laugh so hard, Jenkins. I got a sore lip. Sure, I know all about that end of the game, all about the blackmailing business. That don't bother me. What I want is gravy, jack, mazuma. Get me? I want fifty per cent of the take, and when there ain't any take there ain't any fifty per cent. Get that? All right. I've never been able to control you before, but I can now. Helen Chadwick's the weak link in your chain.

"No, don't interrupt. Listen. Tonight Helen Chadwick is the guest of Paul Boardman and his wife. You know Boardman. He's the real power behind the throne in city politics. Whenever he wants anything he gets it. Here's something you don't know. The Chief of Police is bucking Boardman, knows something about the inside of some of the deals. Boardman is in with the ring that gets the split on the gravy. I'm in with Boardman. Together we're playing the cards to get the scalp of the Chief. I'm going in as the next Chief. It's all slated."

I looked at the man in surprise. Strive as I might to control my features, I could hardly keep my eyes from widening. Such information placed him in my power to some extent, even if I was a crook and he a police official. The Chief would probably credit the information if I should spill it to him. Garret must be crazy to tell me so much of the inside affairs of city politics.

He saw my expression and laughed outright, a gloating laugh of triumph. And then I knew. He felt he was safe in telling me anything he wanted to because I was not slated to leave that room alive unless I threw my lot in with his, became a part of the criminal ring that was splitting the "gravy" fifty-fifty with the insiders.

"Don't worry, Jenkins. You'll never be able to use the information I'm giving you. Here's some more. Helen Chadwick believes that Paul Boardman is framing a crime on you, that you've walked into the trap and are scheduled for the stir. But she also believes that the papers that'll show your innocence are upstairs in Boardman's open safe. Figure it out for yourself. She thinks the safe has been carelessly left open and that there's a lock box in it that'll keep you out of the pen. Good, eh?

"The trap's all laid. When she walks up the stairs tonight she'll be followed. Witnesses are planted in the room. The safe is coated with a special preparation that'll hold her fingerprints like fresh varnish. In addition there's a camera all set with a flashlight so that she'll be photographed in front of the safe, rummaging through its contents.

"Come in with us and we split fifty-fifty. Stay out and you never leave here alive, and Helen Chadwick gets blackmailed out of everything she has in the world. That's an argument you can't overlook, a proposition you can't say no to."

He stopped talking and tossed his cigar into the spittoon. I knew that he meant every word he said. Some people might have questioned his ability to do what he threatened, might have thought he was outlining the plot of a ten-twenty-thirty melodrama. Those people are the theorists of life, the ones who sit back and make it possible for the crooked politicians to run a whole lot of the government. I've been through the police mill many times before. I know.

For a few moments I devoted my attention to breaking crackers into small pieces. I didn't want Bob Garret to see my eyes. Right then I was wondering whether I could stop his scheme by killing him as he sat there at the table.

The China boy that was waiting on the table shuffled up with another order of food.

"Your fliend finish cigar," he said, and deposited the fresh bowl of noodles.

A paper glinted between the yellow fingers on my side of the bowl, and I mechanically watched it as it dropped to the table, screened by the bowl from Garret's eyes.

My fingers slipped it under the table, spread it out beneath the soiled cloth. My eyes soaked in the single line of the message:

"The lights will go out at two minutes past ten."

There was no signature. A red blob of sealing wax, containing the imprint of a dragon, was in the lower right-hand corner. That was all.

I took out my watch. It was but a few minutes of ten.

"Well?" asked Bob Garret.

I stroked my chin meditatively.

"Let me think it over for a minute or two. Go on away from here and give me a chance to think."

I could see swift suspicion in his countenance.

"I hate to get back into the crook game," I continued, doubtfully, as though I were weakening.

He swung to my side of the table, patted swift hands over my clothes.

"They say you never carry a gun, Jenkins, but I'll have to make sure."

I sat still under the search, although the very touch of his hands fired me with an indignation which was more than mere hatred. I could understand how men killed. Damn him—the law had given him the right to paw me over, the right to arrest me on a felony charge if a weapon should be found. There was nothing for me but to submit to the majesty of the law.

Satisfied, he went away, joined the flat-foot at the other table, surveyed the restaurant in smirking arrogance. The three gunmen gave him a questioning glance. The pair of hard-boiled gangsters looked inquiringly at him. To both he nodded, a fatuous nod of complete assurance, yet motioned them to remain on guard.

I sighed and got my feet in under me. The time was at hand. It was possible that Bob Garret, whose eyes never left me, correctly interpreted my preparation for flight—for to stay and fight that crowd was madness. He jerked suddenly upright; perhaps gave a prearranged signal.

The three gunmen got into action first, one of them drew an ugly automatic. The other two had blackjacks. Over at the other table Bob Garret was hurriedly thrusting his pudgy hand beneath his coat. One of the plug-uglies grasped a chair.

It was Bob Garret that I watched. He alone knew how much I knew, how much he had told me. He would see to it that I never left the room alive. No sudden turn of fortune's wheel could divert his mind from the main issue. I knew too much for him to allow me to live. He was too far away to enable me to come to close quarters before he could get his gun into action, yet near enough to be sure of his not missing.

Then suddenly, without a sound, came darkness, total darkness which seemed almost tangible in its velvety thickness.

"This way," came a soft voice; and I sprang from the table, seeking the way I had determined upon.

I avoided both the front and the back entrances. I knew of a secret passageway which led out of one of the windows, on to a roof, to a hidden door, down a corridor and out through an adjoining store into one end of an alley.

A man got between me and my goal. I felt the quick intake of breath as a hand raised back, sensed rather than saw the poised knife, lurched forward with all my weight back of my fist, and hit a glancing blow on the man's cheek. I could feel him reel sideways and backward under the blow.

From somewhere below came the shrill scream of a police whistle, and the cool night air struck my face as I leaned out of the window, rested my feet on the concealed support which had been cleated to the sheer side of the house, dropped to a roof below, ran along a little runway, through a door, down a narrow passageway and into a dark corridor.

I opened a door which led into the storeroom through which I had planned my exit, and, in the dim light, noticed a human form standing very erect at one side of the passageway. The events of the past few minutes had made me prone to act first and question afterward, and I braced my shoulder for a quick punch.

"Soo Hoo Duck wishes you good fortune in your quest," came from the half darkness in the Cantonese dialect. "Water which has been dammed and then breaks through the obstruction carries all before it—but it must rush with great speed."

So he knew then—this wily old Chink, knew that Yee Dooey Wah had been Ed Jenkins, knew that I had a mastery of the Cantonese dialect, and, apparently, knew something of the mission upon which I was embarking . . . also he had known that I was familiar with the secret passageway and surmised that I would be departing by that route.

Perhaps he was a friend, as he said. Perhaps he was a wily enemy, masking behind his apparent friendship a desire to place me in the hands of my enemies. At any rate I was not going to stop and argue the matter with him, any more than I was going to waste time returning his offers of good will. I swept past him like a limited train sweeping past a hobo.

"The alley exit is open and unwatched," I heard him say as I dashed through the back of the store and into another corridor.

I had expected there would be a hue and cry behind me in the store, that the Chinese would raise a commotion, put the police on my track, give the gunmen a chance to learn which way I had taken in making my escape; but they looked at me with beady-eyed impassivity, and went on with their unhurried tasks. Perhaps they had been instructed to expect me, to keep silent as I went through the store. Perhaps I was walking out of one trap and into another.

I had no chance to change my plans. It was the alley exit or the street, and to have emerged upon the lighted street would have been to offer myself as a gratuitous target for the men of the underworld, as a certain captive to the police. And the end would have been the same in either event. I was supposed to either join forces with the underworld on a fifty-fifty split with the police, or to become a corpse. There was no room in their plans for anything different. If I didn't join them they intended to blackmail Helen Chadwick, and they knew that they would never be safe in doing so as long as I was alive.

I hit the darkness of the alley, thought for a moment it was deserted, and then saw that a roadster was parked directly across from the door through which I had emerged.

Another door opened. I heard the soft sibilants of a Chinaman's voice dropped to a cautious whisper:

"Takee car; send um back some day."

I sprinted through the gloom, vaulted into the seat, groped for the ignition switch, and found the keys in the lock.

I pressed the starting motor, threw in the clutch and tore out of the alley just as there came the sound of a whining siren and a police machine ground to a stop around the corner, at the door of the Mandarin Café.

And I saw something else in that brief glimpse I had of the street. A "dead wagon" was parked at the curb, one of those black, box-like affairs in which corpses are transported. On the driver's seat, attired in sombre black, sat the vulture, the human buzzard, his head bent over, his nose twitching, his long neck twisting in his collar.

Only a flashing glimpse did I have and then I had skidded

the corner and was tearing through the narrow streets, gripping the wheel, pressing the foot throttle to the floor boards.

Some time later I swung the car into a darkened street and slammed on the brakes.

I slipped from the car, sprinted to the curb, dashed through the revolving door of a hotel, walked rapidly across the lobby, took an elevator to the second floor, walked down the corridor, sprinted down the steps, went to the side entrance of the hotel and stepped into a taxicab.

"University Club," I snapped at the driver.

I went there, entered the club, came out and into another cab, and went to the Coliseum Theatre. That was only four blocks from where Paul Boardman lived, and I didn't want to be traced too near the house.

For once I was doing but little planning. Action was my cue that night. On other occasions I had had the time to think out some careful plan of campaign, to match plot with counterplot, and always had I kept my back trail so covered that it would be difficult to pin a definite infraction of the law upon me. Now it was different. I was working against time and for the safety of the woman I loved.

Such are the methods by which the police grind down the criminal. One dare not have a companionship with a woman, a love for one of the opposite sex. Such things are tabulated at "headquarters" and whenever the police want a man they look for the woman for whom he has shown a fondness. If they can find him through her well and good. If they cannot, they proceed to hound her day and night, making life miserable for her. Wherever they have the opportunity, they haul her on the carpet, until, in desperation, the man for whom they are looking tries to protect the girl he loves—and walks into a carefully spread police net.

One who would be at war with society must renounce all normal companionship, must have no friendship, must learn to be self-sustaining. And I, for years a lone wolf and proud of the fact, had at last walked into the most common police trap of them all, the one which never fails, the inherent desire of a man to protect the woman he loves.

There were lights in the front of the Boardman house, but the back was dark. I presumed that Bob Garret had already arrived. I felt certain that he was to be one of the witnesses who would trap Helen Chadwick when she went to the safe for the papers, and I never doubted for a minute but that she would go to that safe.

What her feelings for me were I had no means of knowing. This much I did know. Any affection she might have for me could be nothing but a source of pain. Therefore, if I were to act the part of a gentleman, I must conceal my feelings for her, never by word or act cause her friendship to ripen into anything else. The present situation was but a sample of what she might expect if she should show a fondness for me.

For the moment I had the wild idea of storming the front of the house, of demanding to see Helen Chadwick, and warning her, but a second thought convinced me of the futility of such a course. Beyond question Bob Garret would have hastened to the house and prepared for just that. Knowing that I had escaped from the death trap set for me in the Chinese café, knowing that I possessed the knowledge of what was to happen in that house, he could figure out my next move with no uncertainty. He knew what I would try to do as well as though I had told him my plans.

So much had the love of a good woman and this cursed police system done for me. I had ceased to be able to master events, and must, in turn, be mastered by events, not of my own making. I had become merely a pawn. The police had set the trap, had baited it with the one bait I could not resist, and, no matter that I had fought my way to freedom through the smelly darkness of Chinatown, I must throw away that freedom, rush madly to the one place where the police would be expecting me.

And yet I had one ace up my sleeve. I had my years of experience. I was no novice at the game. I had been in tight places before. I had learned the logic of doing the unexpected.

Had I called at the front door I would have been swiftly and quietly overpowered, arrested, started for the jail, and killed en route while "attempting to escape." Had I sought to get Helen Chadwick on the telephone, I would have been kept waiting while the police traced the call and arrested me.

As it was, I violated the law, broke and entered, and I did it without compunction. There was an ingenious burglar alarm, but I had learned my trade thoroughly, and it did not detain me long. One of the back windows slid noiselessly upward, and I dropped into the yawning blackness within.

A phonograph was blaring forth a dance piece from the front of the house. There was the occasional shrill of woman's laughter. Now and then there came a deep guffaw from a man. Evidently there were several guests, guests who could be called as "witnesses" if the occasion demanded. And I felt certain that things had been arranged so that Helen would be making her attempt almost immediately, might be sneaking up the stairs and into Boardman's study even now. Knowing me as they did, the plotters could not help but fear me. Now that I had escaped from Chinatown, they would take elaborate plans to keep me from reaching Helen with a warning, but the best plan of all would be to have her walk into the trap without delay.

There were back stairs in the house, but here I was doomed to disappointment. Such servants as were on duty were gathered in the little hallway at the foot of those stairs. The front stairs would doubtless be near the front door, and they would be guarded.

I had no time to lay plans, no time to do much of any thinking. It was merely a case of doing the unexpected wherever possible and doing it rapidly.

A serving tray loaded with glasses of gin stood on a little table in the pantry and I picked this up, ditched my hat, and started boldly to the front part of the house, toward the noise of revelry. The tray was balanced on my hand, held so that it concealed my face as much as was possible. It was a desperate chance, but one I must take. They might arrest me, might recognize me as soon as I entered the rooms where the guests were gathered, but they would never be able to subdue me until I had raised such a commotion that Helen would be warned. After that, it would be prison of course, for I had broken and entered another man's house. . . .

I kicked open a swinging door. Couples were dancing over a floor from which rugs had been removed. The lights were low during the dance, and the swaying couples seemed engrossed in each other. The casual sight of a man carrying a tray of glasses did not arouse sufficient interest to cause either male or female to give a second glance at the supposed servant.

Fortune was favoring me. She had favored me in the matter of the lights, and she was favoring me as to the stairs. The front stairs forked at a landing, and one flight came down into the very room where the dancing was taking place.

Twisting and turning through the twining couples, I slowly

made my way to the stairs and up, carrying the glasses upon the tray. There was no one to question, no one to comment.

On the landing I set down the tray and dashed upward into the darkened upper story. It would suit their purpose to have it dark here. The trap for Helen Chadwick required darkness. There would be concealed witnesses, a camera set up, with a flashlight all ready. When Helen approached the safe she would touch a string which would click the shutter and release a flash just as wild deer are made to photograph themselves when they approach a salt lick at night.

I knew, from what Bob Garret had told me, that the study was on the upper floor. As to its exact location I could have no definite idea. Also I could appreciate the danger. There were witnesses in the upper story of that house, witnesses who were planted there, ready to pounce upon Helen Chadwick as she advanced to the safe. If I were to explore at random I would be almost certain to stumble upon some of these people.

I determined to play one hunch, and then, if I was not successful in that, to call Helen Chadwick's name at the top of my voice, to shout my warning there in the darkness of the upper hallway.

There was but one chance I could take, first,—that I could pick the room in which the study was located. If I could do that, if I could enter that darkened room and do something that would spring the carefully set trap before the victim had walked into it, then I might be able to escape without divulging my identity. They would know all right, but they wouldn't have proof, and it takes some sort of proof to convict.

Paul Boardman was one of these high and mighty humans who court the limelight. I could rest assured that he would have picked the best room on the upper floor as his study. That would be one of the rooms in the front, one of the corner rooms. There were two doors either of which might lead to the room I sought.

Noiselessly I opened the one on the left which was nearer to me. This was one night when I was working rapidly, trusting to luck—and to speed.

A wall of darkness loomed back of the door. There had been a faint, reflected light in the hallway, but once within the room I might have been on the inside of a pocket, at the bottom of a deep shaft. The darkness was total, a thick syrupy darkness which seemed almost to stick to the skin.

I dared not risk my pocket flash. Nor was there any use in waiting for my eyes to become accustomed to the darkness. There was not enough light to enable my eyes to register anything had I remained in the room for a month.

I stretched my hands out before me, sought to feel my way with the tips of my fingers, and went ahead slowly. Somewhere within me there was a subtle something which told me the room was occupied. I could almost feel the hostile magnetism of crouching enemies.

My hand touched something cold and smooth, explored along it, identified it as the rounding edge of a bathtub. I was in a bathroom then. My quest was futile. It was the wrong room after all, and yet I could have sworn that there were other human beings within a few feet of me, human beings who were sitting tensed, ready, hostile.

For a moment I stood poised, puzzled, and then, with no warning whatever, there came a terrific flash of blinding, white light. In that flash my eyes caught and held a picture.

Before me was rigged a camera on a tripod. A flash-pan stood slightly to the rear and on one side. Just in front of the camera crouched two men, stooped over so as to be out of the field of the lense. I was standing in a bathroom which opened from the hall, and which, in turn, opened into the room that Paul Boardman had fitted as a study, a home office. Before the safe in that room, exploring cautiously, with groping fingers outspread, was the form of Helen Chadwick.

So instantaneous had been the explosion of the flash powder that I saw her as absolutely stationary, held motionless as a marble statue in the green glare of a lightning flash.

And then there came the stabbing beam of a flashlight, seeming pitifully weak after the dazzling glare of the brilliant flash powder.

"Throw up your hands!"

It was the voice of Bob Garret, and it confirmed my suspicions, showed me that he had played the game as I had figured he would play it, had rushed back from the Chinese café to speed up the conspiracy. The other man then would be Paul Boardman and they would be the only witnesses, just these two. They would rely upon their testimony, upon the fingerprints on the safe, upon the evidence of the flashlight photograph.

Garret spoke again, and his voice quavered with excitement and triumph.

"Caught with the goods. Your fingerprints are on the safe, and your picture is registered on the plate. Also there are two witnesses. Attempted burglary of the first degree."

The light played full upon the features of Helen Chadwick, and those features were as calm as though Bob Garret had merely been discussing the weather forecast.

"And what is it you want me to do?" she asked.

Bob Garret thought that she had yielded, that she had placed herself entirely in his power. I could hear the triumph of his voice as he advanced toward her.

"We want your signature to this written confession first. After that, we want you to see that Ed Jenkins is caught red-handed. We have a little trap for him, too."

Helen laughed, a short, curt laugh that had a cutting ring to it.

"What do you offer me in return?"

It was Paul Boardman's heavy voice that answered her.

"We offer you immunity from prosecution, offer you the chance to keep your family name untarnished, to keep from your mother the shock that would send her to the grave."

He spoke with the booming voice of an orator, made his appeal in the dramatic terms of a vote getter, a stump speaker.

Knowing and loving her as I did, I could see her wince, but I doubt if either one of those men detected the slight change in her facial expression. She was more of a thoroughbred than they were accustomed to deal with, and her emotions were foreign to their type, yet they knew the arguments to use to move her.

"I came here to get some evidence that showed that a crime had been framed on Ed Jenkins," she admitted frankly, with the ghost of a pathetic smile twisting her lips. "I would hardly turn around and offer to surrender him into a trap that you were to set."

It was Bob Garret who poured forth a torrent of oily words, seeking to convince her that she was acting for her best interests and was not hurting mine.

"We only want to get some influence to bear on Jenkins," he said. "He's an obstinate chap, and we want to get him where he will listen to reason."

She hesitated, turning something over in her mind and Garret waved the paper before her.

"Go ahead and sign."

"You won't use this against me in any way? Won't try to

blackmail me with it. Won't threaten to show it to my mother afterward?"

I could hardly believe my ears. Could it be possible that she trusted them? She had expressed in words the very thoughts they had in mind.

They were both ready liars, and they chimed their denials in a chorus. It was as though each hesitated to trust to the extemporaneous prevarications of the other.

"No, no, nothing of the sort. Certainly not."

The deep voice of Boardman chimed in with the oily tones of Garret.

"One more question," said Helen, pushing back the paper, "you're sure that you don't mean any harm to Ed Jenkins?"

Again they lied in chorus.

"What is it you want him to do?"

This time there was a second or two of uncomfortable silence. Bob Garret could hardly think of a proper answer, and he left the verbal lead for his partner.

"Miss Chadwick, surely you know me, you know that I wouldn't be mixed up in anything crooked?"

Paul Boardman waited a moment for her assurance of confidence, and, failing to get it, hurried on in his talk a little more rapidly, and with somewhat less confidence.

"I have some things I want Ed Jenkins to do for me, both for me and for Bob Garret here. Surely we wouldn't want anything that wasn't entirely all right, and we control the police politics of the city. Ed couldn't do better for himself than to place himself in our hands. But he's obstinate. He insists on having his own way, being a Lone Wolf, and we've got to have some little argument that will persuade him, win him over."

Her voice was soft, almost devoid of expression.

"You wanted him to help you in the opening of safes? Or did you want him to work in with a gang and split the loot?"

They denied this in unison again. It would never do for them to admit their plans to Helen Chadwick.

She listened to their almost hysterical denials, and then laughed, a harsh, grating, metallic laugh.

"I'm sorry that I was so simple as to walk into your trap," she said, "but it grieves me to see how simple you really think I am. Perhaps you can send me to the penitentiary, perhaps not, but I'd sooner cut off my right hand and go to jail for life than to sign a paper that would put Ed Jenkins back into criminal life. I've been working to get his record straightened out, to show the governors of the other states where he is wanted that he wasn't guilty of the crimes that were laid to his door, that whatever he actually did was the result of the circumstances in which he found himself placed."

Boardman wanted to argue still.

"Think of yourself, of your mother. I'm a hard man to cross. I'm loyal to my friends and bitter to my enemies. You have invaded the privacy of my study with felonious intentions. Your own admission shows that you came after certain private political papers, and the flashlight photograph shows that you were actually removing certain contents from my safe.

"You were up here this afternoon with my wife, and you particularly noticed the location of the safe so that you might be able to come back again tonight and remove the papers in the dark. You were afraid to use a light, and you thought you could get the proper paper in the dark. The party who told you of it told you it was in a small, flat, tin box. The photograph will show you actually touching that box, and the box will bear the imprint of your fingers.

"There will be no question of what any jury will do. Think of the horror of being confined within the cold, gray walls of San Quentin. Think of the shock to your mother . . ."

She interrupted him and every word snapped and stung like the lash of a whip.

"So you had it all framed, you cur. You capitalized on my desire to see Ed Jenkins rehabilitated. It was all a frame-up from the first. Do you think you can get away with that? Why Ed Jenkins would kill you. The city isn't big enough for you to escape him. And don't forget that I'm no common crook to be framed and bluffed. I can and will fight. Don't think I didn't have the woman shadowed who gave me the fake tip about these papers. My detectives can locate her at will, and she'll have something to say when she gets on the witness stand, or before the grand jury.

"It's a good thing for you that Ed Jenkins doesn't know what's going on here tonight—and he probably never will know unless you press things. But God help you if he does!"

Her words disconcerted them. Perhaps it was a bluff about having their tool shadowed. Perhaps she had been shrewd enough to do it. And there was truth in what she said about her ability to fight the case. They had counted upon a woman who would go into hysterics, who would lose her head, beg, plead. Hence the written confession. They would stampede her into signing that first, and then anything she could say afterward would sound like an alibi thought out by a desperate criminal lawyer.

Bob Garret lost his head and rushed forward, grabbing her by the arm.

"Sign, you fool! Sign! Hear the police on the stairs?"

And he was right. He had evidently given some signal and now there sounded the shuffling of heavy feet on the stairs. The police were to enter and catch her before the safe.

But I had not been idle while they were talking.

The beam from the pocket flash lamp showed me other things besides the face of Helen Chadwick. There was the camera, the flashlight stand, a bottle of flash powder setting near to it. The photograph was still on the plate in the camera, and it was their most clinching piece of evidence. With that gone, they would hardly dare to prosecute. Paul Boardman had influence with the city government. He controlled judges by the dozen. The district attorney did as Boardman bade, but there was such a thing as going too far. If they should run into just the right sort of a fight before a jury the whole political house of cards would collapse.

It was a double plate-holder, and I worked with noiseless rapidity. The camera had been set in the bathroom to give the lense a wider field. The shutter was automatic, and the camera focused upon the safe.

I had slipped the slide in the exposed plate, turned the plate-holder, removed the slide, slipped a fresh charge of flash powder into the "gun." All of this I had done while they had been talking.

As there sounded a heavy knock at the door of the study, as the two men pushed against Helen Chadwick, threatening—holding out to her paper and pen, showing by their every attitude, their facial expressions, their gestures, that they were trying to force her to sign this paper against her will, I tripped the shutter and pulled the cord of the flash gun.

The explosion burnt the eyelashes from my face, singed my hair. It was too close quarters for accurate work, and I was hurried.

That second glare of light caught them as much by surprise as the first had caught Helen. They stopped in their tracks. Their faces blanched, and Garret dropped his hand-lamp to reach for his gun.

I slipped the slide back into the plateholder, removed it from the camera, stuck the holder containing both exposed plates under my arm, and was on my way.

Even as I dashed from the bathroom door into the hallway, I had the nucleus of an idea in the back of my mind. In the old days when I had earned my title of "The Phantom Crook" I had always worked on the theory that the police are methodical but not brilliant. They are slow, sure plodders. Given a situation which has become standard, they operate with remarkable efficiency. Place them up against new conditions, however, conditions which change with the speed of thought, and they are hopelessly outclassed. It was up to me to do the unexpected and watch for the breaks.

There were some four or five policemen in the corridor, and all of them were massed about the door which went directly into the study. They had evidently been carefully instructed in the parts they were to play. They were prepared to walk into the room, representing the stern majesty of the law, and bully a helpless girl.

They looked at my back in dazed amazement during that short, split-fraction of a second that it took me to negotiate the distance between the bathroom door and the head of the stairs.

Then the other door jerked open and Boardman and Garret made a leap into the hall, only to become entangled with the waiting officers. There was the usual snarl of arms and legs, the usual commotion of shouted commands, explanations, impatient orders. I didn't wait to see it, but I could hear it, and I knew from past experiences what was taking place. The police had watched me as I dashed down the stairs, their minds functioning slowly. By the time Boardman and Garret had started in pursuit the officers had half a mind that they should have tried to stop me. As a result they automatically stopped my pursuers. Then there were recriminations, orders, confusion, noise, and all of the time the minds of the cops were attempting to adjust themselves to the new developments.

Finally they all wound up by pounding in pursuit, their steps banging in haste down the stairs while the servants and guests ran and screamed. This was exactly the break I had been counting upon. I made but little noise as I ran, and attracted almost no attention compared to the sounds of the stampede from the hallway above.

I ducked back of a curtain while the guests scuttled for cover and the servants rushed hither and thither trying to find out what it was all about. When the servants had vacated the little hallway at the foot of the back stairs, I slipped out from behind my curtain, took the back stairs two at a time in a swift series of noiseless, springing strides, and found the upper corridor deserted, just as I had figured it would be.

Even Helen Chadwick had left the study. She stood at the head of the stairs, looking after the officers as they stormed into the lower hallway, and wasted their time in fruitless questions, contradictory orders.

Silently I slipped into the study and over to the safe. The lights had been turned on now, and the room blazed with incandescent brilliance. The safe, as I had expected would be the case, was coated with some sticky, varnishlike preparation which would register the imprint of any finger upon it. There was a small metal lock box which was also covered with a similar coating.

I had only time for a brief survey, and then I heard the sound of voices, footsteps on the stairs, the booming voice of Paul Boardman raised in a very ecstasy of irritation.

They were coming back.

There was a closet back of the safe and I dived into this. The place was filled with books, papers, old clothes, junk.

I picked a hiding place back of the old clothes, and placed the plate-holder on the floor, under my heel. In the event I was discovered I could merely place my weight upon it and shatter the plates into a thousand fragments. And yet I felt that I would not be discovered. They would never expect that a fugitive would make his escape only to return and conceal himself in the very place from which he had escaped. Almost all of my sensational escapes had been predicated upon doing the thing which was the most illogical for a man in my position to do, yet which, by reason of that very fact, actually became the most logical.

I could hear Bob Garret's voice running along in a continued stream of babbling conversation. Apparently he feared that Boardman would blame him for the miscarriage of the plan by which Helen Chadwick was to be trapped—and he didn't know the half of it yet.

Boardman seemed to pay no attention to the string of alibis which Garret was pouring forth. His voice interrupted the stream of conversation.

"Never mind all that. Get the exposed plate out of the camera. Then find out what that second flash was about. How did it happen?"

Together they went over to the camera. Bit by bit the situation dawned on them.

"I had the lense stopped way down, and used a very powerful flash, that'll give sharp detail."

It was Garret speaking, his words an oral smirk of supreme self-satisfaction.

"Well, where is the plate?" asked Boardman.

There was a period of silence.

"Good God!" exclaimed Garret.

"You mean it's gone?"

"Worse than that. . . . Someone apparently reversed the plate and set off another flashlight, then took both plates. You see there were two plates in the holder, one in each side. . . ."

Boardman finished the sentence.

"And that means Ed Jenkins has a picture of us struggling with this girl before the safe, trying to get her to sign that paper."

There was no further conversation for a moment or two. Each of the men was busy with his own thoughts, thinking just what it would mean to him if that picture should be released at just the proper time.

The silence was broken by Helen Chadwick's voice, and in it there was a happy, triumphant lilt which somehow seemed much more than mere relief. It was as though I had somehow vindicated her faith in me, and had placed her in a position to show these men that her faith had been justified.

"I knew that Ed Jenkins wouldn't let you frame anything like that on me. You men are lucky to have escaped so easily."

It was undoubtedly the way the kid felt, but there wasn't anything she could have said that would have been more like dumping emotional gasoline on the smouldering fires of their wrath.

Boardman answered her, and his voice quavered with fury.

"You and your crook, Ed Jenkins! Who do you think you are? Before another twenty-four hours have passed, Ed Jenkins will be dead, either killed outright, or in jail with a charge framed against him that he'll never be able to explain away. D'you think any man can come in here and pull anything like that and get away with it?

"And as for you—don't forget that you're going to face this thing alone. Ed Jenkins won't be able to help you. We haven't the photograph, but we still have our testimony and the fingerprints you've left on the safe and on the box that was within that safe. It'll take that precious crook of yours a long time to think up some nice, plausible explanation about how your fingerprints happened to be on that safe."

Because of the silence that followed I could tell that Helen Chadwick realized her mistake in seeking to rub it in on these two political crooks. The political crook has forgotten more about double dealing and general crookedness than the average yeggman or gangster ever learns. Yet it would have been the same in any event. They would have reached the same conclusion themselves, even if Helen Chadwick hadn't spoken. It was a cinch that I had been the one to take that second flashlight, to remove that plate-holder, and with what I knew, and the photographic evidence I had, it would be unsafe for these men to allow me to live. Word would go out into the highways and byways of crime. Every crooked cop on the force would receive whispered instructions. Every stool-pigeon would start out with a new hope, a new lease on life, a fresh supply of police-furnished dope. The word would spread like wild fire.

Ed Jenkins must die.

How the news would trickle through the sub-strata of society! Cops would know that I was to be arrested, and that I was to be killed while "resisting arrest." Every gangster would know that should he be the one to speed the fatal bullet he could write a ticket of immunity from prosecution until he cleaned up his pile. Every stoolie would know the most valued information that could be given to the police.

Bob Garret was in virtual control of the police.

Paul Boardman was in virtual control of the city.

These two had willed that I should die, and many and varied would be the instrumentalities that would bow to their will.

Boardman spoke in a low tone.

"Get her fingerprints, Bob, and turn her loose. She can't run away, and she won't dare to talk."

Garret had a worried note in his voice.

"We don't even need her fingerprints. It'll look better if we haven't got 'em. The prints are on the safe, and she can't ever change her fingertips. If we decide to have her arrested we'll throw her in, tell our story, and then let the fingerprint men examine the safe. We'll pretend we don't even know there's a fingerprint there. But we've got to be careful. She's our hold on Ed Jenkins, and he knows too damned much to live. If we can't get him any other way we can always get him through her."

I could hear the throaty rumble with which Boardman growled his assent.

There was a rustling from without, a rustling which signified the motion of human bodies. Apparently they had left the police outside, such as had not started out to scour the neighborhood for me. They had taken the girl back in the room with them, seeking to browbeat her once more into submission, and then the discovery of the stolen plateholder had made them realize just how precarious their own position was. That second photograph meant disaster to them. If that photograph should find its way into the hands of the Chief, for instance—if it should suddenly appear in one of the hostile papers—Oh, they had their hands full of their own affairs right now.

"I have it!"

It was Garret's voice again, and there was a note of confident triumph in it. Crouched there in the dark stuffiness of the closet, I wondered what had happened. I had heard nothing but the faint rustlings of moving bodies. For a moment I wondered if Helen Chadwick had suddenly thrown a gun down on them, if she had some wild idea of arresting them, some hope that it would be possible to start the ordinary machinery of justice grinding in the case of a man of such political influence as Paul Boardman. For a second I was almost in a panic. Green in the ways of politics, knowing nothing of the extent of civic depravity which exists in so many of our cities, the kid might have thought she could find some channel of justice which would lend an ear to her story.

"Get her out of here. Send her home. We've got the trumps in our hand after all. It's simple."

Bob Garret could hardly speak without stuttering, so eager was he to get the words out. His voice rose to a shrill pitch which was almost hysterical. "Get her away. Have the police take her home. Jenkins will be dead before morning!"

"Are you crazy?" It was Boardman's rumble. "Jenkins has shown he can outwit you at any stage of the game. We may get him, but it'll be a long, hard chase."

I could hear Bob Garret's feet as they pattered on the floor. So eager was he, so excited, that he could hardly contain himself.

"I tell you I've got it. It's simple, too. It's the very simplicity of the thing that makes it so certain. We've got the trumps in our hands and we've been so foolish we haven't realized it. Send the girl home, and be sure we keep a police guard about her house. Don't let her get out."

Boardman was getting interested.

"Shall we have her telephone disconnected?"

"No. No. Listen, and do as I say. When you hear what I've got on my chest you'll see I'm right. . . . Here, wait a minute. . . ."

There was tense silence for a moment, and then I heard Garret's voice shrilling a number into the telephone. I had noticed the instrument which set on the study desk, and I recognized the number as police headquarters.

Garret got the photographic department, left instructions that a man was to be sent the first thing in the morning to photograph the fingerprints on the safe, then slammed the receiver back on the hook.

Something in his manner had convinced Boardman, for I could hear them escorting the girl to the door, instructing the policeman who waited without to see that she went to her house and did not leave.

Within the closet I tensed my muscles, made sure my heel was on the plateholder.

Probably Garret had reasoned it out that I was hiding some place in the building. If so, I would have to give him credit for more intelligence than I had originally figured. Perhaps he knew that I was hiding in the closet. Then there would be but one thing for me to do, to smash the plate and fight it out, trying to rush them before they could gather their forces.

They dared not let the police in to hear any conversation which might take place between us. No. Their play would be to enter the closet with drawn weapons and riddle me with bullets before I could say a word. They could always square themselves before the public. After all, I was a known crook. If they should find me in the closet, what more natural than that I should resist arrest, perhaps try to kill them? They could concoct a pretty story, all right.

Very well, I would go close to the closet door. If they came to it I would meet them more than half way. They would find no cringing, crouching figure hiding behind the clothes, a man whom they could shoot down with impunity. They would find me charging forth to meet them, and, if I could possess myself of one of their weapons . . . well, we would wait and see. They had me in a corner, and the happiness of Helen Chadwick was at stake. I could fancy no more sacred altar upon which to sacrifice my life.

The door into the hall closed.

I could hear the rasp of the key in the lock.

Upon the stairs sounded the descending heavy tread of the policeman, the light steps of Helen Chadwick.

Within the room I could hear the two men approach the closet door, and I lowered my shoulders, took a deep breath . . . and then I relaxed.

They were not coming to the door. Garret was speaking, the words fairly tumbling out of his mouth.

"Can't you see it? He's protecting her. He must have been concealed in the bathroom all of the time. He knows of the fingerprints on the safe. He stole the plate, took another one of us—but he's not after us. He's trying to protect the girl. He's bound to get in touch with her tonight. Probably he'll use the telephone. She'll tell him we're going to photograph the fingerprints in the morning. . . . But he won't even need to telephone her. He's a clever crook, and he knows of those fingerprints. He'll figure we'll wait for daylight. I tell you, Boardman, it's a cinch. *Ed Jenkins is going to return to this safe tonight.* He'll come back to remove those fingerprints. Some time tonight he's going to *come through that door!*"

There was silence for a moment.

After all, Garret had doped things out right. He should have carried his reasoning a step farther and known that I had never left the house. For a moment I tensed myself with apprehension. Perhaps Boardman would begin where Garret had left off and make the logical deduction. If so, he would know that I would never have fled from the house while there remained those fingerprints on the safe. Regardless of the cost to myself, I would have removed that evidence.

But Boardman was so swept away with Garret's idea that he failed to add to it.

"Great smoke, Garret, you're right!"

"Sure I'm right. I know him and I know his type. It's only for us to arrange to kill him when he comes back."

Boardman rumbled in his throat.

"Wait a minute. I've got an idea to add to yours," he said, and then became silent.

Once more I listened in an agony of apprehension, wondering whether they would figure out the real situation. They were on the very threshold of the correct conclusion. It only remained for them to add the two and two and get the four.

And then Boardman's heavy chuckle sounded to me in the darkness of the closet.

"Well?"

There was a note of impatience in Garret's voice.

"Just leave the front door open when you go out," boomed Boardman. "Jenkins will be watching the house, waiting for you to go. You can walk as though you were wrapped up in thought, and leave the front door open. We'll nail up the door through the bathroom and nail the window shut. That'll leave just one entrance for Jenkins to use in coming into this room. That entrance'll be the door into the hall, and we'll leave that door partially open."

"Well, I still don't see what you're driving at."

Again Boardman chuckled, and there was something in the supreme self-satisfaction of that chuckle that made me long to get my hands on his throat.

"I'll arrange a gun in the hall, a shotgun. It'll be up out of the way, and there'll be a fine wire stretched across the door, stretched back and forth, up and down. When anyone tries to go through that door there'll be a charge of buckshot sprayed into him.

"That'll simplify matters. You go home and I'll go to bed. We'll say we left this man-trap because we knew a desperate criminal was seeking to murder me, and that this criminal expected I would be sleeping in the study."

"It'll be a cinch. No one can accuse us of framing Ed Jenkins and killing him. He'll be killed while he's walking into my house in the dead of night, apparently seeking to murder me because I caught Helen Chadwick trying to get into my safe. It's an iron-clad idea."

I heard Garret's hand whacked down on Boardman's shoulders.

There followed excited whispers, surreptitious chuckles, the scraping of chairs. Then, after a bit, there came the sound of pounding, as nails were driven home.

After that I heard them checking things over. It had taken them more than an hour to rig the death trap to their liking, and they had been painfully careful in the construction of each detail. They both knew that their safety depended upon my death, and they knew that I was bound to return to that room, sooner or later. Now that the idea had occurred to them, they realized that I would attempt the removal of those damning fingerprints from the safe before morning.

At length the light switch clicked off, and I could hear their voices from the hallway as they put the finishing touches upon the death trap. Then there sounded steps on the stairs, a door slammed, and the house became silent.

I waited an hour and then slipped stealthily out of the room. I dared not press the light switch, but relied upon my pocketflash, and I kept the beam of that shaded as far as possible.

A hurried survey showed that I was in a veritable death trap. The bathroom door was nailed shut, nailed from the outside. The window was nailed down and it would take considerable time to remove the nails, and the removal would be accompanied with as much noise as though I shattered the glass. Nor did the window offer any great hope of escape. It had been nailed shut to prevent my placing a ladder against the side of the house and entering by that manner. There was a sheer drop of some thirty feet from that window, and a cement courtyard loomed beneath.

As for the door into the hallway, it stood invitingly open, and it was a veritable door of death. In constructing their death trap they had done a better job than they knew at the time. Not only would it be impossible to get in that door without springing the trap, but it would be impossible to get out. They had used a fine wire, and the slightest touch upon that wire would discharge the hair-trigger shotgun which was so placed as to spray the entire door with buckshot—and that gun was out in the hall.

In building a death trap to kill Ed Jenkins when he came into the room, they had unwittingly constructed a trap which would kill him when he tried to leave the room.

I completed my inspection, shrugged my shoulders, and turned to the safe. With the blade of my knife I scraped the surface free of every fingerprint. The small box I treated the same way, and then, lest there should be anything I had missed, I rubbed both the safe and the box thoroughly with my pocket-handkerchief.

That much was finished. I had completed the task which

they knew I must accomplish, which they had determined should mean my death.

Then I turned to the trap once more, and, as I studied it, my rage mounted against the human fiends who had sought to frame a crime on Helen Chadwick, and had willed that I should die when I tried to rescue her from their clutches. I determined that these men should not escape punishment. True, they were clothed with power, shielded by the so-called majesty of the law, while I was a crook, an outlaw who was frowned down by society. A jury or a judge would laugh me out of court if I should use the channels of justice to redress my wrongs. A crook seek the protection of the law? The very idea was ludicrous. Who would believe my testimony? I would be a joke. The newspapers would feature me as the prize comedian of the day.

No. It was up to me to handle my own justice, to be my own court, my own judge, jury, executioner.

I stepped to the desk, looked up the residence number of Bob Garret, and breathed the number into the instrument.

I could tell from the sound of the detective's voice that he had not been asleep. He had been waiting, waiting for news of his trap.

One of the most valuable gifts which I have received from nature has been a natural talent for mimicry. Let me hear a voice once or twice and I can imitate it after a fashion, imitate it well enough to get by under favorable circumstances. And the booming voice of Paul Boardman was an easy one to mimic, particularly when that voice would naturally be blurred with excitement.

"Quick, Bob. He came in, walked into the trap and is dead as a mackerel. Get the police and then hurry over, help me see it through."

"It worked then!" shrieked Garret into the telephone. "I tell you, Boardman, I feared that crook. There was something almost supernatural about his abilities."

"Yeah," I growled in my best imitation of Boardman's heavy accents. "Well, you don't need to fear him now. He's croaked right. But hurry over here. I'm up in the study and I've kept the servants out of it. You'll find the whole place quiet. I'm a bit nervous about the police—the Chief, you know. Telephone for a squad, and then hurry on. Come right into the study as soon as you get here."

Garret laughed.

"Say, to hell with the Chief. And why should the police worry you? You were within your rights, a crook in your own house, you know. Buck up. This strain's got you unnerved. I couldn't sleep myself. I'm coming right over. You're in the study now?"

"Yes," I told him. "I'm using the study phone. Hurry!" and hung up.

For perhaps fifteen minutes I sat there in the darkness, the plate-holder with its precious contents buttoned under my coat. Almost anything might happen now, and, as far as possible, I was ready for anything that could happen. There could be no escape from that room until those slender wires across the door had been broken. So ingeniously were they arranged that even the slight pull a man would make on them in trying to break or cut them would discharge the gun. I could only sit within that death trap and wait.

There sounded the rapid throb of a motor. Tires screeched across the pavement as a machine skidded to a stop. Steps dashed up to the front door, and then, more cautiously, I could hear the tread of feet on the front stairs, down the corridor.

"Boardman?"

There was almost suspicion in the voice as Garret paused before the dark doorway.

"Come in, Bob," I boomed, imitating Boardman's heavy voice. "Don't touch the light. I'm watching a shadow who's hiding over behind the hedge. Come over here and peek out the window."

Garret didn't even hesitate. He was so relieved to think Ed Jenkins was dead that he could hardly speak.

"We'll get him, too. Say, I'm glad we got Ed Jenkins. I somehow had a hunch he'd get me. . . ."

The rest of the sentence was lost forever.

There was a double, spitting stream of ruddy, stabbing flame, a terrific roar—and a body pitched heavily to the floor.

I ducked back into the closet, as running steps sounded from the corridor below. An electric flashlight shot upon the sprawled, twitching body, and then Boardman was in the room, chuckling.

He turned on the lights.

"Got him, by George! Got the Phantom Crook at last. . . ."

His deep voice trailed off into a throaty gurgle. I could hear him gasp, stagger over to the form on the floor and then slump into a chair.

"Oh, my God! My God! My God!" he moaned, over and over. "Oh, what shall I do? How could it have happened?"

For ten or fifteen seconds he moaned to himself and then his eyes must have fallen on the safe.

"What!" he yelled. "The fingerprints are gone!"

And just then there sounded the wail of a siren, the roaring exhaust of a police car, and heavy steps began pounding up the walk. The police had arrived in response to Garret's orders.

If Boardman hadn't gone to the door to let them in I'd have walked out and wished him a good evening. His spirit was broken, his nerve gone, and I had nothing to fear from him right then. I could have walked out and twisted his nose with impunity.

However, there was no need. The thought of the police caused him to awake to the necessities of the situation, and he fairly leaped from the chair and sprinted down the stairs.

"You see it was this way, officer—" I heard him saying as I slipped out of the death trap, and into the hallway. I'd rather liked to have stayed and listened for a bit, but it was no place for Ed Jenkins. I melted into the shadows, slipped down the back stairs, and into the night.

Half way down the alley in the next block I stopped to look back at the house. Lights blazed from every window I could see. Paul Boardman was going to have a great time making his explanations. But the real fun would commence after he'd told his story. Then it would develop that the police came to the house because Garret had telephoned them that a man had been killed there—and then, when the police arrived, they found the corpse to be Garret himself.

That would be some little hurdle for even Boardman to take.

I hunted up a friendly photographer, developed the two plates and put them in a safe and secret place. Then I climbed back into a Chinese disguise. Somehow I felt that I could take a chance with Soo Hoo Duck. I didn't step back into the character of Yee Dooey Wah, however. I picked an older man, a gray-haired sage. The Chinks respect gray hairs.

Eight o'clock found me digesting a morning newspaper and sipping coffee. Headlines all over the front page announced that Ed Jenkins, famous criminal, known as the Phantom

Crook because of his ability to slip through the fingers of the police, had shot and killed Bob Garret, one of the most efficient detectives on the force. There was a reward offered. Indignation ran high, and the police had thrown out their "dragnet." It was predicted that the murderer would be in custody within another twenty-four hours.

The account was a bit blurred as to details, but I gathered that I had broken into Boardman's house to rifle a safe, had been caught red-handed by Garret who had been trailing me, and I had killed him with a shotgun.

So they had framed that on me, had they? Oh, well, it's all in a life time. That would knock my California immunity into a cocked hat. And, in the meantime, Boardman would be waging a relentless war. He must get me now or I might get him. He had seen something of my methods. There were other crooked detectives to take the place of Bob Garret, but there was in Garret's death something of a grim warning that must have caused ripples to run up and down Boardman's spine.

Anyhow, Helen Chadwick would read that paper and know that she had nothing to fear. There was only one witness to her attempted safe robbery left alive. It would be her word against Paul Boardman's, if anything should ever come up now—and there was the matter of that photograph. . . . No, Helen would read the paper and know she was safe. Boardman would do nothing, dared do nothing, until he had murdered me, either by due process of law or by the bullet of a hired killer.

I became conscious of someone standing by my side.

Casually, yet with every nerve alert, I peered up over the top of the paper. Soo Hoo Duck was standing beside me, his face wrinkled into its parchment smile.

"Good morning, my brother. You are a stranger in the city?"

I regarded him gravely. There was more than coincidence in his spying me out. He must have the eye of an eagle for piercing disguises. Did he know me as an imposter, or did he know me as Ed Jenkins, the one who had recently posed as Yee Dooey Wah? I couldn't tell, could only take a chance.

"One needs but to know human nature," I reminded him, "and he is never a stranger in any city."

He bowed gravely, with great dignity, his clawlike hand pulling his coat the tighter about his hollow chest.

"Ah, yes, human nature," he said meditatively. "One moment it is like a rushing stream, then it meets an obstruction and is dammed into a lake. Finally the lake bursts through its obstructions and carries all before it. My brother, I wish you pleasure in your visit here. In my small way I have some influence among my people. If there is anything I can do for you, pray command me."

With that friendly word he was off.

I stared at him, speculatively—wondering. Upon his middle finger was a jade ring, and upon the ring was carved a great dragon, similar to the dragon which had been imprinted in the red wax on the paper I had received in the Mandarin Café.

Perhaps, after all, he was a powerful friend. If so, I might need him.

We had engaged in a duel to the death, Paul Boardman and I. He had unlimited influence, money, position, power, and he was frantically combing the city, seeking to bring about my death. On the other hand, I had no power, no influence, was listed as a crook, forced to be always on the outskirts of society—and yet I was fighting for the safety of the girl I loved. There was danger ahead, there would be adventures. Never before had I been in such need of a cool head and a quick wit.

If the man who made the mark of the wax dragon was an enemy, he would be merely one more enemy to outwit. If he should prove to be a friend, something seemed to tell me he would be a powerful friend, a friend not of mine so much as a friend of Helen Chadwick; and more than all, a friend of fair play. And there was the buzzard. Beyond doubt he was an enemy. He lived up to his appearance, a vulture who hovered about, companion of killers—and he had fastened his attention upon me.

All in all it would be a busy time—the next few weeks, or, perhaps, months. I would be back in my element, hunted by the police, trailed by gangsters. There would be a price on my head, both in crookdom and with the police. Yet, through it all, I must find some way to protect Helen Chadwick.

In any event, the die was cast. The future was on the lap of the gods, but, in the meantime, the first trick was mine.

Grinning Gods

CHAPTER TWENTY-ONE

Seated in the back part of the Yat King Café, I dipped my chop sticks into a bowl of chicken noodles and listened to the hum of conversation about me. As long as I could keep in a dim light I felt safe. Color of skin, hair, eyebrows, clothes, would pass muster anywhere. It was only in regard to the eyes that my disguise was weak. It required a little grease paint to give the necessary slant to the upper corners, and grease paint has a habit of glinting a reflected gleam under the rays of a bright light.

The back of the Yat King Café was the gathering place of Chinese politicians. Those who controlled the destinies of Chinatown were accustomed to meet there in the early part of the evening. On this night they had come earlier than usual, a significant sign.

I raised my bowl of rice to my mouth and scooped down the white grains, Chinese fashion. For years I had studied the Chinese, learning the eight tones of Cantonese dialect, studying Chinese manners and customs, learning as much as possible of their habits of thought; all in preparation for the time when no ordinary disguise would avail, and I must assume a role which it would never be suspected a white man could assume.

". . . san man chee."

The words came as a drifting fragment of conversation which eddied from the table behind me where three of the prominent men of Chinatown swapped gossip over their tea.

It was the second time I had heard those three words in the course of ten minutes.

Why should these Chinamen be talking so continuously of

the newspaper? The Chinese paper had come out in the morning and had excited no comment. They were, therefore, referring to the evening newspaper, the *Clarion,* probably.

I beckoned the young Chinese boy who waited on the tables.

"Ngo yiu Fa K'ei san man chee."

He gave that brief flicker of slanting brown eyes which passes for a nod of the head with the Oriental, and slippety-slopped away.

In telling him that I wanted the American newspaper I did not risk discovery. I appeared as a Chinaman of the younger generation, and might be interested in things of the *Fa K'ei* without exciting comment.

And in the next moment, I would have given much to recall the words. The lad slipped to the table behind me, the table where the conspirators of Chinatown sat in conference, and made the courteous suggestion that if they were finished with the *Fa K'ei* newspaper the gentleman at the other table would like it.

My last wish was to invite any unnecessary attention to myself, particularly the attention of such men as the three behind me.

However, the damage was done.

There came the sound of slippered feet, the rustle of a newspaper, and it was spread before me, folded just as it had been at the other table.

Headlines stared up at me.

ED JENKINS LOCATED IN CHINATOWN . . . PHANTOM CROOK DISGUISED AS CHINESE MINGLES WITH YELLOW RACE.

"It is believed that Ed Jenkins, wanted for murder in this state, will be in custody within the next forty-eight hours.

"Captain Ransome, who is in charge of the investigation, states positively that it has been learned that Jenkins is in hiding in the local Chinatown, disguised as a Chinaman.

" 'Jenkins has earned the reputation of being able to slip through any police net,' said Captain Ransome to a reporter of the *Clarion.* 'This reputation has given him the nickname of *"The Phantom Crook."* It now appears that many of his escapes have been because of his uncanny ability in the art of disguise. But when he murdered Detective Bob Garret, he signed his death warrant. Never has any police search been conducted with such thoroughness as the search for Jenkins. Never has such an air-tight net been thrown about the city to prevent the escape of a criminal. Jenkins should be in custody within forty-eight hours.' "

Then there followed a blurb about my criminal history, and the circumstances surrounding the murder of Bob Garret, who had been found dead before the safe in Paul Boardman's private study. It was the theory of the police, supplied by Paul Boardman, that I had come to that safe, that Garret had been awaiting me, and that I had killed him with a shotgun.

They didn't have much evidence, and they didn't need much. All they needed was to play up my criminal record in the newspaper a bit, and emphasize my flight. That and the statement of Paul Boardman was all that would be required to hang me.

If I should raise my voice to tell the real facts of Garret's death I would be laughed down, hooted to the gallows. Garret had been a prominent detective, Boardman was one of the political powers of the city. If I, a known crook, should try to tell my story that Boardman and Garret tried to get me in their power by framing the girl I loved, that I had rescued her from their clutches, and that the two had then baited a trap for me with a shotgun planted to kill me when I came to the room, that I had tricked Garret into entering the trap—well, I might tell my story, but it would be considered worse than a pipe dream. A good lawyer in my behalf, would insist that the truth was too improbable to believe, would have forced me to plead insanity or self defense.

In one thing the newspaper article was right. Never had such a search been conducted for any criminal. Boardman feared me. I could not raise my voice against him, but he had seen something of what I might do. As long as I was free he was in danger. And there was a chance that I could convince some of the higher officials of the truth of my story. I had a photograph that he would have trouble explaining.

Oh, he had directed a search all right! It was a search that included every different angle. The police officers were instructed to shoot first and arrest afterward. The underworld had received the mysterious tip that the yegg who crashed a bullet into Ed Jenkins' heart would have immunity until he had made his pile.

Boardman wanted me out of the way all right. He wanted my lips sealed in death. Conversely, I wanted his life spared. Boardman was the only witness living who knew the real inside of Garret's death. I could never be cleared until I had obtained a written confession from him—and dead men can not sign confessions.

A short time ago clearing my name before the world meant nothing to me. I had let the police frame what crimes they wanted to on me and said nothing. When things got too hot, I slipped into California and availed myself of a loophole in the extradition laws. They couldn't send me back, and they had nothing on me in California.

Now things were different. There was Helen Chadwick. Not that I would even allow myself to think there could ever be anything between us. She was of the upper crust, the inner circle of society. I was a branded crook. True she had once been the object of clutching tentacles which had twined up from the dark subsurface of crookdom and sought to drag her down—and then was when I had met her, had cut those tentacles, managed it so her name never appeared in the subsequent developments. All of her life she had been free to do as she pleased, had looked the world in the eye, demanded her rights. Now she could not understand why I could not see something of her, return the friendship which she was willing to offer.

Perhaps she thought me indifferent, when I would have laid down my life for her any time. But friendship with me was dangerous.

Probably Helen Chadwick realized it by this time. Boardman had sought to strike at me through her. He couldn't get his hands on me directly, but he knew that if he threatened Helen Chadwick with danger I would come to her rescue. Where he had slipped was in not realizing the desperation with which I would come. I had walked into his trap and demolished it, but first I had his accomplice spring the trap, collect the two barrels of buckshot which had been loaded for me.

I laid the paper to one side with a sigh.

There could be no rest for Ed Jenkins until after Paul Boardman had been mastered. Just as there could be no safety for Boardman until I was out of the way.

And then behind me, cutting through the air with the hoarse sibilants of danger, came a swift sentence in Chinese.

They were taking the roll call of the tongs!

Instantly I sensed the trap that had been laid for me. No matter how much I might study the habits of the Chinese, there was one chapter that was closed. The tong life was safeguarded by initiatory ceremonies that a white man could not hope to pass save and except as a white man, taking an honorary membership. Any disguise would be penetrated in the ceremonies preparatory to initiation.

That article in the paper had been fiendish in its effect, masterly in its simplicity. That was the reason those three Chinese at the table behind me had been mentioning it with such interest. Chinatown had been offered a big reward to smoke Ed Jenkins from his hiding place. After all, it would be simple. Somewhere within Chinatown was a white man disguised as a Chinaman. The police offered a secret reward to the political heads of Chinatown. They would make their own search, take a roll call of Chinatown, call the tongs together. The white man would be located by the process of elimination.

The tong messenger was approaching, going from table to table, bending low, giving a secret summons, getting a whispered password, a password concerning which I knew nothing.

I arose, left the price of my meal on the table, and slipped toward the rear of the half-lit room. Chinese do not like to have white men penetrate their inner lives. Such knowledge as I had secured had been at the expense of infinite patience, untold effort. The very extent of that knowledge was a source of danger. It would not need the promise of a reward to spur the Chinese on to getting rid of a foreigner who had penetrated the intricacies of their language, the secrets of organized Chinatown.

Behind me came shuffling steps.

Someone followed, calmly, unhurriedly.

I dared not quicken my pace. To do so would be to confess my identity.

The man behind followed with the remorseless certainty of Fate herself.

I slipped through the rear door, into a narrow, ill-smelling passageway which led to the back alley. My stomach muscles sucked up against my backbone as I waited for the feel of cold steel within my vitals. Mechanically my feet kept the regular, shuffling gait of a Chinaman.

Behind me other feet slippety-slopped with the same rhythmic regularity.

I reached the alley, turned the corner, saw that the street was virtually deserted. Some mysterious summons was penetrating through Chinatown. Each and every Chinaman had become a spy in the great round-up which was taking place.

To my ears came the clashing of cymbals, the boom-boom-boom; boom-boom-boom of a tom-tom; the wailing skirl of a reed pipe whining forth its harmonious discords.

The Chinese theatre.

It would be out in fifteen minutes, but much might happen in fifteen minutes.

I paid for a ticket and slipped within. The performance had been dragging through the afternoon, and many of the higher class Chinese had left the theatre before the finish of the show. The rear of the place was well filled, but up nearer the front, in the higher class seats were scattered vacancies.

I slipped into a chair.

Feet slip-slapped down the aisle, and a body rustled into a vacant chair behind me. I dared not turn my head.

Throughout the darkened room was the subtle aroma of incense, the close human smell of packed bodies, the scent of Oriental perfume. On the stage, the performance was in its final spasm. A warrior hurtled a big sword about his head. An actor rolled to the floor dead. An assistant came and placed a pillow for him to lie upon. There was no scenery, not much pretense. The dead man listened with blinking delight to the staccato voice of the warrior as he made his final speech.

A man dressed as a woman smirked and simpered, reciting lines of squeaky Chinese in what was probably intended to be effeminate tones.

Throughout the audience came a rustle.

There would be a big gathering of the tongs after the show. Ushers had probably spread the word earlier in the evening.

Behind me sat my shadow.

By leaving the Yat King Café at just that time I had attracted attention. A tongman had been planted within the building, instructed, doubtless, to shadow anyone who left hurriedly. Throughout Chinatown hundreds of such spies would be on guard.

Ahead of me a man turned a wrinkled face and peered back over the sea of humanity behind. I would have given much to be able to do the same. The identity of the man behind me puzzled me.

The old man with the puckered face was Soo Hoo Duck, himself a mystery. He had gravitated into Chinatown from Pekin, and there was some strange power about him. Within a few short months he had become the uncrowned king of all Chinatown. Men did his bidding unquestioningly. In some uncanny manner he knew everything that went on in Chinatown. Twice before I had encountered him. Each time I had wondered whether his shrewd, old eyes had penetrated my disguise.

He stared at the people about him, and, of a sudden his eyes seemed lidless, so sharp did his gaze become. He was looking at something behind me, perhaps at the man who had followed me into the theatre.

As for myself, I kept my eyes upon the stage, trying to show my utter unconcern.

There was a rustle of motion. The man behind me had made some sign.

And then the wrinkled countenance shifted slightly, the glittering eyes dropped squarely to my face.

"Your name?"

The comment was addressed to me. There could be no evasion, no escape. I was surrounded with a crowd of packed Chinese, and the word of this man was law.

I must bluff it through.

My reply was in the Cantonese dialect, and as my voice rippled through the four tones which are in each of the two octaves and which comprise the eight notes of the Cantonese dialect, I could feel my heart beats quicken.

"The name by which I was christened was Ah Klim, Oh Worthy One; but, compared to the eminence of your learning, I have adopted the name of Dust Underfoot whilst I converse with thee."

There was a ripple at his side, and a pair of twinkling, mischievous feminine eyes were turned in my direction.

"Father," said the girl at his side, "I like the sound of his voice."

Was she taunting me? Had my voice failed to catch the subtle tone inflections of the language, revealed me as a foreigner, an impostor?

The old man turned to her with a gesture.

"Peace. One does not judge of the contents of a chest by an examination of the cover."

She was not a whit abashed.

"But one judges the quality of the silk by the sound of the rustle."

I knew her then. She was Soo Hoo Duck's daughter, whom he had christened *"Ngat T'oy,"* Little Sun. She had been educated in Stanford, and her modern flippancy was the scandal of the old-timers in Chinatown.

The old man did not turn to her again. Instead he began to blink at her words, blink slowly, solemnly, as though he was thinking out some problem which required deep study.

"You will accompany me to my residence at the conclusion of the performance," he said, slowly.

I could hardly believe my ears.

From behind came a voice which contained respectful protest, a voice which came from the seat occupied by my shadow.

"But, Excellency, is it right that water from the streets be elevated to heaven?"

Again there came that lidless look in the old man's eyes.

"Yes. When it is drawn by the sun."

"Then," came the voice of the other, "it is returned to the gutter as rain and the street knows it again."

There was subtle satisfaction in his voice.

The girl shifted again, her eyes slipped casually over my face, back to the speaker behind.

"Not always, Chuck Gee. Sometimes it descends in the form of hail, strengthened by its sojourn in the high places, causing those below to rush under cover of some protecting roof."

I gasped.

The man behind me was Chuck Gee, then. Reputed to be head of the gunmen. Chinese regard murder as a profession, just as law or dentistry. If one has an aching tooth he goes to a dentist. If he desires to eliminate one of his neighbors he employs one of the hatchetmen who make of such things a profession. And Chuck Gee was the head of the hatchetmen, a past master of the art of murder.

The brass cymbals crashed forth one terrific, final blare, the beating of the tom-tom rattled into a hysterical rat-a-tat-tat, and the reed pipe wailed up into a veritable crescendo of sound. Once more the great cymbals clashed, and then there was silence, a silence in which the tortured air writhed and quivered from the sudden cessation of unearthly noise.

And then shadowy figures got to their feet. The play was over.

I escorted the girl down the narrow street. On the other side was Soo Hoo Duck. Behind us walked Chuck Gee. Behind him came the motley rabble from the theatre. In that throng there may have been a spy, there may have been a hundred.

I doubted if Chuck Gee had as yet penetrated my disguise. He had, however, detected something suspicious in my departure from the café. He wanted a word or two with me, and at his own convenience.

Doubtless, when Soo Hoo Duck had turned around, Chuck Gee had made a sign, pointed me out for Soo Hoo Duck's inspection.

What did Soo Hoo Duck want of me? Had his keen eyes penetrated my disguise? Had his daughter caught Chuck Gee's sign? Did she suspect my identity? Time would tell, and it would be a short space of time. Meanwhile Chuck Gee trailed along behind me, patient, deadly, suspicious.

That newspaper article had been inspired!

We turned down a side street, and I knew that I was entirely within the power of Soo Hoo Duck. Whatever his reason had been for demanding my company, his request was a most imperative command, and his word was law in Chinatown.

Generally, I knew where he lived. It was said that the entrance to his house was merely a blind, that the door which opened upon the dark side street concealed many secrets. Perhaps I was destined to find out.

Here and there we encountered groups of Americans. There were restaurant parties who sought a thrill from investigating the quaint, Chinese cafés. There were the outcasts, those men who were forced to live in the haunts of an alien race—liquor, lottery, opium; sometimes it was one thing, sometimes another. They looked the part, bleary-eyed, shabby, shuffling, furtive.

And then, as we made our last turn, we encountered two men who were different. Upon their smug faces was stamped an assurance of superiority. They looked about them with patronizing sneers as they elbowed their way along.

"Hello. Look at the bright eyed Chink kid!"

There was no attempt to lower the voice. The man glared with brazen effrontery at the girl.

She lowered her eyes, and endeavored to hurry past.

The old man muttered some soothing bit of Chinese philosophy to her under his breath. It was evident that they were accustomed to these insults.

The two men barred the sidewalk.

"Well, give us a smile, slant-eyes."

She shook her head and made as if to go around them in the gutter.

Somehow, I rather fancied her feminine vanity was not entirely indifferent to the masculine notice, even if it was in the easy, sneering manner of men of that type.

"Not so fast, cutie," said the man, as he grabbed her by the arm.

It was the other who furnished the insult. Neither of them seemed to pay us the slightest heed. Soo Hoo Duck had barely enough strength to carry his wizened body about the streets. He was old with that premature age of the Chinaman, that age which seems to shrivel the body at the same time it gives to the mind a detached, philosophic outlook. As for myself, I was merely a "Chink," one to be bullied about as they chose.

"Aw, come on, Bill," said the companion in the full-mouthed tones of burly insolence. "She ain't nothin' but a damn, yellow-bellied Chink. Come get a white girl."

She raised her face at that, and never have I seen such an expression in the eyes of a woman. There was rage, and there was more; there was the expression of baffled helplessness which sometimes shines through the eyes of a caged creature who has wearied of buffeting the bars.

I could feel cold rage in my eyes. The girl had stuck up for me. I sensed that had it not been for her words I would have been exposed there in the theatre.

I glanced back. Some fifty yards behind us Chuck Gee was smirking, watching, waiting.

It has been my habit never to carry a weapon of any sort. I rely upon my wits, and wits are of more value than a gun any day. But not always does an ingenious solution of a difficulty present itself.

As a rule the Chinese abhor physical violence. A Chinaman is constitutionally organized so that he can't hit.

He can become fairly clever with knife or gun, but with the fists their habits are opposed to efficiency. That was why the two men regarded me as a negligible quantity.

The first man recoiled from the stinging blow which I

landed on his mouth. The second gave a vile oath and rushed. It was over in a space of seconds. The hardest punch I saved for the man who had been so deliberately insulting. I felt his teeth give way under the impact of my fist, and knew that some dentist would have a good job in the morning.

Both of the men rolled sprawling into the gutter. The girl watched me with wide eyes. It was old Soo Hoo Duck who clasped my sleeve gently.

"This way, my son," he said.

We slipped down a short flight of stairs, through a door into a basement, to the back, up a longer flight of stairs, through a mysterious room where there were lights, circling streamers of tobacco smoke, yet no visible occupants, and found ourselves in a long, dark corridor. A bolt rasped at the other end of this corridor, and we entered a room so sumptuously furnished that only the Oriental mind could have patterned it.

Indirect lighting shed a glow as soft as moonlight upon rare tapestries, rich silks, great, thick carpets which muffled the sound of steps. There were huge mahogany and teakwood furnishings; cut glass glistened, and the dull white of ivory shone mysteriously forth.

Soo Hoo Duck slumped in a chair, motioned the girl and myself to be seated, and then spoke words of such bitterness as only the very old can speak.

"For myself, I do not care. It is for her. I have sacrificed everything. She has been to college, has absorbed the education of the whites, has learned even their habits of thought. With the right friends she would be happy; but, on every hand she is insulted. Those who notice her are fortune hunters or worse. In my own country the curse of caste would brand her as a coolie of the lower strata. In this country she is a source of ridicule. In Chinatown there are no friends for her. The Americans treat her as a curiosity, as something to be insulted, as though she were a monkey chained to a hand organ."

The girl placed a soothing hand on his forehead.

"There, there, Father. You cannot judge from the attitude of those two men."

He shook his head, slowly, mournfully.

"It is not they alone. It is typical. And we must thank our friend."

I had been taking in this conversation with wide eyes. The significance of it penetrated to my mind. Its significance was not in sentiment nor in word, but in the fact that the entire conversation was in English, and in the purest diction which could be learned in the colleges. There was none of the pidgin-English, none of the halting accents, none of the garbled pronunciation, which almost invariably characterizes the Chinaman who seeks to talk our language. He spoke as a man of my own race.

And then, suddenly, he seemed to realize the situation. He straightened in his chair, and when he again spoke, his words were in Cantonese, and his voice was that of the old philosopher immune to emotion.

"The water of the gutters is very muddy," he said.

I recognized that the words were for me, and bowed.

"But muddy water splashes as far as clear water, and it leaves a stain," he went on.

Again I nodded. My cue was silence, as much of silence as I could maintain throughout the interview.

"And you have saved my daughter from being splashed, you who call yourself Ah Klim.

"Back there in the theatre Chuck Gee made me the sign of the knife and pointed to you. I thought that I recognized you, wanted a chance to talk frankly with you, to find out what you did here. A man may receive much information from another, but the knife of Chuck Gee would have destroyed the source of information which I desired. But, after all, one should not pry into the affairs of his friends. The greatest compliment one friend can give to another is to allow him his independence. And you have proved a friend, perhaps more than you appreciated."

He was speaking pure Cantonese now, the dialect of the lower classes, however, with all of the coolie idioms.

"Take this, and go," he said.

With the words he pulled toward him a teakwood stand upon which was a slab of China ink, a little water, a brush. Picking up a piece of red paper he moistened the brush tip and began to spread out those weird lines which form the Chinese written language.

When he handed me the paper I bowed again. What it contained I had no means of knowing. Whatever it was, I had no intention of using it. I have played as a lone wolf, and I do not blindly exhibit things others have written without at least knowing their contents.

It seemed that he sensed this feeling, for, suddenly, his manner changed, and he shook his head.

"No," he muttered, "that will not do. There are many hands who can make strokes of the pen . . . Here. This is better. There is only *one* of it."

His yellow-nailed hand slipped a ring from his middle finger. It was a ring I had noticed before, a ring of soft, yellow gold, and on it was a jade dragon, a dragon of exquisite workmanship. There were fiery rubies for eyes, small diamonds for teeth, a long ruby for a tongue. The rest was jade and gold. It was a huge affair, and I fancied it had been used as a seal once or twice, a seal to imprint a signature which all Chinatown respected and obeyed.

"Take this. Wear it," he said. "I am weary. I would not talk more tonight. My daughter will escort you to a safe exit. There was much I would have asked, but I shall remain silent. It is better so. Ah Klim and Soo Hoo Duck will meet in the future as casual acquaintances, but here you have sanctuary. Here you have friends. Yet, beware of Chuck Gee. Good night."

There was a finality in his tone which allowed no argument. I wanted to mutter some thanks, to make a formal farewell after the fashion of the Cantonese, but the hand of the girl was on my sleeve, and there was something in the atmosphere of the place which made me remain silent. I bowed, and followed the girl.

We went through two rooms, each of which was furnished with lavish splendor. As we walked, I studied her, and, as I studied her, I came to like her. There was a blending of the ancient and modern in an entirely incomprehensible manner. She was a baffling combination.

We left the magnificent rooms, entered a gloomy corridor of bare boards, and I spoke to her.

"Ngat T'oy," I said, using the language of the Chinese, "one who finds a pomegranate upon a raspberry bush thinks it is a raspberry. If you would have *Fa K'ei* friends who will respect you, you must get away from Chinatown."

She stopped. There in the dim light of the echoing corridor she came close to me.

"Thanks for those kind words."

Her speech was in English.

I made no comment. I would wait and see what her next move might be.

"You see, my father has his life here. I wouldn't want to buy my happiness at the expense of his. And your white society snobs don't pick up Chink women for friends."

She was right at that. The old man enjoyed his power. White society might receive her, but only when she had found an open sesame. It would never open to the old man. After all, it was none of my affair. There remained the fact that both she and her father had used English as the language in which to address me.

It was as though she read my thoughts.

"You might as well take off the mask, Ed Jenkins."

"Yes?" was all I said, but I was tensed, ready for anything at that moment.

"Yes," she said with a low laugh. "My father thought you were in disguise. He felt it would be a bad thing for Chinatown to have you hiding here, and he was going to surrender you. But he knew Chuck Gee intended to kill you. He felt you were entitled to be turned over alive to the police. I liked your voice and tried to save you. Perhaps I could have done so, perhaps not. Of course we were not sure it was you until after you whipped those two rowdies. A Chinaman would not have done that."

I remained silent. She was right. Anyone who had seen that incident or heard of it would know that the man who struck those blows was not a Chinaman. And Chuck Gee had been watching.

"Come," she said, simply.

I followed, followed with wary steps. In the dark passages of Chinatown many things happen. I was an outlaw. A price was on my head dead or alive, and the word had been passed that I was not to be taken alive.

The Chinese love to make secret passages. It is racial habit. They make 'em even when there's no reason. Usually there's a reason. I wasn't surprised to find that the entire block was honeycombed by little runways. I'd have been surprised if it hadn't been.

"There is this flight of stairs to the alley," she said.

With the words she stopped at the head of a narrow stairway, slid back a panel in the wall and peered without. Then her hand strayed back to my sleeve, groped up it to my elbow, and gently pulled me to the peep-hole.

I peered through—

Below appeared the dimly lit alley. At first I could see nothing except streaks of weak, reddish light, blotches of dark shadow. Then something moved. Someone coughed, a suppressed cough that seemed bit off in the middle. The shadows were alive with men.

Again a pressure on my sleeve. I was pulled gently back and the window closed.

"I am afraid it was because of the blow," she said, and there was something almost tender in her voice.

I felt that might have something to do with it, but in reality it was the newspaper article, Chuck Gee and his confounded spy system, that and unlimited quantities of money which were being poured into Chinatown. The police must have me at any price. Paul Boardman, whose word was law, must have my lips sealed by death.

The girl showed a calm efficiency. Technically she was an accessory after the fact, could be held on a most serious charge, sent to San Quentin for what she was doing. And she was smart enough to know it, must also have known she would later be called to account; but she was as cool and calm as though she had been merely showing a visitor through her house.

"There is another way over the roof and down to a basement that comes out on the next corner," she said in that queer, lilting voice of hers.

No wonder her father had christened her "Little Sun." It was a name I liked and I addressed her by it.

"Listen, Little Sun, you don't need to pilot me around. You may make trouble for yourself. I'll work my own way out of this, thanks, all the same."

She paused in the door of a passageway; slender, graceful, attired in semitransparent silk that emphasized the slim lines of her pose, she reminded me of a deer poised for flight from pursuing hunters.

"You don't know just what you're up against," she remarked, casually, and again led the way.

She was wrong. I knew what I was up against—the combined efforts of the police and Chinese. Those blows had established my identity as well as though I had left my calling card. A Chinaman who tackled two rowdies and smashed them into the gutter was pretty likely not to be a Chinaman at all, and then there had been the matter of Chuck Gee . . . The police had learned too much of my reputation. I might have earned the nickname of The Phantom Crook in the East because of my ability to slip through the fingers of the police, but they were taking steps to see to it I did not live up to the name here.

I knew exactly what we should find before we found it—the other corner was watched. A veritable cordon of men were thrown about the entire block. There were police and Chinese gunmen. As yet they had not entered the houses for a search. They preferred to catch me on the outside. Why?

Of course it would be more difficult searching each nook and corner . . . but that would hardly be the real reason. Nor did the men without seem anxious. They acted as though they were waiting for something, some new development in the situation.

I stretched, yawned, and tapped the girl on the shoulder.

"Listen, Little Sun, I've been interested in seeing how far you would go to help me. I've found out, and I thank you. Now is no time for experiments. I'm getting tired of so much police interference. I'm on my way, and it's going to be no place for a lady, so you beat it back to your dad, give him my compliments and tell him I'll see him again some day."

She looked me over appraisingly from those slant eyes of hers, and then slipped me a bit of American slang.

"Go to it, big boy," she said, bowed, smiled at me and vanished through a doorway.

I slipped into another room and took stock of the situation.

The whole upper floors of the block were honeycombed with passages. So far so good. The whole block was surrounded. Not so good. The guards were both Chinese and police. Probably there were underground passages, but Chuck Gee's men would be guarding them. However, there was one thing in my favor. We hadn't seen a single Chinaman in the whole tour we had made of the upper floors. We had gone through dining-rooms, sleeping-rooms, gambling rooms, little corridors, rooms of all sorts. In none of them had there been a single human being.

That meant but one thing. They were getting the Chinese out as fast as possible. In some mysterious manner word was being passed for the Chinks to get in the clear. Did that mean they were going to set fire to the block? Perhaps. It would enable them to get me dead rather than alive; but more probably there was some other scheme. A block on fire would be a little hard to handle, even if they did have the fire department under Boardman's thumb. No, there was something else.

Anyway, I had one thing to go on. The Chinks were being removed from that block.

I opened my blouse and took a wide belt from around my waist. In this belt were many small, compact articles that had been of value more than once. If the police thought I had earned my nickname of The Phantom Crook by depending on one disguise, they were crazy.

Calmly, leisurely I went to work on my features. A white beard, horn-rimmed glasses, a skull cap of blue silk, a stick of grease paint and lines drawn across my face, and I'd do in the right kind of light—an old Chinaman, bent with age, wrinkled of skin, gray of hair and beard, seeking my way out, with trembling, halting steps.

I started for the main flight of stairs that was nearest. Not by any secret passageways would I come down; but right out in the open, down the main stairway.

From a doorway ahead a swift-moving shadow darted into the half-light, poised for a moment, then shuffled to the stairs. Good. I would have a pilot. The Chinaman in front of me would go through the mill first, give me an idea of what to expect.

He opened a door to the street. I was right behind. Hands grasped him. He was held at the doorway for questioning.

"You savee Ah Klim?"

It was the voice of Captain Ransome, the police Captain, who had taken active charge of the man hunt and who had promised that the fugitive would be in custody within forty-eight hours.

"I heap no savee."

"All right. You stickum fingers in ink, puttem on paper."

So that was it. They were fingerprinting the Chinks as they left the building.

I hesitated for a moment while they were daubing the fingers of the man ahead.

"We've got him trapped sure." Ransome was talking to one of many bluecoats near him. "Every outlet is blocked. The men are instructed to shoot on sight. However, I'm going to try for him myself. We don't want him wounded, you know. When you see me shoot, empty *your* gun in him. All right, let's put this next fellow through."

There was a purring complacency about Ransome's voice which characterizes the crooked police officer when he is wielding a terrific power that is his to use for good or evil.

I turned and darted into a branch hallway. This was no place for me. The disguise might get by for a minute, but the fingerprints would identify me. I was trapped.

From behind came a cry.

"One of 'em's going back. He'll warn Jenkins!"

I could never mistake that deep, booming voice. It was Paul Boardman, the orator, the politician, the crook, who controlled half of the governmental agencies in the State.

"Let him go. He can't get out."

That last from Captain Ransome.

So I was surrounded, every channel of escape blocked, and they were fingerprinting the men who left the building. Well, I had been in as tight fixes before, doubtless would be again, but this was the first time I had ever encountered any such organization of pursuit. Beyond doubt I was badly wanted.

I slipped back by another flight of stairs, into the deserted rabbit warren of the upper floors, and heard the voice of "Little Sun."

"Couldn't you make it? . . . Oh, it's not . . ."

I straightened and smiled reassuringly at her.

"Yes, but it is, though. I just aged a bit."

She came straight to me.

"Do you know a Helen Chadwick?"

At the question I stiffened. Helen's name must not be connected with mine. The police knew something—too much. The underworld, Chinatown, the rank and file of crookdom must never know.

"Helen Chadwick?" I repeated the words vaguely, sparring for time.

"Yes," went on the girl. "The police were in our apartment a few moments ago getting ready to start a search of the upper floors here. My father told them you had escaped. They telephoned from our apartment to a Helen Chadwick, told her you were dying, and had asked for her. She is on her way here."

For once I could feel the blood in my veins turn to luke warm water.

Helen Chadwick, drawn into this trap!

The girl saw my expression.

"Perhaps I can help," she said, simply, and her hand patted my arm.

God knows what there was about this paradoxical character, this girl that had all the mannerisms of the West, all the habits of thought and appearance of the East, but there was a steadying something that nerved me for what was to come. No longer was I under any illusions. They were planning the death of myself and of Helen Chadwick, the two who knew too much to live. I would be killed "while resisting arrest." Helen Chadwick would disappear—another tourist who had gone into Chinatown and failed to return.

"Go back and try to get in touch with her. Then, don't let her out of your sight," I said, after a moment. "I'll either be out of here or dead within a few minutes."

She didn't argue, didn't ask a lot of questions, didn't pull any fainting fits. She arose to the emergency with the true Oriental impassivity, and I knew I could depend on her.

Back to the head of the stairs I went. No time now for planning any subtle schemes. I must get out, and I must use my head to do it. Boardman had struck. He wanted to kill two birds with one stone. I must have my liberty. Helen would need help. Boardman needed a lesson.

I had a straggling wisp of white beard fastened to my chin, one of the long drooping beards which strings down from the chins of very old Chinamen. I slipped this beard off, held it in my hand, ready to readjust.

I had noticed a heavy bronze idol in one of the rooms, on a little family shrine. I went back to this, and checked over the last details of the plan in my mind.

The idol sat there, cross-legged, gazing out upon the world through his mask of fatalistic indifference. Before him, little joss sticks gave forth curling wisps of perfumed smoke. Red papers, covered with grotesque Chinese characters, were impaled on sticks and stuck into cans filled with earth. Pieces of roast pig and bowls of cooked rice were before him.

"Old man, I want you to do me a favor," I told him in mock seriousness.

His enameled eyes stared straight forward in complacent serenity. I stooped and hoisted him from his dais to my shoulder. Then I dashed down the hall. I was working against time.

At the head of the main stairs was a door, a door that opened inward. Gently, I pried it open a foot or two, placed a chair, climbed up and balanced the bronze idol on top of the door, resting slightly against the wall behind, ready to fall at the least motion of the door. Carefully I got down, then made a swift trip of inspection to the little slide which covered the peep-hole.

They were still working the same system. Boardman was slightly to one side. Captain Ransome was at the foot of the stairs. They were grabbing the men who came out, taking their fingerprints and passing them on to a fingerprint expert who sat within a sedan, curtains pulled. Chuck Gee's men were scattered through the shadows. A cordon of police were in the background, ready to receive any customers that trickled down the main stairway.

Everything was ready. My scheme would either work or it would not, but I was desperate, had no time to put on finishing details.

Carefully, so as not to dislodge the bronze idol, I stuck my head through the crack in the door, blinked down the stairway.

To all appearances, in that half light, I was a feeble old man, clean shaven, a Chinaman who had nearly rounded out his span of life, blinking with Oriental stupidity, failing to take in the situation, frightened, yet harmless.

For two minutes I waited, cursing the police captain below for his carelessness in not watching the stairway. Had I been carrying a revolver I could have shot him. But they knew I didn't carry a gun, and they knew I was trapped. Their carelessness was the carelessness of supreme self-confidence.

Then he looked up, blinked, and stared.

"Come down," he ordered, and his gun came out and up.

I made no move.

"No savvy," I said, with the calm, emotionless stupidity of an old Chinaman who has supreme contempt for the ways of the *Fa K'ei.*

"Come down, hurry you!"

I blinked slowly.

"No savvy."

Captain Ransome started up, gun held before him.

"Well, here's something you will savvy. Make a move and I'll blow your damned head off. Come down, I say! No!" he added suddenly—"Damn your slant-eyed impudence, stay there. Move that head back or show a hand, though, and you'll be laying on a marble slab inside of an hour. Here, John Chinaman, don't you move."

I thought of the conversation I had heard, remembered Ransome's boast that he would be the one to kill Ed Jenkins. He wanted to empty his gun into me. They wanted me not merely wounded, but dead. Possibly he suspected my real identity and wanted to get back from the street so the others would not see him shoot me down in cold blood.

He was cautious as he came up the stairs. Evidently he feared a trap. I had started the play, must see it through. If I had so much as even jerked my head back he would have fired through the door. He was taking no chances.

I waited until his gun was almost at the tip of my nose, and then I drew slowly, an inch or so at a time.

"No savvy," I said, querulously.

He kept the gun trained on my head; as I drew back, the gun followed. Finally, I was clear of the door, his arm was through it. He could see me in the hall, twisted, stooped, hands upstretched, behind me the vacant corridor.

"Damn you! Take this!" he said and lurched forward, tightening the finger which rested on the trigger.

As he thrust out his arm, his shoulder jostled the door.

My bronze god slipped noiselessly and smoothly downward, straight as a plumb.

As I heard it crack on his skull I grabbed him by the collar, dragged him inside. The gun exploded once, then fell from his limp hand. My fingers sought his pulse. My next move depended on circumstances. If he was clean out I would put on his uniform, take a chance of getting down one of the other stairways.

Damn him, he had a hard head. Even as I knelt beside him, he was stirring, and Boardman's voice was calling uneasily up the stairs. I could hear a shuffling sound which I knew was made by the feet of the cops as they closed in to the entrance. They had heard the shot.

There remained only the most desperate course. It was sink or swim.

I rubbed yellow stain on Ransome's features, took my grease-paint pencil and doped up his eyes. It was a crude job. The gun I put back in his hand. Then, as he struggled to his knees, dazedly, gropingly, I stuck the white whiskers back on my face, and boldly opened the door.

"Help!" I screamed in the shrill falsetto of a Chinaman. "Police, come quick!"

They blocked the foot of the stairs, eager, tense, yet suspicious, a dozen guns trained on me.

I gave them the story on the road down, gave it to them in a quavering voice, shrill with excitement, babbling pidgin-English, yet seeing that the words were sufficiently distinct to give them the idea.

"Policee man he come. White man with face painted like China boy hit him over head. He take off policeman's clothes, dress himself up allee samee cop. You catchum."

The idea was logical. They could see something had happened when Ransome had started through that door, and the possibilities of the situation dawned upon them. Attired in the Captain's uniform, Ed Jenkins could dash through one of the exits and gain the shelter of the rabbit warrens across the street before the guards could dope out the situation.

They started up with curses and cries.

Above me I heard the door open.

That would be Captain Ransome, and he would be wanting a pot shot at me as I went down the stairs.

I risked a look over my shoulder.

He was standing there in the doorway, still half dazed, an incongruous sight. His face was stained yellow, his eyes doped up with grease paint. He had on his uniform, and in his hand was a gun.

He saw me, and he saw the cops. He raised the gun. In that minute he knew that I was Ed Jenkins, and he wanted me to be taken—dead.

The cops on the stairs were looking for Ed Jenkins, his face doped up to look like a Chink's, wearing the uniform of an officer.

Of course, Captain Ransome didn't know that I had doped up his face. He felt the boys below would recognize him.

He raised the gun, and I dove headlong for the feet of the cops on the stairs.

Over my head guns crashed and bullets spatted.

There could be but one end to such a fusillade. When Ransome had raised his gun to shoot at me, it had, of course, been pointed toward the cops and he had started the merry fireworks. Two seconds later his dead body was slumping limply down the stairs, riddled with lead.

The cops crowded by and up. Someone stepped on my hand, another kicked me to one side. From the street came excited cries. I rolled over, jumped to one side and then I was scuttling through the night, my white beard streaming, while Boardman's exulting cry carried the tidings to the waiting men, to Chuck Gee and his crowd of cut-throats.

"He's dead. Jenkins is shot!"

It was the end. Excited Chinamen broke cover and scurried about through the shadows like dry leaves in an autumn wind. By the time the shouts above changed their tune to incredulous rage, I was safely across the street, up a flight of stairs, and exploring about through unknown passageways which were thronged with jabbering Chinese.

My whiskers had come off, some of the grease paint wrinkles had been wiped, and I was walking erect, a younger Chinaman, babbling hysterical inquiries, scuttling for cover, with the rest of the frightened covey. The Chinese are great for cover in excitement, and this time I was with the vanguard.

There was but one more duty I had. To look for Helen Chadwick. Had I staged my escape before she arrived? Would they seek to molest her now that I had broken through their cordon?

I slipped to a latticed window, glanced hastily at the street, and then stopped short.

Helen Chadwick's red roadster was parked a short distance from the corner. She was somewhere within, then. Would she come out? Had Little Sun been successful in keeping her safe?

There were a hundred highbinders slipping through the shadows, scattering out through Chinatown on their mission of murder—Chuck Gee's men, deploying for the purpose of assassinating Ed Jenkins.

And what a police shake-up there would be! Captain Ransome shot down by his own men! Would they be able to hush it up? Probably not. The Chief of Police was on the square, was fighting Paul Boardman. Boardman had been grooming Captain Ransome for the Chief's job. . . . How the papers would be filled with the story of Ed Jenkins' wild escape, the trickery by which the police had turned their guns upon their own captain while the real quarry slipped through their fingers.

It was a wild night, and my work was not over. I must watch that red roadster.

I had thought I knew Chinatown; but, during the next fifteen minutes, I was swept through places I had never dreamt of. Chattering, gibbering Chinese scuttled like frightened rats through the district, breaking away from the vicinity of that fatal block. It was fear of those gunmen who were released for action.

Chinese react toward a hatchetman or highbinder just as a

covey of quail react to the silent shadow of a swift-flying hawk. And now Chinatown's shadows thronged with men who made of murder a specialty. Chuck Gee had combined the tongs, concentrated their energies upon ridding Chinatown of this man who mingled with them, yet was not of them.

I emerged to the surface some three blocks away, stepped to the street, and started working my way back, walking in the open, not with furtive glances over my shoulder as the other Chinese were doing, but with head thrust forward, slipping purposefully through the shadows, my attitude that of the hunter rather than the hunted.

And it worked. Chinese ran from me like mice from a cat. Everywhere was a constant jabbering of excited comment. Chinese were afraid to remain on the street, afraid to stay at home. It was, for Chinatown, a night of terror.

Police were throwing a cordon about all Chinatown. Tourists were gathered up and told to get out of the district. Licensed guides were notified to go on home and forget Chinatown for a night. Grimly, determinedly, the police were continuing the hunt.

I slipped past the fatal corner, swiftly, noiselessly, yet not as though I was seeking concealment.

The red roadster was still there.

And there was more.

Sitting atop one of those sinister, black dead-wagons which are used to convey corpses to undertaking parlors was "The Buzzard."

Who he was I did not know, except that he was, in some way, in with the ring of crooks that were in control of many branches of the city government. He was tall, angular, awkward, long of neck and with a constantly twitching nose. Twice before I had seen him, and each time an attempt had been made on my life. Evidently he furnished a convenient method for relieving the crooks of such corpses as they found it inconvenient to dispose of.

But if they should kill me, they would no longer need to be secretive about disposing of my body. They could and would blazen it forth to the world that Ed Jenkins was dead . . . and the sombre dead-wagon was parked next to the red roadster!

My lips set in a grim line, and at the same time, I could feel the cold sweat on my forehead.

Once more I must take a chance. Trap or no trap, I would go to her.

There was the flutter of a skirt.

Ngat T'oy walked up and down the street, casually, as though she wanted to get out of the close atmosphere of her living quarters.

I waited until she turned, and slipped along behind her, walking slightly faster.

"Little Sun," I whispered, when I was three feet away.

She did not move her head, made no slightest sign of having heard, but one of the hands which was clasped behind her back wriggled slightly, and I saw a piece of paper in the fingers.

I took it as I slipped by. A watcher could not have told we had any interest in each other.

It would have been more prudent to have waited before reading that message, but I dared not risk delay. I turned in at a café, ordered some tea, and spread the paper under the shelter of the table cloth.

"I warned her, tried to get her to come, remain with me for an hour or two; but Chuck Gee had a paper which he slipped her and then she disappeared. I think they forged a note from you. Boardman has gone home and the police were ostentatiously careful to tell her she was at liberty to leave, and advised her to get out of Chinatown.

Chuck Gee is the custodian of the Joss Room and I think you will find him there. If I can help I will.

Here is a map of the entrances to the Joss Room."

The note was unsigned, save for a small circle with radiating lines—a little sun. The accompanying diagram was full and complete. Generally, I knew the location of the joss room. In it were kept a great assortment of various gods. There were the six great Chinese idols that were carried in the parades, and there were twelve boxes of assorted ivory idols, each group having some peculiar significance to the Oriental.

The situation was desperate. Helen Chadwick in Chinatown! Chuck Gee, head of a hundred gunmen, doing the will of Paul Boardman, safe in the knowledge that any police investigation would be controlled.

It is not unusual for people to disappear in Chinatown.

Such white persons as roam the narrow, crooked streets after the usual tourist traffic has ceased are expected to know the risks they take.

Boardman had a perfect alibi. He had merely been a visitor in Chinatown, waiting to see justice done to Ed Jenkins. The killing of Captain Ransome had upset him. He had gone home. He didn't even know Helen Chadwick was in Chinatown, otherwise he would have been only too pleased to have escorted her home.

The police had advised her that the telephone call had been a mistake; that not only was she at liberty to go home, but she was advised to do so at once. They had probably offered her a police escort.

Then had come Chuck Gee, shuffling along, and grinning that evil, pockmarked grin of his. He had slipped a note in her hand, a clever forgery. It had purported to come from me, probably telling her to trust the bearer and he would guide her to me.

After that, a hidden signal, Chuck Gee shuffling away and Helen Chadwick following. Another white girl disappears in Chinatown. The newspapers dish up the news to readers who want to feel the creeps going up and down their spines, the police make an "investigation," and finally unearth the "information" that the girl was really mixed up in certain matters which made her want to disappear. They guardedly suggest to anxious friends that it is better not to press the matter too far, that it might unearth a scandal.

Such is the usual course in such matters. A murder crowds the story off the front page, the police drop it, and the mystery remains unsolved.

That is where outlaw undertakers come into play. An obscure undertaker with a shabby "funeral parlor" in the cheaper part of the city seems to be doing a big business. He buries paupers who are interred simply in the Potter's field. And he becomes rich. Forged burial permits, a political pull, a dead-wagon that rattles forth at night on mysterious errands —and the body is legally disposed of. There is none of the burial in cellars, none of the amateurish weighting of bodies and chucking them into a lake where they eventually rise to the surface. It is all handled smoothly and efficiently. The burial is in broad daylight. The papers are all in order. Another pauper without friends or relatives has slipped over the great divide and finds a legal resting-place in a shallow, unmarked grave.

Such is the murder system of the big cities when men such as Paul Boardman lend their political influence to ways of crime.

Now I realized why the Buzzard's dead-wagon waited in Chinatown.

Because I was being hounded from pillar to post; because my life was in constant danger, with a cordon of police thrown about Chinatown, while a hundred highbinders explored the shadows, Paul Boardman thought he was safe, that I dared not try to rescue Helen Chadwick.

Fool!

I am an outcast of society. The courts are closed to me because of my criminal record. I would be laughed out of court if I should try to present even the clearest case. It would make a feature story for the newspapers.

Very well. Society had closed its doors to me. I would organize a society of my own. I would be my own judge and jury. Yes—if occasion demanded—I would be my own executioner. I would condemn Paul Boardman to death.

I left the café and turned my steps toward the gambling house of Lip Kee. From a rear exit of Lip Kee's place a passage ran to the joss room, the room of which Chuck Gee was the official custodian, the room whose innermost secrets were in his exclusive control, the unofficial headquarters for the gunmen of Chinatown.

I paused for a moment at Lip Kee's gambling tables, listening to the click of Chinese dominoes and the rattle of Chinese tongues. Gossip was rife. The Chinks were all excited. Play was slow and talk was fast. A police line had been established about the Chinatown district. Every person who sought to leave was being finger-printed. A great census of Chinatown was being taken, a hundred Chinese spies were scouting the shadows. Somewhere in Chinatown, disguised as a Chinese, was Ed Jenkins, the Phantom Crook, and the police had him surrounded, bottled up, were gradually closing the net.

I listened, yawned, and slipped through the back entrance, into a corridor, and then on noiseless feet toward the joss room. Within me, all emotion seemed suspended. I had never been a killer. I had always been on the defensive in a war with society on the one hand, and the underworld on the other.

Occasionally I had slipped out of some trap and some other person had taken my place as the corpse—witness the killing of Captain Ransome. Had he not left positive orders that I was to be taken dead rather than alive he would not have fallen victim to the bullets of his own men.

But now I felt differently. Had Helen Chadwick been harmed, Chuck Gee would die, and Paul Boardman would die, and their deaths would be brought about in such a manner that they would know the reason they were being executed.

And yet I did not even have a weapon, nor did I have time to find one. I must depend on my luck and my wits, my ability to turn a situation to my advantage. Single-handed, I must see that justice was done.

As became a humble worshiper, I slipped with bowed head to the teakwood door which guarded the joss room, pushed it back and entered.

At that moment I was ready for anything. Perhaps Chuck Gee figured that I would come, perhaps he was lying in wait with his men. Perhaps there was a police trap set for me. I was not at liberty to plan, to pick and choose. I was working against time, and for the safety of one who meant more to me than life.

This much only did I know: the joss room was open at all times to devout Chinese, and once within the door, I must trust to my wits.

I stepped within.

There was murky gloom. Incense laden half-darkness. Wicks floating in peanut oil gave a weird light. Grouped in a great semi-circle were the six great idols who dominated the room. Each idol a creation of tough, colored paper on a bamboo frame. Each god grinning into space with the same fixity of expression. Behind the gods distorted shadows danced upon the rear walls of the room. Nearer the ceiling were boxes of ivory idols. Before me were bowls of rice, red prayer papers impaled upon pointed sticks, thrust into cans of earth, smoking incense sticks.

The room was silent, impregnated with that heavy blanket of suffocating silence which hints of hidden menace. There was no living soul within the room that I could see, but my vision was cut midway by the great semi-circle of paper gods. That part of the room which lay behind them was shrouded in gloom, and some intuition warned me that it would be death to step back of that sacred semi-circle.

The six gods stood shoulder to shoulder, barely four feet between the bases of each, forming a great semi-circle. They were some twelve or fifteen feet high, massive in appearance, yet light in weight, made to be readily transported at times of festival parade.

I advanced to the center of the semi-circle, bowed down as though to worship, lifted a prayer paper or two so that my hands might be legitimately occupied in case I was questioned.

One of these gods was the god of battle, and while I bent there I almost breathed a prayer to him. There was something heartening in the manner of those huge idols as they grinned away into space. After all, life is but a game, the significance of which is not in the result but in the playing. These gods stood cheek by jowl and grinned fixedly into space, seeming to see beyond the feverish futility of mortal action. Their grim humor strengthened me at the same time their huge bulk emphasized my puny insignificance. I could feel my face twist into a grim grin which matched their own, and, with that grin, I felt a confident strength in my mind. It was as though the god of battle had smiled upon me.

The six great paper gods sat there in a semi-circle, grinning fixedly. I crouched at their base, facing an unknown danger which must be mastered, and, also, grinned. And in that minute I sensed that death was close, knew also that death loses its terror to him who grimly grins into the face of the unknown.

As though moved by inspiration, my hands sought my pocket, took out my razor-edged pocket-knife, and then I bowed reverently before the huge girth of the center god and inserted the knife.

The paper cut easily, silently. My blade was sharp and the paper held on a tension by the bamboo frame. Quickly I cut a little flap, wide enough for a door, looked about to see if my motions were detected, and then crawled inside.

Within was a circle some seven or eight feet in diameter, surrounded by hoops of bamboo, covered with painted paper. Crouching in this circle of darkness, I listened carefully. There was no sound.

I took my knife, crept to the other side, inserted the blade, surreptitiously cut a small peephole.

Behind me I could hear the teakwood door of the chamber

open and close. Another worshiper? I turned toward the flap I had cut in the god. I had pulled the paper back into place, but a fine line of light showed where the cut had been made. It would stand casual inspection, but a close examination would result in instant detection. Tensed, ready, I waited.

The steps did not approach the idol, but worked toward one end of the semi-circle of grinning gods. I returned to my peephole.

From the darkness of my concealment I could see what was taking place in the back part of the room, back where the shadows of the huge gods blended into a thick gloom of invisible menace.

At first my eyes made out merely a huddled patch of darkness, but a flicker of motion showed, the darkness separated into forms, outlines. Someone was in a chair, sitting with the rigidity of a bound captive. Two other forms moved about, looking like black witches getting ready a hell broth.

So there were only two, then?

I reached forward with the knife, and then another shadow came into view.

"Soo Hoo Duck orders that the woman be released at once and returned unharmed to her car."

The words were intoned in excited Cantonese.

A match scraped, a light flickered, another taper floated around in its container of peanut oil.

Two Chinese inspected the newcomer, and the light of the floating wick illuminated the three faces. There was Chuck Gee, heavy of feature, the broad nostrils of his coarse nose shadowing his cheeks as the light flared upward. His eyes glittered above the shadow of his nostrils; weird, evil eyes.

One other, his face an impassive mask of incarnate evil. He looked at Chuck Gee impassively. A jade-handled dagger was in his hand.

The newcomer was one of the hatchetmen, one of the outposts.

"And does Soo Hoo Duck know that his instructions will reach their destination? Is he, perhaps, like the wireless stations of the white man to send forth noise upon the night air and have it received in all places at once?"

The hatchetman shrugged his shoulders.

"It was Little Sun herself who gave me the signed order and told me to run with it to the joss room."

Chuck Gee scowled, his eyes squinting in thought. Dared he

disobey the mandate of the uncrowned king of Chinatown? With a hundred hatchetmen at his back he was supreme from the point of physical power, but Chinese politics are tricky things to monkey with.

And then there came another sound from the teakwood door. Momentarily I was expecting that my disappearance within the worship chamber would be noted, reported, a search started. But events were piling up with too great rapidity for the disappearance of one worshiper to attract too great attention.

The two men who strode into the back part of the room were important actors. One a Chinese guardian of the outer passage. The other a tall, loose-jointed, flapping figure of ungainly awkwardness, a white man so far as skin went, black as coal as to heart—he whom for want of a better name I had called The Buzzard, the driver of the black death wagon.

"I've got the wagon backed in the alley behind Lip Kee's. It's dark there and you can load her, see?"

The Chinese who accompanied him shrilled forth a swift sentence.

"There is something strange. One came to worship and did not return, nor is he before the prayer papers. . . ."

Chuck Gee shut him off. His mind was balancing a nice problem. Should he take the gold of the white man and chance the displeasure of Soo Hoo Duck; should he strike first and explain afterward, or should he meekly accept the mandate of the old man?

He reached his decision swiftly.

"He has not the right to give such instructions except in the proper method," muttered Chuck Gee. "I will go to him for an explanation. In the meantime, perhaps a man will come who has not heard of the instructions. Perhaps he *may* carry my orders into effect before he learns that they have been irregularly countermanded.

"You," to the Buzzard, "wait at Lip Kee's. If you do not hear from me within fifteen minutes take your wagon and go."

"You," to the guide, "make a search for this man who has vanished. It may well be that the man who vanishes is he who vanishes from the white men, the man who is like the phantom. There would be much money for the capture of such a man, but it is orders that his lips shall cease their talk before his capture is made."

With the words Chuck Gee swept to his feet and made for

the door. At his heels came the Buzzard, flapping, ungainly, the taper lights illuminating the long, thin neck, the black clothes, the prominent nose, the red-rimmed eyes.

The teakwood door slammed and I was crawling out through the idol, out through the flap I had cut in the front. There was a chance for me to take. I left the paper flap slightly open and against it I placed one of the peanut oil lamps.

Behind me, they gabbled a bit before starting their search. Had Chuck Gee meant for them to strike home with dagger before he could countermand instructions, or had he intended to send in a new executioner?

As they concluded that he dared not send in a new man, but that he had meant for them to proceed in his absence, I reached the teakwood door, opened and closed it, so it would sound as though I had just entered there, walked with rapid, confident steps straight past the semi-circle of grinning gods.

"Soo Hoo Duck has spoken, and I am his messenger," I said, as I made toward the lighted taper.

They fell back, muttering. The man with the dagger fingered it hungrily.

She was bound to the chair as I had surmised.

To falter would be fatal. Nothing but sheer American bluff would carry it through. And time was short. I surmised that the first instructions had come from Little Sun rather than from Soo Hoo Duck. How far the old despot dared go in thwarting the organized gunmen was another question.

My knife confidently cut the cunningly knotted ropes.

"Your authority for this?"

It was the highbinder with the jade-handled dagger, and the knife was pointed at my throat, balanced.

Carelessly I extended my hand. The gold ring of the green dragon caught the dancing, reddish light, glittered up at him.

In that moment I was ready for what might come. Helen was free, there was a back passageway. These men could never get past me until she had escaped. It was only my own life that then hung in the balance.

They grunted incredulous surprise.

With confident feet I made my way toward the back entrance, the one which led into the dark alley. One of the men slipped from the group, started on swift feet to seek Chuck Gee to apprise him of what had happened, to gather reinforcements, perhaps.

And then he caught the significance of the flickering shadows which danced upon the front wall of the room. And it was time he did so. The other men had started forward, grim, determined.

It is a peculiar quality of the Chinese mind that it cannot function in the face of unusual events. Given an ordinary situation and they work with efficient cunning. They would have held me, or tried to hold me, had the significance of those flickering lights not dawned upon them.

The center god was afire. The flap of paper soaked in peanut oil, caught in the flame of the taper, was blazing up. Momentarily the room became lighter.

The Chinese stood, dismayed, confronted with the greatest danger Chinatown can face with its huddled tinder boxes, its rabbit warrens of flimsy partitions—fire!

"You come thisa way, ladee," I muttered to Helen, and darted for the back entrance.

Behind me I could see the semi-circle of grinning gods staring calmly out over the peanut oil lamps, out over the ruddy flames that twisted and licked up around the paper base of the center god, could see the influx of excited, jabbering Chinese figures with Chuck Gee in the lead.

She followed me, but I could see she was on guard against treachery. For aught she knew, this was a scheme to entice her into some hidden passageway and murder her without witnesses.

"Faster," I said, and increased my pace.

The cold air of the alley came upon my face. At one end the Buzzard would have his death car parked. The other exit led to a main street down which Helen's red roadster was standing.

I led the way through the darkness.

"You savvy Mister Jenkins?" she asked, and there was a hunger in her voice, hunger and anxiety.

"No savvy, ladee," I said, trudging onward through the dark alley.

"I must learn if he is safe," she muttered.

I saw that I must improvise.

"One piecee white man he sent me turn you loose. He heap makum laugh policee man. He heap smart."

That reassured her.

"Will you tell him I am safe?"

It was like her, thoroughbred that she was. She had just

been rescued from certain death, and her thoughts were with The Phantom Crook, with his safety.

"Maybe so. You hurry."

She held back slightly.

"You will see him then?"

She was frittering away precious seconds. I reached back and touched her arm, trying to force her to greater speed.

Who can tell of the subtle psychic organism that we call woman? I was disguised so that I could flit through Chinatown at will. More, I was disguised as a Chinaman, one of the coolie class who would be repulsive to a white girl, and yet no sooner had my hand touched her arm there in the darkness of that smelly alley than she knew me.

"Ed!" she cried, then quivered slightly and stopped in her tracks.

"Quick, if you care for your own safety—or mine!" I told her. "Little Sun, the Chinese girl you met tonight, is a friend; get her to accompany you out of Chinatown if possible. Get into your roadster. Hurry!"

She started to run for the alley exit then.

"You come, Ed. They are watching Chinatown. You will be unsafe here. Come with me. I'll drive you out."

I shook my head.

"They are watching all streets out of the Chinese quarter, and they'll have your car spotted, give it a thorough search. I'll give your telephone a ring later on."

She saw the sense of that, gained the street and started for her car. I remained within the shadows, watched her anxiously. Her red roadster was still parked at the curb. I saw that, and saw something else that warmed my heart. Little Sun was patrolling the street, and she ran toward Helen Chadwick with outstretched arms, calling to her. Helen was safe.

In that moment I saw other things.

Red cars were roaring about filled with blue-coats. They were keeping a reserve force in Chinatown, ready to throw out a police cordon whenever I showed myself. Firing those gods had been all that Chuck Gee needed to proclaim my identity. He had tipped off the police. Once more a dragnet was being thrown out. Once more I was surrounded.

This time, however, I had only myself to think of. Helen Chadwick had learned her lesson. She would get out of Chinatown and stay out of it, and she wouldn't be obeying mysterious telephone calls. Also she realized just how much and how little she could depend on the police force.

There was gladness in my heart as I stepped lightly back into the dark shadows of the alley. About me the night air trembled with the wailing of sirens, the barking of exhausts, the shrilling of police whistles. Apparently they were surrounding a space of four blocks.

I skipped down the dark alley.

As I had expected, a dark shape loomed among the deepest shadows, the dead wagon of the Buzzard.

I threw back the doors, climbed within, closed the doors behind me, lay down and lit a cigarette.

A minute or two later the springs swayed as a figure climbed into the driver's seat.

The engine started and we jolted away over the rough streets of Chinatown. I sat up within the jostling interior, once more opened the pouches in my belt, and took out a mirror, some cotton and a bottle of alcohol. I swabbed my features carefully, washing off the stain.

Chinatown was getting pretty hot for me. It would be some little time before I went back there again—not until after I had convinced the police that I had definitely escaped.

The wagon was halted at the police lines, halted long enough for the Buzzard to show his pass.

"Anyhow, we've got to finger-print you," came the words of a gruff officer. "Them's the orders from headquarters. They say this Jenkins can disguise himself so he looks like anything from a lamp post to the Prince of Wales."

There followed a jostling about on the seat while the Buzzard was being finger-printed.

I sat within the wagon and chuckled softly.

Nor did I do as I had planned at first and slip out while we were traveling. I decided to have another look at this Buzzard, this illicit buryer of the murdered dead. It was not until he had parked the wagon at the curb that I slipped open the doors and stepped out upon the sidewalk.

He was just climbing from the driver's seat.

"I have never got your name. I've always had to refer to you in my thoughts as the 'Buzzard,' " I told him. "It's embarrassing, because you seem to have taken quite a prominent part in some of my more recent adventures, and I want to know who to send the flowers to in case I see any more of you. I'm Ed Jenkins."

He stood there, arms flapping outward like the ungainly wings of an unclean bird, his red-rimmed eyes open until the whites seemed to bulge out over the red, his narrow, thin-lipped mouth sagging open beneath the hooked nose, his Adam's apple racing up and down in his dry throat.

A sign was thrust in the scanty strip of lawn, and on it appeared the gold letters,

"ABE GRUE—UNDERTAKER."

"Good night, Mr. Grue," I said, and strolled away, striving to give to my walk the appearance of a careless saunter.

Two days later I read my newspaper with interest.

Disguised as a South American millionaire, staying in the splendor of the best hotel in the city, with my paper propped before me upon a table covered with the whitest of linen, the most glittering cut-glass, I read two items which interested me strangely.

One was that Mrs. Loring Kemper, the leader of society, had given a party for Miss Helen Chadwick, who had brought with her as a joint guest of honor a Chinese girl, Little Sun. There was an elaborate description of the charming Chinese society girl, and a prediction that she would be very much in evidence at the most exclusive affairs during the coming season. Mrs. Kemper had been particularly gracious, and her attitude was open sesame to the higher circles of inner society.

The second item was a brief description of a complete nervous breakdown by Paul Boardman, the public-spirited financier, who had been devoting so much of his time to civic betterment that his nerves had given way and his doctors had ordered him to the seclusion of a secret sanitarium. It was not mentioned how long he expected to remain, but I knew that only one thing could ever perfectly restore his shattered nerves, and that would be the obituary notice of one Ed Jenkins, sometimes known as The Phantom Crook.

Grimly I folded the paper. I would find out the address of that sanitarium. I needed from Paul Boardman a complete statement which would clear my name of the murder of Bob Garret. After that. . . . well, after that much might be possible; but while I was a fugitive from justice, while I had a price on my head, I could hardly hope to justify the faith that Helen Chadwick and Mrs. Loring Kemper had shown in me.

However, all in good time.

The newspaper contained a front-page story of the steps

that were being taken to apprehend Ed Jenkins, The Phantom Crook.

I crumpled it and threw it aside. The piece concerning Paul Boardman I carefully clipped from the second section and put within my notebook.

I was not finished with Paul Boardman. And then another item caught my eye. It was an account of a mysterious fire in a Chinese joss house. It had been extinguished without damage.

I was glad. I liked to think of those six painted gods standing in tranquil silence, grinning into the future.

"Monsieur is pleased?"

It was the voice of the waiter. And then I realized that I, too, was grinning into the future.

"Monsieur is pleased," I told him.

Yellow Shadows

CHAPTER TWENTY-TWO

The hotel lobby hummed with activity. Plain-clothes police, detectives, special detail men appeared and disappeared like scum upon boiling syrup. Once more Jenkins had slipped through the police net, and the police didn't like it.

After a while things quieted down, but I knew they would be watching, guarding every exit as best they might. They would make no commotion, but everyone leaving the hotel would be inspected carefully.

A very short while before I had been a guest of the hotel as a South American millionaire, dark, swarthy-skinned, indolent. Now it would take sharper eyes than those at the moment looking for me to discover the same man with carefully trimmed mustache and Van-dyke—a tourist who wanted to see much and had little time for it.

I strolled to the desk. Here a Chinatown party was made up every night. A licensed guide was on hand and a knot of people had already gathered. At the proper moment I paid three dollars for a ticket and joined the crowd.

A luxurious bus, glistening with plate-glass and polished brass, drove up to the side entrance, the guide signaled the party, and we filed out into the car, some eighteen of us.

A plain-clothes man watched us sharply. A motorcycle cop stared at each passenger. I met the stare frankly, curious.

The bus lurched forward, rounded the corner and slid down the boulevard. Behind us sounded the bark of an exhaust, the wail of a siren. A police car slid alongside, packed with officers.

"Pull over to the curb," ordered the man in charge.

The bus pulled in to the curb and stopped.

The police car waited. Had a man made a break for liberty he would have been riddled with buckshot.

A policeman climbed out of the car, walked impressively toward us. He searched each of our faces, then paused—and drew some pasteboards from his pocket.

"Your last chance to get tickets to the policemen's masquerade ball, folks," he said. "It starts tonight and the hotel management asked us to reserve tickets for any of the guests who wanted to go."

I chuckled. It had been a great police bluff. According to their theory if I had been in the car I would have tried to escape.

As it was, I held up two fingers.

"Give me two," I said.

Fifteen minutes later we were in Chinatown. The guide began his stereotyped lecture consisting of a garbled mass of misinformation. The Eastern tourists thrilled with the atmosphere of mystery, rubbered at the red signs with their weird characters, and followed the guide about like sheep.

I waited until we were on the sidewalk where a secret passageway came from the back of the Yat King Café. Here I pressed a concealed button, heard the click of a lock, and stepped inside.

The guide turned sharply.

Once within the Yat King Café I enjoyed more leeway. Many white people as well as Chinese were dining. My evening clothes attracted but little attention, and I obtained a curtained booth.

My dinner at the Clearview had been interrupted, so I ordered some of the more palatable Chinese dishes. At the entrance was a telephone booth, and I risked a call to the residence of Soo Hoo Duck, the uncrowned king of Chinatown.

Luck was with me. His daughter, Ngat T'oy, whose name, translated, meant "Little Sun," answered the call. She it was I wanted. I knew that I could count upon her as a friend. Guardedly I suggested that if she would join a gentleman in booth twelve at the Yat King Café she would meet an old friend.

"Does this friend wear a ring?" she asked.

I knew she was referring to a great dragon ring her father had given me, a ring which was well known in Chinatown. I had earned this ring at the old man's hands by resenting an insult to his daughter. At the time, I had thought but little of it. Later, I realized the ring was the symbol of his power in Chinatown. It had some sacred or political significance.

"Your friend has a ring," I told Ngat T'oy, "but it is not for the vulgar gaze. He carries it in a pouch about his neck."

"Tell my friend that I will come at once. I have much to tell him," she said, and hung up.

Feeling well pleased with the world, chuckling at my last escape from the police, I stepped from the telephone and into the curtained booth.

And then, suddenly, my feeling of security underwent instant change. A stoop-shouldered, hawk-faced man entered and swept the diners with cold eyes.

Something special had called Captain Mansfield to the Yat King Café.

I stepped within the curtains, adjusted them so I could see the entrance to the café, and waited anxiously. This was different from the Clearview. The police would be under no compunctions about disturbing the trade here. Given the right incentive, they would bring up the wagon and take every diner there to headquarters.

Mansfield was reputed to be the cleverest crook-catcher in the department. He had worked up to a position of power by framing such men as the police wanted put away, and making the frame-ups stick.

Did he suspect I was in the café? The police had noticed the Chinatown party leaving the Clearview. They might well have planted a plain-clothes man in the crowd. Then when I had left and a check-up showed seventeen instead of eighteen. . . .

No need to speculate longer.

A pock-marked, evil face flitted across my range of vision. It clung to the shadows back of the entrance, and was itself a shadow. Chuck Gee, head of the hatchet-men, the organized killers of Chinatown. He was there for a reason, and I was the reason.

Two and two make four, and Captain Mansfield and Chuck Gee added up to the grand total of discovery.

I gathered my feet under me, wondering if I had eluded the police of so many states, almost at will, to be finally trapped in this Chinese restaurant by a crooked police officer and the head of the Chinese highbinders.

At any rate, I could only do my best, and that quickly. . . .

Ngat T'oy was in the doorway.

In the excitement I had almost forgotten my appointment with her. She was decked out in Chinese finery, pink silk trousers, an embroidered jacket to match, a box-like hat, Chinese slippers. Under her arm she carried a pasteboard box, and her attitude was that of one who was hurried.

I wondered at the Chinese costume. Usually she dressed as a graduate of one of the best Western colleges should dress. And her clothes were just as flapperish as the law allowed.

She was pure Chinese. Yet she had been educated in California, and she combined the East and the West, the education and air of the flapper, the reasoning processes of the Oriental.

She slippety-slopped her embroidered slippers directly to my booth, parted the curtains and entered.

I arose and extended my hand.

"Greetings, Little Sun."

"H'lo, big boy. How's tricks? You're in a jam."

I grinned at her.

"I always am. What now?"

She scowled, then shrugged her rounded shoulder.

"Sergeant Hollman telephoned my father. He said that you had again come to Chinatown. You escaped an hour ago from the Clearview Hotel and have been traced to this block."

I sighed. Damn it, life was just one mess after another now that Paul Boardman had decreed my death. As a fugitive, wanted by that powerful politician, the police trailed me with a relentless efficiency they had never displayed when they sought to capture me as a mere crook.

"Little Sun, you shouldn't have come here. There'll probably be trouble. If they know I'm here they'll be watching the whole district."

She nodded and grinned.

"That's why I'm here. To help."

I patted her hand.

"Ngat T'oy, you're a pal worth having, but there's nothing you can do, and you might get hurt."

Her dark eyes flicked over mine in a gaze of whimsical humor.

"Key down, big boy. The worst is yet to come."

I met the smile in her eyes.

"Break it to me gently, Little Sun. You know my nerves are weak."

And then, even as we sat there, grinning at each other, her dark eyes lost their smile, became as impassive as polished ebony. Her face assumed the mask of the Oriental, and a veil dropped between us. When she retired back of the Western veneer into her Chinese psychology she was a closed book to me.

"It is written that gratitude is a noble emotion. It is also written that respect and honor of parents come before all else in the world. Because of you, because of my gratitude to the girl whom you love, I have violated the teachings of my race and have committed a great evil."

I searched her face with narrowed eyes. It was a bland mask of Oriental impassivity. She might have done anything from murder to treason.

"Yes?" I prompted.

"I have brought disrespect upon my house. Yet it is the only way. I placed a sleeping powder in the tea of my father."

I frowned.

"What was the big idea in doing that?"

She unwrapped the pasteboard box which had been under her arm.

"And I brought you his clothes, his spectacles, his hat."

As she spoke she took the articles from the box and laid them on the table.

"You are to dress as my father. For the evening you will be safe. I have seen something of your skill in disguises and you should be able to make yourself look enough like him to leave the café unmolested."

It was a good idea. Perhaps it was desperate, but it was the best chance that offered. Having Ngat T'oy with me, I would not be subjected to as close scrutiny as though I had tried the disguise unaccompanied.

"I will turn my back while you make your change, and do not hesitate," she went on; and then, suddenly snapped back into her flapper manner. "In other words, make it snappy."

I waited for no second invitation. No false modesty was going to stand between me and my freedom. My dress suit came off in record time and I slipped the loose blouse, the wide-sleeved jacket and the baggy trousers on, adjusted the spectacles, took out my make-up outfit and put on the finishing touches, the grease-paint about the eyes, the puckers over the lips, the gray on the hair.

In a pinch I'd get by—as long as the girl was with me.

She turned out the light over the table so that the booth was illuminated only by the lights from without.

"That's better," she said.

With the words there came an increase in the light, a shadow danced about the booth, and I looked up to find a form in the doorway.

Police Captain Mansfield, the hypocrite, the fixer, the framer, known and hated by every crook in the profession, stood upon the threshold.

"Well, what's the idea of the darkness? Come on. Let's have a look at you. The police are making a search. Turn on that light."

Ngat T'oy turned toward him, partly arose from her stool, stood in such a position that her shoulder was between the detective and myself.

"The subdued light is for the resting of my father's eyes," she said. "He has a headache. Your assumption of the right to order us about as though we were cattle will doubtless go far toward curing it."

He peered at her, then laughed.

"Hello, Ngat T'oy. How's the little spitfire? I didn't know you folks were here. We're after Jenkins again."

"Again?"

His eyes narrowed.

"All right, *yet,* if you want it that way."

I thought it best to add a word to the conversation. I have always had the gift of mimicry. A voice which I have once heard I can imitate fairly well, particularly if it has some individuality of timbre.

"That which is worth finding is worth seeking," I husked, imitating the dry, almost expressionless, tone of Soo Hoo Duck.

Mansfield's reply was casual. Already he had accepted me. By monopolizing the conversation at the start, the girl had drawn his attention. Now he accepted me without bothering to even look closely.

"Yeah, you birds are great on philosophy. I'm strong on results. . . . Say, Soo Hoo Duck, you and I can talk a little business profitably."

Ngat T'oy swung about with a lithe motion, interposing her body between the detective and myself.

"You forget that we came here to eat, and that my father has a headache."

Mansfield's smile faded from his lips as though the grinning veneer had melted under the heat of his wrath.

"Say, listen, don't hand me no razzberry because I won't stand for it. You folks may be pretty high an' mighty in Chinatown, but you need the police back of you, see? When I say I want to talk, I mean I want to talk, see? This is important. If your dad has got a headache he can turn out every damn light in the place if he wants to. But I want to talk, savvy?"

I knew there was truth in what he said. Soo Hoo Duck needed the friendship of the police. Moreover, if he should penetrate my disguise now, he could arrest Ngat T'oy as an accessory after the fact. All in all, it was a pretty kettle of fish.

And I needed Ngat T'oy there with me.

So long as her vivid personality dominated the situation Mansfield would take me for granted. With her gone, he stood a good chance of penetrating my disguise. The dim light was a protection. It had enabled us to get by so far—that was all.

I glanced through the slit in the curtain again.

The café swarmed with activity. Plain-clothes men were making a swift search, peering into the faces of the diners, looking into the curtained booths. They had trailed me to the café, and they were determined that The Phantom Crook should not escape them this time.

Once more the light grew stronger. The curtains were being parted. I raised my hand as though to shield my eyes, and, by doing so, covered my features.

A plain-clothes officer was in the doorway.

"Here, turn on that light. . . . Oh, it's you, Captain Mansfield. Pardon me, I didn't get yuh at first. Nope, we haven't anything so far, but the place is surrounded. He wouldn't be here in the main dining-room, anyhow. We'll catch him in one of the passages. Chuck Gee's watching all the dark spots. We're going through the light places. Savvy?"

Mansfield nodded.

"Yeah. That's all right. Make a good job of it."

The curtain dropped back into place and I lowered my hand. Any minute now he might discover the truth. His eyes were becoming accustomed to the dim light. I must work fast.

The officer's eyes suddenly grew frosty as he turned to me.

"Soo Hoo Duck, there's a rumor about Chinatown that you're helpin' Ed Jenkins in his getaways, see? We know that he knocked down a couple of wise crackers that tried to get fresh with Ngat T'oy on the street, an' yuh probably felt grateful to him for that little turn. I know how you Chinks are. Yuh love your friends and hate your enemies, an' when a bird does yuh some little good turn like that yuh think yuh have to cut off your head if he needs it.

"Well, forget it. That's out of the picture. The word's gone out that Jenkins is all through, see? Don't mix around with him. You play ball with me an' I'll see yuh through; but yuh try any funny business an' I'll make Chinatown too hot to hold yuh, see?"

It was vital that I say something, yet I wondered just what they had on Soo Hoo Duck. He had helped me. Ngat T'oy more than the old Chinaman. There had been the matter of that jade dragon ring Soo Hoo Duck had given me. . . .

I got my feet in under me and toyed with a water glass, ready to crash it down on his head at the first sign of suspicion.

Then—"What you hear about Soo Hoo Duck?" I asked, following the custom of many of the Chinese in referring to themselves in the third person during a conversation in which they have little interest.

His eyes narrowed.

"Well, for one thing, you had a ring that represents some heathen power, some sort of a combination of all the tongs. It's supposed to be a symbol that every Chink has to obey. If what I hear's true, that ring got into Ed Jenkins' possession somehow. Now suppose you just tell me how."

I fumbled within my blouse, hoping that the shadows would conceal the lines of my hand.

"Daughter, show the man that which he seeks," I said, and tossed the ring over to Ngat T'oy.

She was quick to perceive the situation.

Calmly, the girl took the ring, slipped it securely upon her middle finger, then thrust her delicate hand into the tobacco-stained fingers of the detective.

"Observe," she said.

He held her hand while he studied the ring intently.

"Humph," he said, at length, and released the hand.

A shadow loomed on the curtain over the door. Once more I ducked my head as the curtains parted and light streamed into the room.

The situation was dangerous. I dared not let the light strike my features, yet every time I lowered my eyes, raised my hand to my face, I knew I was courting discovery. Mansfield was no one's fool and it would not be long before his suspicions were aroused. We were sitting on the edge of a volcano, the girl and I.

"It's no use, Captain, he's given us the slip again. We've examined everyone in the restaurant and Chuck Gee has sent men through every passageway. We've finecombed the block."

A less dangerous man than Mansfield would have cursed, made some outward display of his emotion. Mansfield sat calm. His gray eyes bored steadily into the table, his head bowed in thought.

"That's all, then, Saunders. We'll go ahead with the other."

The man in the doorway seemed uncertain.

"The other?"

Mansfield scowled.

"The *yellow shadows,"* he said, at length.

The curtain dropped back into place. There was cold sweat on my forehead. Mansfield was thinking, and when he thought he thought clearly. I had been trailed to the restaurant. I had not left. Every nook and corner had been searched. Therefore, by the process of elimination, I must be in the only place they hadn't subjected to a detailed examination, to wit, sitting there with Mansfield.

Would he put two and two together? If the faintest flicker of suspicion ever crossed his mind he would instantly appreciate the significance of my "headache," of my lowered eyes and raised hand every time the light came into the room. It seemed so plain to me that I couldn't understand why he hadn't tumbled before.

It was not for myself I feared. It was for the girl. She would be trapped as an accomplice.

There was only one hope. Ngat T'oy had carried off the situation so far simply because she held herself in the foreground. She was so unmistakably genuine that she carried me with her—and she kept Mansfield from considering me without constant interruption.

Now she rose to the occasion once more.

"In a way I am glad," she said brazenly.

Mansfield flicked his cold gray eyes over her youthful features.

"I know it," he said.

There was silence for a second or two. I had not liked the calm way Mansfield took that statement. She had sought to draw him into a discussion, to anger him—and she had failed.

"You are friendly with Helen Chadwick," went on Mansfield, after a pause. "She is in love with Jenkins. Perhaps you have seen Jenkins, for all I know. Probably you were the one who interceded with your father for him."

Ngat T'oy shook her head quickly.

"You should not say such things of Miss Helen Chadwick," she asserted.

I heaved a gentle sigh of relief. I was glad she had said that. The police were not entirely sure as yet of just where Helen Chadwick stood in my affections. Had they known, she would have been doomed. But they suspected, and that was almost as bad. She was of the upper social strata, one of the best families in the city, friendly with Mrs. Loring Kemper, the society leader of the charmed, inner circle. The police hesitated to drag her into the thing; and yet they had made one or two futile attempts.

Mansfield let his eyes bore into the inscrutable almond-shaped eyes of the girl, then shrugged his shoulders.

"You can have your opinion, see? I've got mine. The department can't stop you bein' friends with Helen Chadwick, but I can give you fair warnin'. Keep out of what's goin' to happen. See?"

His eyes left the girl and turned to me.

"As for you, Soo Hoo Duck, let me give you a word of advice. You keep your hands off from Chuck Gee. Savvy? He's helpin' the department in this thing, and Jenkins has got to be caught, savvy?"

I bowed my head in dignified acquiescence.

There was a steady, ominous silence until I raised my eyes again. Mansfield was staring at me with a peculiar expression upon his face. It was not entirely suspicion, but it was a recognition of something that wasn't exactly as it should be.

For a moment we faced each other. Discovery was near at that instant. The slightest false move would have crystallized his mind to the present.

But he was preoccupied with his own schemes. His message fitted in with some carefully laid plan, and he was a thinker. That alone saved us, for his eyes clouded with thought and he repeated his warning advice to us.

"Whatever happens, Chuck Gee is to have a free hand at the policemen's ball tonight. Do you savvy that?"

Ngat T'oy took advantage of the opportunity again to attract his attention.

"At the policemen's ball?"

There was puzzled curiosity in her tone.

"At the policemen's ball," he said, and from the ring of his voice I knew that he had accomplished what he had in mind all along. That note of curiosity in Ngat T'oy's voice was what he had been angling for.

I puckered my brows in thought.

Why at the policemen's ball? Why would Chuck Gee be there? Why must he have a free hand? What were the yellow shadows Mansfield had mentioned to Saunders? Why had he sought to arouse curiosity in Ngat T'oy concerning what was to happen at the ball?

Mansfield was smooth, smooth and diabolically clever.

He arose.

"Better let me take you folks out to the street. There'll be a bunch of my men scattered around the place; and if anybody's going to be manhandling little spitfire here I want to be the one."

Together we descended the stairs to the street, Ngat T'oy walking stiff and straight, her beady eyes looking into the distance, as impersonal as a waxen figure; Captain Mansfield inclined to swagger a bit for all that Ed Jenkins had once more slipped through his fingers.

As for myself, I preserved a grave and dignified demeanor. Keeping my shoulders bowed as became one of my assumed years, trying to feel just as Soo Hoo Duck would have felt in order that my actions should be entirely in keeping with the part I had assumed, I shuffled down the stairs and out upon the sidewalk.

There was a crowd of curious spectators about the place, and the police were breaking these up into knots, forcing them to walk on. Men in uniform and men in plain-clothes were gathered about, waiting further instructions. On the outskirts jabbering Chinese flitted hither and thither, conversing in their sing-song dialect. Some of these were doubtless the men of Chuck Gee, some were merely curious spectators.

I attuned my ears to the varied tones of the Cantonese dialect, seeking to pick up some information which might enlighten me, getting my mind away from my own problems and into tune with the difficult language, knowing that at any minute one of the men might address a remark in Chinese to me, and that I would be forced to reply in kind, giving to my voice just the right tonal inflection.

A Chinaman wriggled his way through the crowd, made as

though to pass in front of us, then paused to let us go by. His eyes were upon the police.

"Ho sheng!" he hissed as we went past, a sharp word of Chinese warning.

I did not turn my head, but scattered my reply over my shoulder, Chinese fashion, letting him know that I had already received my lesson and would be very cautious, a reply which was sufficiently indefinite to satisfy him whether he intended to convey some specific warning or was merely cautioning Soo Hoo Duck against too close an association with the police.

Ngat T'oy flashed a roguish look from her almond eyes at me, but I shuffled onward, head lowered, face grave.

We passed through the outer ring of the police, mingled with the knots that were being dispersed and sent on their way, and still Mansfield remained with us. Now I was certain that he was playing a game, some game which had been previously planned and decided upon when his assistant had reported that Ed Jenkins had once more slipped through his fingers.

Ngat T'oy sensed the electric suspense of the moment, realized that we had not yet made our escape, and once more that mask of inscrutable calm descended upon her features. In silence we three walked on, walked until we were well out of the crowds. The side street down which we were to turn opened before us. For one wild moment I thought that Mansfield was going to insist upon accompanying us home.

And then, abruptly, he changed his manner.

"Well, I guess I've gone far enough with you folks, no need of my takin' you clean home. Remember, now, and play along with me and I'll treat you square. Get funny with me and you'll find that I'm a mean fighter. Savvy?"

I bowed courteously to him, a bow which might have been taken as a sign of assent.

Ngat T'oy stepped out of her Chinese impassivity long enough to resume the flapper manner of a flippant generation.

"Bologny!" she said.

He grunted at that, but turned and went away.

What had brought about his sudden change in manner? Why had he been so intent upon arousing the curiosity of Ngat T'oy as to what was happening at the policemen's ball?

Why had he ordered Soo Hoo Duck to let Chuck Gee have a free hand at that ball?

Helen Chadwick would never attend such a ball. It was absurd to think that I would be there. Ngat T'oy did not go to public dances. A cabaret party once in a while, perhaps, but not a policemen's ball.

As I tried to puzzle out the answers to the questions, feeling that they were all inter-related, all having the same answer, my eye noticed a shadow detach itself from the side of a wall and step out on the sidewalk.

I had seen him as soon as we rounded the corner. He had shown as an indistinct patch of darkness against the half-lit street, and he contrived to give to his manner that surreptitious something that marks the skulker.

A thought flashed through my mind.

Had Captain Mansfield seen this shadow by the wall? Had it been the sight of the shadow which convinced him there was no use of escorting us farther? If so, he had accompanied us to the corner in order to make sure the shadow was there. This man was a pawn in the game he was playing, and a vital pawn.

I had time for only a word of warning to Ngat T'oy, delivered in the Cantonese dialect after the manner of a parent chiding his daughter.

There was time for no further conversation. The shadow was abreast of us. The light from a street lamp disclosed a battered countenance, a face in which evil had plowed deep furrows.

"Got a message for Ngat T'oy," he mumbled from the side of his mouth as we went past.

She stopped.

"Yes?"

"Not here, not here. Five minutes from now in the Tsoy Far Low Café. And be alone. Not a soul with you. Make it snappy."

That and he was gone, absorbed in the street shadows as ink is absorbed by a black blotter.

The girl turned to me, a question in her eyes.

"He is Sammy Sneed, a stool-pigeon. He works hand in glove with Mansfield. He had been planted here to wait for us. I would not go to meet him."

She took a few steps in silence, then threw back her head and laughed.

"Well, I'm going to meet him. That'll leave you free to make your escape. Otherwise, they'll be shadowing us to see why and what."

There was truth in that. Mansfield was running this affair, and he had use for Ngat T'oy.

"Promise me you won't walk into any trap. Go to the café if you want. Listen to what he has to say. I'll be waiting across the street, disguised as a fortune-teller. Stop by and let me tell your fortune."

Her slant eyes widened a bit.

"You'll do nothing of the sort. Get out of Chinatown and stay out. Chuck Gee is after the price that's on your head, and he'll get it if you hang around here."

It was my turn to laugh.

"He will be worm-food when he gets it," I said; but it was sheer bluff. Too well I knew the danger I was running; but I felt the fingers of police corruption were clutching at this girl, and I wanted to see her through.

"Would Helen Chadwick go to the policemen's ball?" she asked abruptly.

I shook my head.

"I should think not. Anyhow, she's promised me not to go out without a dependable escort—some one who has sufficient influence to keep the police from framing anything on her."

Ngat T'oy extended her slim brown hand.

"Well, 'father,' your daughter's stepping out for the evening. You run along home and read a little philosophy until you see me again."

"Across the street—remember, the fortune-teller," I told her, and then shuffled along the dim sidewalk, keeping to the part of old Soo Hoo Duck, Chinese philosopher, father of Ngat T'oy, the Chinese flapper.

I was not followed. Whatever Mansfield's plans may have been, he apparently had not questioned but what I was the man I seemed. No, his business had been with Ngat T'oy.

I rounded a corner, stepped into an alley, whisked off part of my hastily assembled disguise, adjusted stringy white whiskers, great horn-rimmed spectacles, grayed my face, painted in a few more wrinkles, and risked a light long enough to survey the effect in the little mirror I cupped in the palm of my hand.

I would pass, and this time I would stand a closer inspection.

Shuffling along slowly, moving with bowed head, heedless of the flitting forms which scouted through the shadows, I went to a place opposite the Tsoy Far Low Café. Having procured a stool and a small table, I set myself up as a fortune-teller.

Minutes passed.

A party of gawking tourists, under the escort of a licensed guide, came around the corner, blocked the narrow street, then slowly moved on.

One or two paused before my little table, making some patronizing comment. Two furtive Chinamen slipped around the corner as silently as shadows. Gunmen these, paid killers in the employ of Chuck Gee. I watched them from the cover of my horn-rimmed spectacles. They moved as men move who have a purpose, some definite goal before them.

One took up his station some ten feet from the corner. The other went to the next corner, and then sought to mingle with the shadows.

There sounded the harsh clickety-clack of heavy-soled shoes, contrasting with the whispering feet of the Chinese.

Almost before he rounded the corner, I knew whom to expect. Captain Mansfield, more stoop-shouldered than ever, yet walking rapidly, cold eyes flickering through the shadowed doorways, mouth grimly set in a thin line.

Had he discovered the fraud I had worked on him? Did he now realize that the real Soo Hoo Duck had been asleep in his rooms while I masqueraded in his clothes?

I could not tell from his expression. This much I did know. He was laying one of his slimy plots, plots in which he pitted the emotions of men one against the other, set the stage for his human pawns, and then watched from the wings, subtly directing the action that was to follow. No man on the force had ever possessed a tenth of his uncanny skill in manipulating human emotions.

He slowed his walk as he came opposite the entrance of the Tsoy Far Low Café, looked casually into the grimy interior of a shop window, stopped to light a cigarette, flicked a little dust from his coat, and looked for some one whom he could engage in conversation.

My table offered him his opportunity. He came to me.

"You savvy me, John?"

He was not in uniform, and I put as much hostility in my voice as I dared.

"Heap no savvy. You likum see Chinatown you catchum guide. Me no savvy."

He laughed at that.

"You tellum fortune, John?"

He carried on the conversation in the pidgin-English which white men use in conversing with the lower, coolie class, and I could see he was enjoying the situation.

"I no savvy white man's fortune. Heap savvy China boy's fortune."

Again he laughed and flipped open his coat.

"You savvy police badge?"

I grew sullen.

"Heap savvy."

"All right. You lookum badge. You heap tellum my fortune. You no tellum, makum you get off street, buy license, make lots trouble."

I stroked my beard.

"What for you come Chinatown? You come for makum arrest me?"

He shook his head, his frosty eyes twinkling.

"No. I come to pickum poppy. You savvy poppy?"

"Pickum poppy?"

"Yes, pickum poppy."

"How you find one piecee poppy Chinatown street?"

Again he laughed, a cold, remorseless laugh.

"Maybe so, pickum two piecee poppies. Use poppies catchum wolf."

I turned that over in my mind while he chuckled to himself at having mystified an old man.

I glanced up, and, as I did so, I saw a taxicab swing around the corner, come to a stop before the Tsoy Far Low Café, and the driver dash up the lighted stairs, carrying a package under his arm.

Mansfield watched that cab driver, too, watched him with preoccupied, veiled eyes. Seemingly he had forgotten me.

The cab driver came back down the stairs. Almost at his heels came Sam Sneed, the police stool-pigeon. Mansfield stiffened to attention.

Sneed saw him, nodded his head, turned sharply to the right, slipped along the sidewalk close to the buildings, and vanished in an oblong of darkness which marked the entrance to an alley.

Mansfield heaved a sigh, and his mouth relaxed into a self-satisfied smile.

And then there came a flutter of pink, a flounce of skirts.

Ngat T'oy, in the costume of a red poppy, was running swiftly down the café stairs.

One bare suggestion of a glance she flashed me, hardly a pause in the swift motion of her eye, and then she was in the taxicab. The gears clattered, the wheels spun, and the cab hurtled around the corner and was gone.

I sat there, puzzled, apprehensive.

On the curb Captain Mansfield nodded his head and smiled, then turned and walked rapidly away.

Ngat T'oy had been in a costume of the kind that can be readily rented for masquerades. A cap made of red buckram fluttered imitation poppy petals in the air. A collar of green fringe merged into great green leaves which extended over her arms. Her legs were attired in green stockings.

And I dared not fold up my table and leave just then.

Too many people had watched me while I was conversing with Mansfield. Chuck Gee's spies were still stationed on either corner of the block.

Whatever had happened it had caused Ngat T'oy to rush from the place in too big a hurry to pass any word to me. It had been planned by Mansfield, and her hurried departure had fitted in with his plans. And he had spoken of picking poppies.

Impatiently I plucked at my false beard, and contemplated my next move.

Fifteen minutes passed, and I gathered up table and stool and started shuffling down the street.

In the alley back of the Tsoy Far Low Café I removed my stringy beard, straightened my carriage somewhat and approached the café entrance. I knew that I would be taking risks, but I wanted a taxicab, and aged Chinese fortune-tellers do not telephone for taxicabs to come to them.

There was still an eddy of excitement about the café. I did not take a cab which stood near the entrance, but waited until one came cruising up to the stand. From a point somewhat to the rear of the line I gave the driver a signal. He swung over to me, and I popped into the door.

The ten dollars that I pressed into his hand gave him far more speed than any story I could have concocted. There was a newspaper upon the seat, one of the late evening editions, and I raised this in such a manner that it completely covered my face as we went past the lighted café entrance. To an observer on the sidewalk I was merely a passenger immersed in the news, suffering from our twentieth century complex which demands that we must have our morning papers issued the night before, and must read them "on the run."

With my eyes on the printed page before me, but with my mind on Ngat T'oy in the red poppy dress, I soon began to see a big light.

I set the paper down on the seat and gave the address of a costume company to the driver. Events were moving rapidly, and the next two hours would see much accomplished. I must discover Mansfield's game and block it. A trap had been set, and I must slip through that trap. I had my own plans for the future, and the first step was to convince Boardman that I could laugh at his efforts to apprehend me.

At the costumer's I secured the costume of a clown and changed into it at once. I have always been partial to such a costume. The big nose, the peaked cap, the baggy trousers and blouse make recognition almost impossible, even when one has unmasked; and the costume is easy to slip on and off.

At the curb I found another taxi.

"To the policemen's ball," I told the driver as I fished one of the oblong pasteboards from my pocket, the sale of which had tested my nerves earlier in the evening.

It was late, but cabs were still arriving and departing. The stairs were thronged with a laughing, chatting crowd. Masks were everywhere in evidence, and costumes represented every form of disguise which the mind of man could conjecture. There were comic-strip characters, moving-picture policemen, hick constables, lizards, chanticleers, fiction characters, caricatures, all thronging about the immense hall, rubbing elbows, chatting, laughing.

I looked at my watch.

Ten o'clock. They were to unmask at midnight.

On a raised dais in the center of the hall were seats for guests of honor. These guests were not masked, and Paul Boardman was among them.

I knew that my costume wouldn't win any of the prize money, but I felt pretty certain it would enable me to circulate through the crowd long enough to find a red poppy, and to dance with her until I could learn something about the trap that was being set.

No sooner had I started to mingle with the throng than Paul Boardman began a speech.

As a member of the police commission he was in his element. Nor could there be any doubt of his political power. His moves were made with shrewd insight. His influence was extended day by day until he had dominated every branch of the police department except the chief and one or two of the old standbys. The chief had been a prominent figure, had done much to stamp out the crime wave which had swept the city under the previous administration, and the people would not stand for his summary removal, without some good excuse.

In the meantime Boardman was greasing the skids for him, making friends in the force, pretending to act with wide-eyed impartiality. In reality he was establishing a deep-rooted system of graft which reached down into the lowest dive in the city. From hundreds of such dives, from gilded cafés, from big-time criminals, from exclusive gambling joints, Paul Boardman was mulcting graft. The men who worked with him would stop at nothing. They were bound together by mutual profits, illegal activities, quick riches. Murder was as nothing to them, and the underworld knew it. Never had such a system been built up in the city. And this system had been built up under the guise of a reform administration. So smoothly did it function, so well were the newspapers controlled, that the average citizen on the street believed Paul Boardman had done as much as any man in the city to stamp out crime, to abolish graft and to increase police efficiency.

Now he was indulging in his forte, making a political speech.

Officially it was a statement of thanks on the part of the police department for the wonderful support which the citizens had given to the ball. Really it was a skilful piece of propaganda, patting the police commission on the back, commenting on the increased efficiency of the police officers, intimating that the old regime must be absolutely swept away.

Just as he finished, and there came a roar of applause which shivered through the walls of the place, I found the costume I was looking everywhere for.

She was in a corner, her eyes covered by a red mask, the poppy effect startlingly real as she stood, feet together, slender, well-formed legs indicating a sweep of green stem, leaves blossoming out where the arms left the body, the face furnishing the bud, and the hat sweeping upward in an expanse of quivering red petal.

"Ah, little poppy, may a clown claim a dance?"

I disguised my voice slightly, not wanting Ngat T'oy to recognize me too readily, fearful that she might be watched, and knowing that I must appear elaborately casual.

For answer she stretched out her arms as the music swung into the catchy melody of one of the popular airs, and couples swayed out upon the floor.

I knew the truth as soon as I touched her.

"Ed!" she breathed, a happy catch in her whisper.

This was not Ngat T'oy! This was Helen Chadwick herself!

"Helen!" I exclaimed. "Why did you come here?"

The eyes behind the red mask glittered.

"Because I had the strange idea that you would be here."

Mechanically my feet followed the music. My mind was seething with a mass of seemingly unrelated facts, trying to co-ordinate them.

Mansfield had arranged the whole thing. He had arranged that Ngat T'oy should be given a similar costume to that which Helen was wearing. . . . He had insisted that Chuck Gee's men should be given a free hand at the ball. . . . He had known of an ultimatum that Paul Boardman had given to the Chief of Police—Get Jenkins or Quit. . . . But what was the connection of it all?

Those questions pulsed through my brain, keeping time to the cadences of the music. And through it all was the intoxicating sense of physical contact with the girl who swayed in my arms, dancing with thistledown feet.

"Who is your escort?"

"Mr. Loring Kemper. I told him that I was coming and he decided that he had better come, too. He's in the costume of the monk. He's got his eye on us right now. See him, over there? There, he waved his hand."

Inwardly I heaved a great sigh of relief. Loring Kemper was a power in the city. He never dabbled in politics, but he represented one of the wealthiest and oldest families. He was independently wealthy and numbered his friends by the thousand among the inner circle of bankers, professional men, executives, and clubmen. The police would hardly dare to question the word of such a man.

Yet there was the ultimatum to the Chief—*"Get Jenkins or*

Quit." And there was some mysterious plan of Captain Mansfield, a plan which could be counted upon to be devilish in its ingenuity.

I let it slide for the moment, gave myself up to the spell of the occasion. With Helen Chadwick in my arms I felt the music throbbing through my soul, and police chicanery, plot and counterplot, were left behind as I soared to heights which lifted me out of myself, attuned me to a great peace.

I have no idea of the time of that dance. I seemed in a place where there was no time. The rhythm of the music rippled through every fibre of my being. Human affairs dropped away. There was only a great peace, a perfect understanding. . . .

And then the music stopped.

There came a clapping of hands. People started chatting and laughing.

Once more the physical necessities of everyday life enveloped me in a great surge of revulsion. I was Ed Jenkins, the Phantom Crook, a price on my head, surrounded by enemies, standing within a trap the nature of which I could neither conjecture nor comprehend.

The monk drifted toward us. There was no particular exchange of words, merely a commonplace greeting which might have been witnessed or overheard by any of the masqueraders who were crowded about. But the hand which rested lightly upon my shoulder gripped in a warm clasp of steady encouragement.

"Let's go where we can talk," I suggested, and led the way to the balcony.

"I don't want to talk," protested Helen as she followed me. "This is to be our night together. Please, Ed. Let's dance and forget."

The monk held back, apparently feeling that he was intruding, but I continued toward the balcony, and he reluctantly followed us.

The cool air of the night struck our faces with foggy freshness. Wisps of fog trailed around the eaves of the building, streamed out into the night. The street lamps shone redly through a moist halo. The band struck up another dance, and we had the balcony to ourselves.

Quickly I told them of Ngat T'oy, of the events of the evening, of Mansfield's remarks concerning the picking of poppies.

I could see Helen's lips set in a fine line of pink determination.

"Very well, Ed. She has not come here yet, I am sure, for I have looked at everyone, watching for you. And if she has not come by this time, she must have been kept away. You must go to her. She is in danger."

Loring Kemper added a thought, speaking with the calm deliberation of one who is accustomed to take his time in pondering over any given situation.

"But don't you think that the whole thing is an elaborate trap, Helen? That Mansfield is counting upon something of the sort and is waiting for Ed Jenkins?"

Helen made a gesture of worried impatience. "There are two sides to this, both leading in the same direction—Ngat T'oy. It is evident now that they learned what my costume would be and had it duplicated for Ngat T'oy. Therefore, knowing how I would appear, they will watch for some one paying me special attention. It is dangerous for you, Ed, to remain here a moment longer. Furthermore, my coming here at all is the cause for whatever scheme they have against that sweet little Chinese girl. And I already owe her too much not to be willing to sacrifice almost—anything to save her. It's our luck, Ed—our—"

I caught her to me, held her tight for one swift, throbbing second, and then I was out, over the edge of the balcony, catching my hands in clinging vines, keeping within the foggy shadows cast by the protruding corner.

I had no particular idea as to my next move, other than that I would strive to pick up the trail of Ngat T'oy and follow it as far as possible.

I sprinted for a cab.

Several officers in uniform were standing about the entrance to the hall, and one of these caught sight of me, scowled, said something to his companions, and they all turned.

The door of the taxi slammed, and I waved a hand to the officers, waved with the careless familiarity of one who is sure of himself, who knows his position.

"Going after another quart," I shouted, as the cab pulled away from the curb.

My assurance got me by.

Whatever their purpose in guarding the door they remained there, probably deciding I was a cop myself, out for a lark.

One thing I had as a starting point, the number of the cab in which Ngat T'oy had left the café. It took me half an hour to run down the driver.

"I'm from the policemen's ball," I told him importantly. "Give me all the dope on that fare from the Tsoy Far Low."

He needed no second invitation.

"Say, boss, I'm sure glad you showed up. The guy that hired me was a dick, had a star and all of the credentials, but it sure was a funny set-up. He said he was layin' a trap to catch a crook, an' that it was all right, but I got to wonderin' afterward."

"Can all that," I interrupted, after my most hard-boiled police manner. "Never mind the alibis. Tell me what happened, and tell me quick."

"Well, boss, I was to be waitin' with a poppy costume for a call. When I got it I went an' delivered the package. The jane went into the dressing-room an' made the change, an' then came out.

"She seemed all hopped up about something an' kept tellin' me to make speed. She wanted to go to the corner of Second and Helmold and after that to drive slow. Well, I'd had my instructions before, so they didn't surprise me so much. I got to Second street, and then I drove slow through the Chink quarter, taking the alleys about half the time.

"Along about halfway in the block back of the Mandarin Café four or five Chinks with guns stepped out and stopped the car, an' pulled the jane out and into another car that was standin' there. An' will yuh believe it, boss, she was actually glad to see 'em. I heard her say 'Thank God!' when the Chinks stepped out an' grabbed her.

"But she went through the motions of makin' a struggle when the Chinks pulled her out of the car. Still, she didn't scream none, nor do much fightin'. Of course, they had a gun throwed down on me, an' I sat there with my hands up in the air.

"I'd been told in advance what was goin' to happen, an' I could see this jane was a Chink an' the four or five men were all Chinks, so I figured it was none o' my funeral. When they got her out they told me to drive on an' keep my mouth shut, an' I drove on.

"That's all I know, boss."

I could see the man was telling the truth.

That had been nearly an hour and a half ago. And it had all

been planned with diabolical cunning. But why? Ngat T'oy must have had some big reason to overlook her promise to me and leave the café without even attempting to let me know where she was going. She had taken a cab dressed as a red poppy, and had apparently expected to be kidnapped en route. Why?

And a cold, clutching fear began to creep up around the vicinity of my heart.

Helen Chadwick was at the policemen's ball dressed exactly as Ngat T'oy had been dressed.

It was all part of some subtle scheme, and Mansfield was a wonder at subtle schemes. In some way—easy to him—he had assured himself that Helen Chadwick was going to do this extraordinary thing—attend the policemen's ball—and found out what her costume would be. Upon these facts his scheme was built.

But what his scheme could be was beyond me. Loring Kemper was with Helen Chadwick. Kemper was a man who could not be trifled with. His word would be accepted at face value anywhere.

I pondered the matter and the more I pondered the more perplexed I became. There seemed but one thing to do. I climbed into the taxicab, ignoring the anxious queries of the driver as to whether he had done right, and gave him the address of Soo Hoo Duck.

Would the old man surrender me to the police when he once became certain of my identity? Would he blame me for what had happened to his daughter?

If Soo Hoo Duck wanted to surrender me to the police he could do so. Helen Chadwick would be safe. Ngat T'oy would be safe after I made my confession to her father. *I* would take what Fate had in store for me.

To try and hunt through the maze of Chinatown for Ngat T'oy would be like hunting for a needle in a haystack. There was only one person who could command instant results, and that was Soo Hoo Duck. Regardless of what the girl may have thought she was doing, I knew she had walked into a trap. Twice before she had risked her liberty to save me, and now I would return the compliment.

Would Soo Hoo Duck let me in?

I had been in his apartment once before; but it was so planned that it was impossible to gain access to it unless the owner was willing. Now, disguised as a clown, I stood before the massive door, the center of interest for shifting, beady eyes which surveyed me in sudden silence.

A panel in the massive door glided back, then slammed closed. There was silence. Then, without warning, the door noiselessly swung back. A black oblong loomed before me.

"Wait, there," I told the taxi driver, and stepped forward into the darkness.

Behind me, the door slammed shut. There came the click of an electric lock. I advanced a few paces. Another door barred further progress. I turned and tried the door behind. There was no knob on it, nothing but a smooth surface. It was worked by an electrical connection somewhere. Was I to be held prisoner in this passageway with the two barred doors preventing any further progress?

"Who are you?"

The voice was that of Soo Hoo Duck. It came from the darkness, perhaps through some speaking tube, perhaps through an opening in the inner door. I have always been acutely sensitive to voices, and I could tell not only that the voice belonged to the old Chinaman but that he was laboring under some intense emotional strain.

"I bring news of Ngat T'oy," I answered.

"*Who* are you?" the question was repeated.

Damn it, I couldn't stand there all night while every second was precious. Hang the old philosopher, anyhow. I'd give it to him in bunches. After all, Ngat T'oy had risked everything for me.

"I'm Ed Jenkins, the crook," I snapped.

There was a draft upon my face as the inner door swung open. A faint light disclosed a long passageway, and the faint odor of heavy incense came to my nostrils.

"Soo Hoo Duck will see Ed Jenkins, the crook," said the voice, sounding almost at my elbow. Yet there was no other person in the passageway.

Impatient, weary of all this Oriental mystery, sensing that great events were impending and that every second of delay was an additional handicap, I walked rapidly along the passageway, climbed a flight of stairs, and then knew my ground. I had been in this passageway before.

Quickly I turned to the right, took the first turn to the left and knocked at the door.

It was opened by Soo Hoo Duck, himself.

"I see that you have been here before," he said, his eyes boring into mine accusingly.

"I have been here before," I said, giving him as steady a gaze as he sent.

And then I caught the faintest flicker of a smile in the beady eyes.

"It is well. The gods favor a truthful man," he remarked, and stood to one side.

I was in no mood to waste time.

"You have seen me several times, disguised as a Chinaman," I said. "Once or twice I think you suspected my identity. At any rate I have come to look on you as a friend."

He bowed without either affirming or denying.

And then I plunged right into the middle of things, giving him briefly an account of the adventures of the evening. I even told him of Ngat T'oy's assistance with the disguise by which I escaped from the Yat King Café, masquerading as old Soo Hoo Duck, himself. I went on, told him of the conduct of Mansfield, how he had escorted us until he was certain that Sam Sneed was waiting with his message, how he had been before the Tsoy Far Low Café to make sure that the plans worked right. Then I told him of the ball, Helen Chadwick's presence in the costume of a red poppy, gave him the story of the taxicab driver who waited below.

He heard me through without comment. So far as I could see there was no change in the expression of his face.

When I had finished, he picked up a small ebony striker, and tapped a gong which hung suspended before him.

Instantly, a wicket slid to one side in the wall, not over a foot from my head, and a gray bearded countenance was framed in the opening. It was the face of a Chinaman, but it might as well have been carved of bronze for all the expression that was on it. The beard was of the two-stranded variety which grows on aged Chinamen. The head was almost bald. There were thousands of fine wrinkles about the face, particularly about the eyes. The eyes were compelling. They glittered with cold impassivity.

"You heard?" asked Soo Hoo Duck in Cantonese.

"My Lord, I heard."

"Then go at once and use the information."

The wicket slammed shut.

Soo Hoo Duck's eyes bored into mine.

I met his gaze without flinching. If he had meant that the

aged listener should summon the police that was his privilege. I knew how much old Soo Hoo Duck thought of his daughter. She was more than the apple of his eye. She was his sole reason for living.

Finally he spoke again. His voice was now as calm as his countenance.

"There is a Fate which masters the efforts of puny man. Yet such powers as we have were given to us for use."

I nodded. Personally, I was in no mind to discuss abstract philosophy. Yet I knew how much more he suffered than I did, and I was willing to let him take the lead.

"You knew, perhaps, that Chuck Gee had gone to his fathers?"

Perhaps it was because he slipped in the statement so casually, sandwiched in between bits of philosophy. Perhaps it was because I had been thinking so much of Ngat T'oy that I was listening mechanically. Whatever the reason, I could feel my eyes widen in incredulous surprise.

"Chuck Gee!" I exclaimed.

Soo Hoo Duck bowed in grave assent.

"Chuck Gee. He is with his fathers."

"Who did it?"

His eyes suddenly raised from the teakwood table and bored into mine.

"He was shot down from an automobile which drew up close to the curb."

"Did they see who was in the machine?"

He nodded, his eyes as hard as two pieces of polished ebony.

"Yes. The shots were fired by a man who yelled that he was Ed Jenkins. He was accompanied by a girl who was dressed as for a masquerade ball. She wore the costume of a red poppy."

I clutched at the table.

What hellish scheme had Mansfield planned? What was the diabolical significance of his plot? Why should these two girls who meant much to me, who had sacrificed much to help me, be placed in red poppy costumes, and on a night when Chuck Gee had been murdered by a man who used my name, who was accompanied by a girl in a red poppy dress?

A sudden thought came to me.

I arose and made for the door. Dimly I was conscious of the heavy teakwood chair toppling over backward. Almost as one in a trance, I saw a huge, half-naked Chinaman stand before me with a curled scimitar upraised. I plunged madly forward, and, for some reason, he made no attempt to strike, but fell back. I took the steps two at a time, pounded impatiently at the smooth surfaces of the doors which barred my way.

There came a faint clicking as though an electrical contact had been made and a magnet had pulled a piece of steel. Then the doors opened and I was once more out in the night.

The taxicab was still there.

I pulled the startled driver close to me, lest some other ears should hear the question I asked.

"Was there an undertaker's wagon parked near the alley down which you took your poppy?"

He scowled for a moment in contemplation, then slowly nodded.

"Yes, I believe there was, boss. I ain't sure just whereabouts. I remember seein' a dead-wagon parked near the curb, an' a tall chap was sittin' on the box."

I climbed into the cab.

"Drive out Grower Street," I told him, "and make it just as snappy as the bus'll stand."

Twice before I had crossed the trail of the tall man who drove the dead-wagon. He was in with the police in some manner. Boardman used him as a tool, and such bodies as the police did not care to officially account for were removed in this sombre, black-boxed automobile and eventually received regular interment in the pauper's field, officially recorded as "indigent dead."

The last time I had crossed the trail of this man I had managed to track him to his place of business. Abe Grue, undertaker, were the words that appeared on the sign which was thrust in the scanty lawn of the cheap house.

Very well, that information would come in handy. Boardman did not know that I knew the identity of his scavenger. Certainly, Grue would not divulge the information. Far be it from him to kill the goose that lay the golden eggs by admitting that I had tracked him to his lair.

Perhaps he had been in on this thing. It was a clue well worth following. The hidden interior of that black wagon could be used to transport the living as well as the dead. There was a chance that Ngat T'oy had been given a ride in that gruesome vehicle, either as a captive or as a corpse.

If Abe Grue knew where she was, he would tell. That I vowed. Ngat T'oy had been the victim of some scheme because of her friendship for Helen Chadwick or me, and I quivered with rage at the thought. I had been too long on the defensive. Now they could see me fighting back.

Then and there, in the interior of that swaying taxicab I determined to fight back, and fight back hard.

I stopped the driver two blocks from Abe Grue's place. Everything seemed quiet. The neighborhood was not of the best, but it was one that went to bed early, and had received rigorous training in minding its own business.

I took to the alleys and back yards. If there were any watchers keeping vigil on Abe Grue's place of "business" they could have their pleasure for their pains. I didn't know just what my interview would lead to, but I knew what it would be about, and I wasn't advertising my presence.

I still retained my clown masquerade, and the white clothing caused me a little uneasiness as I slipped through the shadows. However, I made a back window undetected. None of the windows was open, and all of them were latched on the inside with the conventional catch. There was little to choose from between them so I picked a wide one.

The catch yielded to a little persuasion, and I raised the sash and reached within.

Then I got a surprise that sent little tingles up and down my spine. The darkness back of that window was artificial darkness, caused by a thick felt curtain which hung from some point on the inside of the window. At the touch of my hands the curtain pushed back and I sat, framed in the window, looking upon such a scene as caused the hairs on the back of my neck to tingle and bristle.

It takes something well out of the ordinary to make the cold waves ripple up and down my back-bone. But this time I'd run into something that was an utter stranger to the word, "usual."

The window was wide because it opened into the buzzard's "workshop." During the daytime it doubtless furnished him with ample light. When he worked at night he covered the window with felt to keep the white light of the incandescents in the ceiling from arousing curiosity in the neighboring houses.

Below me was a marble slab.

On either side stretched a row of big bottles.

On the marble slab was the body of a young woman, a young woman who had met a death of violence. Her face was bruised and scratched. There was a look of wild horror in the open eyes, and her throat showed as a ghastly slit.

Bending over her, his long, ungainly arms seeming all elbows, his long-necked head wagging back and forth, performing some technical trick of his gruesome trade, was Abe Grue, the outlaw undertaker, he whom I had labeled "the buzzard."

In a chair, tied hand and foot, gagged, her eyes absolutely inscrutable, was Ngat T'oy, still attired in the costume of a red poppy.

While he worked, the buzzard talked.

"It won't be long now, little one. I'll just get this body fixed up, and then I'll attend to you. My, my, but they expect a lot of me. Think of having to fix this body up so it'll look natural if anyone opens the casket. A high-necked dress will do it, but high-necked dresses cost money. Why can't they learn to do their stuff below the shoulders?

"But it'll be different with you, little one. I'll fix you so you'll be a credit to the profession. There won't be a wound that'll show on your whole body. Just an opened artery or two and they'll believe that was done in embalming."

"I'll have to readjust rates, though. I'm only supposed to attend to a removal of the bodies, not to go into the murder business. But they were so insistent that you must absolutely vanish . . . and old Abe Grue's the one to fix that up, all right.

"When I get done with you you'll be a poor little pauper that's buried all regularly as an indigent dead. Six feet of earth between your face and those who are looking for it. Ha, ha, ha! That's the way old Abe Grue does things."

I sat there on the sill, crouched, frozen into immobility. Directly below me was the marble slab and the body of the girl. Her wide eyes, glazed with death, yet staring in horror, seemed to hold my own. I could not jump down without lighting directly on that marble slab.

And then the felt curtain which I had thrust to one side came loose from its fastenings, and fluttered down, coming to a rest directly over the face of the corpse below, covering it completely.

Abe Grue, looking more like a buzzard than ever, crooked his long neck and raised his red-rimmed eyes.

What he saw was a clown, his face dead white, a permanent smile painted in red, thousands of smile wrinkles grinning from the eyes, a peak cap on its head, grinning down at him.

Doubtless the sight startled him as much as what I had seen had startled me.

"Eh?" he said. "What's that?"

I twisted my lips, broadened the painted grin on my face. "Death, Abe, death. You always thought of me as a skeleton, didn't you. But I'm not. I'm just a clown, a big joke, and the biggest part of the joke is that it's on you."

The words as much as my appearance puzzled him. He blinked rapidly, and then, suddenly, snapped back into the world of reality. His awkward elbow croked into angular action. His hand started back toward his hip pocket.

My own hand reached out, seeking a handhold to aid me in my spring, caught on one of the big bottles that sat on the shelf, and furnished me with an inspiration.

I gave every ounce of strength I could muster into a sweeping throw that took the heavy bottle from its place, plunged it forward and down. It caught the buzzard's upturned face in a crashing impact of broken glass and ill-smelling fluid.

He toppled backward to the floor amid the jagged fragments of glass, the pistol falling from his nerveless hand.

And I made a great spring, cleared the marble slab, and was at the side of Ngat T'oy.

She was conscious, and she recognized me at the first words of reassurance I poured into her ear. My knife cut the ropes and gag, my hands chafed circulation into her numbed limbs, and I raised her to her feet, turned her so that her eyes did not, perforce, take in the gruesome marble slab and the sprawled form of the outlaw undertaker.

Her arm clung around my neck, her weight resting largely upon me, and I could see she was physically weak, mentally shocked; but as to the thoughts that went on in her mind I was totally ignorant. The almond eyes which she turned upon me were as inscrutable as her father's had been, as I led her to a couch in an adjoining room.

"Tell me everything, Ngat T'oy. Make it short, sketchy."

Her face became perfectly expressionless, her slant eyes fixed upon some point beyond the four walls of the room, and she recited, in a matter-of-fact tone a tale of adventures which would have driven a white girl to madness.

"The man you called Sneed told me of a plot against Helen Chadwick. She had been inveigled to attend the policemen's ball as a red poppy. She was to be kidnapped. A taxi driver had been bribed. He would take her down Second Street, and

Chuck Gee was to have men there to take her from the cab. Of course, I suspected a trap. I excused myself and telephoned Helen's maid. Then I learned that he was right. Helen had just left the house, dressed as a poppy.

"An idea came to me. Perhaps Sneed suggested it. I cannot remember clearly. I would secure the costume of a red poppy. I could get a cab and reach Second Street before Helen did. The Chinese would kidnap me and then leave. When they found out that I was Ngat T'oy, daughter of Soo Hoo Duck, they would release me.

"I asked Sneed where the poppy costume had been obtained, and he said he could find out by telephone, and have a duplicate sent at once.

"The cab driver brought the costume. I changed in the dressing room. I did not come across the street to the fortuneteller, because there was but little time. I told the driver to hurry to Second Street, then to drive slowly, and not to resist anyone who tried to hold us up.

"We met five men who took me from the car. I struggled a bit, but kept my mask on. They took me into another car and drove me off. At the next corner a man got in who was dressed as a monk. He said something in a low tone, and the car whirled around a corner, swung swiftly to the wrong side of the street, and there stood Chuck Gee and three of his men.

"They looked up, and the man who was dressed as a monk leaned forward, over the door of the car. 'I'm Ed Jenkins,' yelled the man dressed as a monk. Chuck Gee took a swift step toward us, and then the man who was dressed as a monk shot him. The driver stepped on the gas, and the car whizzed away.

"The man took off the monk disguise and I saw he was Sam Sneed. A black wagon such as is used for the dead was parked in the alley and they forced me to crawl into this, slammed the doors and then drove me here. A man sat with me in the car, tied and gagged me as we traveled.

"I told him there was a mistake, that I was Ngat T'oy, took off my mask. He laughed. Then I knew I had been trapped. But I fear for Helen Chadwick.

"We came here. I was taken out under a sheet. The man instructed the undertaker to see that I was properly prepared for burial. I was to be underground at nine o'clock in the morning.

"Then you came. That is all I know."

There was silence for several seconds. I noticed that the room we were in had been fitted as a funeral chapel. A huge clock mournfully clacked off the seconds of passing time. Through my mind there ran the philosophy of the Chinese, that the present is a part of eternity as much as the future.

"Is there anything you wish to ask me?" she inquired.

I shook my head. I wanted to think.

"Very well," she said calmly, and fainted—abruptly, without warning.

I opened her clothes, fanned her, placed pillows under her head and opened the window. It was of no avail. I could not bring her to.

Sitting there in the stuffy funeral chapel of the outlaw undertaker, the clock clacking off the seconds, audible evidence of man's puny effort to measure eternity, I wrestled with the problem, moving from one fact to another.

And then I reached a solution.

There were probably fine points of the game which I did not have, but in the main I could see the plan.

Chuck Gee knew too much. There was a shake-up in the police department impending. The Chief was slated for the discard. They must reach me at any cost. Helen Chadwick knew too much. Ngat T'oy knew too much. I was making powerful friends. Hourly, I was in a better position to fight back. Boardman was becoming afraid. Afraid not only of Helen Chadwick and her friends, of Ngat T'oy and her friends, but afraid of Ed Jenkins, and what he might do.

Therefore Chuck Gee must die. Helen Chadwick must die. Loring Kemper must be removed. Ngat T'oy must tell no tales. And Ed Jenkins, the Phantom Crook, must vanish forever.

They tricked Ngat T'oy to wear the costume of the red poppy when they had found out that Helen Chadwick was going to the ball so attired. A car carrying two people, a monk and a red poppy had boldly driven to the curb in front of the Bing Gung tong house and the monk had shot Chuck Gee. That eliminated Chuck Gee. There were a hundred highbinders who would seek vengeance. What more natural than that they should suppose the two costumed occupants of that murder car were at the policemen's ball? Vindictive Chinese, bent upon revenge, would slink through the shadows about the hall where the ball was being held. At the proper moment they would strike. The monk and the red poppy would fall, riddled with bullets.

How easily the police would explain the murders.

It was a typical Mansfield plot.

I arose and took stock of the situation.

Ngat T'oy stirred, heaved a troubled sigh, and sat erect.

"I feel rested now," she said, calmly, sat up, took a compact from her stocking and began calmly powdering her nose, touching up her lips. Her fingers were as steady as those of a graven image. Her eyes contained no expression beyond one of utter and absolute calmness.

"You have reasoned it out, Ed?"

I nodded.

"It is Mansfield?"

Again I nodded.

She closed the compact and slipped it back in her stocking.

"I shall kill him," she proclaimed with the utmost calmness, "by the method of a million cuts. I shall sharpen a knife, and slice him, a little at a time until there is nothing left but the quivering, red flesh and the white bones," and in the next breath:

"Tell me, Ed, is my mouth straight?"

I nodded, nor wasted time in argument seeking to dissuade her, nor in mental comment upon the incongruity of her remarks. Some one had made a psychological hybrid out of her. To the base of a pure Oriental character, with its thousands of years of ancestral habit, had been added a veneer of western education, flapper reactions. She embodied both the East and the West. And she would, beyond doubt, kill Captain Mansfield by the method of a million cuts, a choice torture of her native land. That is, she would unless I killed him first.

I stepped back into the workroom of Abe Grue.

We had left the human vulture stretched on the floor, lying amidst jagged glass, completely dead to the world.

Now he was gone. Nor was there any trace of his going. The only door from the room was the one into the chapel.

He had not come through that. It was as though the human buzzard had flapped his awkward wings and whisked himself out into the night, through the open window above the marble slab.

I knew then that time was limited, every second counted.

I went back to the chapel.

"You will have to play the game, old girl," I told Little Sun. "Grue has gone to warn the others. They will scour the town for us. Now we *do* know too much, and we may block their plot. Do you feel well enough to stand the gaff?"

She grinned.

"Lead me to it, big boy."

I led her to it.

The front door was locked. A side door opened into a passageway and in front of this side door was parked the gruesome dead wagon which Abe Grue used to carry off the victims of illegal activities.

I climbed to the driver's seat, motioned Ngat T'oy to my side, stepped on the starter, and threw in the gear. I had one consolation. Abe Grue had slipped away, but he had escaped on foot, while we had the automobile, such as it was.

I took corners on two wheels, skidded across boulevard stops, violated traffic rules, and made time. Ngat T'oy asked no questions. I removed her poppy hat and threw it away. She crouched at my side, bareheaded, hair streaming in the breeze, her dark eyes fixed on the road ahead, as inscrutable as the eyes of a bronze Buddha.

She saw where I was going.

"Can't I come, Ed?"

I shook my head.

"There is danger. You can't help. You'll go home."

She made no further comment.

I skidded to a stop before her house.

I had dreaded that moment when she would have to leave the car, when the loitering Chinese would see her costume, the green stockinged legs, the dress with its green collar, the green sleeves made to represent leaves.

But there was no need.

The heavy door swung open and Soo Hoo Duck stepped to the curb. A robe was over his arm, and he threw this over his daughter's shoulders, helped her from the seat of the car.

It seemed that the old bird had some uncanny way of knowing everything. How he had been advised of my coming was more than I could tell. Yet there he was, a robe over his arm. Perhaps he, too, had been doing some thinking. Certain it was that he had hundreds of points of contact in Chinatown.

He crooked his withered arm about his daughter, and raised a perfectly bland, expressionless face to my own.

"You will have to hurry, my son," he said in Cantonese, then, inscrutable as ever, turned away from the car.

There was no word of thanks either from himself or from Ngat T'oy. They turned into the darkness of their mysterious hallway with no other word.

I sighed, slammed in the gear and stepped on the throttle.

The ride with Ngat T'oy had been wild. This was worse. I took everything the car had and prayed for more. It was approaching midnight, and I fancied there would be something doing at the policemen's ball before midnight.

I ran the gruesome dead-wagon up an alley which ran back of the hall where the ball was in progress. There was a police officer on duty at the entrance to the alley. He saluted and stepped to one side. Evidently there had been given strict orders concerning the dead-wagon of Abe Grue, the official buzzard of the underworld.

I parked the car, but did not enter the ballroom at once. I wanted to verify one fact first.

It took me but a few seconds.

A figure crouched in the foggy shadow of a hedge. Another skulked behind a palm tree. A third clung to the shadows cast by the side of the huge building. The street light glimmered redly through the wisps of fog, but failed to show any white blur of faces. They were yellow men, these skulking shadows who waited some word, some signal. The yellow shadows of Chuck Gee, intent upon avenging the death of their leader.

I found a back entrance where refreshments had been unloaded from caterers, and slipped within, rushed through deserted passages, through a kitchen where there was a great clatter of dishes and tableware, up a flight of stairs and into the ballroom.

It was approaching midnight.

I looked about the room. Within ten seconds I saw the waving red mass of a poppy hat across the room. I saw the advantage and disadvantage of that red hat. It could be located without delay towering, as it did, a good eighteen inches above the heads of every masquerader in the place.

I made my way toward that hat, moving through the swirling throngs as fast as I dared. I did not wish to attract attention to myself. My costume looked as though it had been through the mill.

They were serving spiked punch, and the odor of perfume and perspiration mingled with the acid smell of crushed fruit.

A monk worked his way toward me, and then the red poppy turned and saw me.

"Ed!" she breathed softly, a question and a greeting in one.

Loring Kemper's strong fingers gripped my arm in an agony of silent apprehension.

I nodded slightly.

"All safe so far; but we've got to get a change of costumes at once."

That silenced them. It was a big order, getting three new costumes on a moment's notice, but it must be done. The red poppy and the monk were marked for death, and any moment Abe Grue might arrive with the warning that would identify the clown as Ed Jenkins, the phantom crook.

"But, Ed, how *can* we get a change of costume?"

I grinned cheerfully. "Oh, we'll manage somehow."

The words were brave enough. It wouldn't do to let her realize how desperate the situation was.

"I know what!" she exclaimed. "You and I'll change costumes. We can get in one of the necking corners and make the change. If you're in danger you can slip out in my costume and they can arrest me in yours. They won't hold *me* long."

Poor kid. She didn't know that all three costumes were marked by death! I think Kemper did. He flashed me one of those silent glances of swift interrogation and read the answer in my eyes.

And, at that moment, there was a swirl of figures about the entrance. A woman screamed—a thin, shrill scream. A long, ungainly figure, forehead streaked with blood, arms and legs working with awkward angularity, pressed through the crowd, working his way toward the dais where Paul Boardman sat.

Abe Grue had arrived with his warning.

I stiffened with apprehension. In the swirling crowd I was caught in as close a trap as I had ever experienced. Boardman would doubtless raise an immediate alarm. I had but one consolation. I had arrived in time to warn Helen and Loring Kemper. They would be saved from death. The commotion that would follow, the posting of police guards about the building, the alarm that would go up if I should escape, or the excitement that would be caused by my death, would lessen the menace of those yellow shadows who crouched without.

I started away from them, trying to move casually so Helen would not appreciate the danger. Kemper could be trusted to take care of her. If new costumes were a possibility he would get them.

"Whatever happens, don't leave the place in those costumes," I said, trying to make my voice sound casual, and started to elbow my way through the packed mass of humanity.

Immediately I sensed the futility of such a course. People were wedged tightly into a small space. I could work my way slowly through the crowd, but rapid progress was out of the question.

And then a new voice came to my ears.

"Big Boy!" came the soft, liquid tone, "come back!"

I turned swiftly.

A girl attired in glittering Chinese robes, a package under her arm, stood at the side of the red poppy.

Ngat T'oy had followed me!

There was a conventional mask over her face, but her dark eyes glittered with excitement. That was why she had left me with no word of thanks. She and her father realized there remained swift work to be done.

I heaved a sigh of relief and turned, following my little group into one of the dark, palm-protected alcoves.

Ngat T'oy worked with unhurried swiftness, a swiftness that was a marvel of efficiency. The package, ripped open, disclosed three coats of flowing, Chinese silk, coats that were embroidered in writhing dragons, gaudy butterflies, spreading flowers. Each one of the coats was a work of art, and each one was virtually priceless, the genuine handiwork of a race which has never been excelled with the needle. Here were no cheap, machine-made garments for sale to curio dealers. These were genuine, priceless silks.

The whole thing took less than ten seconds. In part the silks slipped on over our other costumes. It needed but a few swift adjustments, a fitting of Chinese box hats, tasselled on the top, glistening with fine silk—and we were out, back in the crowd, a crowd that was already milling with excitement.

And then an excited voice spoke close beside us:

"The clown. He was here a moment ago. They're looking for him. Where did he go?"

Word had spread. Trusted officers, grim of face, their hands held stiffly at their hips, were circulating through the throng, seeking to locate the clown who had been seen but a minute before. They wanted to get him without a general alarm, and they preferred him dead to alive.

We made our way to the exit.

Paul Boardman, acting the part of a professional politician, pretending to know us with that ready semblance of friendship which is the stock in trade of all politicians, waved his hand affably.

"Have a good time?" he asked, but his hungry eyes were watching the group of officers who were searching purposefully. He did not even notice that we failed to answer his question.

And so we went out into the night, past the yellow shadows who were crouching, waiting; out of the clutches of the searching officers, making good our escape by a matter of split seconds.

Ngat T'oy had a car waiting at the entrance, a high-powered creation of swift speed. The motor was running and a young China lad, his eyes looking straight ahead, crouched over the wheel.

There were tears glistening in Helen Chadwick's eyes as I helped her in, but Ngat T'oy's face was as expressionless as a full moon.

"You will come to the house of my father . . ." she started to say, and I knew she meant business. The Chinese are a race of square shooters. Gratitude with them overshadows all other emotions. Felon that I was, I knew Soo Hoo Duck would shelter me regardless of the risk to himself or to her whom he loved more than himself, his daughter.

My eye caught the eye of a taxi driver, and I was impolite enough to slam the door of the glittering closed car on the middle of Ngat T'oy's sentence. Hang it, they must understand! I was a criminal, wanted by the police, and I brought danger to my friends.

I sprinted for the cab and jumped inside.

"Away from here. Drive like the devil," I snapped at the driver.

He was a youngster with youth's desire for adventure and youth's disregard of consequences. He slammed the gears in, snapped back his foot, and the car lurched forward.

At the same time Ngat T'oy's car purred smoothly away. She had realized the truth of what I said, and yet I knew, and she knew that I knew, that her father's house would always be sanctuary for me, regardless of what it might cost them.

From behind, there came the faint sound of a police whistle. I glanced apprehensively at the cab driver. His attention was concentrated on the job of taking a corner on two wheels and he had not heard it. Bracing myself, I looked back. The hall was debouching police who ran with drawn revolvers to the curb.

They had discovered my escape.

And then the lurch of the car threw me against the cushions. There followed a series of jolts as the machine gathered momentum.

"Where to, boss?" yelled the driver without looking back, his hands wrestling with the steering wheel.

"Anywhere," I called back, and felt a tug at my heartstrings as I yelled the word.

Once more I was out in the world—alone, a menace to my friends.

I snapped my teeth together.

Very well, I'd show my enemies that I was a menace to them. Mansfield and Boardman would pay for this night's work; but, in the meantime. . . .

I settled back in the cab cushions, my thoughts leaping ahead, while the driver obeyed instructions, piloting the lurching cab to his conception of anywhere.